Printed in the United States of America

Originally published on kdp.amazon.com 2012.

Second Illustrated Edition Printing 2021. ISBN 978-0-692-11402-5

jim gabour moving pictures LLC   www.jimgabour.com

for Faun

Unimportant People

Activity at the Criminal District Courthouse slows after midnight, but as Mutt leaves, the newspaper vendor in the lobby is awake and actively hawking tabloid reports of serious celestial activity:

"Da stars, honey! Dem stars! Read ya horrascopes inna Comet. Rat now it be Happy Hour at dat Cosmic Conjunkshun Bar, doncha know? Got alladem planets bellyin up for a lil taste a dem haff-price Coincee-dental Cocktail. Takem wit a twist, dey do. Da wurl be rockin. Read bout it rat here inna Comet, fiffycent thankewbaby."

The last hours have been a trifle chaotic, even for New Orleans. L Mutt Jeansonne – for the last month AKA Orleans

Parish Criminal Court Juror #34278 in the duty pool system – does not realize that a wild universe has been frantically banging at the door. He only knows that he's dog-tired. And that his wool pants are chafing his balls. He walks from the protection of the Criminal Courthouse's thick stone walls with measured, unhurried steps. His last day of jury duty now happily behind him. Walking back to loose-change work at a French Quarter strip joint and sweaty sleep in a warped plywood box under the Ponchartrain Expressway.

Yeah, not much of a life, but Mutt he can deal with it. He goes on. It's the only thing a guy like Mutt can do.

Except that on this steamy August night the world is merrily out of control.

UFO sightings have risen some forty percent since the beginning of the summer. According to various media to whom such things are important. The Government says: "It's the heat. People get hot and see flying saucers. Naturally-occurring sort of phenomenon," they say.

PhDs specializing in mass psychology are making highly official-sounding statements on network news about "minor thermal hysteria." The PhDs wear long white coats to the press conferences. The coats always clinch their theories. The authority costume is very reassuring to everyone. No one could doubt the coats. They work really well. American made. 100% natural cotton fiber. Pre-shrunk.

People like the heat idea. The affliction sounds good to them. The public is also happily in the mood for hysteria.

Low-level bankers and lawyers have started missing work at the full moon. Middle-management executives as a group are taking an inordinate number of sick days, doctoring themselves with the yogic purges increasingly available at most homeotropic health clubs.

All of society is affected. During the final twenty-four hours of Mutt's jury duty, thirty-odd thousand Galactic Evangelicals had trooped into the sinful heat of New Orleans for their annual religious convention, delegates from all over the world maintaining their physical and spiritual health by doctoring themselves with 500mg salt tablets imported from the site of James Abram Garfield's last apparition. The twentieth President of the United States, his body allegedly taken away in a saucer, had seen fit to reveal his essence as a drawing on a vending machine in an Exxon ladies room near Elko, Nevada. A church scholar versed in apocalyptic visions of former chief executives said Garfield appeared to be advocating salt tablet use in blood-boiling climes. $21.29 for a hundred-count UV-resistant bottleful, direct from the blessed station attendant's hands, with an equitable percentage to the church's soul-revival fund. On sale in your hotel lobby.

Much to other local businesses' chagrin, however, the convening Evangelicals came to New Orleans with only the Ten Commandments and a ten-dollar bill, and broke neither during their visit. It was too hot to do anything fun, they said.

It isn't just resident humans of religious persuasions who are feeling other presences in the heat, however. Commercial and residential real-estate agents are claiming in ever-increasing numbers that the visitors' rays are lowering their sales totals. Ned Rander of Little Rock, Arkansas, spoke for the industry in his desperate keynote speech before the Suburban Realtor's Convention in May. The gist of his plea was quoted in cutlines under a two-column picture of the speaker's dais in Property Movers' Gazette:

"Heat rays!" exclaimed Brother Rander (above right, with toaster) in his emotional closing remarks. "The scientists know they are there. Massive rays shining right down through this planet's stagnant, inflamed atmosphere, for

Godsake! The alien thermal beams become more intense
every day!

"And we, we see the results: single-family-dwelling sales
drop to nothing! We Certified Housing Agents, we're out
there doing our noble but futile best to preserve democratic
life as we know it, in an uncaring world being transformed
by power-mad aliens into a global tanning booth!"

The trade paper dutifully reported that Ned has been
known to have mild bouts of paranoia since a recent bladder
surgery, but his message rang true and strong with the
concerned realtors hearing and reading those prophetic words.

The beacons are reportedly also touching other
vulnerable white-collar brains, causing insurance sales forces
to have disturbing en masse daydreams about interplanetary
abduction. And the settlements required by such actions. Their
only hope is that the aliens can soon be legally defined as God,
and their Acts, by definition, exempt. Worship services are
being encouraged.

Tabloid newspapers stained with the chicken blood of
supermarket check-out stands report "Unconfirmed Air Force
Sightings" on a daily basis, publishing fuzzy photos of dark or
light rounded or square-edged space craft every other cover
throughout the summer. The photos, usually taken by a trucker
named Derek Wizzer from Wyoming or a housewife named
Aline Lodenlach from the suburbs of St Louis, are quite
artistic. They are inevitably accompanied by line drawings of
the inhabitants of the dark or light round or square vehicle. To
Mutt these aliens always look like Xavier Cougat. His canine
friend Fred thinks they more closely resemble Louis Prima.
Most of their acquaintances agree that the alien planet is
definitely Latin and musical.

Rodrigo the Street mystic saw one of the drawings a
few days ago and posted it at his Church. He is sure the
illustration is modeled after the meter maid who works the
Dauphine street night shift. Rodrigo has always suspected the

portly woman with the nose mole has a bigger purpose in the Universe than collecting quarters. Since finding the picture, he has resolved to spread a message of tolerance to aliens. Especially since they're already here. And writing tickets.

Having no car, Rodrigo believes the visitors can do little social harm.

Another Street named Virginia knows differently. She zealously guards the entrance to Bourbon street, occasionally stopping tourists to search their pockets for signs: "It's a whole new world out there. They should all have passports. I need to see some ID."

Unlike Mutt, Virginia has no ID. Not at the moment.

Rodrigo, long the resident holy man of the Quarter and the intermittent astrological adviser of L Mutt Jeansonne, often engages eager audiences outside the Can-Can-Do Lounge at 265 Bourbon Street, Mutt's current place of employment. This evening a visiting psychologist from Yonkers is listening. He tells his wife that he finds Rodrigo's "patterns of disjointed speech, especially those parts referring to extraterrestrial forces" extremely interesting. The shrink continues lecturing disassociation theory to his uninterested spouse while his libido is finding fulfillment in lingering, clandestine glances over Rodrigo's shoulder, through Marty the barker's partially opened door. Inside he can see Melodie LaGrande again doing her thing, which involves slowly disrobing, and in the process enrolling her covert new fan who watches outside, from the street.

Rodrigo himself notices what is really happening, as the New York tourist hands him an unsolicited dollar: "...yityityittrivial incidents treated with too much respect travesty vaudeville nudity burlesque Milton. Naked, sir, naked thanks for the buck you will undoubtedly be kept alive for your knowledge of the terran psyche here let me buy you a chili dog

I have a buck right here yit yityit yes, sir, I have burnoose bushmaster bustard nice shoes, sir..."

Inside, not only is Mutt still AWOL, but two of the girls have failed to show up to dance the night shift. One of them is Mia, the star night-time attraction of the Can-Can-Do. The daytime number-one dancer, Melodie LaGrande, is preparing to leave, already well past her scheduled departure time.

Day Manager Abu Chaudhuri   a well-dressed Pakistani of little social grace and questionable moral fiber who is himself doing a double shift, goes crazy. Begging Mel, "You are being the star tonight, my lovely Melodie! Be the Star and I am promising you, I am promising you the top of the daytime billing! Within the next month. Or so. With certain reservations. And of course I have to talk to the third cousin Nawaz. I am promising. As soon as I am able to be clearing it with Nawaz. I am promising. The star."

Mel is wild-eyed and not too rational. Being ever-so-slightly under the influence of a long convoy of the house specialty drinks called Dump Trucks, she says yes. She calls in sick to her second job at Benny's soon after, and stays on at the Can-Can-Do to fill in for the missing dancers. The money is better at the Do.

Her guard dog Fred figures it will probably work out fine being loyal   even though any semblance of loyalty to the notoriously ungrateful management of the B-drinking lounge is usually wasted   except for the fact that Mel is already drunk as a post at the end of her regular shift.

Closing in on one in the morning Mel is staggering up for her tenth or twelfth stage dance of the night. She hasn't even changed outfits since around ten. On and off and on. She doesn't care. It is a bad sign.

The boys are flocking to her. The club's flyers have done their job advertising her show, but Mel is well past doing the "tie stands up tie falls down" routine with her suited admirers. She seems to be getting a bit liberal about the administration of the club's secret two-drink digital reward to its customers. Her hand is touring a rapidly-mounting number of Brooks Bothers laps. And correspondingly, she is making a lot of money.

Since midway through the shift, every twenty minutes Mel has come over to Fred with another wad of bills. She has taken to wrapping them around Fred's collar, because the money won't fit under her garter belt or g-string any more. Plus she is too drunk to make it to the dressing room to stash the notes in her wardrobe or makeup bag. Knowing the ever-ready Abu would probably steal it if she left it back there, anyway.

So eight hours after Fred is supposed to be home and fed, she is still sitting on a barstool, watching Mel carefully if a bit uncomfortably. Fred has now not been outside for a bit of relief since two in the afternoon. But she is determined not to move from her spot until she gets Mel out of the Can-Can-Do safely. Unmolested.

To that protective end, Fred has her ferocious face on. Being both female and canine, the result is an immediately communicative snarl. Which she fancies looks a bit like Doc Wolf's pose on his canned product, Doc Wolf's Doggie Ration. A picture of Doc Wolf himself on the front. The Doc a rather rabid-looking wolf. Fred is a fan. At this point, though, she can barely breathe, much less bark out warnings. There is so much money twisted around her collar that she makes a high whistling noise when she inhales. But she can still growl just fine. Quite well enough to keep hungry hands away from Mel. And the dough.

There are cops, however, close by. Just in case. It isn't Marty the barker's favorite brand of insurance, but as he stands at the door to Bourbon street pulling in customers, he figures that with the crowds this big and the drinking this heavy, the presence of a little law enforcement is a good thing. Even the plainclothes boys from Vieux Carré station are working the street in force tonight.

Marty discusses the situation with Rodrigo around midnight. "Probably breaking in some new rookies coming in and out of here every five minutes, acting solemn, scaring the customers to death. Audience is a little more in control than I would expect under the circumstances."

But the observant Rodrigo also notes that the girls' frequent acts of manual dexterity on their customers have eluded detection by those same valiant officers of the Law. So far.

"Grappling hook," he confides in Marty.

Marty understands.

Rodrigo is not sure this bit of luck will hold. Not at all. He isn't sure how to convey his feelings, even though he knows Marty is a sympathetic listener. Rodrigo is verbally stuck somewhere in Volume Eight of the supermarket encyclopedia he carries around with him.

He tries anyway. Marty is worth the effort. "...nixnixnixnnNNNNyx goddess of the night, sir. Mythology, sir."

The collegiate barker looks in need of a translator this time.

Rodrigo hopes Mutt will arrive soon.

Inside Fred is also praying for the missing Mutt to walk in the door. Something is up. She has noticed that Rodrigo keeps sticking his nose in every few minutes and anxiously looking around. Fred hadn't realized that Performance Art interested Rodrigo. She can barely tell he's a male, and as are many of her species, she is usually quite good at determining such things.

It's not that odd an occurrence, the Street dweller Rodrigo showing up this night. He normally gravitates toward chaos. Everyone assumes that is why he is in New Orleans. For his residence he has been rewarded. The City has refined his senses to such an extent that Rodrigo can now feel the onset of greater and lesser degrees of chaos. He moves decisively toward the greater. Rodrigo is a scientific register of deviation. A lunacy seismograph.

He is carefully watching the Can-Can-Do insanity brew this particular evening. The seismographic needle is fluttering madly. He is making notations in the volume he has tucked under his arm. Volume Eight(supplemental): *Imbrocado to Kapellmeister*.

Rodrigo looks into the Can-Can-Do again, just as Mel starts her move. A tourist walks in front of him. "...onon-ononingenue the girl ingenue," he sputters, "... just rolling along sir just rolling along thank you for the coins sir would you like a hot dog no cheeese no..."

Inside, Mel is performing a move she calls The Titty Cyclone. Swinging those silicone spheres around like she is going to send them into orbit. Whoop. Staggering a little on that last twirl, but she doesn't go down. Regaining her composure now.

Fred is worried. She knows that Mel sometimes exhibits the same trait that Fred so despises in cats. Whenever they make a gigantic goof they have to immediately toss off an even grander gesture. So that nobody will remember the goof. And here Mel goes.

The twister expands in scope.

Mel is really getting into it now. She is also relating to the audience a little too heavily for her own good, bending over and talking in fairly explicit terms to her admiring male fans. The breasts are most definitely and simultaneously atwirl.

The Cyclone may be actually getting out of hand this time, thinks Fred. Where is that Mutt when I really need him?

Mel is in prime form, coaxing a customer sitting stageside.

"I bet you never see anything like this back home do you, handsome boy? Check these out, sugar plum."

She takes off her pasties and tosses them to the audience.

To the two plainclothes officers in the audience.

The cops immediately begin yelling loudly through megaphones, turning on lights and pointing outside.

An hour later, a throng of partiers, perverts and hangers-on block the front door of the French Can-Can-Do Lounge. Mutt arrives back at the Bourbon street club, his place of employment, worn out from the hard realities of law and its administration as a juror, only to find that the very same legal system has now intruded into the lives of two of his closest friends, an ancient dog and a not-quite-so-ancient stripper. Who have both been forcibly removed by the police.

Rodrigo has not been removed. The Street seer is trying to maintain some semblance of control. He runs up as soon as he sees his friend Mutt. Rodrigo sputters, spits, attempts to relate the facts. Through the web of his own tangled universe.

"... Iiiiahhhhh I got it now, sir. I got it now. Cops. Got 'em. Melodie and Fred. Got 'em. Took 'em to the parish lockup, sir," he says. "Night court nightcourt know it well been to nightcourt I have. Know it well a small leaping rodent of northern Africa and Asia jerboa... patience patience patience I got it now I got it Mutt sir I got it. Cops crawling all over Melodie. Fred making weird noises like she was strangling and trying to get her mouth open to bite those cops and off comes her collar and all this stuff wrapped around it falls on the floor but I got it. Got it cops cops cops oh they were cops yelling and in comes the uniforms NOPD I got the stuff got it here in my... I got the stuff oooooOOOOOIIii I I remember, sir. Mel awful drunk. Cops grabbing Fred this Uniform squeezing her hard trying to hold her and she just lets go and shits all over the policeman like she's been holding it for a week and the cop he's yelling like the Universe ended, but it hasn't no way not for a while yet... E-EEEE EEEEE eeee ii II I got it I got proof. I, sir. Everybody screaming those old men in the bar thinking it's a raid and they've got to call their wife back in Milwaukee going to have to bail them out of the New Orleans jail just listening to jazz Maybelle and they bring these naked women onto the stage I thought it was a jazz club jazz coming from jass coming from jism coming from all those slaves dancing in Congo Square I sleep there sometimes because I can feel all that power all that sound all those bodies slapping together in the night under the giant yellow moon and they feel like they're alive like they're not slaves like they're back in the motherland and happy with all their families raising cattle and soybeans not in chains a prisoner locked up in Parish Prison they'll have them over in the Parish Prison on Tulane Avenue right now waiting to see if old Judge Cannalo will get them in the Night Court put them on the docket unless they've got poor Fred loose from Mel and sent her to the animal pound down on Wadley street get her locked up jugular June bug Ikikikikikikkkkk kk KKcan't put her to sleep for three days. Got to wait until they see if she's got rabies. Unless she starts eating folks. Took Fred in the same cop car with Mel. Couldn't separate them Fred taking a hold on Mel's arm with her mouth holding tight tight tight cops couldn't pull her mouth open she's growling at them like she could eat them but she won't let Mel go anywhere without her Mel pleading saying don't you fuckers hurt my doggie Fred growling louder then howling like a wolf between her teeth aaaaaAAA-ooooo-ooooo-OOOOOoooo those cops getting scared pointing guns throwing them both in the back of that cop car Fred attached but good to Mel but Mel not yelling like it was hurting or anything just didn't want to be separated. Parish Prison. We got to go sir got to run Mutt me and you sir. Here got got Fred's collar got Mel's bag out of her dressing room too figuring she might need stuff out of it like I need my bag in the slammer letting me bring my book let me read my book in the holding cell I even know how to get messages in the women's side kaolin making porcelain teabowls and medicine to keep you from shitting all at the same time that's good stuff to have that many good different uses in the universe poor Fred should have had some before she got arrested.

"Parish Prison. Now, Mutt. Sir."

Across town in the slammer, Fred's digestive tract is feeling much better. She feels vindicated. That rookie should have known better than to go around squeezing delicate members of the opposite sex. Especially after they've had half a dozen jalapeno chili dogs. Earlier in the evening Marty, playing the part of the doorman at the Can-Can-Do, had given in to Fred's pleading looks. Stagnant Bourbon Street vapors had wafted in the door of the Lounge, carrying the gustatory invitation of a steaming hot dog cart into the strip joint. Marty fronted the bucks for the six chilidogs, but his generosity resulted in a massive siege of canine gastrointestinal rumbling.

Melodie LaGrande, her head still bearing an overflowing burden of the cheap bubbling wine Dump Truck cocktails she was responsible for hawking to customers, is returning to sobriety in grand form. Communicating with her fellow political prisoners in the parish Criminal Court holding area. At the moment, though, she has turned her attention to the cell-block matron's ear jewelry. The matron had just entered, and now patiently stands outside the bars holding a piece of paper toward Mel. The obliviously festive detainee continues her fashion critique.

"They are absolutely stunning!" Mel raves. "My ears are not strong enough to hold up anywhere near such a bold statement. And they go with your lovely body so well   Fred, have you ever seen anything so Karen Carpenter? Frieda, you are the number one! Bringing me legal communiqués and being the best-dressed matron this side of Fire Island!"

Mel takes the paper, looks at it briefly and turns to Fred. "Freddy, we have an attorney! Raymond Burr will walk through that door any minute now! Can Andy Griffith be far behind? I'll save this little missive until we have some private time." Mel puts the piece of paper in her pocket without reading it. She returns to her audience.

"Now, Darlings, I know I'm a little tipsy still, but I'm a good girl and I have a great deal of self-respect. I just will not be sitting in a room that is filled with envy and malice. We all must be sisters here, if we are to get through this medieval torture system."

A bedraggled young coed whose vomit-stained University of Mississippi t-shirt is also adorned with a Tri-Delt pledge pin stands nearby. She moans loudly at Mel's last statement. "It's all right, sweetie," reassures sister Melodie. "Just kidding. Right, Frieda, liebchen? No torture. Unless they make you eat the food. I don't need it, though. I'd rather lose a few pounds off the hips while I'm here at Sing-Sing Spa." Mel looks at the matron. "Do you good, too, girl."

"What are you saying, lady?" queries the matron.

"Now, don't be natty," Mel admonishes quickly. "We've got to get honest feedback from each other to get by in a world ruled by male hormones."

The matron does not seem to be immediately persuaded, pivoting toward the door with an extended "Hummmppph!" A single bobby pin pings to the concrete floor, ballistically propelled from the civil servant's twisting coiffure by the sheer centrifugal force of her turn.

"Leaving, Frieda? All the best to the boys in your life." Mel's good humor will not be quashed.

The matron departs with a wave and a head shake, holding the door open as the male bailiff enters the area outside the cell.

The bailiff is not looking particularly genial, either, even considering the hour of the night. This is the third time in the last forty-five minutes he has been back to the holding area to interview Mel. The bailiff has been experiencing a bit of difficulty getting factual information from the inmate in his charge. He needs to fill in all the spaces on his forms before Court comes into session. Judge Cannalo demands completed forms. Neat. With no erasures. But the bailiff has been unable to ask a question, much less retrieve an answer.

"Miss..." he starts again.

"Melodie, baby," she interrupts, still on a roll. "The modern entertainer Melodie LaGrande."

The bailiff jumps. That is an answer, though he had not asked the question. He quickly scribbles down the name and raises his eyes to start again. He is filled with hope.

Melodie, however, quickly dashes any further expectations.

"No, do not look at me that way! I have no ID hidden about my body. I was totally without clothing when they drug me in here, except for these shoes." She turns back to her audience in the cell. "They're not really my first string, these shoes. I don't know why I was wearing them."

"Miss..." the bailiff tries to interject, thinking this might be the key word.

It is not.

"No, you sick little mind-prober! No, I do not know where my G-string went   your vigilant comrades-in-arms needed a souvenir, I suppose. Is this what the media is crying about? Is this it? The World News was right! 'Alien Invasion Imminent!' You're from Mars, and you've come to steal the heart of our culture! You've got my performance costume, haven't you? Sent it on its way back to your scarlet planet. Some sickly, institutional-grey lizard is this very moment trying to arrange my pasties on its scaly body! They'll undoubtedly crave the real thing after seeing that! I suppose I'll have to get an agent there, next thing you know."

Mel turns to Fred, and is suddenly diverted.

"Baby, you can testify that they're the ones who wouldn't let me get my bag. I could at least have worn a decent smock for this little affair   delve into the more conservative areas of my wardrobe for items that would fit the occasion. I've got something quite modest in sky blue. Lovely. Subtle. Jailer! You will notice this dismal green thing you gave me does absolutely nothing for my skin. Makes me look much older than 23."

The bailiff's ball-point is scribbling again. He is finally making progress.

"Yes, you may put that on your form. Melodie LaGrande, 23. Who'd you think I was, Grable? Notice, though, Betty and I do have similar legs. And those forties shoes! I would die for the sandals she wore in those pin-up posters! Just die for them. All those handsome GIs dreaming about her limbs. Too romantic! I want her shoes! Wouldn't you, Freddy?

Jailer! You can also note down that I wear a petite 6B, if the shoes are sized properly."

The bailiff has already written down "6B" before he suddenly howls with frustration, crumples up the top form and starts filling out a new one with the small amount of information he has already gathered.

The noise causes some commotion among the other residents of the cell. Sleepy groans accompany the turning of bodies on the concrete benches. Then as the momentary disruption subsides, a large twitching woman, well over three hundred pounds and wearing her prison dress backwards, moves from the wall of the room toward Mel and the bailiff. Her eyes shift focus every few moments, as another rippling surge of neural activity runs through her body. The twitching resembles the muscular shivers produced by large jolts of electricity applied to unruly farm animals. Mel openly inspects the bottom of the woman's dress for dangling cords as the Twitcher approaches. A girl can't be too careful. The Twitcher might not be grounded. The woman sits next to Mel and extends her hand toward Fred. Mel quickly clutches Fred to her chest.

"No, you can't pet my friend right now, Madame ElectroVac. Look, Freddy, here's the Home Appliance Queen of New Orleans." The old dog begins to rumble. "Shush, Fred. Easy, my darling."

Mel raises her eyes to her fellow inmate, radiating no small amount of ill will. "You see what you've done, Miss Buzzbucket. My companion's upset now. I don't think the poor baby's ever been put in jail before. Me, I'm a veteran here, though I don't show my years now, do I?"

She turns again to the waiting bailiff, asking sweetly, "How old did you think I was, sweetheart?"

"Forty-five, miss?" the bewildered bailiff ventures, without thinking of his own safety.

Mel explodes, "How? HOW old! How old did you say I was?!" She swivels completely away from the bars. "Well, the same to you, Auntie Mame! You can take your nasty paper out of here if you intend to insult me."

She looks for sympathy from the electric Twitcher, who is once again trying to touch Fred. This time she reaches for the spot where Fred's mouth is wrapped around Mel's arm. Mel is diverted.

"No, Miss Hoover Dam, leave her alone. She'll let go when I tell her. She's a willful woman, just like me. Like Oprah, except we're both thinner. She's just not healthy looking, Oprah. Now Fred here she's a trim little baby, even at her age. Yes, she's elderly, you know   now Fred, don't be grumpy. We girls have got to be honest with each other, especially about things like age."

"Fred?" says the Twitcher, after a belch that reeks of ozone.

"Yes, you absolute biddy, Fred is a girl's name. Fred is a great deal more a lady than you'll ever be, you AC-DC tramp."

Melodie emphasizes her point, slapping the Twitcher sharply on her extended wrist.

The huge woman gives a quick "Yeek!", and runs quickly to the rear of the cell, nursing her injury and twitching even more furiously than before.

Fred is sure she sees a blue arc snap from the side of the woman's head. Fred   AKA in some more bureaucratic circles as Mrs FT Jeansonne   is a very sleepy dog. All this late-night activity requires recapturing a bit of canine energy. She relaxes and is snoring before her eyes are closed. Melodie strokes the grey muzzle lovingly.

The bailiff shakes his head, clicks his ball point into its retracted state and, in a well-practiced movement, adroitly inserts the pen into its proper slot in his uniform pocket.

He is giving up on this one. He has a name and an age and a place of employment. Has the dog's name. That'll have to do.

Bailiff Larry Purbush knows that the Judge won't be happy, but Purbush can see no way to get a hold on this woman's runaway train of thought. Jump on and get run over, dragged along the tracks.

However, the man is a trained professional, a deputized instrument of the people and the Government of the US of A. And America will have the last word.

"Lady, I don't think you realize how serious this is," he says, in as ominous a voice as he can muster. "You could lose your cabaret license. They could stop you from ever working a club in this town again. Then where would you be?"

"Quiet, boyfriend! You'll be waking my sister Freddy. Such a nuisance," says Mel, looking to the rest of her cellmates for confirmation.

The bailiff is already at the door, wishing the security lock would work quicker. *Shee-yut. I can't think straight any more. My head's all banged up just talkin' to her. Woman's a damn menace. A menace with gee-GAN-ticko knockers, but still a menace.*

The bailiff is trembling as he locks the outer cell door closed behind him. He looks at his hands. *That damned coffee. I got to give it up. Or get a day job.*

Fred can feel the pressure of the chisel on her toe. It is cold. She won't let go.

There is the pain.

"Freddy, honey, ease up on Melodie's arm, sweetie. That's better. You had a nightmare, Freddy, but it's OK now." Fred looks around the cell, sleep-fogged, and realizes where she is.

Inside a cell Waiting for another Trial.

Miss Melodie LaGrande continues her lecture. She is nervous now, though trying hard to conceal it. *Lose my license. What would I DO?* She has not even noticed the bailiff's departure. Her mind is elsewhere as her banter continues.

"I can't believe they didn't let me go back for my makeup. Just how am I supposed to get a fair hearing in court if I must go waddling in looking like an absolute trollop.

"Fred, I know you've always hated these shoes. I should have worn the black sandals. You were right. I know that now."

She turns again to the semi- and ultra-conscious residents of the cell for consolation.

"You see, babies, the one time I don't listen to my best girlfriend's advice and I get stuck out in public with just the most indecisive of wardrobes. No statement here, at all. Hospital chartreuse with a drab grey monogram. I suppose it is rather butch. What does the 'OPP' stand for, anyway?" she asks.

Mel waits for an answer. This is a quiz.

"Orleans Parish Prison," volunteers the Twitcher.

Mel waves her hand: "Thank you, sweetheart. What an utterly droll sense of humor. I wonder if sweet Frieda will let me keep it? Fred-dy, I've just had the most marvelous idea for the act!

"I suppose it's in situations like this that those of us with a true flair for fashion can really shine. Just make do, you know. Fred, sweetie, you don't have to hold on so tightly any more   they are simply not going to separate us now, and I think they know it.

"Those horrid detectives would probably pull a child from its mother's breast   though, did you see the blonde one? Fred-dy! The young boy was trying to hold you and look at me at the same time. He raised a rather magnificent Trouser Tent while he was getting an eyeload of yours truly."

Mel turns to the locked door to the Courtroom.

"If I could just get the right man, babies, life would be so much simpler." She whirls back to her captive audience, Loretta Young fashion.

"But thank god for Sisters. We have to help each other through this absolute vale of tears. Like that sweet nelly who booked us. She knew we had to be together, Freddy baby, you and I. Knew how important it was to my emotional well-being to have you close, close by. You shouldn't have made such a noise when she called you a Poodle. The poor woman simply doesn't have the background to handle rare mammals of your special breed. My sweet baby Freddy. Here, let me rub those ears. Poor baby protecting her momma. Just love her to death, I do."

Mel's monologue is broken by the metallic squeal of the door opening. The bailiff re-enters the room with another deputy immediately behind. The second man announces loudly, "Melodie LaGrande!" The bailiff points timidly at Mel.

"Miz LaGrande?" asks the other deputy.

"It's me, alright honey. Oh, joy, We're to go in tonight that's a relief."

Melodie stands, holding Fred and straightening her clothes. She feels a lump in her prison dress pocket, reaches in and pulls out a scrap of crumpled paper.

"I must first prepare to meet my attorney. It is my legal right to read this important message as brought to me by the official hands of your own Shtupmeister Frieda."

Mel grasps the note with her left hand, the hand that protrudes from Fred's mouth, while she unfolds it with her right.

She calls to the bailiff, "Just a moment, O Grand Inquisitor."

She begins reading, her face brightening as she reads. "This is an absolutely mysterious message, Freddy! The Frau said this came from our lawyer, whoever that is! But what lawyer would write 'steatopygia' and 'steenkirk' to an unknown client! What vivid imagination would possibly think that I would enjoy a picture of a steamroller at this moment of high drama? Not a mention of the charges. And unsigned. I love this man! Trying to cheer me up with wit and wisdom. The medieval barrister clamoring to haul me up from the Pit of Despair!"

Mel primps her hair, not pausing in her thought or speech, "I do hope it is one of my more masculine admirers the body of a Greek god to go along with this lively mind would be a treat beyond belief!"

She begins walking toward the waiting deputies, still talking. "Life is so refreshing at times, Fred. Just when you think things are desperately maudlin, along comes that special someone from out of the blue with just the right take on all the madness. A girl needs that kind of companionship to get through it all, you know."

She pauses at the door, "That, and the proper height pumps, of course."

Mel and Fred sit in the docket of the justice factory. Judge Robert Armstrong Cannalo presiding.

Judge Cannalo is running through people's lives on automatic pilot. The bailiff has barely read the charges when the Judge finishes rambling through the pleas, throws out a sentence, and gives the formerly-innocent accused a one-way elevator trip to hell. The basement of the Courthouse holds the Prisoner Processing Unit, and Cannalo keeps it humming, even at night. Due process takes maybe three minutes in this room.

Mel seems a great deal more together now, especially since she's spotted Mutt Jeansonne and his unknown   to her companion Rodrigo sitting in the Courtroom. Mutt is wearing his dress clothes, a gas station tshirt and holed tuxedo pants, accessorized with basketball sneakers and baseball cap. Still dressed up, since he was here in this same courthouse building just a few hours ago in his role as jury member.

In his swarthy arms Rodrigo cradles a briefcase bulging with multiple volumes of Professor O's All-Fact Encyclopedia. His reference library is ready. The All-Fact's English editors overcame haphazard translation from an original Korean edition by tailoring the encyclopedia's contents to the sensationalist hordes of free-spending American parents who roam the aisles of supermarket chains in search of knowledge to pass on to their progeny. The All-Fact remains Rodrigo's philosophical touchstone. And if casual observers don't immediately notice that he is both barefoot and stark raving mad, they'd probably say Rodrigo himself looks rather like a slightly bedraggled, though refined, barrister this night.

Fred is a bit shocked, though, when she gets a look at the very back of the courtroom. More of the friendly Street population is arriving every moment, as word of their incarceration spreads. Noonie and Virginia enter the Courtroom to nods and greetings, and the two smiling though unwholesome-looking Streets now sit side by side. Both are muttering rhythmically in different directions. To no one in particular. There are at least four seats vacant between them and the rest of the late-night court-watchers. Fred sees a small feathered head rise above the wooden seats in front of Noonie. The dog begins to get excited. Noonie has brought her pet duck to Trial.

Mel might not realize it yet, but Fred can sense that there is not a Norm in the audience.

The armies of liberation are present! Can justice prevail? Can I get a WERF, brothers and sisters? Fred wonders.

Mutt also has Mel's bag on his lap.

Now there is a considerate boy, Mel thinks when she sees her portable dressing room. It's all the girl can do to keep from leaping across the docket. Running over to that bag and freshening her lashes. Changing to her other shoes for indictment.

She has already done her best to adapt, stopping repeatedly on the walk to the courtroom to accommodate flashes of apparel inspiration. She tied the waist of her prison dress tightly and stretched the neck of the faded cotton garment just enough to allow her womanly figure some subtle display. Doing her part for the dignity of the American legal system.

Rodrigo keeps pointing his briefcase at the defendants. His planetary orientation is not altogether apparent tonight. Mel does not realize that her mysterious, intellectual, admiring legal correspondent is this same shoeless wonder. In spite of Rodrigo's occasional rambling, however, Mutt Jeansonne feels it bodes well for their case to have the unleashed forces of the universe on their side.

While waiting for the two defendants to be eaten alive by the snapping jaws of the nocturnal judiciary, there is opportunity to check out the other players on the scene.

The courtroom itself is now completely jammed with the most unsocial, wild-looking and filthy humans that inhabit the City. Fred & Mutt's kind of people. Vagrants, mostly. But there are also middle-of-the-night insomniac housewives and 24-hour sales clerks who come down to watch the proceedings because they don't own TVs. There is a sprinkling of victims who have been called to court to testify, and a few police officers here for the same reason. Mel's arresting officers are waiting, too. Drinking courthouse coffee in the back row while they fill out paperwork.

Mel keeps batting lashes at the blonde one. He is trying very hard not to notice the woman he arrested for public nudity. He knew it was a clean bust: the law in New Orleans requires these women who strip for a living to wear pasties on their nipples. Mel had removed hers, and he had witnessed the act.

A novice, "cub" newspaper reporter is sitting up front, bored to death and trying to chat up a hooker who is in line to bail her roomie out of jail. She stares at the hand the newsman has placed on her shoulder as if the meter is already running.

Two old ladies are eating Popeye's Fried Chicken in the row in front of Noonie and Virginia. Watching them lick grease off the bones, Noonie's duck Ellis D has acquired a concerned look. He twists his bill from side to side contemplating the implications of a number three dinner. Three pieces of spicy-style dark meat with batter-dipped french fries and coleslaw. Two thighs and a drumstick. An extra jalapeno pepper.

From the dock, canine Fred is looking too. Starving.

She is trying to send that message across the room into Mutt's brain. Doc Wolf, Mutt. I need the Doc's doggie ration. Fred watches intently for results, but Mutt and Rodrigo seem occupied, at the peak of some sort of plot. They sit on the second wooden bench whispering wildly back and forth. Rodrigo holds up two volumes of his library and makes cow sounds. *Mooooooooooooo.* A very pastoral touch in this ultimate urban setting.

Fred has to once again admire Rodrigo's sensibilities. Very calming effect. She wonders what his feet smell like this evening. She thinks that walking Bourbon street all night had to have added some extra depth to his normally fertile scent.

Moooooooo to you, too, Rodrigo. The dog makes a noise around Mel's wrist.

The Judge slams his hammer down. Mel is startled. Rodrigo gets quiet and looks around. He suspects some planetary collision might have occurred. Rodrigo does not understand much about Judge's hammers.

Fred is restless   the chicken dinner is making her stomach shiver and mouth salivate   but she resigns herself to her situation and looks hopefully at Mutt.

Mutt has stopped talking to Rodrigo and is now inspecting his friends' captors. Besides the usual complement of overweight and under-intelligent goons hired as Sheriff's Deputies to guard the august proceedings, there is only a handful of official personnel in the room   the court reporter, the judge's assistant and the public defender. Mutt has never seen any of these individuals during his juried tenure on the day shift, but he is familiar with their jobs.

Then, a revelation. He spies, all by herself at the prosecutor's bench, a young woman, extraordinarily beautiful considering her present situation.

The sensitive Mutt put out feelers, takes a reading on her: this woman is simultaneously entangled in the mechanism of the court, dominated by this monster judge, and carrying a bit of the monster herself. She wouldn't have been able to survive here otherwise.

Obviously the Assistant District Attorney has been assigned to the lowest of the low jobs in prosecution, carrying on the will of the State against the human slime of the Night Court. Trying cases simultaneously more trivial and more grotesque than anything Mutt had witnessed as a juror during the day. Mutt does not understand why this woman should have such a job. Ex-juror LM Jeansonne does not know that many unseen powers are at work here.

A mountain of files obscures the ADA's profile. Mutt comes to for a moment and cranes his neck. This woman is by far the most interesting Norm in the room.

She stands. The bailiff is reading the charges against Mel as Mutt continues to stare at the woman.

It is only then that the Judge spots Fred. Cannalo bangs his gavel, yelling, "Bailiff, Bailiff! Why is there an animal in my court?"

That gets a laugh from the people in the back. One of the old ladies drops a drumstick.

The bailiff whines quietly, "Judge Cannalo, your honor sir, we just haven't been able to get that dog off the defendant's arm   there ain't no animal doctor on call at Charity Hospital this time of night. But the Chief Deputy and me will get the dog knocked out as soon as we can get a vet down here with a needle. Probably around seven, when the morning shift comes on, Judge. I did get that dog's name, though Judge. Name is Fred."

Judge Cannalo audibly grits his teeth. "Did I ask for the dog's name, Bailiff? Do I need the little doggie's name to carry this trial forward?" he says, a slightly crazed look in his eyes. A low growl goes unnoticed under his question.

The bailiff slinks away to the protection of the bench. Cannalo resumes his routine. "I am going to continue with this case and get this..." pointing to Fred, "...abomination out of my Court, and... Bailiff, you will get that veterinarian in here before you transfer the accused to the main lock-up."

He pauses significantly while he looks straight at Mel, then finishes, malevolently, "...if incarceration is indeed the disposition of this case. Now let's proceed. Clerk, Assistant District Attorney Reed, you're on. Now."

There is a loud "Quack" from the back of the room. The Honorable Judge Cannalo has already gone back into automatic mode and luckily does not hear the fowl expletive.

Mutt had also done a character assessment of the Judge on first sight, having seen nine different judges over the progress of his month's jury duty. Cannalo definitely has the dubious honor of ranking at the bottom of Mutt's top ten. At least as far as attitude goes. Mutt can tell this judge has the corncob of life lodged solidly in place. In his legal briefs. Another individual who lacks essential biologic rhythm.

The trial goes on.

Cannalo acknowledges the public defender and then the ADA.

The defender is a muddled-looking fellow in a muddled suit, scruffing through handfuls of more muddled paper. He doesn't hear a word the Judge says, though he is standing directly in front of him.

The Assistant District Attorney is a different story. As the Judge enters into the record that the prosecuting ADA is Christine V Reed, she hears her name. The dazed look in her eyes retreats. She looks besieged as she comes to grips with where she is and what is happening, but is still organized and steadfast.

She looks determined to continue. And win whatever is to be won, Mutt notices.

She is interested in winning, he thinks.

Another interesting addition to his information database clicks into place. Observing and interacting with other humans in a jury pool for four weeks has honed his sensitivity, focused much of the input he is used to receiving. This has allowed him to sort, and reason why certain things have effects on one another.

It all means something.

Melodie LaGrande is also appraising the opposition. She notices that Reed carries a set of sizeable bulges in key locations under her tightly-buttoned raw silk suit and wears much more makeup than an aspiring career DA would ever have on her face. Plus the woman attorney is adorned with a solid gold Rolex and can invoke a dimple in each cheek at will. Mel watches as Reed flashes those dimples at the Judge. There they go again. Each and every time he yells about what he considers to be one more dropping of the legal ball. Mel stores her own observations for later use.

Fred is getting interested in the proceedings, too. She doesn't exactly want Reed to win. Fred harbors some mild hope that Prosecutor Christine V Reed will not have an elderly dog put to sleep as a result of whatever transgression a Bourbon street stripper might or might not have committed.

There was a catchy jingle on New Orleans radio and TV a few years back about the lovely animal compound on Wadley street, played often during a campaign to raise money for the shelter. The jingle failed to mention that Wadley street is also the place where quite a few four-legged creatures start their undistinguished journey to the pet netherworld.

"Eeeth-chch," lisps Fred around Mel's arm.

"Now, Freddy, easy, darling, nobody's going to hurt you," whispers Mel soothingly. Mel can sense Fred's moods instantly. There is some primal link between them, something bigger than tooth and gum pressure on forearm. "Looks like we're going to do something now, honey. Be brave," Mel tells Fred.

It starts.

Reed tells the Judge that Mel's "bust is a violation of the City of New Orleans Health Code".

Another huge laugh from the back of the room as several uncouth sorts cup their hands over their chests for the more obtuse members of the court.

Reed is embarrassed at her own unfortunate phrasing, which seems to afford Judge Cannalo a small flash of entertainment. The crowd is waking up.

Reed continues her argument by rote, noting again for the record that a violation of the city's Health Code is the basis of arrest.

"I am trying to be fair to the defendant, Your Honor, but the covering of certain female body parts in such public places, while a convoluted and antiquated law, is still held in force and is administered at the discretion of the individual officer of the law."

Mel stares at Reed like she could chop her into bite-size morsels, though Reed ignores Mel totally.

Rodrigo, on the other hand, has taken to directing certain rather awkwardly suggestive upper torso movements at Mel, while silently shaking his briefcase. Mel notices, but it is not apparent whether or not she is reading the clues. She gives no sign she knows that Rodrigo the Magnificent is also her prison correspondent and admirer.

On the machine goes. The arresting officer is sworn in, wearing a new uniform unsullied by processed chilidogs. The policeman glares with some irritation at Fred, who seems to be smiling. The Judge asks then asks the lawman to step forward and testify to the facts of the case.

The blonde officer testifies nervously, "Your Honor, I saw the accused expose her nipples..." He stutters twice on the word, prompting another unnoticed "quack" from the courtroom. "...at the French Can-Can-Do Lounge located at 265 Bourbon street on this night. I noted a violation of the Code, arrested the defendant, read her her rights and brought her in to the central lock-up holding area where she was further questioned."

"Did you read the dog his rights?" the Judge asks. He allows a brief period of laughter from the Court for his own comment, then silences it with one look.

Blondie gets even more flustered. The Judge seems to be having a good time now. He hasn't even begun to get the house hot.

Mel stands up unasked, to a gasp from the court, and says calmly, "Excuse me your honor sir, but this is a lady dog, and she is also my loyal and loving companion, sister and wardrobe consultant. Don't you think she's ever so darling? I take her everywhere. She makes any occasion festive."

To which Fred responds with a hearty "Moof!"   the best she can do with Mel's wrist still embedded in her mouth.

The Judge replies without a lost beat. "I won't hear evidence of crimes against nature at this point, only violations of the Health Code, madam."

Da da DUM.

There is a solid laugh from the courtroom this time, unchecked by the Judge. After all, it is his room and he is definitely on.

He has the crowd going. They have been waiting around forever in the stuffy courtroom, and now they are ready for anything. If the Judge has decided to wake up and entertain himself here at the corner of Tulane Avenue and Broad street at 4:15 in the morning, it could be nothing but fun. Regulars observe that Cannalo has quite an evil grin spreading across his rough red face.

The fun might potentially be a bit brutal.

The Times Picayune reporter is up to the railing in a flash, copying Mel's name off the books. He is praying that this little gathering of miscreants is headed toward a messy ending. A story nasty enough to earn him a page-one byline in the afternoon editions. Maybe get him interviewed on the local tube. "Bimbo and Mongrel in Bourbon Street Love Nest" ought to get him off this god-forsaken night shift. The media child is hungry for some big-time splash.

Fred sees the vultures gathering, and suddenly feels she may be riding on the fast track to The Big Dog Doze at the Wadley street SPCA, after all.

***********DOCKET CASE AO-51674B*********

CITY OF NEW ORLEANS VS Melodie LaGrande
VIOLATION OF CITY HEALTH CODE
STATUTE 978, ARTICLE G

****

NIGHT COURT DIVISION B, CITY OF NEW
ORLEANS
THE HONORABLE ROBERT ARMSTRONG CANNALO,
PRESIDING

LAWRENCE R. PURBUSH, CHIEF BAILIFF

[TRANSCRIPT CERTIFIED A TRUE AND ACCURATE
COPY BY: GERALDINE R. MOUTON, CLERK OF
COURT]

PRESIDING JUDGE INTRODUCED OFFICERS OF THE
COURT INTO RECORD, IDENTIFIED DEFENDANT
AND CHARGE. COMPLETE RECORD ATTACHED AS
ADDENDUM A.

Judge Robert A. Cannalo: Miss LaGrande, I
presume that you plead Guilty in the face
of the overwhelming evidence against you
and the testimony of the arresting
officer, and so I...

L. Mutt Jeansonne [subsequently
identified]: [coming forward from public
gallery] Mr. Judge Your Honor sir, I am
sorry to interrupt these legal Government
proceedings here, but I believe you, sir,
are about to be making a serious bad
mistake.

Unidentified male accompanying Jeansonne:
[unintelligible]... rheumatism
rhinoceros... [unintelligible] got it got
it innocent sir.

Judge Cannalo: Order! I'll have order in here. Quiet! Now, just who the hell are you, fellow, and why have you interrupted this Court?

Jeansonne: I just spent the last month locked up in this very same building on jury duty, Your Honor sir. Sitting down there in the basement waiting, I saw a lot of folks come in and out of here guilty as sin of doing some things I can't even mention in public. But this lady here she's done nothing to hurt anyone. She's a good citizen and you ought to be letting her go.

Public Defender Steven R. Wagner: Your Honor, I have not had the opportunity of interviewing this gentleman. It could be that he...

Judge Cannalo: Quiet, Wagner. [to Jeansonne] Your name?

Jeansonne: L. Mutt Jeansonne, Judge. Got me my Registered Voter ID right here to prove it. [Jeansonne offered card for inspection by Judge Cannalo]

Judge Cannalo: Well, very good, Mr. Jeansonne. You are indeed a voter in Orleans Parish.

Jeansonne: Just call me Mutt, Your honor.

Judge Cannalo: Mr. Jeansonne. Do you think you have anything relevant to offer the Court in this case?

ADA Christine V. Reed: Objection, your honor, this man is not a recognized officer of the Court, nor has he been requested by the defendant to represent her interests in this case.

Public Defender Wagner: Judge, as the legally-appointed representative of the Office of the New Orleans Public Defender, I believe I have precedence here. I have my rights. As you yourself well know, in my three years of office I have faithfully served over two thousand clients. All with distinction, many successfully. I have accomplished this feat while maintaining both the traditions and the dignity of the State of Louisiana's system of legal jurisprudence. I do not see why this August Court should listen...

Defendant Melodie LaGrande: I want Mutt. He's my man.

Unidentified male: Piragua! [spelling uncertain]

Judge Cannalo: I said quiet, son. Quiet, or I will have you removed. Miss Reed, it seems the defendant thinks this man has something to add to her case. Seems sensible to make sure the defendant receives the defense of her choice, doesn't it?

ADA Reed: Judge, I would have to agree with you. In my opinion, this gentleman can certainly — and adequately — substitute for Mr. Wagner.

Public Defender Wagner: This is uncon...

Judge Cannalo: So ruled. [Public Defender Wagner left the Courtroom at this point] Mr. Jeansonne, I warn you that if this is frivolous, I will take great pleasure in placing you also in the custody of the deputies. Contempt charges are a lot more serious than health code violations. Now what is it you want to say? And make it brief.

Jeansonne: Judge, I just want to know what it is that she is being charged with.

Judge Cannalo: Mr. Jeansonne, we have already read the charges. If you had been paying attention to the proceedings, you would know that. We still have a long docket ahead of us. I am allowing you this extra attention only in the interest of properly serving justice to your client. You will listen this time. Miss Mouton, I believe you have the statute. Read it to the gentleman, please.

ADA Reed: Judge, I don't know what purpose this will serve.

Judge Cannalo: You have a problem with giving this lovely woman a fair trial, Counselor? Not your sort, is she? You will humor me.

ADA Reed: I have no problem with Ms. LaGrande at all, sir. Except the legal problem she has presented to this Court.

Judge Cannalo: I will determine that, won't I? Miss Mouton, the statute, please.

Clerk of Court Geraldine R. Mouton: [Clerk of Court presented City Statutes, Volume 3, to Court] Yes, Your Honor. The applicable law is stated in the New Orleans City Health Code Statute 978, Article G, and specifically Subsection 3. The statute reads, and I quote, "Female service and/or entertainment personnel employed in public places of business that are subject to the articles of Statute 302, namely the City Liquor License, required for serving beverages of high alcoholic content, shall be subject to health rules specifying the wearing of approved hair nets and shoes in food preparation areas, and the sanitary covering of both the pubic region and breast nipples, to include the aureoles, in applicable entertainment areas."

[Clerk of Court replaced City Statutes, Volume 3]

Judge Cannalo: There you have it, Mr Jeansonne. Miss Reed. The law.

ADA Reed: Exactly, Your Honor. Miss LaGrande did, in fact, remove her pasties. She exposed her nipples, including the aureoles, in the presence of officers of the law. She is therefore both guilty of violating the law, and subject to its penalties. Judge Cannalo, we both know that this statute is a bit of self-righteous demagoguery that was snuck in the political back door with a Republican-dominated City Council back in the Eisenhower era. They put restrictions on the Bourbon street strip bars to try to convince the general population that government was setting a good example – keeping public mores from deteriorating by keeping female body parts under cover. It is indicative of the misguided social legislation of the nineteen-fifties. That said, I am sorry, Miss LaGrande, but the law remains both on the books and quite applicable in your specific case. Judge, the District Attorney's office asks that you rule Miss LaGrande guilty as charged.

[disruption in the courtroom]

Judge Cannalo: Quiet. Quiet! Stop that booing back there. And no more of those ridiculous noises! I will have order in this courtroom. If you people can't keep silence while this court is in session, I'll have you all tossed out into Tulane Avenue where you can talk as loudly as you want. Purbush, I want you to keep these people orderly. Pay attention. And Mr. Jeansonne, I would appreciate it if you and your companion would also refrain from muttering so loudly while I am doing you the courtesy of acceding to your own request.

Jeansonne: Sorry, Your Honor. Me and my buddy here just realized something we think you'll be interested in. We realized that not only is this lady not guilty, but she ain't even supposed to be here in the first place. If you'll let me come up there to your bench again, I can show you what I mean.

Judge Cannalo: Proceed. But in an orderly fashion. And let me warn you again: you had better be right about this.

Jeansonne: Yes, sir. Yes, Your Honor, sir. [to ADA Reed] Maam, would you identify the person who supposed to have committed a crime here?

ADA Reed: Of course. Counselor. [pointing to the defendant] Melodie LaGrande, present here in this court.

Jeansonne: That's what I thought. Judge, there ain't no Melodie LaGrande here.

Judge Cannalo: Bailiff Purbush, identify the defendant.

Bailiff Lawrence R. Purbush: Melodie LaGrande, 23, address unknown, place of employment French Can-Can-Do Lounge, shoe size 6B, Your Honor.

Judge Cannalo: And how did you get this information?

Bailiff Purbush: I got it from the defendant herself, Your Honor. In the holding area. She was pretty drunk, flashing them big boobs and that butt all around and...

Judge Cannalo: Purbush, any more talk like that from you and you will walk yourself down to the holding cell, and spend a little time as a guest of this Court. Without pay.

Bailiff Purbush: Yes sir. Yes sir. I'm sorry, your Honor. It's just she made such a scene back there. The lady she did tell me her name. We haven't been able to prove that she is who she says she is yet, because she didn't have a proper ID on her when she was brought in. Judge Your Honor sir, she didn't have nothing on her when she was brought in.

[courtroom disruption noted]

Judge Cannalo: Order! Quiet, you people!

Bailiff Purbush: But we got her prints, and we sent them off to the Feds for ID confirmation. Regular procedure in a case with no solid proof of identification. Should have something in the morning. But I wouldn't think it matters who she is as long as we know what she did.

[courtroom disruption noted]

Judge Cannalo: Order, dammit! [to Clerk of Court] I apologize, Miss Mouton. [to Courtroom] I won't tell you people again. Bailiff, you will keep your astute legal opinions to yourself in my Court. And Mr. Jeansonne, if the gentleman with you becomes unruly just once more, I will find you both in contempt.

Jeansonne: Yes, sir. Of course, Your Honor, sir. My associate here was kind of overexcited about some fine points of the law. And though I just sat here thirty days getting my education in the way things work in a courtroom, I still don't know how to do stuff. What I'd like to do is I'd like to enter something into evidence if it's OK with you and the lady.

[at this point Mr. Jeansonne placed a large bag on the defense table; he pulled a wallet from this bag, and then removed a Louisiana Driver's License from that wallet which he subsequently placed on Judge Cannalo's desk]

Judge Cannalo: Well, Mr. Jeansonne?

Jeansonne: Judge, just look at that picture on the license. Pretty, ain't she? Do you recognize the person in that picture, sir?

Judge Cannalo: Yes, it is the defendant here in Court.

Jeansonne: Judge, sir, if it's OK with you, I'd like this lady here [indicating ADA Reed] to get a look at that license.

Judge Cannalo: Alright, son, but I am telling you, you better have a damn good reason for what you're doing. We have wasted enough time here already. [to ADA Reed] Miss Reed, come over here, please.

[Jeansonne handed license directly to ADA Reed. There was a short further disruption as the ADA dropped the proffered evidence.]

Jeansonne: [to ADA Reed] Yes. Yes. Maam, I know all about the importance of having an ID of some sort. I been having mine a few years and I know it helps the Government keep track of us, among other things. This is a legal document, ain't it?

ADA Reed: Um. Yes. If issued by the State.

Jeansonne: And this one you got in your hand is, ain't it? Legal?

ADA Reed: Yes, it seems at first glance to be authentic. And if it is authentic, it is therefore a legal document in the eyes of the court.

Jeansonne: Would you mind looking carefully and reading me the person's name off that license?

ADA Reed: George Hotard.

[a longer period of general disruption noted in the courtroom]

Judge Cannalo: Order, dammit! I said order in the court! What the hell are you saying, Mr. Jeansonne?

Jeansonne: I'm getting there, Judge, sir. Maam, would you mind reading to me what the State of Louisiana certifying as to being this here person's sex?

ADA Reed: Male.

Judge Cannalo: Holy [expletive deleted from the record by Clerk of Court at Presiding Judge's subsequent request]

Jeansonne: That does it, Judge, sir. This lady just read me the law, and you yourself identified the person on this legal document. That law she read don't say a thing about a male needing to have his nipples covered in a public place, does it?

Unidentified male: Oblong!

Bailiff Purbush: Judge, there is a goddamn duck back here.

[another period of severe and prolonged general disruption followed this last statement, during which four people were ejected from the court, including the reporter from the Times-Picayune]

Judge Cannalo: I will have quiet! [to defendant LaGrande] Maam. Sir. Is this really you?

Defendant LaGrande: That's what I was trying to tell them when they first brought me in here. They just wouldn't let a girl have her say.

Judge Cannalo: I am sure they were a bit overwhelmed by the [Presiding Judge pointed to Defendant LaGrande] physical evidence in your particular case to think there was any other possibility. [to arresting officers] I think we tend to forget where we live once in a while, gentlemen. This is New Orleans, you know, and the French Quarter... well, the French Quarter is what it is. We must regard the law as flexible.

ADA Reed: Objection, Your Honor.

Judge Cannalo: Quiet, Miss Reed, I think I have this one under control. The law is clear and Mr. Jeansonne is correct. You are free to go, Mister Hotard. And on that questionable note, ladies and gents, let's pack it up and call it a night.

ADA Reed: But, Your Honor...

Judge Cannalo: The magic word tonight was Get a Life, Reed. Court adjourned.

****

THE ABOVE CERTIFIED A TRUE AND ACCURATE COPY.

GERALDINE R. MOUTON
CLERK OF COURT

CASE AO-51674B DISPOSITION:
CHARGES DISMISSED.

DEFENDANT RELEASED.
CASE FILE CLOSED.

From the September 1 Times-Picayune

Homeless man defends topless 'woman'

NEW ORLEANS (AP)   Shortly before sunrise today, City Night Court Judge Robert A. Cannalo dismissed charges of misdemeanor health code violations against Melodie LaGrande, 23, of this city. Cannalo ruled for dismissal despite the protests of both arresting officers and a representative of the Orleans Parish District Attorney's office. In an unusual and lengthy session at the Tulane Avenue Criminal Court Building, Judge Cannalo cited a technical misapplication of the law as the reason for his ruling. Officer T.E. Fortenberry of the New Orleans Police Department was issued an informal reprimand from the Court for failing to determine that Ms. LaGrande is in fact legally male, and not prosecutable under the so-called "nipple coverage" ordinance.

Making the decision more significant was the fact that Ms. LaGrande, an exotic entertainer at the French Can-Can-Do Lounge on Bourbon street, was represented in the legal proceedings by L. Mutt Jeansonne. Jeansonne, allegedly a homeless person, refused to give a local address, though he described himself as a "registered voter" of this city.

After the adjournment Assistant District Attorney Christine V. Reed commented on the acquittal, saying she believed the incident was "the first time an untrained indigent person has willingly and successfully participated as a principal in this City Court's trial process. I am happy to have been a part of this precedent-setting session, even though I was on the losing side, thanks to Mr. Jeansonne's legal insight," Reed said.

The trial was often interrupted by an unruly late-night courtroom crowd, some of whom made loud "barnyard" noises to indicate their approval or disapproval of the proceedings. There were, in fact, a number of animals in the Court. A duck and its owner were among those expelled as the Court's docket was called to a close.

Ms. LaGrande attended the trial clad in a green prison-hospital gown. Bailiffs provided the defendant with the clothing after she was booked at Central Lockup wearing only high heels and with a small grey dog attached to her left wrist.

On questioning by the Associated Press, LaGrande claimed the dog to be her wardrobe stylist.

* * *

The Picayune reporter's initial six paragraphs on Melodie LaGrande's acquittal was picked up by a wire service and in a matter of hours went out to two hundred newspapers around the world to be used as a curiosity, a filler, a substitute for blander UFO reports which contained no mention of Elvis.

The night's activities would bring other, more significant, developments.

L Mutt Jeansonne's slow, month-long metamorphosis as a juror, then a jurist, in the Criminal District Courthouse ended with the emergence of a new human on that October 1 morning. He felt awakened, empowered, alive for the first time in his life as dozens of people slapped him on the back and congratulated him. He beat the Government. He beat the System. He could handle the Norms.

He had no idea at all what to do.

Assistant District Attorney Christine V Reed is headed home after losing a public nudity case to a street bum. She does not, however, seem concerned. Her dark blue BMW filters all the bumps out of Tulane Avenue as she drives methodically through sparse early-morning traffic. The riverbound lanes are spotlessly clean, their asphalt patchwork shiny with moisture as it is each Tuesday and Thursday morning.

Tulane remains pristine for perhaps an hour after the streetsweepers pass, giving Mid-City New Orleans a fresh face that only a handful of her residents ever see. By 6am the glut of trash-laden commuters once again fill the gutters with disposable coffee cups. Decorating the lanes with the flattened remains of Breakfast Burritos and Popeye's morning-only Buttered Biscuits.

But at the magic moment of the BMW's passage, Tulane Avenue is dreamily perfect.

Reed's face is blank as she drives. Her jaw set solidly in place on fifteen thousand dollars worth of porcelain caps. Daddy's appointive position on the Louisiana Insurance Commission has allowed her access to an exceptional dental policy not offered to the general public. She isn't even sure who pays the premiums. All she knows is that some things in her life are always taken care of by others. Allowing her the time to concentrate on important matters. This morning her teeth fit together perfectly. She rolls through the streets of New Orleans, her driving unconscious and intuitive.

Christine Reed thought she had finally found the proper balance of wake and sleep. Twelve hours of each, on a daily basis, allowed her to heal from the unsettling demands of Night Court.

But now with the added pressure of catering to Judge Cannalo's erratic demands, and the scrutiny of the DA himself, Chris needed to be prepared well in advance for each night's cases. She was forced to take work home. Her sleep was cut to eight hours immediately, quickly dwindled to six, then less. Unfortunately, her conscientious research and newly-respectful demeanor in court didn't seem to make a difference in Cannalo's temperament. He remained the source of nightly fits of pique.

And well-prepared Assistant District Attorney Christine V Reed was still inevitably the subject of one or more of those fits.

Her stress level had escalated significantly. She worked harder at regaining equilibrium, even using the twenty minutes of car travel to and from work to separate the tortured ADA from the recovering human Chris Reed. The drive wasn't bad. Her father had bought her a brand-new BMW when she submitted to his will and took the job with his friend, District Attorney Bronner. But as always, the paternal gift was not without strings. Her father had specified that the car was to stay in his name until he thought Chris truly deserved full ownership. It was hers when he determined she had become a real lawyer. He would allow her the use of it until that time.

She used it hard.

Reed's mind is working full-tilt elsewhere, even as she drives. Filtering out the night's bumps in much the same way her car's suspension deals with potholes. She looks up for a moment. An illuminated Tequila billboard flashes the multiple yearning smiles of its painted inhabitants at her passing. Reed relaxes. Her mind wanders.

These street signs are probably holdovers from the same era as that idiot Nipple Law, and a homeless nobody just knocked the teeth right out of that one. So I lost. Big Deal.

Wish we had set a precedent.

First order of business, all laws made between 1950 and 1960 in the City of New Orleans are hereby invalid. As they were made by jerkoffs, are enforced by assholes, and are therefore subject to civil disobedience. Second order of business, kill all the judges from that decade who still occupy judicial benches.

Clear the decks. Starting with that wise-ass sexist shit-head Cannalo. How do I always get stuck having to deal with men like that piece of trash? Get rid of them! Put in people like that man Jeansonne. Real people.

Reed turns the steering wheel sharply. Aiming the car to cross left in front of the illuminated "No Left Turn" warning onto Elk Place. Looking directly at the printed law as she purposely breaks it.

The thought of the Judge makes her jerk the steering wheel even harder into the illegal left turn.

The car obeys immediately and without effort. Wide Teutonic wheels hum around the corner noiselessly. The Beemer never questions her whims, no matter how sudden or contrary to logic they are. She guns the engine to speed up even more, skidding just a bit into the far left lane.

And there, dead center in her headlights, stands Mutt Jeansonne.

Mutt had taken all the congratulatory hand-shaking and goodbye pats-on-the-back as he could from the Courtroom folks. They were all very nice people, but Mutt hadn't quite perfected a method of how to stop input. He had never before had the occasion to think he would need such a skill. And yet, there he was, inundated. He got another life story from the touch of new flesh every time someone grabbed him. The whole and complete life story. It was an odd ability he had, one that he seldom used, since he had so little human contact. Sometimes it frightened him.

Like the feeling he got from Assistant District Attorney Christine V Reed. When he had passed Mel's license to her during the trial, Reed had briefly touched his hand. Mutt was embarrassed when she jumped back. He could tell that Reed had somehow felt him get a reading on her. She had acted like she had received a shock of static electricity. Mutt had never realized anyone got feedback from his gift. He was rather amazed. He hadn't much experience at touching Norms. He wondered if maybe she had some part of the gift herself and didn't know.

But there wasn't much for Mutt to get a hold on. Reed had most of herself locked up tighter than the offering box at a tent revival. Mutt could tell, however, that closer to the surface, she really cared about the people in her court and that... she somehow admired him. Insane. Him. L Mutt Jeansonne, registered voter of the City of New Orleans. He was astounded, but managed to continue. Then when the trial was over, he was overwhelmed with congratulations. The Chris Reed person was lost in the flood of new people and old friends. The moment was gone.

Now he remembers the jury manager earlier in the evening, handing him a crisp rectangle of paper as he leaves. He sits around for a month watching others go into service, waiting to be selected himself, then when he is chosen the court pays him ten whole dollars for his single day's active jury service. Pays him with a check.

Great. Government helpful as always.

I'll need to find a place to cash it, so me & Fred can get some decent food. Hard this time of night.

Mutt's hunger adds to his confusion.

The walk back to the Quarter starts to clear his head. After the trial Noonie and Virginia ran off in one direction, Rodrigo in another. Mutt is stuck, as usual, carrying a tired dog and supporting a hung-over employer. As Mutt warned her would happen, the innocent Melodie LaGrande is maneuvering with a great deal of difficulty. Now that she has donned a fashionable pair of midnight-black Milanese stiletto sandals.

Here he is again, next-to-blind and with a bad leg, dragging friends home in the wee hours of the morning. At this pace it will take them at least an hour to make it back to the French Quarter, he estimates.

Maybe even until sunup.

It does not seem like so bad a prospect, though. Fred is asleep in his arms, and Mel is almost sleepwalking as she slumps along beside him. Mutt is thinking about the lawyer woman. Studying her in his mind like he would study a new billboard on the expressway. He relives the moment when he discovered that she was thinking about him. And relives it again.

He stumbles off the curb as he crosses onto Elk's Place, helping Mel step down. He can see even less at night, and Fred is getting heavier. He raises his head from the street.

Even as bad as his eyes are, he can see the headlights coming quickly toward him. They are in his lane and only ten feet away.

* * *

Mutt Jeansonne fidgets in the passenger's seat as the BMW rounds another corner. Fred moans briefly at the force of the turn, tucking her head further under Mutt's left arm and going back to sleep. Mutt hopes she will stay there. He has things to think about.

First he has to deal with this woman, and her car. In spite of being in his jury duty outfit, Mutt is all too aware that even his cleanest clothes might at this moment be soiling the spotless interior of the luxury car. And his furry companion smells downright ripe. Fred having managed to extract a complimentary sampler of the various scents handed out by the courteous representatives of the parish prison holding cell. "*Parfums des Femmes Extraordinaires*", Melodie had dubbed the stench. Mutt is sure that Mel savors the most fragrant of human smells almost as much as Fred.

Mel. Mutt turns to check on her. She fell off balance on the last turn and is now sprawled across the dark padded leather of the back seat. With her beloved wardrobe bag under her head. Snoring loudly. Her green prison dress hiked up to her waist pockets. Which bulge with a dozen wads of money wrapped around pieces of a dog collar. Mel's last night's earning salvaged by Rodrigo.

As Mutt watches, Mel snorts awake at a passing car's headlights, looks around groggily, and then like Fred drops back immediately into a shallow sleep. She seems content.

Mel is dreaming sweetly, recreating the whole scene in her sleep. But this time wearing her Anne Klein neon pink business suit with matching hat. And those exquisite little Italian satin pumps.

Melodie giggles as she sleeps. Dreamily musing that it was actually a treat to see her Mr George Hotard surface this time. To think she had totally dismissed him. *The boy does have his uses.*

Mutt wonders at how quickly Mel has recovered her good humor. He could tell she was nervous in the courtroom. She gave off all the signals. But here she is, totally healed, as if she never even approached the cataclysm. Nothing seems to faze her. He envies that.

His mindset on the Street itself is far different. Mutt knows intuitively that he is being hunted. Pursued by something. At least he has felt that way. Before tonight.

He's not feeling stalked at this moment, and for good reason. As he turns back to the front, L Mutt Jeansonne steals a sideways look at Christine V Reed.

Another first in a day and night of firsts. First time actually on a jury. First time in a courtroom when he didn't have to be there. First time speaking out by himself in front of a group of people. An unimaginable first time arguing   and winning   a case in a Norm court of law.

Now, topping even that, the very first time in his entire life he has ever sat next to a real woman. A Norm to the nth degree. Beautiful. In private. She even offered him the opportunity.

"A ride home for the victor," she had said. "The least I can do."

Mutt is torn between staring at Christine Reed and desperately trying not to stare. It is quickly apparent to him that the not-staring option is not working out.

He finds new resolution, admits to himself that he is incapable of turning his eyes away from her. Mutt decides to cover his embarrassment with talk. Even that is difficult.

"Well, me & Fred and Mel do want to thank you, Miz Reed, for the ride," he says quickly. There is an awkward pause as he looks inward for another subject.

Reed nods, a wave of her salon-highlighted blonde hair falling across a freshly-rouged cheek. "Mister Jeansonne, I almost ran over you!" she whispers, her voice breathy and low with wear after the long night's legal discussions. "If the brakes on this car hadn't been so good, you might have been on your way to the hospital, instead of heading home to celebrate your victory."

"Maam, I'm sorry. I didn't mean to be disrespectful," Mutt stutters.

She smiles. "You did a great job tonight, Mr Jeansonne. You beat me and Judge Cannalo. And we deserved to be beat." As she finishes speaking, Reed turns toward Mutt. Looking him directly in the eyes.

The move takes just a moment, but Mutt is suspended in time. When he recalls the sequence of events later, he is sure it took at least an hour to travel the last few blocks into the

Quarter.   He feels like he has fallen headlong into an ever-tightening spiral. His receptors go crazy.

This is a new one. Beyond his experience. Beyond his imagination.

Tonight his mind is suddenly jerked into motion, then pulled in exactly the opposite direction. After decades of passivity. In the courtroom it had suddenly become apparent to him that he could actually have an effect on his own life. He could actually do something in the Norm world. And yet minutes later here he is, rendered powerless as a child.

Again, he doesn't have a clue as to what is happening. He sees his body sitting rigid in the car seat. He knows he has no control.

Mutt Jeansonne wonders if it is possible that he has died. The nuns had hammered into him that lust is the doorway to hell. Is this lust? Is he damned?

"If this is it, then hell isn't anywhere near as bad as those nuns were saying," he says out loud.

Holy Christ on a crutch! I said that out loud!

"What?" Reed asks, "What about hell?"

He becomes aware of the woman's presence again and is immediately lost.

Got to get it back together here!

Her eyes hold him. Thin turquoise circles border dark pools. Edges seem somehow out of focus. He is being pulled down into the dark. Getting lost in the darkness.

He is... jerked upwards with a start. She has parted her lips. Preparing to speak to him again. He has heard the flesh of her lips make a sound as they draw apart, amplified to the threshold of pain. He can hear everything. The interior of the car becomes his world.

She pauses, draws in a slow breath.

Mutt waits.

To him this person is the woman on the cigarette and liquor billboards. The only standard of comparison he possesses outside of Mel. And Mel is disqualified from the current Norm-world study group. Even though she does look like the billboard girls in some ways. Mutt's favorite highway signs are loaded with twenty-foot tall women. Made up of hundreds of thousands of colored dots.

Unlike the old faded movie posters in Mel's dressing room, when these picture walls contained women, they always seemed too intimidating to Mutt. He hadn't become bold enough to talk to any of them. But he had been forcing himself to at least look at the oversized images. He felt it was a necessary part of his continuing education. Norms could talk to anybody. Mutt, as much as he could sense and feel about the world around him, had trouble trying to communicate with the Norm world. He simply had very little experience with it, except for the highway signs. Until now.

Billboards had shown Mutt much of the little he knew about the opposite sex. The pinnacle of American womanhood is smiling in a bikini on a beach. A cigarette in her hand. Lungs quite large enough to hold the smoke. Looking happy and in control of her destiny. Mutt had never dreamed that the billboard women might exist in three dimensions. And without the dots.

The car continues, passing through an endless succession of magnesium street lights. Time continues to stretch.

Like standing in front of a department store TV, but being inside the picture.

She is beautiful.

And she is looking at him.

Mutt feels his heart make a weird sound. Then his stomach. He feels like he might throw up. He sees that his own mouth is open.

"Are you all right, Mr Jeansonne?"

He comes to abruptly, and finds that he is unconsciously stroking Fred's ears. Hard.

"Yes, maam."

He coughs deeply, trying to clear his throat. Sees that they are nearing their destination.

"Take us to Mel's car, if you please, maam. Just around the corner from the Lounge. On Dauphine street between Bienville and Conti. Please, maam."

"No need to call me maam, Mr Jeansonne. I'm Chris." Reed takes her right hand off the steering wheel and touches Mutt's arm.

He pops backwards so hard that the headrest reclines a notch.

"And I know you're Mutt," she says, willing her dimples into existence once again.

Chris Reed is in control of the situation. Her smile is broader now. Dimples deepening. An easy exercise for a young woman schooled in social-surgical procedures. She had learned advanced southern belle charm from her mother and Louisiana politics from her Daddy. But she realizes she is doing this for herself.

This is exciting. Jesus! Am I reading this right? This isn't just your average bag lady with a history of vagrancy, is it?

Chris stops to think on that one. No. She had read the cues right. As soon as he handed her the license, she knew that he was right. There was a flash of real insight there. She had known he was right.

There is something here she rather likes, too. This man is altogether an innocent. She keeps her predatory reflex subdued in the face of his willingness to show and say exactly what he is feeling. He doesn't seem capable of deception. But the jury is not yet in on that premise.

She can also tell, quite easily, that he is sexually attracted to her. And she has called only the most marginal bit of charm into play.

Charm is another reflex that she never has to consciously engage. Part of the business of life, it comes naturally, emanating from the same system of simple feminine politeness that has been used for the better part of three centuries in Louisiana. To crush the balls of countless southern gentlemen. And claw the eyes out of even more numerous rival southern gentlewomen. It is a defining characteristic of true southern aristocracy.

Totally-heartless soul murder done politely.

Funny. I finally run into a man I don't find offensive and he's a street bum without a penny to his name. Daddy would be furious.

"Where did you ever get the courage to jump up in front of Judge Cannalo, Mutt?" she asks. "He makes most people scared to move."

Mutt feels panic rise a notch. He is afraid he might have pissed his pants when she said his name.

"I don't really know, maam," he says, inching his right hand into his crotch to see if he can detect moisture. "I guess I kinda got used to being in the courtrooms after my month of jury duty. I had to get my two best friends out of that jail, and I forgot about being scared."

"You learn quickly," she says.

What is it I feel about this man? What is the connection here? Not sexual. Definitely not intellectual. Something, though. Might as well gamble. I've got nothing to do but sleep all day. Get back into that same deadly rhythm. I can skip reading through all the court material for just this one night.

Daddy will be furious. I'll tell him I was just trying to avoid a lawsuit. I was being nice to a man I'd almost run over.

Chris looks in the rear view mirror at the sleeping Mel.

No way he's gay, and surely not fooling around with that thing.

Her eyes snap back to the road as they cross Rampart street. "Why don't we have some breakfast after we drop off your friend? Just you and me."

Mutt's stomach answers for him with an involuntary, immediate and loud rumble. He is out of his body again, watching this moment in time progress. Becoming more confident. He somehow knows his lines now.

"Yes, maam. I haven't been eating too regular this last month. Neither has Fred here." He scratches the dog's chin.

"But I got me my jury money to get us a meal later today, and I'm afraid we'd both drop off if we stayed up too much longer this morning. How's about we meet up tomorrow , say at the Suds & Duds? That's been Fred's favorite place for breakfast, the few times when we got enough money to eat there.

"Fred?"

"Fred's got to come, too, Chris maam. I can't be leaving her. She's my roommate, you know."

Reed sighs. *I knew it was all going too easily. But if dealing with unsanitary pets is the worst I've got coming, this is still a situation I can handle with my eyes closed.*

"I am sure we can get some breakfast for Fred, too," she answers quickly, then heard a mental replay of Mutt's last statement. "She"? This might be kinkier than she had expected.

"Is Fred a girl, Mutt?"

"Yes, maam. Long story."

They are approaching Mel's car. Mutt seizes the opportunity to divert attention from himself.

"That's it right there, Chris maam, if you want to pull over. Just let me see if can I wake Mel up. See if she can be driving this car by herself. You see, I usually am the one driving her. Part of my job."

Fred raises her head groggily as Mutt moves his arm and pushes the door ajar.

"Mrrrf?"

He picks the sleepy dog up, gets out and gently puts Fred temporarily back on the BMW's front seat, then opens the back passenger door, ever-so-slowly lifting Mel upright and pulling her dress down to a more modest position.

Fred's eyes clear as she realizes where she is. An open-mouthed dog yawn ends in an abrupt throat-clearing cough. Gagging a small projectile of dog phlegm onto the previously immaculate carpet. Fred sniffs at it, barks once with authority at Mutt, then looks across the car at Chris Reed.

Reed is staring at her car rug with horror in her eyes.

* * *

Four hours later, the moment the Central Library doors open, Virginia and Noonie rush in. The two Streets have been waiting beneath the azalea bushes outside the Library entrance ever since they were expelled from the Night Court, and are eager to carry out their mission. Ellis D, stashed in Noonie's voluminous cloth bag, sleeps contentedly through the stampede. The duck has made a comfortable nest of the dozens of cigarette butts in the bottom of the bag, and apart from being banged about a bit, he enjoys being carried.

The two women, both talking furiously, push past the guard and sprint through the reference section directly to the Ladies' Room.

The toilets at the Central Library are the community center of the Street people of New Orleans, who had long ago in a spirit of governmental participation dubbed the rooms "Shitty Hall".

Amidst the air-conditioned comfort of the scarred marble stalls, messages and community news are posted and gathered. Long lost friends are found and reconciled. Evicted nighttime squatters are hidden from the daytime Law. Marathon sink baths are indulged. And the occasional biologic function is exercised.

Shitty Hall's Street-use rose dramatically after the financially troubled 1984 World's Fair, which only served to draw more Northern unemployed to the snowless streets of New Orleans. New Orleanians had never seen Street people like this before. No one knew how to deal with what became a growing tidal wave of disenfranchised humanity. The people of the City could not understand how the problem simply appeared overnight. There was a rumor of free one-way bus trips being offered that winter by the Mayor of New York. To any of the homeless of Manhattan who wanted to relocate to the Sunny South.

The Fair's failure was closely followed by the '85 oil bust. Which further glutted the blue-collar workplace with thousands more unemployed offshore riggers and local petroleum executives. Who had thought the good life on oil company payrolls would never end.

The Library and the City made several legal attempts to curb the Street people's aggressive take-over of the restrooms, but had been unable to come up with a formula that would simultaneously curb the toilet monopoly and yet not curb constitutional rights. The ACLU grew to be an avid defender of the Free Toilet Movement. After two years of effort the authorities were still unsuccessful in unseating the squatters. Since 1988 the restrooms had remained primarily in the hands of the homeless.

As is the way in New Orleans, this small action had an escalating ripple effect on the community at large.

Other more affluent library users began walking across the street to the lavish WCs of the Wade University Medical Center when the need for such a facility pressed upon them during their scholarly research. Shortly after the onset of these impromptu toilet tours, the Med Center found its donations from the private sector rising significantly. Never one to miss an opportunity   especially in those days of slim funding   the Med Center promptly instructed its security staff to welcome to the johns anyone looking wealthy enough to handle the Patron Level of donation. To the Friends of the Center. For $100 and up, benefactors received a membership card plus a free "I Love to Go to the Hospital" t-shirt.

Books under the arm merited immediate and unquestioned admission. Except to the unshod Rodrigo. Street people could not check out books, since the application for a library card required a permanent local address. The Friends of the Wade University Medical Center were rapidly infiltrated by the Friends of the Wade University Medical Center Restrooms. There was talk of establishing a walk-in outpatient clinic. With valet parking, of course.

But the Library toilets were left to the Street people, and Shitty Hall became an institution.

It continued to provide the dominant means of communication among Streets, especially in its bank of half dozen mirrors, and the regularly-replenished stock of soap bars on its sinks. Which were a product of the generosity of Mrs Alice Bedusky, an 82-year-old non-Wade library volunteer whose side mission had become helping the Street people of New Orleans stay a bit cleaner. At her own expense, Mrs Bedusky furnished the Library's maintenance staff with two new cases of of magnolia-scented, 100% antiseptic Wonderbar soap each and every month.

Most of which was actually used in non-hygienic fashion to inscribe messages on the mirrors.

The headline story this morning, thanks to Noonie and Virginia, boasted multiple narratives of an incredible victory over Norm law enforcement by one of their own. Plus a sidebar mention of the heroic efforts of a neighborhood duck and dog in an animal-unfriendly court of law.

All in all, it seemed that L Mutt Jeansonne was well on his way to notoriety among the Streets of New Orleans. And many many others.

As noon approached, Mutt, forever the complete outsider, did not know that his name was suddenly in print in newspapers around the world, or that every Street in the city was now speaking his name. Up until that morning, Mutt had been the sole source of his personal story. He was the only one, other than the tight-lipped and loose-bowelled Fred, who could relate anything at all about L Mutt Jeansonne.

That would soon change.

Mutt at the moment he's hanging out under the Expressway looking for a decent conversation. Unlike Fred, he hasn't been able to sleep, in spite of being exhausted from the events of the previous long day and night. The Reed woman has loosed something odd within him. Something that keeps him thinking, reminiscing. He's nervous. It's not hard to spot him out here. The boy sticks out like a prom-dressed debutante at a soup kitchen.

There he is. L Mutt Jeansonne. Standing all by himself again. This time below the dark fluorescent tubes on a "Jerry's Trailer City" billboard. The long lights below a huge but dim Satisfied Customer smile are buzzing with a flickering noise the sound of flies straining against a windowpane. The tubes are audibly responding to repeated prodding by electronic sensors, but they resist. Even this late in the morning they are not quite ready to fully darken. They do electrical battle to stay alight.

There are plastic and metal devices that know when the day, and the night, is over. Mutt has that statement firmly ensconced in the sacred mystery category. He suspects the power company employs an itinerant gypsy switchman. Very stealthy person. Very small and quick on his feet. No one ever sees the fellow as every day he turns things on and off all over the city.

Neither the buzzing nor the mystery has slowed Mutt's intensity. Mutt, he's looking for clues, like usual. He's being very careful, taking his time examining the smiling sixteen-foot-tall face of Jerry's "Satisfied Customer". For almost an hour now. Nose. Eyes. Mouth. A freckle on the giant right ear shaped like the waning moon. Asking to be studied. Asking to be quoted: "Satisfied since I bought my double-wide, and proud of it."

Mutt stares, wide-eyed, taking the information in.

Then, BOOM, an explosion of light. The summer sun pops into view over the metal sign frame. Hello, Mutt. The old boy doesn't even flinch. As he watches, a beam flows across the face, warming the painted surface. Shadows on the sign pause briefly in their time travels to show the sun is directly overhead, then move on. The monumental sundial nose of the Satisfied Customer reads noon.

Mutt squints. He knows that twelve o'clock brings the prime heat of the day. And yet here he is, exposed.

His eyes do a quick recce, leftright. Even the idiot pigeons have already disappeared. Not a grey-feathered roofrat in sight. Sensible creatures wait out the noontime, Mutt. They doze in the shade. The heat passes.

Fred is asleep back at the Box. Has been for the better part of an hour.

But Mutt Jeansonne stands his ground. Intent. Not moving a muscle. His shirt, saturated with sweat, has become his outermost skin. The paper bus transfer in his chest pocket is easily readable through the thin polyester. At one time it said "Canal Cemeteries Express Bus." Expired 4:30pm Thursday the nineteenth. The dead transfer now in the process of dissolving as the moisture trapped in Mutt's clothes refuses to leave. Soon the paper will disappear completely, leaving only portions of the inked words suspended in the cloth of the pocket:

CAN CEMETERIES PRESS US

The important words don't dissolve so easily, even in New Orleans.

Water seems to have a direct effect on how Mutt views the world.

It is late summer. Evaporation is a fool's pipe dream at this point in the Delta moisture cycle. That stinking, bubbling Gulf of Mexico stew has already reclaimed the air as its own.

Mutt Jeansonne lives in New Orleans. Yes he does. And in Summer New Orleans lives below the surface of the ocean. As it once had and always will.

At the moment it is mid-August, Summer's pounding heart.

Mutt's body gives proof enough to the fact. Rivulets of salt water pulse down his cheeks. A stream works a course over his chin, pooling behind his collarbone.

Hands hang at his sides, pointing to the somewhat hotter core of the earth.

Sweat drips intermittently off his ten fingertips, making a pattern of uneven circles in the dust near a pair of worn cloth shoes. You can hear a gentle "plop" sound as each droplet makes contact with the ground.

The August sun brings heat. Heat demands water. Mutt gives the heat its due.

Shade would be nice, Mutt.

But even though he looks old and stupid out there in the sun, he's smart. He knows the cool of the elevated roadway is well beyond his eye range. The Trailer City Customer would be a dark blur from back there. Mutt stays put.

I need a good look at this fellow.

Mutt's thinking. It's written right on his face. The man is an easy read if you know him.

He has to make sure, and that's OK. He's never spoken to this particular billboard before. He needs to think about the possibilities, just for a few moments more. Then he'll be ready.

Anything new is always traumatic for Mutt Jeansonne. The man is more than just sensitive. Mutt is an antenna, the earthbound flesh equivalent of NASA's giant radio-telescopes. Snow-white electronic ears pointed out at space, listening for minute gaseous expulsions from enormous black holes. Excited scientists listening carefully to the results.

"Celestial flatulence! Star farts!" as Rodrigo so delicately and succinctly explains.

Mutt and Rodrigo discuss interstellar goings-on regularly. Infinitesimally small happenings, billions of miles away. Everyone eavesdrops as Betelgeuse scrapes his chair pushing back from a great meal at the Orion constellation cafeteria. M42 picks her teeth. Rigel flosses. The space ears hear it all.

Mutt's just like that. Anyone on the Street can tell you. Loose human electrons stick to his cuffs as he passes through the weed-ridden, abandoned lot of his daily life. He can feel them, zeroes right in on any sort of communication. The source doesn't matter.

Mutt is in touch with so much of his everyday environment that even minute quantities of unfamiliar input often confuse him. They get to be too much for him. He weaves through his day, dodging this and that stray bit, but continually picking up transmissions most people don't know exist. He reads lengthy messages in places that normal people the Norms of the world   wouldn't even think to look.

His pants, for instance.

Tuxedo pants. Twenty years old, by his own estimates. Bought on sale for four bits at the French Quarter Volunteers of America Thrift Store. An ex-State Treasurer was working behind the counter, fulfilling the community service portion of his fourteen-count felony embezzlement sentence. Nice gent. He found the pants for Mutt. They fit perfectly. The moth holes are hardly even noticeable when Mutt darkens the thigh skin underneath. He uses a number one pencil. This, his long-time-favorite writing device, once had "Krewe of Karnival" printed in gold on one purple-and-green-striped side. He systematically freshens the dark graphite leg pools twice a day to disguise his pant cavities. This regular use of the soft graphite has already left only the "Kre" of the original Mardi Gras title. Mutt knows he will miss that pencil when it's gone. He has become reconciled to loss. The pants require pencil use.

But if Mutt had suspected the hidden price carried by those trousers, he would never have laid down his hard-earned money.

They cost him his nights.

The pants wouldn't let him sleep for months after he got them. He was always waking up thirsty. Or having to pee. He immediately sensed that the former long-time owner of his pants had a drinking problem. Mutt nightly relived the hundreds of drunken fly-openings the pants had been subjected to. The head spinning. The numbed fingers trying to deal with five buttons and thick prickly cloth. The anxiety of trying to not look the fool.

A broad sweep of pant history came to Mutt the first time he put them on. A distinct gin feel to them.

The details came as he slept, the director's cut of a vivid biopic running in Technicolor and Panavision in his drowsing head screening room.

The Story of Mutt's Pants

They were genteel pants. A Rockfield's label inside the left front attested to their pedigree.

Rockfield's, the ultra-expensive five-floor clothing salon on Canal street, has been at its current location for one hundred fifty-five years. Even while they pillaged the rest of the city, the Yankees had not dared to harm the Rockfield establishment. To this day the aging night custodian will tell the story with only the slightest prompting. He proudly prefaces his tale by noting that up until the onset of the War Between the States, Union General William Tecumseh Sherman had Rockfield's clothing artisans tailor Louisiana cotton shirts for him on a regular basis. His orderly cut ever-expanding paper size-patterns each month, folding them precisely into small envelopes for their trip south through the US Mail. Rockfield's shirts traveled the same route in reverse, heading north from New Orleans to find their new owner and drop comfortably onto his shoulders.

Then came the War.

Four years later, the general sent a letter by personal courier to the Rockfield family, explaining his sad but necessary part in the defeat of the Confederacy. For his courtesy Mr Sherman was allowed to anonymously continue as a customer during his later term as president of Louisiana State University. It was rumored that the Rockfield family secretly admired the man who had had the good taste to burn Atlanta. An act for which he is no less revered in contemporary New Orleans.

To those allowed to shop there, nothing can take the place of Rockfield's.

As a setting for purchasing clothing, few establishments can call themselves its equal. The walls of the spacious private dressing rooms are draped in multiple layers of deeply-colored velvet, ceiling to floor. Persian carpets cover the polished hardwood floors, the fiber so ornate and thick with design that few customers ever dare set foot upon it. Most normally choose to tip-toe around the room's edges on a narrow six inches of floor not covered by a subtly-woven reproduction of Hannibal Crossing the Alps. Hannibal's bearded grimace remains to this day a bit unsettling for those unfamiliar with the gentleman's legendary personal charms when off-elephant. Even incidental pieces of furniture are vintage British antiques. Chandeliers hang in the ladies' and gentlemen's lounges, illuminating hundred-year-old ebony rollers fitted with polished brass. The rollers cradle tissue for unmentionable but occasionally undelayable biological functions. Rockfield's prides itself in being as tastefully well-decorated as any of its patrons' homes.

Uptown New Orleans society has clothed its denizens within these sumptuous confines for over a century. Credit accounts are preferred by management to the extent that cash is considered not only gauche, but unsanitary. The sales staff do not want to touch it. "My dear madam, that soiled paper could have been almost anywhere." Besides, there is rumored to be a wooden chest filled with century-old Confederate currency still sitting in the Company vault, continually reminding the owners of a lesson on the shortcomings of a cash trade. As modern American economics begin to encroach on the rest of the City, Rockfield's has maintained its stance that nothing so democratic as plastic cards is needed or wanted.

It is difficult for a stranger to buy things at Rockfield's, no matter the expanse of wealth or the depth of lineage. Things can become even more difficult if the intruder is suspected of Not Being a Southerner. The uninformed tourist walking in the doors of the marble-girded temple can wait hours to be acknowledged.   Much less be served.

But, oh, family.

Most regulars never sign for their purchases. A word is, of course, enough.

Mrs Cleona Louise Bagatelle has been assisting her ladies for forty-one years. She has refused promotion to management on six separate occasions, preferring to remain on her own third floor. "I have a responsibility to my clientele, sir. They would be lost without me," she firmly asserted to the Assistant Manager in 1987, all the while inspecting his administrative suite. "Besides, I wouldn't be happy up here. These offices are so dismally uninspiring. You could really use some plants in this room, something to distract from this dreadful carpeting. We've the most lovely mauve drapes just come in to Home Furnishings. I could help you with your selection if you like."

This was the last occasion on which Mrs Bagatelle was invited upstairs to the Executive Offices.

She is not put out in the least. Mrs Bagatelle is getting a bit short-winded for the climb to five, and as a lady of character she hasn't much use for elevators.

She places her energy in attention to detail.

"Yes, all your information is completely up-to-date, Missus Beaumont," she says, making notes on her ivory index cards. "Not to bother. Alterations ready first thing in the morning. Rather this evening? Fine then." A discreet lowering of the voice. Leaning close now. "Put on say an inch in the waist, two in the hips, shall we? Should be more than sufficient. Won't say a word to anyone. Mrs Gutierrez is the most discreet of seamstresses. No problem whatsoever. Love to the handsome hubby Bruce and that lovely little niece. Susan. We never see her any more since she's gone away to Vanderbilt. Chi Omega, isn't she? First in her pledge class?"

This was not a solitary familial inquiry on the part of Mrs Bagatelle. Rockfield's sales people always make a point of inquiring after customers' obscure relations by name. The research shows they care. That much is expected as routine courtesy. The inputting of such information, clothing sizes or even account balances, into a computer would be considered profoundly intrusive and socially unwise. As a trait essential to its existence, Rockfield's will forever be an analog universe.

About five years elapse before a new clerk is fully accepted by both clientele and management. But from then on, the sales people know they will always get a card   with a crisp new and very clean hundred-dollar bill enclosed, if not a fruit cake   from their society Regulars each holiday season.

This also is expected. Forgetfulness might result in alterations to little niece Susan's Winter Cotillion frock being excruciatingly slow next December. Possibly a duplicate Comus ball gown might be sold to one of milady's closest friends, without either woman's knowledge. It has happened. It can happen again.

Alienate a Rockfield's sales clerk? The Missus would never be able to stand the stress. She would have to leave the City immediately to recuperate from her spirit-crushing depression. Run off to the summer house in Pass Christian, Mississippi. There she would mope, watching the listless brown water. The madame of the household, the matriarch of an entire Uptown neighborhood, sits hiding amidst the omnipresent stench of another coastal fish kill. At the height of the social season.

An entire year ruined for lack of a fruit cake. And a grubby bit of currency.

The end.

Fade to black. Up house lights. Touching bit of cinema verité. Mutt Jeansonne has the britches' story now.

The pants had carried pocketfuls of life's loose change to their current Downtown owner. The emotional jingling kept him awake all night every night.

But Mutt didn't like taking off his pants to sleep. Not any more. He'd had a good pair stolen just last year, from right beside him. And then a second pair a month later. Fred never woke up either time. In the process of recovery from the losses, Mutt discovered a new Street rule: *It's hard getting a pair of pants when you don't have a first pair to wear.* No, he didn't want his pants stolen again. That was Reason Number One for sleeping in his pants.

Reason Number Two was that he liked to always be ready, just in case. Ready.

But the lack of proper sleep distressed him. Made him feel goofy all day. That, and all this Gulf humidity. Disorients a fellow. Mutt pondered his predicament for weeks, finally solving the tuxedo pants karma problem by taking them off at night and tying the legs around his waist.

That way he can ignore the pants' riotous history. Not as much contact. His privates have more freedom. He can scratch his balls. And the pants still remain secure from thievery.

He has slept soundly ever since.

Aided by this   his ongoing sensitivity to even the minutest output from supposedly voiceless inanimate objects he is here, confronting the Satisfied Customer. Mutt has vowed for months to expand his circle of acquaintance. Today is The Day. He is determined.

He is patient.

When he is finally and completely certain that the Customer is a willing audience, Mutt looks up to the billboard and begins.

Yessir. Name's Mutt. Given name. Just four letters. Up until a few years ago I had no Doe no Smith no Jones. Just Mutt.

Stop right now, please. Don't you be sayin' it. I've heard those jokes, all of 'em. I don't really need to hear 'em again, thank you.

Somebody give me the Mutt name fifty-something years ago. I don't know who. Don't think it was my momma. From what I've been hearing about her all these years, that is. Nuns said she was alright, my momma, though they told me they only saw her once.

Probably one of those Boy Home jokes, my name. They're supposed to give you Church names in there, but I know for a fact that there ain't no Saint Mutt in the Bible. So I didn't get me a patron saint. No Saint Mutt. And I never did have an official last name. Nuns said that's the way I came, anyway. A shame.

I have had hell to pay about having nothing but Mutt for a name, what with me moving through one Boy Home classroom after another. My whole school life. Lot of fights. Not much name.

Then the US Army decided that Mutt could be an official name, way back when. They give me an ID and all kinds of government numbers. But that was a long time ago, and the US Army has forgotten about me now. I've forgotten about them too, I suppose. I lost or sold all my Army things ten or twenty years ago. Ain't had anything in the way of an ID for almost as many years as I can remember.

But now the Mutt name is sitting in print right here on a Voter's Registration Card. Look here. Almost the Mutt name, anyway. It does have an M in it. Only ID I got. Too bad there ain't no picture on it. Now this would be one handy piece of paper if it had a picture.

Mutt can put things off like nobody else. The old boy's been intending to get a decent pair of eyeglasses for months. He needs a driver's license badly, but the driving is secondary. He really just wants a legal ID. With his picture on it.

Streets know how important that really is. A picture makes all sorts of difficult transactions easy. Out with the Streets, there's cash. Then there's everything else. And the biggest everything else is checks. Nowhere near the same thing as cash. Mutt gets his cash from handouts or from an on-again-off-again job with Melodie LaGrande. Or quickie odd-jobs he stumbles onto in the decrepit neighborhoods near the box he and Fred call home. Nothing much in the way of steady cash coming Mutt's way these last years. A meal or two's worth here and there, then nothing substantial for weeks.

Though the work for Mel seems to be getting more regular.

Temp work is better than scruffing around the neighborhood looking for yards to clean. Mutt sometimes can work long enough on a temp job to actually accumulate a few bucks, live more than two days at a time without scrounging grocery store dumpsters. Luxury. As often as his funky leg allows, he goes down to one of the temporary workforce halls and sits in a plastic chair. He prints "L Mutt Jeansonne" in the book and waits for a job. Sometimes he hangs around for a week or two before picking up a gig. The waiting is occasionally worth it.

The problem is that temp work pay comes as a check.

Temp work companies don't care that Mutt's got no driver's license, no Social Security number, no government ID. No nothing. They don't care. They don't ask questions. They get their work done and pay the very same day. The temp companies are good about that part. But they pay by check, and if the temp worker can't get that check cashed within 30 days, the temp company automatically cancels the payment. That's written in tiny print right below the signature. Thirty days and the check is no good. Many the rookie has been burned by not seeing those few little words.

So, the company naturally doesn't care one bit that Streetfolk have a hard time cashing their checks. The bosses figure they've usually got nearly a 50-50 chance of getting their temp work for free when they hire a Street.

When a check drops into Mutt's hands, he's got only one raggedy piece of paper to turn that check into cash. A paper that says LM Jeansonne with an address in a bad neighborhood, no phone, no any other sort of number. Still, that paper's the best bet he's got to turn the check into cash.

And then the cash into food.

Food's pretty hard to come by, too, what with the vultures swirling around after what little money he earns. "Papa Jack's No ID Check-Cashing and Fried Chicken" is like Death Valley on a bad day for the wagon train. There are some real buzzards circling at Papa Jack's. Mutt knows it. He also knows that for him there is nowhere else to go.

Oh they take his checks. And take him. Two old men sitting behind a bullet-proof glass window, subtracting twenty-five percent of the Mutt check for their risk. The old men know they're the only bank available to a Street.

The chicken isn't much good, either. Bland. Breaded, cooked and frozen in Wisconsin. Nuked for three minutes in New Orleans a year later and handed over on a limp paper plate. No salt. No napkin. So sorry. Just ran out.

But Mutt does have that one official government card, proclaiming in black and white that Mutt & Fred are New Orleans registered voters. Mutt & Fred both feel this paper proclamation means they are finally two somebodies. Somebodies to be reckoned with. Even though the Government doesn't exactly know who they are reckoning with.

That's what's on his mind this afternoon. That's the philosophical agenda: the Government's part in creating his identity in one way or another. Heading LM Jeansonne down a path without him even knowing it. He acquires a name and all of a sudden he's worrying about losing what little control he has over his life. Maybe he's getting a feel of what's down the road. Those Mutt antennas are always out there sniffing the wind.

Like now. Mutt isn't altogether sure about the Customer yet. He is proceeding cautiously.

Appreciate you keeping all this to yourself, you know. Private stuff, but I got to talk to somebody about it. Maybe stop me worrying. Fred don't want to hear another word on the subject, I know. So maybe I can trouble you to just listen up for a bit and help an old man get along.

Thanks.

Back just a while, without us even asking, the Government sends us these registration cards in the mail certifying that me & Fred we are Mr & Mrs Jeansonne. Yeah, we're living at the same address, but they've got it a little screwy. Like they've got me being a girl and Fred being a boy. They got that seriously wrong.

Me, I'm the boy and Fred the girl.

Fred, she's also a dog. Me, no. In spite of the Mutt name. I don't think being a dog makes Fred any worse a voter. The cards say we are Democrats. But a label doesn't change the way we think, me'n Fred.

Like I said, we both get those voter cards, along with this nice last name   Jeansonne   oh, a pretty good while ago. When we were living two-three years in that falling-down empty used-to-be whorehouse just past where the bridge on-ramps cross Carondelet street. Mailman was nice enough to let us get mail there. Good-heart fellow. Lot of nice pictures of TVs on sales and ladies in underwear smiling like somebody just give them a prize. Good mail like that come nearly every day. Then here come these two envelopes. To the Jeansonnes.

Jeansonne. Somehow, the name stuck in both our heads. We liked it just fine.

Seems the Jeansonnes were the last folks who lived in that place before us, but they were long-gone when we got there. Me and Fred talked to one old man, Mr Claude Vigreux was his name, man who lived in a camelback shotgun house on the corner of Carondelet and Melpomene, before we moved in. We had to feel our way around to see if it was safe for us to live in the Jeansonne house, you see. We weren't exactly what you would call legal residents right then.

Mr Vigreux says the Jeansonnes they were elderly folks, a widow and widower. Good neighbors. Like him to us. Old lady Jeansonne could cook a mean gumbo z'herbes. Had her own way about things, like using both file' and okra at the same time, he says. Real real old. Smart, though. He says them two come up with a plot to get married. They were gonna combine their Social Security and retirement checks. So they'd be more independent from their families. They did get married, sure did, both of them sitting in wheelchairs down at City Hall. Claude was best man. Wheeled them into a taxi and down to the government offices with a United Cab man helpin', he says. I could tell he was getting a little sad telling the story. Claude tells us the Jeansonnes got no chance to enjoy their new married life. Less than a week after the ceremony, their kids shipped them both off to separate nursing homes somewhere in California. The Jeansonnes didn't even know it was coming. Without so much as a thank-you-ma'am this lawyer showed up one morning with two ambulances and carted them away. Mr Jeansonne didn't get no coffee that morning. Ain't got no real coffee in California, I hear. Just pulled them old folks out they house with half a bag of clothes and that's that. Made me mad just to hear about it, and you know me, I don't get mad.

No, I forget. You don't know me, do you?

Pitiful, though. Kids weren't even there to say goodbye.

Mr Vigreux he was the only person left in the City who knew the first Jeansonnes. Now he's gone, too. Died four-five years ago. So I guess we're the only Jeansonnes now. Least on Carondelet street.

I think those two folks would have liked the idea of me and Fred keeping up their voting tradition. FT Jeansonne. LM Jeansonne. Computer wrote them right out, just that way.

Two letters, two cards. Me & Fred found them, we started getting excited. See? Look at all those letters.

Great, huh?

There's an M and an F there already. So, Fred gets to be the FT, and me, I'm LM   fine for me, even though the M is last. Call me L Mutt. Very classy being L Mutt Jeansonne.

We've been keeping up our voting, though Fred she does hers absentee. She hates them loud machines they make you stand in.

I took her with me my first time going in a voting machine. Voting for the Mayor of New Orleans.

Fred, she had already sent in her ballot by mail. I raised the stamp money myself. You know, the government makes you pay to send in that vote? Took me a hour and a half standing round on my game leg by the First Federal Bank on Baronne street, but I got me that cash. Yeah yeah, that was a helluva long time for that little bit a money, 43 cent, but Fred wasn't in much of a good mood that day   possibly constipated again, I was thinking at the time. She was sitting by me just a-growlin' at all the potential donors I was trying to hustle to the cause a democracy.

Monkeying around with Fred's biologic rhythm makes her grumpy. Folks won't give money to a grumpy dog. You can write that one in stone. Could be costing you the vote, I tried to tell her. But I hung in there. I got that cash, bought the stamp, and sent in the FT Jeansonne vote. Fred was proud, in the end.

Me, too.

Mutt is momentarily disturbed from his talk with the Customer when the men in suits come by again. The older man is familiar. He has visited the empty lots around the Expressway regularly over the last few months. Each time with a different companion. Always pointing, pacing, measuring. Always dressed in a perfect, unwrinkled three-piece suit. With faint and thin, thin stripes. No cuffs. And rapidly growing, dark sweat stains under the arms.

The older suit always seems a bit uncomfortable. Even though he does bring companions. A large angry-looking young man   presumably a bodyguard   usually is close by his side, every time he visits. Possibly the old man is frightened. Of Mutt, and the rest of the Streetfolk living in the no-man's-land around the roads. But he needn't worry about being hurt. No.

Mutt has never hurt anyone. And the Streets, they are all much smaller than the bodyguard. Maybe the old suit is afraid that these dirty people will give him the poverty disease. That he'll suddenly get poor by being near them. The Streets are not offended, though. No, the fear is fine with them.

At least, the result of the fear is fine.

The fear means the bodyguard always gives them money when the old man comes. The big young fellow walks around handing out quarters. "Stay away from the boss," he always says, pointing to the older suit. The old man is buying a ticket to be here, they all think. A ticket to their mud-filled amusement park.   The price of all rides included in one low, low price. Just keep your distance.

Mutt has no wish to approach any closer. But he accepts the quarters the man offers. Mutt pockets the coins with no idea what the suits are doing in his hot dirty home land.

The intruders are gone now, though. Everyone is gone except L Mutt Jeansonne. Only Mutt continues to withstand the noon heat. He has reason. He is rolling again. Enjoying this part of the telling. Gesturing as he speaks.

We didn't know what it was going to be like, voting in a machine, though. Neither of us. Me, a US veteran getting up in years, never voting before. Then I get me this good solid last name. Lots of letters. Jeansonne. Nine. More than Mutt.

There was three real nice ladies and an elderly gent down at our precinct. Gent was proud to announce that he was the Commissioner. Ladies were nice about letting him have his way a bit, since he's so old and all. Said his name was Cyrus R Gladstone, of the Thirteenth Ward Gladstones. He and the ladies were all set up in a grade school gym on Martin Luther King Boulevard. I liked the way it echoed in that big room but the sound made Fred a little nursey. You know, skittish. Mr Gladstone he asked about my not walking so good   just curious like those old folks can be   and I told him I got hurt in the war. True. I did. I wouldn't lie about that. Said mm-hmm. He was thinking that getting a hole shot in my leg had made me into a better voter. Especially when I told him and those ladies that FT wasn't well, that she had some terrible constipating going on, was never leaving the house any more.

Yes, that last part I know was a lie, about Fred not leaving the house. Since she was standing right there and all. But I had to protect Fred's registration, you know. Once you get to know me, you'll know I don't lie so easy. Don't lie often, either. It's just that the Street makes it hard to tell the truth sometimes, you know, and still get along.

Anyway, while I'm telling this little lie, old Fred was hanging around under the voting people's table making snuffling noises like she was thinking this whole thing real funny.

I made a good story, saying "My Sweet FT"   when I was saying this "sweet" word, I thought Fred was going to pass a hot one   I was saying that though she was sick, FT always voted by mail, being a responsible citizen.

They liked that. Family stuff, vet husband and sick wife voting, no matter what. "Good stuff," Mr Gladstone was saying. "Good for the cause a democracy." Said it just like that.

Just fine. They was signing me in. But then Mr Gladstone he looks up and tells me City Hall must have got some records mixed up like usual, because it looked like on the books that LM was the Mrs and FT was the Mr. Me, I just laughed and said folks make that mistake all the time. I'm the L Mutt. He said he'd fix it right up. The Mr and the Mrs and all. Said he knew all about this new computer system they give him to keep track of the voting. Must have, because old Mr Gladstone just started pecking away at that computer thing the minute we headed to the voting booth.

I asked the ladies was it OK if my dog Fred come into that booth when I'm doing my voting, and the biggest lady she said she didn't think it would cause any of those City Hall government people to stop stealing her money for one single minute.

"That dog can watch anything that dog wants to, long as I have my say," said the lady. "Nice looking dog like that."

Mr Gladstone he looked up from his computering when she said that. "Democratic process probably help that dog," he told me.

So Fred come right on up to the machine wagging to beat Dixie. But when I throw this switch that closes the curtain, that voting machine all of a sudden made one helluva big banging noise. I mean, one big ka-BAM!

I thought Fred was gonna soil a official government polling place right then and there. Made one helluva racket herself, yipping and carrying on. I understood. She was thinking she was locked up in a cage, in that noisy curtained booth, all closed up. She figured it was making all of that noise getting ready to eat her or something. Some pre-historic fear of voting machines, I guess. Fred come running out underneath the curtain before I got anywhere near through voting. Democrat.

Registered Independent because of the Jeansonne family heritage   that was a done deal before we got our cards or last name – but in spite a being free thinkers, me & Fred really are what local folks around this town call "Yellow Dog Democrats." Old saying goes you'd vote for a yellow dog if it ran on a Demo ticket.

Be funnier if Fred was yellow.

She might have been once, but she's been mostly a real light grey all the years since I've known her. Still a lively old girl, though. Probably outlive me.

Me, I'm kinda grey too. All over, I suppose. I get me a few extra jobs at that temp work because they do the occasional writing on the working papers that I'm a black man or a hispanical man. The words don't mean much to me, since I don't much know what color that hispanical is supposed to be. One time they even wrote down that me I'm a oriental man.

Sounded kinda like a sailor word. I'd like to be a sailor. They use me as a temp when they got a need for a certain number of a certain color of men, and they shy a few. Though they never seem to worry bout gettin too many a them white men. Shoot, I fill whatever bill they got, and gladly.

But I'm telling you the truth when I tell you I never found out if I got me one of them official colors. The Nuns that took me in the Boy Home, they said they never got any kind of papers at all from my momma. She just dropped me and run off, they said. They didn't know nothing about her, not even her name. Didn't really get a good look at her, they tellin' me.

So I got me no birthday, no momma's name, no daddy's name, no color. I hadn't ever put anything down on the pieces of paper they give me when it says race because I don't rightly know. And I'm not going to lie about something like that either.

Unless it means I won't eat.

Sometimes I think it's a damn shame I hadn't got me an official color.

The US Army they never said a thing to me, anyhow and it don't say anything at all on that LM Jeansonne registration card. Most of the time, though, it's pretty good just letting other folks decide for themselves what color I need to be for their own reasons.

Like I was saying, though, I'm mostly a Yellow Dog Democrat.

That first time me & Fred voted, we saw that there was two Democrats running. Made it easier for the voting process. We picked the candidate with the most letters in her last name. We knew it was a lady because neither of us ever heard of a gent named Delores. Delores Pontevecchio. Nice long name. Twenty letters, if you count the space.

We saw in the Picayune a few days later that a Mr Roland Clemenceaux got elected Mayor. Eighteen letters. Even though she had twenty, our lady didn't win. We were still proud because we voted.

Besides, we still got a Mayor with eighteen letters in just two of his three names. Pretty good. Also leading me to speculate on our number threes   just what my L and Fred's T might stand for. Something long, for sure.

Mutt is sitting now, more relaxed with his audience. The Satisfied Customer had been a gamble. His face was a new addition to the long gallery of thirty-seven billboards filling the Streetfolk's hidden no-man's-land. Tucked away beneath and around the Ponchartrain Expressway, right in downtown New Orleans.

Mutt knows all the huge signs. They are his family members. He knows that eight have the same faces on them all the time. That another dozen never have people, only writing. Leaving seventeen with rotating newcomers. Mutt likes meeting new faces, but he is careful. He watched the Customer for two months before approaching him. Fred often reminds Mutt to be cautious in letting go with strangers.

The Customer seems OK, though. Mutt doesn't feel like going back to the box for a siesta. Fred is already snoring away up there. So here he is.

The hottest part of the afternoon has finally forced Mutt to retreat to the shade beneath the roadway. He can't really see the billboard, but he recognizes familiar colors in the blur. Trailer City. Satisfied Customer. Mutt knows who he is talking to.   *Feels safe now.*

Pedestrians, except for the occasional touring suit, seldom come under this part of the Expressway, so he is for the most part undisturbed. Left alone, Mutt's feeling of empathy with his audience grows.

We had a damn good life as Registered Voters on Carondelet street, in spite of the place being a bit rundown. By the way some might think anyways. No electricity, no gas, but I figured out how to turn on the water, so we had a fine working toilet and a cold water shower working right through the heat of these New Orleans Augusts.

You may not know it, being as you might be from out of town, but the scientific armpit of the universe relocates to right here in the Crescent City come every single August. Comes from somewhere else out there in the Milky Ways some New Orleans Jr on Saturn maybe and it drops right on down here in south Louisiana. Giant armpit. Scientific fact. Ask those astronomers. Ask them weathermen. They'll tell you.

Living around here all of my life, and I still haven't gotten used to these Augusts. I don't think anybody does.

The house on Carondelet is tore down now. Me & Fred had to move quick. Machine just showed up on a trailer about sundown. Me 'n Fred we took a good look at it and we could tell that there wasn't but one use for such a machine. And that was for tearing stuff down. By the time they got it unloaded the next morning, we was already getting some lumber together to make us a place. Took me the better part of a month scouting and climbing up and down to hammer us together our box. It's OK, but no water.

Can't get mail at the Box, either. We're lucky we got us a understanding postman. All this time, he's still sticking me & Fred's mail under a slab of concrete where the stoop of that house used to be. Keeps us Registered. Never did build nothing on that lot. We heard tell that the city government people just tore down the Jeansonne house 'cause they was supposed to be squatters in there. Safety hazard. Me & Fred. Figure it's a bigger hazard to this town the way we smell nowadays. Cause we can't get us a regular shower. Not to mention the lack of them toilet facility.

We moved almost two years ago   two? Something like that. Been hard the both of us living in this ratty plywood box, but it's OK, I guess. I got it wedged up good under the Ponchartrain Expressway. Little better than cardboard, but just a little.

It's like a tree house stuck in the pilings and beams about ten feet up in the air. Got a good ladder   those metal rings they stick in the concrete pilings so workmen they can climb up and reach the electric junction box. Got the letters NOPSI, six numbers and a skull and crossbones painted right on it. Skull & bones in white, the rest in a really pretty red color. Nobody has ever come to look at that box since we've been living there. But I think that box it's important to somebody. Makes clicking noises all night, so I know it must be doing something somewhere, though what the hell it's doing I just don't know.

Takes me a while, what with my leg and all, but I climb up there just fine. Old Fred can climb up all by herself. Smartest dog in the whole universe, Fred. She has her a bit harder time going down, so I usually carry her, but she can do it, yes she can. She can climb down there if she's got a mind to. She just prefers to go down in that lady-like fashion, and I don't mind accommodating her. Doesn't weigh but thirty-thirty-five pounds. About the only time she lets me lay hands on her, that and when I'm holding her up to see stuff. Though she's my buddy. Best one I have. Or ever had.

When we aren't scrambling for cash or food, we're back home at the Box and I'm talking to Fred. Telling her everything. Like now to you. Only I got to yell it out loud to her when the traffic is getting heavy. It helps her constipated condition, my talking. Noise can mess with those biologic rhythms.

Noise all the time makes a man get a bit loony too echoes bouncing around in this big pile of concrete. The pilings and beams and all. Makes a man's head ring like a church bell sometimes.

Same with Fred. She's more in touch with the biologic rhythms, though. Especially since she's a dog. Closer to the bio parts, I guess.

I help with the rhythm, since she's older than me, at least in dog years. I figured it out once, with the help of my friend Rodrigo. We figure that Fred is 135 years old. Civil War dog, Fred. I sing "Dixie" for her every so often, but she don't seem particularly inspired. Hate to think she might have been one of those Union collaborators   or something even worse. Probably too young to care who was shooting who, especially knowing Fred's attitude toward government. Dogs got no governments. She's just adopting mine to be accommodating. No President Freds, at least none she's willing to tell me about.

Loud as the engine of hell under here, sometimes. Probably one reason why nobody comes here except us. Don't do much entertaining under the Expressway, me & Fred.

She doesn't worry so much about noise any more. Fred she used to howl all night every night. Just went berserk any time a eighteen-wheeler passed over us. Now, with my talking to her, she's much calmer. I got the right rhythm, you see. I'm younger in dog years.

Except sometimes. My age shows a bit.

Like I know it's rude to be saying this right after I just introduced myself and all, but I got to go take a dump worse than the Queen Mother on her second day in Calcutta.

And, wouldn't you know, right in the middle of the New Orleans daily thirty-minute four o'clock rainstorm. Ain't summer fun?

Time out. Now don't you be worrying. I'll be seeing you again. Real soon.

Some twenty minutes after the rain stops, on his way back to wake his sleeping roommate, a sodden but refreshed Mutt decides to take the time to stop for a few words with an old friend.

Unlike the newly erected Satisfied Customer, John Feinman of "Feinman's Nothing-Down Furniture" has been a permanent fixture in the billboard arcade for twenty years. Feinman's hair never grays, is never mussed with the passage of weather and time. His skin is always clear and unwrinkled, except for friendly-looking "laugh lines" carefully outlined at the corner of his mouth.

Twice a year a sign-painting crew climbs up the ladders to freshen Feinman's smiling image. The furniture mogul's face is comfortable for Mutt, in spite of the fact that the eight-foot smile has become a little twisted in two decades of over-painting.

Mutt even knows some of Feinman's life history, or at least he has pieced together an impression from newspaper sales ads. The old Mutt sensor bank has mentally mixed the graphic messages with snatches of jingles from car radios. Cars are often poised above his head without moving for long hours at a time. The daily traffic snarls offer a wide range of input, and Mutt has often heard Feinman's ads blaring from open automobile windows.

Then there is his own inspection of the store through its massive front windows. Feinman's is only four blocks from the Expressway, sitting right beside the Dixie Brewery. Mutt takes the Brewery tour every three months, just like clockwork, to get his free six-pack of Dixie. The rules say you're only allowed the free beer once, but Mutt knows the quick turnover of high-school-age tour guides insures that he will never be recognized on his return visits. Fred isn't much on Dixie, which makes it even better. Mutt can stretch a six-pack out to a two-week experience.

The regular Brewery runs have allowed Mutt to become familiar with the content and changes in Feinman's store. He had been captivated by a leather "pub-style" sofa on his very first pass   it looked quite comfy. Three months later he saw John Feinman himself sitting in the very same sofa, right by the front door, waiting for a customer to enter.

Feinman looked very very old in person, but just as friendly as his billboard. Feinman waved at Mutt. Mutt waving back said, "Hi, Mr Feinman," as he waved. Feinman seemed very pleased to be recognized. Mutt didn't tell him that they were already old friends. Had been talking for years.

The "Nothing-Down Furniture" radio and newspaper advertisements have one thing in common. The presence of an eight-year-old girl. The closing four seconds of every thirty-second Feinman's radio spot is always the same, the little girl's Gentilly-accented voice singing the store's address: "Fif-teen-thir-ty-two Tu-lane." A cartoon of the little girl, with the musical address suspended over her head in a balloon, graces Feinman's print ads.

Mutt is sure the girl in the ads is Feinman's granddaughter, even though he has never seen a child of any sort at the Tulane Avenue store. There is just something grandfatherly about the aging furniture salesman.

Mutt Jeansonne knows who he is dealing with when he speaks to John Feinman. Mr Feinman will understand.

Used to have a regular john when I was just a kid. Wasn't just mine, of course, like the one at the Carondelet street house. Was in the Manus Boy Home. Catholic, like I was telling you.   One of the few things I appreciated, living with all of those different people. I try remembering those days. Most of my kid time is just kind of a blur in my memory, but let me tell you: a warm and quiet place to take a dump is something I will always be remembering.

I can get a good picture of those toilets in my mind better than I can remember birthday parties. Of course that's likely because I never got one myself. Birthday.

You probably got your own. Birthday and toilet. But let me tell you that when you don't, and when you got to go, ohlordy.

But never go too close to home. That's a Top Ten Street Rule. I learned that over the years. Fred she been knowing it since she was a baby. She's very particular.

Funny about how something you didn't want to even deal with in the first place just carries itself over the air. Haunts you. Can't get away. Life of its own.

Lot of things like that.

Smelling confuses me. I mean, I don't understand it. Fred seems to, but me, I think smelling stuff is just like electricity zapping along wires or big metal airplanes flying through the air. I don't care how many times you tell me how it happens or show me how it happens, it makes no sense to me.

Big puzzles in life. You figure out those puzzles, you're going to heaven. No sweat. Fred's going to heaven. She knows about that smelling part. Maybe the other parts too, but she's not telling me a word about them. She smiles and her pink tongue curls up from her teeth when she smells something so bad that it's good. Breathes funny. Says "Theeee-yewt!" real low, speaking down that curled-up tongue tube. Another little sacred dog comment on that mystery condition, I suppose.

Like I said, godknows I myself don't smell too good to start with, and the damp here in New Orleans don't help my condition. Course, I guess if that really bothered me I sure as hell would have gotten out of this burg a good long time ago.

I'm sure you can guess that I'm not ever going to be ready to give up this town. Not New Orleans. My home. You know.

There's not much in the way of winter here, which is a primary concern when you're not living in the best-insulated accommodations. Big consideration, that one. Don't do much for the pub-style leather out here in the open, Mr Feinman.

And just staying here, I done had me some wild times. I been lucky, you know   a lot of those times seemed to happen at just the right spot in my biologic rhythm.

For instance, I found the weirdest thing under the Carondelet mail slab the other morning. Started this whole thing. Weird, in what it did to me, just when I thought I was headed in the right direction. My rhythm just got busted totally up.

I found three different pieces of paper telling me come to Criminal District Court, each one with a date just a few days after the other. Government sent the letters, and they were just getting madder and madder at me for not coming by to visit. But here I was, I just got the invitation.

I don't walk all the way over to Carondelet street now but once every two to three weeks to look for mail. Fact is, nobody but the Government writes me. Because nobody but the Government knows the registered LM Jeansonne me.

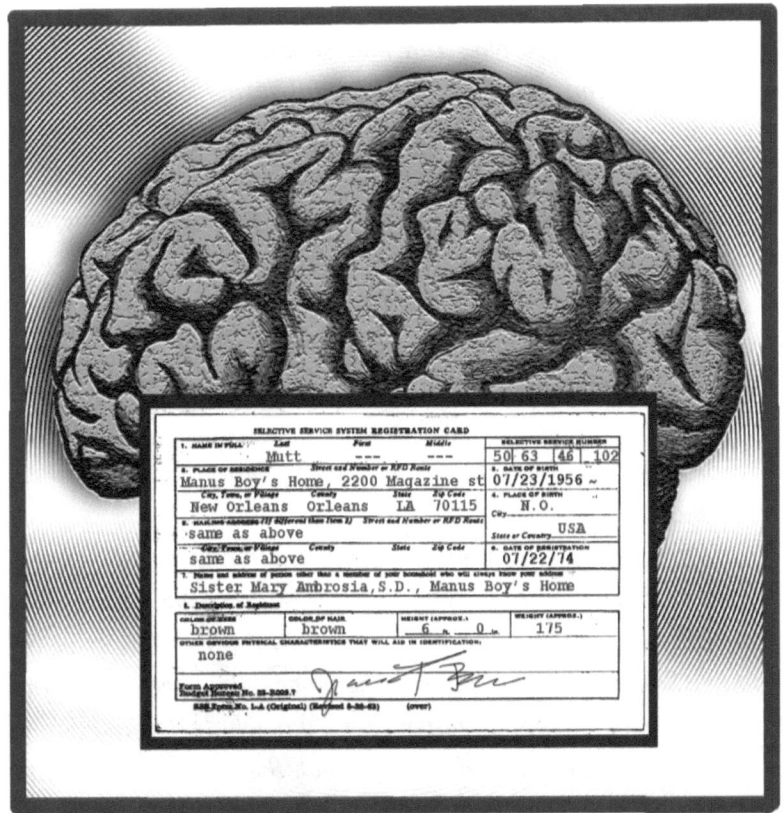

Lemme explain.

Government found out about the plain ole Mutt me a long time ago, though they still lose that one now and again. Pretty much all the time for the last bunch of years. That's the Mutt boy who's got no last name. Mutt. Gets them unsettled, me having just those four letters. Government even tried calling me Mutt Doe for a while, but that messed up their machines worse, so they gave up an called me just Mutt. Official. Mr "Mutt". Me.

That was later. I guess I gotta talk about the beginning.

Sorry. You may have noticed I got some real trouble dealing with time. Maybe I'm just simple. I can't tell. These last years it seems my life has gotten all scrambled, and I need to get me some order put to it. I need to remember my story. Hell, I'm not even sure any more whether I got a story. That's why I'm telling you all this. Because it helps me with getting my time straight. Once the time gets in order, it'll put my story all in a nice row. Right here and now. I mean, I ain't got much else. I ought to at least have a good story. Right?

I'm working on it.

So.

Long time ago when I'm a young man, the Government writes me.

It give me chillbumps, having the Government writing me. Knowing something always comes besides the paper when somebody writes you. I saw it happen with all the boys at the Home. Something happens whenever the letters come. Naturally, when I get a letter from the whole United States Government, I get spooked. Pretty much the same weird feeling I had with those three new letters. I was happy before, when I thought they had lost me.

Now that I'm an old man, I know a little about the nasty way things work with the Government. So when I pick that first official letter out from under the concrete slab, I didn't even open the envelope. I just stood there, looking at it. Knowing something was coming.

Waiting for somebody to stick their finger up my ass.

That's the official seal of approval of the US Government. You're laughing at me again. You ought not, because I know. I got it once. Guess I should have been grateful, but I don't remember it that way.

The United States Army Draft. Wasn't a bit of good in it. Don't even know why they call it that. Because the main draft part I remember was mostly a draft around my balls.

Of course that was a few days after the letters and the phone call.

I'm telling this bass-ackwards.

See what I mean. Damn time. Let me start again.

The United States Army Draft discovered the Mutt me in the Boy Home. Me being a seventeen or eighteen-year-old boy, or close by. Next oldest boy was twelve. I was still just a one-name, no-color, four-letter Mutt at the time. I remember acting like I was named after St Mutt to all those younger boys, saying St Mutt was from China and that's why they never heard of him, Mutt being a Chinese name. I knew there was no St Mutt, and I lied. I try not to do that so much anymore. But then, the Nun they didn't care what I said. They knew that Mutt was the oldest boy in the Home, and that made those Nun nervous. I don't know why. Me I was just mowing lawns, fixing windows and anything else they told me to do. Until the day the Government telephone call came. I got real confused that day, and scared again, like when I was the smallest boy in the Home.

Just like at that Court building, last night. I felt the same way back then. That first letter day in the Boy Home, I sat there staring at it for hours, afraid to even touch it. Just a few pieces of paper, and I was scared to death. Petrified. I couldn't believe a letter was really for me, especially since I never ever got a letter before that day. Then I get three, four of them, all looking the same. I didn't open any of them.

Until the phone call day.

An official Government man called the Nun and he said, "You Nun be bringing this Mutt man to the Government place now or he's going to jail now Yours Truly Mister Draft Board 476."

Something like that.

Those Nun had stuck my name on some list they gave the Government, saying I was old enough to die for my country. Thank you very much Jesus and friends.

They give me fifty-five cents times two for the bus and streetcar back and forth. I had to get me a transfer, you know, and they were letting me come back to the Home, at least for the moment. Until the Government says something different.

I go to the New Orleans Customs House at the foot of Canal street like they said. Right off the bat, they ran all of us must have been a hundred of us boys   into this big room, and a soldier yells out: "All you citizens, you drop your pants, bend over and spread your cheeks. Now!"

No kidding.

Me, I never heard of such a thing, but all of a sudden there I am just like everybody else, bent over sure as hell, gripping both sides of my ass. I'm telling you, as I recall it, I was wishing that they would go ahead and shoot me for my country right then and there. Better than making me stand around in a room full of strangers with my naked butt up in the air.

Those people they weren't making it easier, either. Got some very important-acting men walking around wearing rubber gloves. They're walking around, very important, just looking at all those asses. On the sly I see quite a few ugly ones in that batch of asses, too, let me tell you. First time I ever seen such a display.

Then the important guys would stop, look at an ass and, BAM, stick their rubber finger right on up in there.

Why important Government men got to walk around sticking their fingers up dumb boy's asses is beyond me.

I began my real Government education right then, you know. Civics. Outside of a book, this is how I got my very first idea of what the US Government is like. I remember thinking that these important Government men must be out of their minds.

Not that I was totally all together myself that day. I had listened to the voice of experience. And got myself totally messed up.

It was James. He worked on the pipes and wires at the Home. James was almost as old then as I am now. I could be wrong. In those days I wasn't too good at judging old, you know. I had me no time experience at all. James he told me he had Government experience, though, and that I need to make sure I got myself a little buzz for when I go see the Government people.   I wondered about that "little buzz" business from the start. He said, "You start acting like you're healthy, boy, they gonna send your ass away someplace where folks shoot bullets at you for no good reason." It didn't sound right at the time, but James he never lied to me before, so I took his advice. He gave me a couple of these "speedball" things. I took them, too.

"Take 'at medicine so you be sick, boy," he told me. I took that speed medicine an twenty minutes later I'm so dizzy I almost fall down the steps of the Broad Street bus. James also give me two glasses of stuff to drink. This was the very first alcohol drink I ever had. Rum. It was called something like "K&B Brand," probably made behind a drugstore or something. Got a picture of a pirate and a ship and a bird on it. Picture was pretty nice. Rum, pretty nasty. James kept it behind the water heater in his work room. He told me that a big glass

of K&B rum and a little speed medicine would keep me out of that rice paddy, no problem. I told him I'd seen rice paddies all around New Orleans. I always thought they looked OK.

But he told me about a war that was hooked up somehow with this drafting business. Way across in Southeast Asia. First time I heard tell of it. Said I might have to go fight, instead of being at the Boy Home. Of course I'd rather stay right there at the Manus Boy Home in New Orleans, Louisiana. I didn't mind mowing grass for my keep. I liked my life just fine right then. Knew I liked it much more than running around doing any Government war stuff. I knew that even before I got in it.

I tried looking it up, to see if that James was yanking my squid. There wasn't no Southeast Asia in my old beat-up Nun-school geography book. Found it, though, after James he tells me Southeast Asia is the same as French Indochina. Which is the same as Vietnam. Don't know why they keep changing the name all the time. How you gonna find it if they keep changing the name? Seemed to me it might be a Government strategy   that would pretty well stop the war right then and there, if nobody could find it. I figured maybe that was the reason they kept changing the name. That Government can be smart sometimes, I guess. Except everybody still seemed to find Vietnam.

New Orleans always has the same name. I remember it was on page 63. All the time. But Southeast Asia was hard to find in the geography book.

Wish I had that book now. Look at page 63 and say there we are, me & Fred. Right there.

The Vietnam era draft came as something of a surprise to New Orleans. It wasn't like the draft hadn't been around before. But it hadn't really been necessary before. In previous wartimes, the Government had always been able to convince the City that the threat to their homeland, and hometown, was imminent. The idea of the oyster beds in German hands was enough to outrage any true New Orleanian. This was America, for God's sake. This was New Orleans! The oyster beds had to remain in Yugoslavian hands.

Everyone volunteered. Men and women went to war. The Old World Yugoslavs to this day contentedly work the oyster beds.

But a Vietnamese invasion wasn't within the wildest dreams of anyone in the Crescent City. At least, at the time.

After the war ended, of course, the invasion actually occurred. Initial resistance led to the inevitable good-natured acceptance. The Vietnamese liked to fish and drink cold beer and eat rice-based dishes, just like their neighbors. Being invaded wasn't as traumatic as everyone thought.

But in the late sixties, serving in the war in southeast Asia remained a remote fairy tale. Time in the Army wasn't considered to be so bad.

Until some of the boys didn't return from the experience.

Those who did return brought with them nightmare tales of fighting phantoms in swamps. People in the Crescent City could relate to that. They knew about phantoms and swamps. They wanted no part of any activity that held both.

But unlike other urban areas, there weren't massive anti-war demonstrations. There wasn't much draft-card burning. The resistance was more passive.

But there was resistance.

So James he tells me that the Government doesn't want to kill you in Vietnam if you got medicine and alcohol in you. I figured it sounded logical, like I said.

Wrong again. That James had his head up his proverbial butt looking for daylight. I got what I deserved, trusting somebody just because they're older.

When I got to Nam ten months later, the place was full of speed freaks and drunks, all the same folks James told me the United States Army didn't want. My Sarge told me later I should have used me some steroid. Army didn't like them steroid. That's why we didn't have no big body-building sorts out there in the jungle. Just little old scrawny beanpoles like me. And that James he had me drinking all of that K&B Pirate Rum. Stuff that smelled like what I usually put in the lawnmower.

But at the Customs House in the middle of New Orleans summertime, that man had got me all messed up. I rode the rollercoaster of K&B Rum and speedballs until I thought my ticket had surely expired, and then some. Riding too heavy to be thinking about getting out of the draft. At that point I really didn't know what it was all about, me.

There I was, my face looking at the floor, my backside pointing at Canal Street, my head aiming at the French Quarters. I remember looking down there and seeing my socks didn't match. My drawers weren't all that clean, either. Wasn't expecting to be doing a drawer display for the Government. But now I'm just looking at those drawers like I'm reading my history lesson. Not much else to do. Waist size 28-30. Hanes one hundred percent cotton men's underwear. "Mutt." Nuns write "Mutt" on all of my clothes. Use a marker. Red letter "Mutt" looks OK. The elastic in the waist is giving out, though.

I'm standing there, bent over, sweating a Mississippi river down my back over my hips and knees and into my dress-up jeans   they were down around my ankles   and one of the important smiling doctors comes up behind me.

I think: "Ohoh, here it comes."

He says: "Where you from, son?"

I say: "Boy Home, Mister."

He says: "Hmmmm."

Knowing what I know now, I wonder what that doc did in the evenings. Like if he hung out in the Can-Can-Do, or some place like that.

The Doc takes his own sweet time putting on just one brand new rubber glove every time he looks at a new backside. There's a guy walking behind him, his whole job is carrying two bags. One for clean gloves, and one for the important Doc's dirty rubber gloves. I wonder then if there is one of those chemical plants between New Orleans and Baton Rouge that specializes in making only right-hand gloves for this type of Doc. No, probably not. Probably the Government is just stacking up bales of extra left-hand gloves in a Customs House closet somewhere, gloves getting all dusty waiting for a switch-hitting Doc.

Here he comes, finger pointing at the sky. I remember thinking that rum comes from the same place where they get rubber. Didn't help one bit, that kind of thinking.

Then I get it. Cold finger feeling around. Not much in the way of enjoyment coming to mind there, I have to tell you. Me, I got no idea what this man is doing.

Somehow, though, I think I must have really known deep down what was happening.

That this is the sort of thing Government does.

I was trying to get out of Government service all the way back in 19 and 74 75, and here I am all these years later. They still got their finger up my ass.

Then the Government thinks I'm trying to do the same routine all these years later   get out of something. I was hoping they didn't have the same kind of test nowadays. I was glad to serve again as long as they don't have any more of those rubber gloves hanging around. I already walk funny because of my first Government service.

Wait. Is it really twenty thirty years?

Goddamn, I wish I could remember better.

My try at getting out of Government service didn't work so well then. Didn't do so good lately, either.

I'm an old man, and I still had to bum me a quarter just to call up the number on the Government card. From a payphone in the Greyhound bus station. Closest to the Box. Fred she's my lookout. Got to. The bus station ain't the safest place on earth any more.

A not-so-nice lady answered the phone, and she tells me I got to come to the Criminal District Courthouse, wherever that is. Or I lose my Vote. It turned out the Government needed Mr Jeansonne for a month of Jury Duty, starting right away.

No gloves involved.

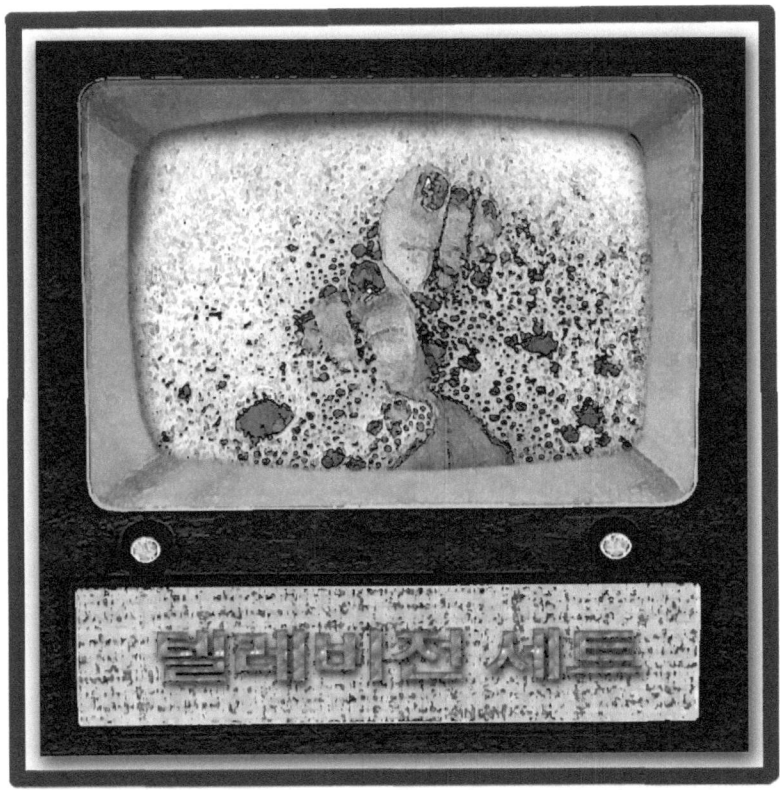

Mel, having slept six hours in her parked car, is still feeling the aftershocks of her night of incarceration as she maneuvers her Studebaker in serpentine fashion on Esplanade Avenue. Her automobile rolls north with the curvature of the earth. The New Orleans Streets Department has not previously measured such a rondure to exist between the wide asphalt lanes. Mel heads slowly toward her house in the Faubourg St John. Very slowly. So slowly in fact, that when she notices her speed has dwindled below 10 mph, she panics and stomps heavily on the gas.

Her logic is that if she stands out in the morning traffic by going too slow, a cop might recognize her for DWI and pull her over. The secret is to blend in. So she speeds up. Quickly.

The reality of her logical action is that in the process of "blending in," Mel lays half a block of screaming, smoking rubber.

Her sudden action startles Robert Salter, 27, a Kentwood Water truck driver from Metairie, Louisiana, into running 2,200 gallons of natural spring water up a sidewalk and through a nineteenth-century cast-iron fence, launching meteors of intertwined rusting roses and corn stalks toward the sky.

In turn, the flying metal and screeching tires cause Lottie Lambaso, 67, an Orleans Parish School Crossing Guard, to irreparably tear her fluorescent "Bunny Bread" vest while diving into a gloriously blooming Crepe Myrtle bush. Pink. Lottie had owned that vest sixteen years. Got it free from the Bunny Bread Company when she first took her Government job standing on the street corner. Red and orange Bunny. She would mourn its loss.

Finally, as he stands paralyzed at the Miro street bus stop ready to be flattened by Mel's swerving red Studebaker, Felix Hernandez, 56, of 2214 Ursulines street, instantly re-converts to Roman Catholicism. Making the sign of the cross repeatedly while saying his mother's name six times in rapid succession.   His life is spared.

Of the survivors, only Hernandez is uplifted by the incident.

Melodie does not notice any of the repercussions of her action. Her mind is elsewhere. She speaks to the road ahead.

"That Oliver Wendell Tramp! Lured my Mutt away. Didn't invite me for breakfast, did she? Me, the law-abiding citizen she tried to stick in the drab, dismal lock-up forever without benefit of a proper wardrobe! Now what was the name of that picture? 'The Man in the Iron Mask'? Yes. So tragic, *tres triste*   it's me in the mask, don't you know, girl! And now this Sandra Day Slut! How could Mutt go along with her Virgin Mary charade? Oh, Mary, what has happened to you?! I detest that budding Perry Masonette, detest her. The way she looked at me! She's no one to be throwing any stones. I could tell those weren't hers, either, not one little cup size. And that pouty little JC Penny mouth. "Not an ounce of style. What my Mama always called a Back-of-the-Woods Shotgun Girl: every one of those tramps is sawed-off and pump-action. She'll never have my legs, this one. Never. Reminds me, I simply must call Doctor Knudsen soon. Fred, Fred, Fred-dy, where are you when I really need you? Work rushing down on me in just a few hours, barely time for a bath and a cocktail, and no idea what sort of wardrobe I can assemble to complement this, the moment of my own personal tragedy!

"This could be my greatest role. Yes, yes, yes! A TV Guide cover! Let me read it: 'Conquest on Bourbon. A simple Faubourg St John maiden triumphs over massive and sustained political persecution. Set in modern-day New Orleans. With Melodie LaGrande, Jackie Gleason and Tony Curtis. 11pm, Channel 12. Rated "R" for explicit sexual innuendo.' Yes, yes! Only PBS would be daring enough to air it! And only late night, for appreciative mature audiences! Oh, Bette! Oh, *Lana!*"

And then, finally, home.

Home means the Can-Can-Do workday is officially over and the courtroom hubbub is well behind her. She decides to ignore the multiple messages from television reporters on her answering machine, at least until she has time to make herself properly presentable for their harsh lighting. Melodie "George Hotard" LaGrande, canned Singapore Sling in hand, lounges happily in her tub. The hollow belly of the deep, four-legged vessel is one of her favorite places to be, and much of her home time is spent in its embrace. Taking the advice of her doctor on the post-operative benefits of therapeutic soaking, Melodie had commissioned a specialty shop on Magazine street to refinish the monumental cast-iron antique in bright red ceramic to match her car and hair. The result was perfect. When the sun found its way through the mountains of bubbles, its reflected light caused the entire room to glow a soft scarlet. It made her feel so good, so clean.

Mel proceeded to further develop the tub's potential as a source of revitalization.

After she returned home from the hospital the first time, the tub became the center of her household. She had Mama's inheritance to do with as she liked. There was the money. Then there was the other part. With the annual trust fund money, she had been able to buy a house in the Faubourg St John and make herself comfortable.

The tub made her very very comfortable.

She had surrounded it on one side with a cut-glass bay window looking out onto her flourishing herb garden. There were three louvers in the window, each level with the edge of the tub, allowing the comforting scents of rosemary and lavender to flow into the room. Above the low window, she had had cabinetmakers build bookshelves to her specifications. The carved mahogany planks were now neatly lined with her most precious books. A gilt-framed photograph of Lili Elbe sat in prominence among them, the photo flanked on either side with delicate glass candlesticks.

Lili Elbe was the first to cross the modern sexual frontier, the Columbus of transsexualism. She found the New World first, in spite of the notoriety of Copenhagen's Christine Jorgensen some twenty-one years later. The photo Melodie owned was inscribed in Lili's own hand "Dresden 1930," the actual year and place of the surgery. Lili had touched and signed the now-brittle print with her own hands, after she had become a woman. It showed. Mel could tell.

Mel bought the picture for an outrageous sum of money from a dear elderly friend who was going through some unfortunate medical problems. It had been the very first thing Mel had purchased after her mother's death, and Melodie made the photo into a shrine to her ever-developing womanhood. Even more than the tub, it was the centerpiece of the room.

Then, to make sure that she could "do business" from her bubbly comfort zone, Mel had installed an unlisted phone extension on the wall next to the tub and an apartment fridge built in under the sink. The crowning touch was a mini-stereo with a wireless remote at tubside. Mel was fond of vintage Lee Dorsey and Otis Redding.

She took special delight in stocking an assortment of bath preparations that would be the envy of any Oriental herbalist. The parfumiers, botanicas and traiteurs of the Vieux Carré were known world-wide for their potions   luxurious, exotic, effective and expensive. Mel's baths were important to her.

At first the baths had been therapeutic. Dr Knudsen had prescribed regular immersion in salts, herbs, and the use of a variety of holistic medicines and supplements. He had designed her recovery period to help speed the healing process, and his prescriptions had lived up to their promise. Her skin was radiant and almost totally without blemish or hint of masculinity, and her brand-new sex was in perfect working order. Even if it wasn't broken in yet.

The recuperation really hadn't taken that much time. She was back in New Orleans within six weeks of the operation, her luxurious red pubic hair completely covering the four dime-sized dimples that were all that were left of George.

The two-month mark was especially encouraging. At nine weeks Doctor Knudsen had been challenged, making use of every centimeter of the old George to "gild the vault of your voluptuous Sexual Cathedral," as he put it in his Danish-inflected Nevadan English.

The Doc was known to wax poetic about his best work, and Mel was his consummate masterpiece. A series of twelve eight-by-ten glossies of George Hotard and Melodie LaGrande, matted expensively and set in art-deco faux-Erte' frames, lined the walls of Doctor Johann Emil Knudsen's high-rise offices overlooking the Strip in Vegas. George and Mel's faces and various body parts were displayed in detail in both these photos and in brochures and advertising material for Johann Knudsen's Heavenly Body Spa. His logo was a miniature map of the Milky Way. Master surgeon "Jo" Knudsen knew the whos, whats, wheres, whens, whys and hows of advertising. Melodie's broad smile and broader cleavage protruded in 3-D from two Melrose Shopping District billboards each April in Los Angeles. Right above the absolute chic-est of the Melrose Harley Davidson apparel shops.

"Those California girls, they always start thinking about rearranging their furniture in the Spring," Knudsen told Mel once.

Melodie had been given quite a large discount on the cost of her operation for allowing the Doctor the use of her image and testimonial in promoting the Spa. She had gone to him on two occasions for "touch-ups," and in return for his special attention, she had joined in round-table discussions with prospective clients to promote his business. It had been an enjoyable experience, and the Southern California clients were extremely supportive of Mel's new life. Of course, not many of them were well-versed in the cultural and social ramifications of Melodie's current means of employment. Still, they were such a sweet bunch of girls.

One of them, a B-movie director's wife, had told Mel that she simply must meet her husband.

"He'll fall in love with you, just as I have. There is definitely a future in Hollywood for a girl with your sensibilities, not to mention this delightfully erotic figure. Jo, you must give me a perky lift exactly like Melodie's."

Mel wasn't sure she really wanted to be one of the LA girls. New Orleans was so snuggly for a woman of her particular persuasion.

Unlike Baton Rouge. Eighty-four miles of Mississippi River had made a lot of difference. Her first couple of decades had been pure hell.

You couldn't blame the town. Mostly her problem had been the people involved. Or not involved. Melodie had come into the world as George Basile Hotard. Melodie/George's natural mother did not survive his entry into the world. His parents were an older couple, his 45-year-old first-time mother gambling on the birth to satisfy a sudden need for company in her long-term marriage. George remained in the hospital nursery an extra week while his father took care of the whiskey-and-tear-saturated intricacies of a Cajun funeral. Then a heartbroken Lavelle Hotard and his handsome new ten-pound son left University Hospital to return to their residence in the eastern suburbs of Baton Rouge, Louisiana.

After two years of mourning and a substantial investment in Wild Turkey 101, Lavelle allowed himself to be cajoled toward marriage again. His prospective bride was herself a widow of only one year. The modestly-dressed matron was a mild and sensitive aggressor in their courtship, and won Lavelle's hand after a brief two weeks' unemotional skirmishing. Lavelle said *"Mais oui, cher,"* and it was a done deal. She had acquired a detailed knowledge of almost every aspect of the two Hotard males' existence. He barely knew her as they walked to the altar.

For instance, Lavelle, himself with only a few remaining vestiges of Catholicism, had taken no notice at all of his prospective wife's religious beliefs. He was simply content to be headed into the safe structure of a marriage again, and to have someone to watch after the growing George. It wasn't until he noticed the lack of a Roman collar on any of the males at their nuptials that it occurred to him.

"Mon dieu, c'est une juive."

Then immediately, he forgot that she was Jewish. It didn't matter. He said "I do," for the second time in his life. And he did.   The rest was not really important. In that way he was very much like his new wife, the former Dorothy Shilberg Goodman. Almost unwittingly, Lavelle had formed and executed a plan. Once prodded into action, he had made up his mind, gone down to that great Used-Wife Lot, kicked a few tires, looked under the hood of a vintage model and remarried. He had acquired both a wife for himself and a mother for his child. Low mileage and in perfect running order. But now that Lavelle had a well-tuned family vehicle, he realized he had no desire to go anywhere. His first wife had taken all the travel maps   and Lavelle's curiosity about life outside the city limits with her. Lavelle lived his final four years sitting in his shiny new marriage with the engine idling in neutral. He left the garage only to be present at his own funeral. Then he was gone. Little George remembered his father as a quiet spot in the living room.

Dorothy had been anything but quiet. She was a bustler. She loved to work, and could find an unlimited number of tasks that needed her immediate attention. George had been many of those tasks from the moment she entered the Hotard household. She and the former Mr Goodman had not been blessed with children of their own. After fifteen years on a strict schedule of attempted procreation, he had claimed she intimidated him. The intimidation causing his sperm count to drop. When her husband himself had dropped, dead of heart attack at 47, the liberal Dorothy had turned back to the comforting embrace of Judaism to get her through what was surely the end of her life. It was with a young rabbi's encouragement that she sought out a replacement husband. A befuddled 52-year-old fallen-away-Catholic Cajun was not exactly what Rabbi Burke had had in mind. She knew that. But a future with Lavelle Hotard projected as infinitely better than a possible half-century alone in a badly-paneled condo, dusting silk gardenias.

And even though Lavelle had terminated their arrangement a bit sooner than anticipated, she still had little George.

The boy had always been a touch strange, sitting on the floor of her closet for hours on end. He had tried on every pair of shoes she owned. She thought that endearing. He wanted to be like his mama. And Dorothy did have a serious weakness for the shoe sales. At the height of the collection, her double closet the "shoe museum," as she called it held 122 pairs of footwear. Every one of them treasured. Little George had actually cut one of his last baby teeth on the stout heel of a beige French lace-up. She didn't mind. She had bought the shoe after five markdowns, the designer label removed after the third. The nameless ones were so much easier to let go. Or so Dorothy reasoned.

On George's confirmation, the widow Hotard had insisted her son have a bris. She felt it was a debt she owed to her faith, that her happiness would in some part be paid for if her son would adhere to such a revered custom. With Dorothy by his side, George was circumcised at age sixteen.

Just over a decade later, George took his mother's gesture a solid step further.

Melodie LaGrande was much happier than George had ever been.

But not at first. George had been what the shrinks all call a "hysterical" drag queen when she first came out. George was a she well before the operations started, and she ran to New Orleans, where the population was much more tolerant of life choices that deviated from the Norm. In that atmosphere George had flagrantly overdone the whole thing. She dressed as her favorite movie star of the week, and picked up drunk fraternity boys in the French Quarter. She had been beaten up more than once, when the final revelation occurred in such eventually-acknowledged same-sexual trysts. Her mother had been terrified, which was exactly the effect Melodie subconsciously desired.

It took a while, but she calmed down. George and Dorothy reconciled. Dorothy actually grew to love Melodie, even advising her new-found daughter on the maintenance of prime leather footwear in moldy Southern climes. Melodie emerged a complete woman shortly after her mother's death. But the unexpected feeling of loss   her mother, rather than her manhood   pulled Melodie into a raging celebration of her new sex. She was hysterical once again, and that hysteria led her into the Can-Can-Do. It wasn't all bad. She felt protected in the Quarter. She knew all the Boy Tricks and could beat her employers at their own game. Her first experience with heterosexuality occurred seated at the bar of the Can-Can-Do, and if limited in scope, it wasn't altogether unpleasant in execution. She had always liked working with her hands.

Besides, she had also inherited her mother's work ethic.

Yes, Melodie had her trust fund tucked safely way. And yes, practical-minded Melodie was making a substantial tax-free living at the Can-Can-Do, in spite of Day Manager Abu's constant attempts to short-change her. And at her occasional second late-night job, pouring drinks at Benny's Raw Bar. But besides hoarding her money with a very definite goal in mind, she was learning the ways of men to a depth not many women of any age could match. After this education she was sure she would know a good one if she found him.

She had decided from the start that she needed the security of a large nest-egg of cash for her future as a woman. Money was a constant. It would make things easier to focus in on just the man, and not the circumstances. So she did what she knew, worked Bourbon street, daily gathering additional packets of knowledge and money.

With the annual cash installment of her inheritance dropping automatically into her account every May, Melodie LaGrande didn't really need to work. Not if she just wanted to maintain a comfortable lifestyle. But Mel was saving for her Grand Adventure. Saving money for the part of her new sex that was still missing. The part that didn't come with Jo Knudsen's scalpel. Mel, too, wanted to have Love. Mad, passionate, absolutely real Love.

And to have a baby.

For that was the second part of her mother's inheritance. After watching half a dozen years of George's cross-dressing, Mrs Dorothy Hotard had finally accepted the fact that with or without her help, sooner or later George would physically become Melodie. Dorothy loved George, and was determined to love Melodie. In hopes that her soon-to-be daughter would then proceed with a Normal life, Mrs Hotard had done some research of her own.

There was much for her to learn about abdominal pregnancy and in vitro fertilization. Not too many places to learn it. She found that the procedure was a bit more risky than a natural female pregnancy. But with proper care, an embryo could be planted inside the peritoneum and the abdominal cavity and develop in fine fashion, resulting in a completely normal term pregnancy terminated by Caesarean section.

Mrs Hotard became excited, and without George's knowledge, she had a few of her own eggs removed and frozen before her death. She trusted Melodie to find the appropriate sperm.

Dorothy had wanted grandchildren so badly. Mel wanted to give them to her, as a posthumous memorial to the woman who allowed George the opportunity to uncover her true nature. The living memorial would cost a great deal of money, but it would be worth every single night on Bourbon Street once achieved. Mel was going to make both herself and her mother a son.

Giving birth to her brother at the same time would be an added bonus. The thought makes her giddy for the hundredth time.

She calms again, part of her solace coming from the completion of a trip in a crimson Studebaker and subsequent embarkation on a dip in a tub of the same color.

Constructing harmonious chromatic nuance is a lifelong hobby for Mel. She was born with the red hair. Might as well go along with nature's suggestion. At least, this particular suggestion. Establishing themes is a mission. She is comforted by continuity. And shoes. And the color red.

Unfortunately, this morning her green eyes are circled by a nest of her favorite color.

Melodie slides even deeper into her heavily perfumed bathwater, arms raised vertically as she carefully holds a crumpled scrap of paper above the Alpine bubbles. Unfolding the prison message slowly. There, among many cryptic scribblings and arcane symbols, her unknown correspondent had glued a picture of a steamroller. It is starting to melt free of its glue in the steam of the tub water. Melodie smiles. Warmed by more than her bath.

Could it have been Mutt's friend   that divinely interesting older and darker gentleman? Mutt's stately comrade had defended her so valiantly in Court   could he be her soul mate?

Melodie allows herself to daydream of the shoeless man. Bouncing a robust tyke on his knee. He looks to her to be a serious candidate for the perfect, loving father.

Melodie's ideas of perfection in a mate are undoubtedly a tad skewed from the Norm. Many factors came into play in the creation of Melodie LaGrande. She found a slightly off-median-curve perspective in both her sexual evolution and the value systems she put in place as she evolved. Then, of course, the French Quarter is not known as an environment conducive to conservatism in the choice of partners, whether in the short or long term. And Melodie's mother, Dorothy Shilberg Goodman-Hotard, added her influence as a uniquely individual and tolerant role model. And finally, in spite of her own occasional lapses, Melodie retains a character that values, above all, originality.

Her attraction to Rodrigo may still seem baffling.

However, there is a further phenomenon that should be noted here. Not as much in Melodie's defense as in further explanation of her tendencies. The people in her profession are predominantly women of a naturally-determined sexual designation. They were born with their parts already in place. By the nature of their jobs, they are constantly pursued by hormone-wracked males. These females make their livings by allowing small parcels of their attention to aroused audiences. Thus encouraging the johns to give them money. Outside of work, the dancers tend to have rather particular personal preferences. Especially when it comes to the men they allow to approach them. Regardless of location, environmental pressures or sexual kinks, the vast majority of them prefer mates who are the exact opposites of their customers.

The last person they want to meet is another grabby, wool-suited television sales executive with four kids and a fat wife. Or a conventioneer, no matter the cut of the clothing. Or one of the numerous and self-designated Studs. No, the working girls want something else.

Bikers. Grease-stained two-wheeled poets tend to be a lifestyle more favored by the topless set. Even bikers without bikes, or in this case, without shoes. Preferably also without the haute couture of the urban brand of yuppie motorcycle enthusiast.

Rodrigo's All-Fact Encyclopedia carries a two-page pictorial spread on the Harley Davidson. Right after eight substantial paragraphs on "hariolation". In some cases the All-Fact understands the predilections of its readers.

As Melodie lounges in her tub in the Faubourg St John, the object of her meditation, Rodrigo, stands motionless on the French Quarter sidewalk in front of his paper-encrusted place of worship. His eyes are fixed on the product of his last hour's labor. Rodrigo is searching for clues that he knows are close by. His fingers are covered with torn ribbons of paper. Held to his flesh by a cracked crust of white school paste. Red marker ink stains his hands all the way to his wrists.

"Stamen," he says deliberately.

The pause in construction had begun only moments before. He noticed a theme emerging from the display, even as he constructed it. Yes, there it is. Undeniable. Though it puzzles him, he knows where it had its start.

Using no small amount of artistic finesse, someone had stapled a flyer for Bourbon street's French Can-Can-Do Lounge onto his previous day's arrangement of encyclopedic excerpts. The flyer, which intimates a certain voluptuous Can-Can-Do artiste's dramatic relations with articles of men's apparel, had been neatly attached next to a cutaway diagram of a piston engine. Eight-cylinder. Water-cooled.

The metal of the staples and the image on the pink flyer has caused a further fluctuation in Rodrigo's mental field. A force   possibly related to magnetism or planetary gravitational systems   directs his life. Pulling him this way and that under Newtonic theorems unknown to him. Completely unknown. His life is directed from the outside, and he likes it that way. He has no decisions to make. No motivation for movement other than a general childlike delight in exploration.

And now this. The night, and now a message.

Rodrigo had been no less affected by the recent collision of lives and energy than Mutt. His own formerly even pace of existence had been totally disrupted by the Night Court drama. He had experienced a burst of revelation. Rodrigo, well into his sixth decade of life research, is carefully examining the unfamiliar runes identifying illustrations in the "CAA to DZERON" volume of Professor O's All-Fact Encyclopedia.

The Encyclopedia is a curious guide to world civilization, produced in Korea for inexpensive by-the-volume sales in that revered center of learning called the American supermarket. Professor O had obviously preferred the spirit of scholarship over either real research or proofreading, occasionally rendering his work less marketable though no less interesting. For instance, in spite of its Stateside target audience, only the text of the entries is translated from his original Korean language manuscript. Information below the rudimentary illustrations remained in Korean. To Rodrigo's delight.

The polished black leather brief case tucked under his arm is full of additional Encyclopedia volumes, a half dozen rolls of wide brown plastic wrapping tape, scissors and string, glue and gumwrappers, cracked cat's-eye marbles and left-over yatcamein noodles in a manila envelope. Rodrigo looks very learned and in touch with the world.

Except that he is not wearing any shoes.

His foot-long white goatee, and to a certain extent his clothes, are clean and fluffed. His ebony face, neck, arms and hands are hairless and well-maintained. But as he stands at the edge of what business world exists in this city, Rodrigo's bare feet cause the early morning suits to roll their eyes heavenward. With the continued heat, they are to a man still in the official Old Money summer uniform, even though it is well into the fall. Pastel-striped seersucker, top to bottom. Silk-clad feet shod in glossy black and white Spectators. Crisp white cotton shirt.

As soon as JazzFest passes by in the first week of May, it is officially summer in New Orleans. Out come the seers and suckers. The suits in the latter category. Rodrigo in the former. With his bare feet treading the paths of commerce.

Fred is an ardent admirer of this small item on Rodrigo's rather gargantuan list of idiosyncrasies   she thinks the heat from the sidewalks make his calloused feet smell quite earthy and pleasant. When they meet she always takes the opportunity to get a good nose-full of each and every one of his scent-laden toes. To see where they've been, and what he's been up to. Rodrigo is happy to oblige. He is known to encourage communication in any fashion.

Thus, his friendship with Mutt.

Rodrigo and Mutt stop to talk at least two to three times a week. It has become a ritual. They call each other "sir," polite as they can be, conversing with the gravity of two Washington DC Supreme Court Justices passing the time of day before deciding that, from thence onward, day was to be called night, and night day. By a 5-4 margin, with conservative dissent.

Both of the New Orleans Streets like to use their hands to punctuate conversation, Rodrigo gesturing ecstatically with his well-maintained briefcase. Usually toward the Lost Pleiades.   Oriented in that direction, he is.

Rodrigo does not speak English exclusively, or even as his primary choice. He prefers to communicate by blending English and obscure tribal dialects with the more melodic sounds of the animal kingdom. His words may have no direct source in either the ancient African tongues of his ancestors or the conglomerate patois of more recent generations of West Indians. Even so, his utterances sound primitive. Powerful. Bantu ululation and Guernsey mooing often enter the same declarative sentence for emphasis. Rodrigo is flexible in speech.

Fred and Mutt seem to understand Rodrigo perfectly. Fred has her nose. Mutt with his own gift is actually in tune with a curious and large cross-section of the population. This is possibly due to his extensive practice on two-dimensional representations. And his knowledge of pant history. Mutt speaks enthusiastically to a select corps of usually non-communicative "non-communicative" in the Norm sense of the word members of New Orleans' Streetworld. They seem to love him for it. Mutt, their translator to the real world. To the Norms.

Rodrigo, on the other hand, is in tune with the cosmos. Big-time. He spends his days subtly and respectfully evangelizing some sort of interstellar movement. He can tell those sensationalist newspapers a story or two about Up There.

Except none of his prospective interviewers would have a clue as to what their informant was saying. Rodrigo will need Mutt interpreting full-time if he really expects to get a message out.

For years Rodrigo has given his friends brown plastic bundles as supplementary communication. Mutt has saved three of the nicest to decorate the Box. No one knows exactly what is in the heavily taped forms. That is what makes them feel so powerful. Rodrigo takes much care in applying hundreds of layers of brown wrapping tape to obscure objects whose identity will never be revealed. For his part, Mutt loves the anonymous messages that seep out to him through the plastic. He imagines infinite possibilities for the contents. Street Poetry.

The last few months it has finally dawned on the gentle Rodrigo that he might possibly be speaking a language different from that spoken by the other inhabitants of this planet Earth. The Norms of the world. His circle of acquaintance is severely limited, even within the Streetworld. Many people know of him, or nod their heads to him in passing, but less than a handful   actually three, Marty the barker at the Can-Can-Do, Mutt & Fred, if Fred is counted as speaking   have ever spoken with him. So Rodrigo has taken to another means of passing on concrete clues to whatever mind-boggling vision he wishes to communicate.

It is actually a place to pass on clues. A boarded-up window on the face of an abandoned Decatur street shoe factory has become The Church of Rodrigo. All the Streets go there for the occasional taste of enlightenment. Rodrigo is quite proud of that.

Possibly there is an important transmission coming my way. A call to meconophagism?

President Garvey would not approve.

He touches his goatee thoughtfully.

A surge, then? Some great cosmic flux. Maybe I have misunderstood the data.

He had not planned any overt message for the window, especially after the spiritually-taxing effort he had made at the courthouse. He had been coherent for his friends' sake. But it hurt. Rodrigo ran to the church to purge himself of images. Not to gather them together. But here they are. A wide, rich vein of continuity dominating today's assembly.

He begins to consider the clues.

It seems to have something to do with gender in general and the naked Can-Can-Do female in specific. That is significant. He had come back to his message board from an experience involving this friend of Mutt & Fred's. And there she is again, right on his board. A flyer with her picture. For the third time he sees her. As he had seen her briefly on the stage the night before.

He did not know the woman, but he had found himself trying to attract her attention in the courtroom. Why?

As Mutt requested, he had sent her a message to let her know that help was on the way. He had done that for Mutt. But the waving the waving he had done for himself.

And now her image has appeared at the Church. Try as he might to put another snippet of encyclopedic information on top of the pink flyer "Esophagus" was ready for the pasting, as was the well-illustrated "Stereopticon" he could not do it. He could not cover her.

"Pistil?" he announces quizzically.

"Polyurethane?" he wonders aloud.

What is the purpose? Is someone trying to disrupt my Field? Of course not. Tonight's theme took off on its own. What then? What?

Possibly the infamous biologic rhythms   those natural phenomena that Mutt finds so fundamental   are taking hold. Though that seems stretching it a bit, even to Rodrigo. The board is riddled with references to political and sociological institutions. That is a natural outgrowth of his recent judicial experience. Also to be expected. Though he is amazed at how literal some of the references are. Re-reading his carefully-written marginal notes, he wonders at their coherence. This make sense. Mostly in his birth language, too.

I am beginning to think in familiar patterns. Something from the past is returning. Staples instead of glue.

Rodrigo tries to focus on the larger scale, on ever-expanding interplanetary relationships. To bring himself up to his optimal level of inspiration. He waits for a message. Nothing. He is befuddled. More befuddled than usual. No, less befuddled than usual.

And that is making him very befuddled.

He puts his hand on the poster-thickened church of images and lets his mind go blank. He would continue to patiently wait for the universe to enter the psychic vacuum. Patience. Waiting.

There is something, finally. Something approaching in the void. Someone. Someone lovingly coaxing a narrow Wembley tie into a provocative variation on a Tudor knot.

The darkness parts.

"Great sparkling rings around Uranus! I am thinking about SEX!" he says aloud, clearly and in English.

Rodrigo promptly faints.

Later that same post-court, post-library afternoon Noonie makes her way to Rodrigo's church after bumming the required handful of cigarettes. The mystic himself has departed, but a tour bus full of lens-laden Japanese pensioners was unloading nearby, and its occupants had coughed up five bucks, eight Marlboros, two unfiltered Camels, and something pink and cylindrical, as it disembarked passengers single-file onto Decatur street. The Nipponese sightseers were easily intimidated into generosity by the high decibel level of Noonie's requests.

Noonie tears a Marlboro in half and lights up both pieces. She stands quietly in front of Rodrigo's display. Allows its calm vibe to soothe her spirit. Ellis, her duck, is also a believer. He squats contentedly in the gutter, bubbling complex duck mantras. Rodrigo has again provided shelter. Even though neither the duck nor Noonie has ever spoken to him.

Rodrigo acquired most of the volumes of his massive, decades-old Encyclopedia in one giant trade. Noonie heard it involved as many as five hundred pounds of aluminum cans, gathered singly from roadsides. Whatever the price, Rodrigo now has fifteen precious volumes stashed at the end of a blocked drainpipe. Near Fred and Mutt's Expressway Box.

Rodrigo works hard all night every night reading those books. Fred often hears him down the way still grunting and moaning with revelations near sunrise. Rodrigo makes some pretty loud noises. That is Fred's opinion. Even with dog ears pressed under the covers. She doesn't much enjoy having her sleep disturbed, but makes allowances in Rodrigo's case. For the sake of theologic advancement. And science.

Then, early in the morning before any one else is up, Rodrigo goes down to his window, the boarded-over window most of the Street people have come to call his Church. In about an hour, he pastes up what he considers to be the exact bits of knowledge from the All-Fact Encyclopedia that relate to that day's planetary involvement with the rest of the Cosmos.

The placement of the information is very important to Rodrigo. He glues the clipped extracts on the window carefully, as befits their importance. He occasionally trims unneeded images, then writes explanatory notes in Rodrigese on and around his new creation. In a lovely cursive hand.

Some people come to the church every day for fresh information. Rodrigo does not begrudge members of his flock who need to commandeer a loose scrap when the message strikes deeply into their psyches. Generosity is a guiding force with the unassuming Street thaumaturgist. In spite of this pilfering, the plywood window is dozens of pages deep in places. An inch or so of one human's knowledge of   and deciphering of   the world around him.

Weather and human wear and tear have placed some very amazing facts in apposition, without the original author's conscious participation. This day Noonie notes that "beguine" is explained next to "anticyclone." The All-Fact, as usual, acts as a catalyst of, rather than a repository for, for facts:

> BEGUINE   a dance native to the island of Martinique. Named for Lambert le Begue, known as the Stammerer, who founded an order of lay nuns in the Low Countries around 1100 AD. Related to the rhumba and mambo, the dance can be continued over a period of several hours, and sometimes, days. Within the context of this larger time frame, the beguine is said to simulate the effects of an equal period of sexual activity. The steps have become very popular on French and Dutch islands in the Caribbean. So much so that proponents of the dance have organized politically in the second half of the twentieth century. Their rallies are recognizable principally by a looseness of the limbs below the waistline. See also: TANGO, RIJSTTAFEL, CONTRACEPTION.

ANTICYCLONE   a recently-synthesized modern antidote to the turn-of-the-century psychotropic drug Cyclone, used to induce clockwise circular walking patterns in laboratory animals. Anticyclone has been found to invariably bring on counter-clockwise walking. Also, a fruit drink served in the French Quarters of the city of New Orleans in the United States. Said to induce similar effects. See color plate XIV, page 167, "Venomous Fruit Drinks of the Northern Hemisphere."

With Rodrigo's annotations and the suggestive swiggles of the Korean titles, this gives Noonie an entirely new perspective on motion, which she immediately communicates to her duck.

"Duckie know all about GRAVITY. Yes duck DO."

Noonie was especially looking forward to Rodrigo's delving into the "M" and "N" regions. The Church should really be thick by then.

Rodrigo is a sculptor of words. Paper is his medium.

Rodrigo has a brother who shows up in town once in a while, offering him a return to a real home and bed up North. Most of the Streetpeople have met the brother once or twice over the years. Even though they may not have met Rodrigo, most are glad for this concrete connection to a Street legend. The brother's a pleasant well-to-do African-American businessman who wants to take Rodrigo home. Take care of the poor deluded soul. Rodrigo won't have any of it. He has become a naturalized resident. Somebody gave him that New Orleans injection. Rodrigo made himself an Earth passport with clippings from the All-Fact Encyclopedia.

But his brother still comes to town every few years, tells anybody who will listen that Rodrigo was once just fine, an upstanding Chicago attorney. That he had beat the Man at his own game. Was a pillar of the African-American community. This same Rodrigo one day left a cigarette burning in the conference room where he had been dictating a memo on tax shelters for minor entertainment celebrities. A married couple who were hosts of a regional radio talk show "Dave and Linda Edelman Love the Love-Lorn" were the final straw for him. Husband Dave ran off to Costa Rica with a male "Strip-o-gram" delivery boy. His ex-wife Linda had asked Rodrigo to handle the divorce and another small thing. She wanted her name changed to Dave. She had started dressing as a man, and wanted to develop a career in television. She'd use her worthless husband's name. And could she write off her new wardrobe?

That was it. Rodrigo stepped off the edge of the universe and disappeared for thirty-odd years. He was thought dead until his brother saw a picture of him in an Associated Press feature "Notorious Street Person in New Orleans Speaks His Own Language" and came south to rescue him.

Rodrigo had forgotten Chicago and his brother, but as always he was very temperate and polite in refusing to leave his present circumstances.

Recently Rodrigo has himself taken to attending a more regular church at the Chinese Methodist Enclave in the Lower Quarter. Not totally Norm, but as close as Rodrigo gets. The congregation of mostly older oriental women, with little or no English, love to hear him pray and sing in his native tongue. He merely walks in and participates when pointed to. The ladies bow to him and smile, since they have no language other than a spiritual reverence in common. They also feed him.

In return he has given the Enclave a total of fourteen of his plastic-wrapped objects. The ladies have arranged the heavy forms on a side altar, as a shiny brown cloud around the feet of St Peter. They have taken to speculating as to the contents. Each package is now labeled in delicate Chinese calligraphy: "fluttering starry moth," "dewy branch of wisteria bloom," "chilling September raindrop," "3/8-inch socket wrench." The churchgoers change the labels often, as the mood strikes them. Rodrigo knows he has found simpatico spirits. Family.

Rodrigo is always most appreciative when people do things for him. Though he rarely has to ask for handouts like Virginia or Noonie or Mutt and Fred. People offer to give him things all the time.

His friends know Rodrigo is a bit magical. He is like those omnipresent sculptures of big-bellied laughing Buddhas people are constantly rubbing the Buddhas' stomachs for good luck. Rodrigo's stomach sticks out in much the same manner, sticks right out from under his four-sizes-too-small 1973 New Orleans Saints t-shirt. '73 wasn't a great year for the Saints or Buddhism, as most fans of either will recall. Noonie figures that one day she will herself speak to Rodrigo. Noonie can talk about food, albeit only loudly.

Until then, Rodrigo remains both stoic and happy on his own.

Maybe that's why the Chinese churchgoers like him so much. And he loves those ladies' shrimp fried rice. Noonie had even overheard him say the actual words "shrimp fried rice" in a conversation with Mutt one day.

It was in the midst of a discussion of the contemporary glut of oil wells and alien fast-food on Pluto, best as she could discern.

* * *

Noonie does not fit the Norm mold herself. Skating by the front door of the Can-Can-Do, soiled wedding gown blowing in the wind and a two-foot-tall partially-defeathered duck squawking madly in tow, she has no idea that the sun is hours from being up.

Noonie, like Virginia and Rodrigo, does not live on Planet Earth.

She lives in New Orleans.

Historically, Noonie is accompanied for brief periods of time by a succession of solitary ducks who follow her about on a leash. Fred has been personally acquainted with seven   four hens and three drakes   and swears that not one was a decent conversationalist.

She suspects the fault could be due to their brief life span. Or the diet, or maybe even their urban environment. Fred believes the adult bird's only proper environment to be egg & milk batter, white flour and heated vegetable oil.

There are possible exceptions to her fowl theorem. Fred has yet to meet a penguin, though there are a few in New Orleans. Over at the Aquarium. She can picture the penguins: black and white birds living in captivity amidst what is probably leftover cocktail ice from Pat O'Brien's bar on St Peter street. The occasional swizzle stick floating by in the Arctic Environment room. Maybe several Maraschino cherries imbedded in a miniature display iceberg.

Fred had heard these particular penguins were born in New Jersey. She is curious enough to go, but Pets are not allowed in the Aquarium. Fred is often considered a Pet to ticket-takers. She has been trying to find a way to get Mutt to acquire a white cane and glasses. You see, Seeing-Eye Dogs are allowed. Fred is anxious to try the scam. Duo-chromed penguins from Hoboken might be worth the effort. Might even try on the shades herself.

Noonie, unlike the penguins, was born in New Orleans. Even a casual observer can tell. Certain small eccentricities given to the population of the City have been amplified in Noonie into full-blown planetary disturbances. UFOs have nothing on her.

This may well be true of each and every inhabitant of the Crescent City   bubbling beneath the polished Southern veneer, absolute madness lurks. Yearning for release. Most residents, of course, find this reassuring, and won't live anywhere else.

No one knows what catalyst releases the demon madness. Big explosion, small step   both seem equally potent when it comes to popping Over There.

Lots of these stories among the Streets. Even the immediate Family.

Virginia the Bead Lady was a high society dame with a wealthy husband, bank account to the rafters and a well-maintained mansion Uptown. Twenty years into the marriage the husband gets caught with his hand in the till of some large genteel corporation, resigns his Pickford Club membership, and blows his brains out with a monogrammed skeet gun. Boom. Virginia hears the noise. Boom. She follows him. Loses contact with the surface of planet Earth herself. Zoop. Flies right off, out into the Street. The Bead Lady is born.

Noonie had relatives, too, a brother being the last alive. He passed on a few years ago, though Noonie found out only recently. She is now the final surviving member of a very old family of very mixed origins. As the sole heir, she owns a big house over on Toulouse street, though the Quarter grapevine says Noonie hasn't been inside the house since 1969. The front door is still supposedly unlocked, but even the toughest Bienville project hoodlums the Downtown Mob are afraid to go in and ransack the joint. Noonie has some serious juju riding with her, and the grave-robbers of this City are much more willing to deal with ten burglar alarms and every cop in the Vieux Carré District than to challenge the sort of protection that covers Noonie's world.

Noonie may be one of those rare instances where the body is born on Earth and the mind is born elsewhere.

Noonie and Fred get along all right, in spite of Fred's not being too intellectually excited by her ducks. Noonie has been working the Streets of the Quarter for two decades, and she is a survivor. She has also had some actual brushes with reality, however brief and tenuous those brushes may have been.

In the early seventies, she sold LSD. This was not a bad thing, not like being a drug dealer today. Hippies who populated the Lower Quarter the old Bank bar on Decatur street and The Roach club at Ursulines and Royal had given her large quantities of the hallucinogen. Noonie was their Tibetan guru. She had no idea what the tablets of LSD were, other than visually interesting little objects, but she soon discovered that people would give her beers and sometimes money for the small colorful pills and shiny "window panes" that filled her pockets.

Then somebody told her "The Police will Get You if they Catch You with this Stuff," and the amorphous Bust concept was born in Noonie's mind.

It was then, in one of the more remarkable bits of deranged practicality ever exhibited by Noonie, that the duck entered the equation. She tied her stash of acid around the neck of her pet duck. "Cops want to Bust somebody, they can Bust the Duck," was her logic. She named it Ellis Duck, Ellis D for short.

The current Ellis is reckoned to be duck number thirty-two by the most long-lived Streets. The birds have come to her from a variety of sources. Some were donated from admirers. Some were convinced that she was their spiritual counterpart in long debates on the essence of reality at the City Park duck pond. Some were outright filched. Some were merely befriended. Noonie had found number thirty-two coated with diesel fuel on the Mississippi river levee. After a bath and two bags of cheese doodles, he had decided to hang around. In spite of the danger.

But the ducks have always been exempt from prosecution. Everybody, including the police, knew what was going on, but those were simpler and more innocent days everybody was considered a Norm then and Michael Rennie had the only interstellar saucer so Noonie was left to enjoy her little cottage industry with a minimum of harassment.

Nobody could tell if she ever ate any of the drug herself. That was an index of the depth of her strangeness, and remains so. It was at about this point in her life, though, that she began wearing white bridal gowns, wide-brimmed straw hats, and roller skates. Not a properly inconspicuous style of wardrobe for a dangerously notorious drug dealer.

The elements of her outfit have not changed in all the years since, though she mysteriously shows up with a new wedding dress, and the occasional new Ellis D, at sporadic intervals. She has always preferred sleeping on the floors of benefactors' shops and bars, but never for more than a single night at a time in any one place.

The LSD she used to supplement her income in former years is long gone, now replaced by posters of Noonie and Ellis.

The posters were her friends' idea. They collaborated. A painter from the Jackson Square Artist Commune rendered the subjects in quick-drying acrylics, faithfully capturing the flowing wedding dress, the roller skates, and the wry look on Ellis' bill. Dozens of Quarterites kicked in small amounts of cash to get the first edition printed, and a friendly graphics dealer distributed them to shops.

It ended up wonderfully for everyone concerned. All the poster shops that sold the piece gave Noonie royalties on each one sold, plus the printer gave her one hundred to sell herself out of each edition. The "Bride Noonie and Ellis D" poster is currently up to an eighth printing.

Noonie is another of Mutt's favorites. He absolutely idolizes her. He contributed almost two dollars to the poster fund. Fred was furious at the ensuing week of lessened nutrition, but allowed Mutt the extravagance.

Mutt also collects cigarette butts for Noonie, even though he doesn't smoke himself. He presents them to her with reverence, wrapped neatly with bits of string. She has taken to carrying pockets full of them, and will sometimes sit on a cool storm drain and smoke ten in a row, often three or four at a time. Noonie likes to enjoy the full nicotine burst.

Noonie only occasionally remembers who Mutt is, though Mutt has talked to her almost daily for years.

Noonie likes Mutt   likes him a lot when she recognizes him   but she has a bad head for faces, even her own. She does seem to recognize Virginia. The two women suddenly appearing in the strangest places in each other's company.

At the moment, now balancing on her skates directly in front of the French Can-Can-Do Lounge, Noonie is unabashedly hitting up plain-clothes vice cops for tobacco. She has long since learned that they enjoy being benevolent to her, and she is quick to take advantage.

Even in this low-pressure situation, Noonie never speaks at anything other than the top of her voice.

"Ain't me Officer. IT'S THE DAMN DUCK. MESSING ALL OVER THE CITY STREET. Duck. Ellis. NICE CIGARETTE THOUGH Officer. Good cigarette. Good job you doin', too, guard the duckie."

* * *

Twenty blocks away, Virginia crosses Canal street toward the Quarter. She is engaged in the constant roll of words that punctuate her waking hours. They are more connected than Rodrigo's, these words. They have a flow that gives an occasional glimpse of a mind at work. Her logical arguments are, however, usually preceded and interspersed with escaping bursts of air. As if the words are pushing from her lungs every unnecessary breath: "SSSSS SSS... SSSSSSS SSS SSSS ...Where ...we ...SSS ...have got to get therefore ...SSSSS ...we know that in life they could be coming any time now... SSSSS SSSSSss... lucky you all have me here to warn you about the radiation. Look here! There could be radiation any minute. Radiation. But I, I have beads! My beads offer protection, protect the brain stem in each and every average human. You, mister, look mighty average. Need Protection. SSSSSSsss... Care for a lucky bead, mister? Small donation only."

She has already made $1.32. Soon, her regulars will hit the Quarter and she will have more money. *Like the guy with the dog. The famous lawyer. He's always good for something. If I could just not get bit by that damn dog.*

Dangerous work, saving humanity.

Virginia is one more example of the Crescent City's overpowering world-view confusion.

Here she comes, zipping back and forth across the sidewalk. Rejecting gravity. Rocketing along in ragged non-directional bursts. Her head up, then down-up-down-up quickly in two more cycles. She maneuvers easily through the glut of people in the first block of Bourbon street. At its onset, the south side is occupied by a Krystal Burger and another tourist-trash shop, the north by a dark-windowed Off-Track Betting parlor and a purveyor of sex toys. Gambling on what you get for your money is the order of the day in all four establishments.

As usual, the street itself is full of sunburnt retirees dressed like Don Ho on mescaline. This apparition is indicative of yet another twentieth-century human malady that flourishes in summer, something Rodrigo calls the Universal Human Tropical-Vacation Body-Covering Syndrome. Virginia has taken its appearance as confirming the tabloids' worst predictions. For her, this disease is much worse than thermal hysteria.

To both Virginia and Rodrigo's chagrin, the Syndrome is sadly neglected in the American medical journals.

Streets recognize the Syndrome in an instant, but even Mutt has a difficult time coming up with the words. In the privacy of their box, he and Fred discuss it by its primary symptom: painful visual relationships in clothing. In males, this is apparent as an immediate darkening of socks worn with

Bermuda shorts, and an increasing occurrence of glow-in-the-dark colors in upper-body coverings.

Females contracting the Syndrome are driven to make multiple purchases of spandex pants-wear in sizes inversely proportional to the size that will actually cover their bodies. The afflicted are inexorably drawn to wearing these pants with spike heels of the exact size that will fit snugly in the holes of sidewalk ventilation grates. Thus the infected females can easily be identified by the unusual gait that comes with wearing one shoe and carrying the separated parts of the other.

On this day, the mass of uniformed ogling tourists do a Universal backlot imitation of the Red Sea parting as Virginia the Bead Lady draws near. She knows she frightens them and takes a certain pride in the intensity of reactions she evokes. Virginia continues forward, making sporadic sharp, cosmic-sounding noises as she plows through the heavy electrons of New Orleans summer.

With intergalactic invasion firmly in mind, Virginia takes great care in assembling herself like the metal and chemical layers of a great regenerative battery.

Some eager young scientist will undoubtedly soon discover the possibilities of using an immobilized Virginia as a graduate project, possibly the basis of an extended doctoral thesis.

For the capture, the scientist will have to hire someone of the caliber of the legendary Great White Hunter of Pascagoula. Anyone less will be intimidated at the prospect of diving into the unsanitary wilds of the Vieux Carré at night.

The stalk is easy to imagine.

The distant echoing cries of a
hardware store owner from Virginia biting

into his first cayenne-hot-sausage po-boy fill the street, as the intrepid hunter examines Virginia's spoor and silently tracks her on the streets of the Quarter. There, hidden in the shadow of a Lucky Dog stand's twin red weenies, he bags her with a single shot. The hunter cautiously remains behind his weenie-blind as the hypodermic projectile a humane stunning compound the scientist has cleverly loaded into the shining chamber of the hunter's powerful rhino gun works its magic and brings Virginia slumping slowly to the asphalt.

The technicians bend hungrily over the Bead Lady's twitching body on Royal street. They smile, eagerly examining an exploratory drilling core. Taken from this unclassified sample of humanity's outer boundaries. The baffled scientists are surprised to discover thick sedimentary layers of expensive late-twentieth century designer clothing decorated with crayons and separated by strata of pre-historic asphalt and twentieth century bubble-gum. Colors cluster mostly at the dark end of the spectrum. The matrix, the street tar and bubble gum, has been carefully applied in small flattened spheres, presumably to keep the other layers from shifting about during planetary movement.

The next to last layer of the core is the most brilliant in color. The subject female's drawers.

Fred herself has conducted preliminary research here, having been dazzled by this anthropologically significant buttock mantle on numerous occasions. The inspection has also facilitated Fred's sex verification process. It seems that Virginia uses the same grassy patch that Fred prefers, when in the Quarter, for biological functions.

This is Virginia's terminal covering. Her drawers actually form a geothermal layer   thick fluorescent orange plastic swaddling her wrinkled loins, top to bottom. An Angola Penitentiary prison-guard rainsuit worn under twenty kilos of other clothing.

At the plastic layer, without protective equipment, scientific exploration ceases. The subject's ancient, leathery flesh is directly and continually in contact with the plastic prison sportswear. This produces a rather pungent and sour scent that cloys her immediate environment, even on windy days. The unprepared have on occasion been rendered momentarily unconscious when caught upwind.

A graduate student from Georgia Tech drops untidily to the street surface as the confused scientists retreat from Virginia's carcass in disarray.

Virginia reminds Fred of her brother Helen. Helen had brown and black stripes and threw up a lot. He and Virginia carry the same basic scent.

Unlike Helen, though, the gaunt Bead Lady always seems healthy and durable. Fred is visited by sporadic nightmares based around the foreboding that Virginia might actually be immune to the passage of Time. That she will always be near the 100 block of Bourbon street.

Fred is not what you would call a bead fan, not when donations for Virginia's protective talismans inevitably mean fewer purchases of dog food.

For Fred there have been encouraging developments in the last months, though. She has noticed what might be taken as evidence of Virginia's preparation for imminent interplanetary travel. The Bead Lady has taken to wearing a scarred black motorcycle helmet, with a faded "Triumph" winged insignia on the back. This has to mean travel.

Virginia moves through the crowd. The Bead Lady's face twitches from side to side, continually scanning the immediate vicinity for intruders. The eyes, set in cave-dark sockets, do not seem attached. Floating below her forehead. Almost colorless. Reflecting what passes in front of them. Encased in scratched and fogged carpenter's goggles.

Just above the goggles Virginia has installed her final line of defense from intrusive cosmic rays: wrinkled aluminum gathered from dozens of fast-food garbage cans, then flattened and applied following the contours of her helmet. The thin metal layer represents the limit of her science. The occasional drip of mayo tolerated for its adhesive quality.

This woman is prepared. If not for travel, for a rain of deadly cosmic debris. A rain that could happen at any minute.

It is all poised up there somewhere.

LM Jeansonne was still a bit tense at the sundown proceeding his night of jury duty and appearance as a homespun legal representative. After cashing his ten dollar check, and having various fees deducted, he had invested the remaining money in a large can of Doc Wolf's for Fred and a loaf of bread and a jar of peanut butter for himself. Fred had eaten gratefully, and gone right back to sleep. Mutt, now well into his second day without rest, returned for a final conversation of the day with the Satisfied Customer.

He noticed that during his absence, someone had scratched a "happy face" in one of the billboard's support posts, with the romantic legend "Jamie fuck Loretta Ray May 2016 she fuckin good" scratched sentimentally underneath.

Mutt talks to inanimate objects much more than he talks to real folks. The feedback from living people overwhelm him.

Representations, no matter how crude, made for much more pleasant conversations. He knew he would be talking to the Reed woman again first thing in the morning, so he had decided to practice for that encounter by actually speaking out loud to the Customer this time around.

I know Fred's mad that she wasn't there for the whole thing. The Jury Duty thing, you know.

See, my first day me & Fred went together to my duty but the Courthouse guards wouldn't let her in the building because she's not a Seeing-Eye Dog. Fred tried to ad-lib a little Seeing-Eye routine, even bumping into walls and all, but they wouldn't fall for it. I don't think she realized it's the person who's supposed to be blind. I told them that myself being an almost-blind registered voter and soon-to-be jury member I thought blind dogs should be able to go into the Courthouse, too, but that didn't change their minds much.

That's why I had to take Fred back to the Can-Can-Do so Mel and Marty could watch out for her until I got through with the Government. Pissed Fred off big time. Not the Do, no. Being there doesn't bother her one bit. She likes watching Mel dance and Marty pull in the customers. She was just steamed about those guards not going for her Seeing-Eye bit. Me, I thought it was a damn good act.

Then the jury people kept me tied up there all day every other day for a month so I couldn't make but less than half a decent living. Slept most of my days off, because I was so worn out from dealing with those Norms all day, and then I'm getting just the littlest bit of nighttime money after I woke up. This of course was cutting down considerably on the purchase of Fred's Doc Wolf.

Her favorite dog chow, Doc Wolf Doggie Ration. I'd take her some of my friend Mr Lee's food, but folks just flocked around once they discovered him and there wasn't ever a bite left. Folks didn't like him at first because he's a Oriental man, but when he started bringing that food, everybody started acting like that Asia place was a regular registered voter suburb of New Orleans. Just across the river. Food will bring folks together. Me and Fred should know, seeing as how little decent food we get our hands on and how much it means to us.

Good thing Mel and Marty were looking after Fred during the day for me. Marty can always catch a chili dog or two off the weenie vendors on Bourbon street. The Lucky Dog guys sometimes give him free food for steering drunk Can-Can-Do customers their way. Marty gave those chili dogs to Fred starting the first day. Filled the old girl up pretty good. Except afterwards Fred farted like some wild and wooly woods goat all night long. Woke me up. Louder than the roaring of the trucks. I suspect she'd been eating her chilidogs with onion. Maybe even jalapenos. That's a sure rhythm buster, feeding a dog those hot vegetables. You bust folks' rhythm, makes them do all sorts of things.

It was a hard month doing that Government job. First off nobody wanted me on a jury, seeing as how I look and smell. And then, just the day when it's supposed to be over and I can get out and make a living, they kept me at Court until this one last trial was done.

Oddly enough, whether he knew it or not, Mutt had come awake during his long stay at the Criminal District Court.

He had been force-fed the acquaintance of several hundred Norms. He had to speak several times a day. He could find no way around it.

Some of the talking was not at all pleasant. This miniature cross-section of the city held both good and bad specimens. There was even a town drunk who barged into every conversation in the jury pool. "Dave Carlsson's the name, murder one's my game," the drunk would say. He hadn't been selected for a jury either. But all the different people had to be dealt with. Then Mutt had to answer to the system, answer questions about himself under oath. Questions from very very serious Norm law-types, even Judges. He didn't know the answers to all the questions, either. Never had known all the answers. The boy was a mystery to himself.

Mr Lee Fat was the catalyst. He and Mutt had met two weeks before, in the second week of their term, over large boxes of shrimp fried rice and duck feet.

"You like eat Chinese food, mista? You like?" Lee asked.

Mutt had been hanging over Lee's shoulder, inhaling deeply as the old man released yet another wave of fragrance from a paper sack. Inside were three large white boxes, their lids neatly folded shut. The old Oriental gentleman gingerly lifted each box by its thin aluminum handle and set it on his lap. When he had the third balanced on his knee, he had addressed Mutt. Mr Lee was obviously proud of the stir that his food smells were causing in the jury waiting room.

"My family have Lee Fat restauran' in French Quattas. Verrr-r-ry good restauran'. My wife she make this food. This here this shrimp fried rice. This box duck feet in oyster sauce. Verrry tasty also. Also got white rice for feet. You like some, mista? I give you some," he said before Mutt could answer.

Up to this point Mutt had found that the Government had not anticipated the possibility of jury starvation.

Mutt recognized the restaurant name from the mad Rodrigo's occasional ecstatic reviews of free church food. Lee Fat's Restaurant often donated leftovers to the soup kitchen favored by many of the downtown Streets. Mr Lee's fried rice lived up to its advance praises.

The duck feet were delectable, but a lot of trouble to consume. They were also the source of a peculiar and all-pervading aroma, a smell that could not quite be categorized as appealing. At least not at first scent.

The sight of the two men eating heartily drew no one else to their side. Lee and Mutt were the only two non-Norms in their group. They had each been isolated without conversation and given little more than perfunctory courtesy for the better part of two weeks. It was inevitable, though, that they finally be drawn together.

For Mr Lee, too, had a gift.

His parents had already known the young boy was a wonder at mathematics when they escaped the revolutionary China of the '40's. He had been at the head of his class when his family abandoned all their holdings and fled the northeastern city of Jinan. The elder Lee's politics were wrong for the emerging China. His father had booked passage aboard a river scow that asked for no papers and held none itself. With his parents and brother, Lee Fat sailed the Huang He River through the otherworldly mountains of Shandong province. Great pillars of rounded black rock, lushly furred in green, rose vertically on either side of the evenly-flowing river throughout the week's voyage. On the eighth day, the boat emerged timidly into the silt-filled saltwater expanse of the Bo Hai. The crew, constantly on the lookout for government patrols, held the boat in tight tacks, creeping along the coast to the small port of Yantai on the great Yellow Sea.

It had taken nine months of scrambling and bargaining for his father to secure passage on a Korean freighter bound for the US by way of the Philippines. The young Lee Fat spent his time amongst the multi-lingual wharf traders and sailors, acquiring a firm basis for what would become a lifetime of wheeling and dealing. This was fortunate, since he arrived in San Francisco with only a change of clothing, an incomplete set of mahjong tiles and three thousand Korean won in his pocket.

In the western United States he had made a substantial fortune by combining his skills with a willingness to work as long and hard as it took to accomplish his goals. He spent his initial months in America in the basement of a laundry, walking away from work each day with a few more dollars and a few more words of English. Night-time employment as a delivery boy broadened his knowledge of western culture and the means to ownership of property. He relished even the most menial jobs if they carried him on his way. Lee Fat learned and earned quickly. To celebrate his third year in the country, he bought the laundry that had given him his first job.

He had worked for his success, and was proud of it. Lee Fat had retired some five years before the day he shared food with Mutt, having given away the major part of his money and possessions to his children. The family secure, he and his wife had moved to New Orleans with their youngest son to enjoy a simple end to life, comfortably working with his hands and enjoying his anonymity.

He was a humble man, Lee Fat, but the old restaurateur had about him the air of a person of substance.

He had registered to vote only a year earlier.

After devouring much of the contents of all three boxes, Mutt and Lee finally sat back and looked at each other. Mutt rubbed his stomach and nodded approval. Then belched loudly in the key of G. Lee lowered his head in recognition of the compliment. Both men smiled. The strong aroma of the duck feet had filled the room. Mutt was glad, as the smell of the food had overcome the scent of a man who had been rather short of bath time for the better part of a month. The gamey LM Jeansonne, prospective jury member.

"You know," said Lee, "I thinking maybe hungry people be talking to me in this room, I get to meet these New Orleans peoples, but nobody say nothing to me. Not until you come over."

"I still haven't said anything sir, but I am now, and I'd like to say thank you sir. For the food. I was hungry. I was." Mutt stopped, amazed that he had spoken, afraid to go forward, afraid of offending the man who had befriended him. He made a decision, forced thoughts through his brain, opened his mouth.

"LM Jeansonne, sir," he said extending his hand. "Registered voter. You can call me Mutt. If you want, sir."

"Lee Fat. Lee Fat my name," said the old man happily. "I so glad meet you. I register voter myself. Me my wife, my son his wife, we all register. Own business. Live in French Quattas. Make verrr-rry good food."

The two shook hands. Mutt experienced a small jolt as he took in Lee Fat's story all at once. He had not thought about the results of a conscious physical contact with another human for a long time before this. Mr Lee was a good man, and much smarter than he acted. Mutt knew it as fact. Lee Fat squinted, taking further stock of Mutt. The two men's smiles grew broader, introductions shared. But as they finished their handshake and withdrew their hands, Lee looked wonderingly at his palm, then back at Mutt.

LM Jon Son remarkable man.

The jury room was unsettled. The overpowering smell had started the discomfiture. A number of the inhabitants of the room looked at each other, sniffing the air and seeking other's reactions to the pungent stench. Then Mutt and Lee had begun talking, both of them prone to rather liberal gesturing. Two people got up from chairs near the pair, and moved to the farthest corner of the room. There were knowing glances exchanged, followed by nods in the direction of the two ostracized men.

The ever-vocal and over-large Dave "Murder-One-Is-My-Game" Carlsson made faces over Lee's head. Carlsson, stimulated by the covert consumption of cheap liquid derivatives of the juniper berry, held his nose, contorted his mouth and eyes and pointed at the old man. Even the more reasonable in the crowd fidgeted in their chairs, tried to ignore his clumsy antics.

"The goon is drunk again," whispered someone at the back of the room.

Mutt noticed nothing, except his new acquaintance. He was full, and he was having a conversation. "My friend Rodrigo told me about this food. He loves it, says it's the real thing. Though I don't know if he's had the feet."

"Roh-doo-ree-goh? Ro-dreego? Yes! Rodrigo? Correct? My wife she know this man! He go to her church! He man make prayer balls! This good you me meet. Our family know each other. This good. Very good. I give you my address, numbers. You come visit anytime anytime." Mr Lee pulled a waitress' pad from his pocket and started scribbling. He hummed as he wrote, clearly delighted with his new friend. He tore off the top sheet and handed it to Mutt.

"Don't worry all Chinese writing. Don't worry. It just say I not there, they treat you like family. Phone number right here," he said, pointing to the printed top of the sheet. Say 'Lee Fat' in 'merican."

Just then the door to the room slammed open, and the jury manager entered with a computer list in hand. Another set of trials demanded twelve honest and true.

"Judge Rogers. Division C," he yelled without prelude. They were all supposed to know the system by now. "Third floor. North end. Come up when your name is called and I'll check you off before you head to court. Eubanks. Ortega. Foster. Lee. Delaney. Now for Judge Smythe. Division E. Roland. Jeansonne..."

Lee Fat stood. Mutt followed suit, and held out his hand again to Lee. "Looks like get to go in there. We got to be here anyway. We can talk more after, if you like."

* * *

At least I finally got a couple of dollars out of it. No motel room, though. I found out early on that you don't get a penny unless you're actually sitting on a jury. You get chosen, then you get ten dollars a day. Not bad. Only, like I say, the fancy lawyer sorts weren't too keen on choosing me most of the month. Hadn't made a dime for all my sitting and waiting. That last day I think this defense fellow wanted me because his client was something of a bum, too.

"Murder trial," they said after they called my name.

Right away I was thinking OK, Mutt, me I'm going to get a free motel room with a color TV and instant coffee pot and the deluxe-quality paper sanitary band on the toilet. Perked up my day considerable while I was thinking that.

Then they said "second-degree murder." Jury pool lady said they don't give motel rooms for no stinking second degree.

Excuse me, but that really got my dander up. Later I found out that even if they give you a motel in the first-degree cases, they don't let you watch TV, because a jury person might be watching TV news and see himself. Make him prejudice. So, I guess that motel wasn't the best thing in the world anyway, you know. But it would have been pretty close.

I would have liked me a bath and some quiet sleeping. Sneaking Fred into the motel for that quiet sleeping. Would have made the rest of the jurors happy, too, me getting a bath. Hadn't had any time at all to go for a clean-up. For the whole month. And the bathrooms in the courtroom building were stripped to the bone. They got those "security concerns," the bailiff people said. They figured you might stay in there and make a bomb out of the toilet paper rolls. A mad bomber might very well disrupt the judicial proceedings of some desperate jaywalker. Bailiffs don't have much to do down here at the courthouse. Mess with folks in the bathroom the best they can do.

Neither did I, until Mr Lee came along.

Thirteen jury members are picked for a major trial, even though the jury is based on twelve votes. The court picks an extra in case one of the regular twelve dies in the box or loses contact with reality or realizes the stove was left on at home.

The Judge addresses the prospective jurors before the selection process even begins: "This is a peculiar brand of law we've got here in Louisiana, this Napoleonic Code. And it has certain peculiarities which you will be asked to consider in making your decision."

The Code is indeed peculiar to Louisiana among all the other United States. The rather nebulous core of what would become this state's legal system sailed up the river in the backpack of the explorer Iberville three hundred years ago, and never left. During his eleven years of ascendancy at the start of the nineteenth century, Napoleon Bonaparte codified the morality of the times, merging it with his own. He then compressed the result into a written document. Juries and courts in Louisiana still enforce the Gallic value system of The Little Corporal on a daily basis.

Mutt's favorite manner of jury selection was the way in which Judge Reynaldo Smythe picked his potential jurors. Smythe had his bailiff shred the computer printouts of names into half-inch-wide strips, then put the strips into a glass box and draw names like it was the Saturday night Lotto. The names drawn were then called aloud. The possessor of the name came to the front of the room, and was questioned as to suitability for the actual trial at hand. A slightly complicated lottery.

Mutt won. His was the first name out of the glass box on his last day of jury duty.

He walked up and stood next to a chair in the back row of the jurors' area, as he was instructed. Answered questions. Was told to sit. He was proud. L Mutt Jeansonne had finally been chosen. It was like a graduation ceremony.

It happened so fast at first.

The bailiff came up and made me swear something. What it was, I'm still not sure, they all talk so fast. But I did my best to make that man happy. Since it's probly my last time up there, I figured I'd take it easy. Get home early.

The bailiff said, "Sit down, Mr Jeansonne." Said it mean, like I'm the one on trial. So serious, and me being so accommodating. But I did that. Sat down. Also in the process tearing another hole in my pants. And me with barely an inch of pencil left.

Then everybody on god's earth asked me question after question after question. They wanted to see if Mr Jeansonne has religious beliefs that might keep him from frying this citizen in the electric chair or putting that citizen in the Angola prison for the rest of his life. Me, I told them that I was once a bad Catholic, but right now I belong to the Church of Rodrigo. Very loose church.

They ask if I'm a Liberal. I say no. It says I'm an Independent on my official card   I pulled it out   but I vote Democrat all the time on account of me being a Yellow Dog.

They laughed good at that one, though I couldn't quite figure why, unless they were all Republican. Judge looked like he was one. Constipated condition for sure. I didn't say anything, though, on account of the way he looked and pointed at folks when he said that word "Contempt". Scared me to death the first time I heard him say it, and he was just practicing that time. It would loosen up most folks' constipated condition right off, if they heard that judge say "Contempt".

A man asked me, "Mr Jeansonne, do you have any relatives in law enforcement or government?

Mutt said: "If I had me one, I sure as hell wouldn't be sitting here for a whole month maybe getting ten dollars." They laughed again. The Judge started to point, so he lowered his eyes and acted like he was real sorry.

Then they asked: "Do you know the man accused of this crime?" *They point at the man who looks like a bum kinda like me. I said no.* Then they asked, "Or do you know the lawyer sitting next to him?" Mutt said, "No, no, no. Don't want to, either."

Final thing, they said: "Have you been the victim of a crime yourself, Mr Jeansonne, within the last six months?" He told them the only thing he remembered was the time a couple of seven or eight years back when two slimy junkies who lived in the Broad street pumping station drainage pipes got sixty-two cents off of him. And two cans of "Doc Wolf's Doggie Ration" off his dog buddy Fred.

The Court people thought that was funny too, but I told them it wasn't no laughing matter being hungry. So they got serious and said, "No objection to Mr Jeansonne, Your Honor."

I got the ten-dollar-a-day job in the government box. So there I sat. Nobody said a word to me any more. Me so bored I could fall asleep. Mr Lee got me used to real folks sure enough.

The trial actually got started about mid-afternoon, and Mutt paid attention to the judge and lawyers once they had finished picking the jury. He tried to sort out what was happening: *I was thinking and thinking, and all of a sudden I realized this was the first time I had ever talked to myself. I don't think my lips even moved once. Though they might have when I finally looked up and saw what I saw.*

The accused man was sitting in a wheel chair.

Yep. This man accused of a violent and cold-blooded murder was paralyzed from the waist down. He's got a giant economy-size Afro, and it's all white. Has a face a hundred years old.

He also has a mind game going   a game he was playing with us jury folks in the box. He looked up at just one person at a time, and when he got that person looking at him, he locked his eyes on that person. He was sending a message, and that message had hoodoo written all over it: "Don't be messing with me now." Then he real quick looked back down at his lap. He picked up his leg and moved it around so the jury could see that those legs don't work.

The man in the chair's name was Walter Taylor.

This Walter they say killed somebody over sixteen ounces of Mad Dog wine.

Ten hours of talking passed. There were witnesses to a death threat that Walter made over the woman calling him a wine thief. There were witnesses to seeing Walter on his porch with a long rifle. There was the long rifle with Walter's fingerprints and a shell missing. And a suited man with a briefcase saying that the bullet that killed the woman came from Walter's gun.

The ballots were passed forward. The foreperson, a large schoolmarm-ish lady named Lerline, read the pieces of paper and made marks on a tablet. The eleven other jurors were quiet, leaning back in their chairs, not talking at all.

"Everybody says guilty," said Lerline, "but one person says maybe manslaughter rather than second degree murder. Doesn't matter. Judge said for now it only takes eleven to convict in the second degree in Louisiana. The verdict is guilty."

Fifteen minutes later it was over.

Eleven o'clock at night. The whole thing took twelve hours. Mutt's jury had made a decision in forty-five minutes. But there was more action to come in the courtroom.

That man Taylor's family is making a scene and all. Guess you can't blame them. But for a minute there after they read the verdict, I thought his brother Charles was gonna climb over the rail and come up to get us. Him yelling and screaming at us because we decided his brother did it. But it didn't scare me like it would have before I came here. His acting that way made me feel even surer about what we decided in the jury room. We had got on down to the truth. That was our job.

* * *

Mutt was still exhilarated an hour after he emerged from the courtroom. Lee, too, when he came out even later and sat by his new friend. He shook Mutt's hand, then attempted to bow. As the old restaurateur stepped back, the alcohol-flushed Dave Carlsson   behind him   extended his feet directly in Lee's path. Lee Fat saw the barrier too late, tripped and fell to the floor heavily. He lay on the worn linoleum rubbing his elbow.

The red-faced man seemed amused at Lee's situation. "Watch out there, buddy! Gotta pay attention in this room. Haven't learned much since you been in our country, son, have you?"

"Sir, you trip me I think," Lee said angrily. "Why you do this, you so stupid man?"

"Stupid! Who do you think you're talking to, buddy?" Carlsson turned to the rest of the room for approval. Most turned away. "You folks hear that?" He grabbed Lee by his collar and pulled him to his feet. Carlsson's breath carried the sweet scent of Mother's Own Brand gin.

Mutt came up quickly. He seized the man's arm, pulling Lee toward him and attempting to support the hurt elbow.

"Let Mr Lee go, sir. He's not hurting you."

"Now we got the other one! Don't you two fools start acting like you own the place, acting like you was real Americans. No, no, no. Don't you start getting too high hat now. Come in here stinkin' this place up with who knows what all," the man exclaimed, again panning the room for sympathy. No one was looking. That made him up his volume again. "Raggedy-ass smelly bum and a nasty-mouth old foreigner. Why you messing with me?" He dropped Lee and put his hands on his hips, confronting the other two men.

Mutt turned his back, straightening Lee Fat's collar and ignoring the rest of the room. Lee made an exaggerated gesture of disdain, lifting his chin away from the large man. Making him even more agitated.

"Listen to me, you sunuvabitch!" he yelled, swinging a giant roundhouse at Lee's head. Mutt somehow saw it coming. He reflexively stepped inside the punch and brought his knee up into the drunk's crotch. Just like he had seen Mel do. Just like his instructors had shown him in the Army, and the way he'd had to do often on the Street.

The man made a deep "Whooooff" sound as all the air went out of him. Mutt gripped his hand and helped him sit.

"Sorry. Very sorry to do that sir. You shouldn't ought to try and hurt folks that done you no harm. Especially not registered voters here in this Government building," Mutt said apologetically. There was the sound of one pair of hands clapping, then another. Mutt helped Lee Fat down the steep stone courthouse steps as they exited onto Tulane Avenue.

But as Registered Voter L Mutt Jeansonne was leaving, a tall blue-haired lady from Central City shuffled over and whispered in his ear that Carlsson DE, had been dropped from the jury pool. "Justice after all," she said.

"Justice," replied Mutt, at that point not knowing that the rest of his night would be even more intensely involved with the principal and workings of the judicial system of New Orleans.

Fred likes the toasted white bread at the Suds & Duds 24-hour Bar Grill & Laundromat on St Charles Avenue. That much is obvious. She is on her fourth order, having also devoured both Mutt's and Christine Reed's toast in the process. Even though Reed ordered whole wheat, Fred is trying to keep an open mind about the woman   she has, in fact, bought them a very nice breakfast and not complained of Fred's table manners once. Still, Fred has her doubts.

Mutt, however, is talking like Fred has never heard him talk before. At least not to a live Norm.

"Yes maam, I seem to be dealing with the Government every time I turn around now. I had doings with the US Government one time only, nearly twenty-five-thirty years before I became a registered voter. All that time since I hear nothing from them. Now I get the vote and they're all over me."

Chris Reed takes another sip of her coffee. She is more awake than she has been in months, revitalized by the puzzle unfolding at the dingy table. "What did you do with the government thirty years ago, Mutt?"

"Eight months one day in the US Army is what I did, Chris maam. And what they did to me. Plus they stuck their finger up my ass," Mutt says, stuffing another wedge of pancake into his mouth.

Viet Nam. Mutt was there only a matter of months. During his brief tenure, he was paid every two weeks, fed every two days and shot at every two minutes.

Mutt is still uncomfortable with most of that particular memory. He is not used to talking about himself to Norms, or saying anything at all to women. Much less discussing remote parts of his past life. The past has all blended and swirled together in his mind. He has a time problem, had it even before the service. But this morning he was telling it all to Chris Reed.

Mutt was the old man in his platoon. His CO told him he was the oldest first-time-around PFC he had ever met. Mutt was also the first person the Commanding Officer had met who had only had one name.

"Even Topot Gigot had two names, and he was nothing but a talking doll made out of balsa wood," was the CO's initial comment on the phenomenon. The CO was from New Jersey, and claimed that he knew all there was to know about Italian dummies. Especially if they'd been on The Ed Sullivan Show more than once.

Training. He had passed through boot camp and AIT Advanced Infantry Training with a minimum of hassle. Once out of the Boy's Home, he discovered he had a knack for fitting in, without even trying. He was quiet most of the time, but seemed to always know the right thing to say to cement a friendship. And, as is the way of the military, the man without a high school diploma was evaluated and judged to be perfect material for an administrative MOS   Military Occupational Specialty   91H10. The numbers and letters meaning a certain kind of job in the Army. He was a 91H10: Administration Specialist, E-3 rank. PFC. A war-zone secretary who hadn't made it past 10th grade. Though he could spell Tanzania. He liked that geography.

One minute he had never been out of Louisiana, then the very next he was sitting in a circle of sandbags in this thirty-yard-wide hole in the jungle. With a notebook, three US Army-issue ball-point pens and twenty-one pounds of mimeographed forms. In a place called Quang Nam, just back a bit from the DMZ itself. The hole he sat in had been made by Navy planes dropping bombs the boys called cheeseburgers.

Frightening things, those cheeseburgers   seven tons, without the lettuce and tomato, the Navies always said. Fourteen thousand pounds of fire and noise. The US Government made them for cutting holes in the jungle. Cheeseburger cuts the hole, then the Government sticks the grunts right in there. Grunt Mutt was immediately put in charge of making smaller holes, places for folks to crawl into to avoid flying metal. He was instructed on how to properly fill sandbags with dirt. A definite secretarial sort of operation.

The company's 47-year-old Top Sergeant enjoyed making light of their situation. Kept them from getting too worried. He stood up on a log to make an announcement. "PFC Mutt, in accordance with Army regs and your qualifications as stated in your 201 file, I am promoting you to Sandbag Administration. You are now officially no longer FNG." No longer a Fucking New Guy like the rest of the replacements. "Better get those bags filled chopchop," he yelled at Mutt, "or old Charlie he'll be shipping your paperwork ass right back to battalion in three different mailbags."

The majority of the men in Mutt's platoon were 91B the B condemned them to life as infantrymen, humping through the jungle with M16s and a heavy belts of somebody else's 50-caliber ammo. They were jealous of Mutt's H, but didn't begrudge it to him. *Whatthehell.* Maybe having someone around who knew how to administrate would come in handy some day. Out there in the boonies.

The first week Mutt and his cohorts didn't pay the enemy Charlie any mind at all. At least they acted that way as much as they could. Mutt made neat clusters of holes, just snug enough for one man and his weapon, then arranged the bags of dirt in a simple maze to keep out ricochets. Two days later Charlie discovered they were there. On the spot the VC commanders decided that the regular US Army, volunteers and draftees alike, would be better off not being alive. The Viet Cong then proceeded to make Mutt's second week in-country a little noisy. He tried continuing with his regular regime. He filled sandbags even while he was hiding in his own hole in a firefight. Mutt pretended it was pretty much the same as yardwork at the Boy's Home. If the Home had been moved to a really bad neighborhood.

Two weeks later the Top called the platoon together and stood on the log again. "PFC Mutt, I am making you an Acting Jack," he said, signaling Mutt to come forward. "Mutt's the only man around here who shows any initiative in trying to keep his buddies' asses from getting blown off. You boys ought to feel lucky you got somebody like this Mutt here. C company lost two men yesterday 'cause nobody thought to dig in properly."

Mutt was thrilled. He didn't realize at the time that an Acting Jack was only a temporary sergeant. He got to wear three stripes, true. But there also was the added luxury of being the first man ordered to leap out in front of bullets when the perimeter needed to be secured. An acting jack does not get any more money for this substantial benefit.

Mutt liked the stripes, anyway.

One day at the end of the first month, Mutt was sitting on a stack of bags at his home base drinking a beer from Washington state. He was learning to drink beer like the rest of his mates, but he always clandestinely poured out all but the bottom third of the beer before he started drinking it. Beer made him silly. He was on his second sip when half a dozen rounds popped the dust up in a line that ran straight across the dirt. Twenty yards of small, evenly spaced explosions, one following another. Stopping right in front of him. The dust from the last slug settled on his shoes, as the entire company started shooting. *Three-sixty degrees, puttin' lead into the trees*. As usual, no one was sure about where the first shots had come from. Mutt, he just sat there. Didn't move, even as the firing bursts erupted all around him.

A thought slowly crept into his head.

There are people out there, people I don't know and never will, and they are trying their best to kill me. That's what he thought.

He had not realized the extent of his predicament.

Mutt tells as much of this as he can to Chris Reed. She knows he is telling the truth.

"You know, maam, I got to tell you something. I was OK most of the time, but those other boys they were trying some kind of hard to forget where we were. Using drugs, all kinds, and going into these bars in the ville to drink and hang out with the ladies. They gave those Viet Nam women names like their girls had back home   Rhonda and Suzie and Jodie. They would stay overnight with 'em, then sneak all the way back out to the compound in the morning. They'd be still stoned and messed up and start shooting at nothing.

"Got me in it once, too. They gave me some powerful powerful medicine, and I stayed overnight in the ville, too. And truthfully, I couldn't even tell you what happened, but they all thought it was funny and that now I was one of them. Me, I couldn't tell the difference, but they all started looking after me then, and listening more when I talked with them.

"Some of those same boys in my platoon took me on a picnic about two months or so after I was in-country. With Vietnamese ladies from the bar in the ville. Not much of a place, that bar, tin roof and all, but the owner was trying to act like he had a big-time operation. I do remember the bar was named after a fancy place in Saigon called The Queen Bee. I heard that joint was real swank. I never made it to Queen Bee Number One. They tell me I made it to Number Two, but I still don't rightly know that I did.

I do remember it was a Wednesday we went out on that picnic. B platoon's day off from being shot at. I was in B platoon.

"Larry, my first buddy I ever had from Tulsa, he was already past what he called the PCOD, so he didn't have a lady along with him, like me. PCOD meaning Pussy Cut-Off Date. See, Larry he was Short, meaning he was going home in 28 days. Like all of us, he knew that if he got the clap between now and the day before he shipped out, the Medics were going to keep him in the Nam until he got well again. Took five weeks to get rid of the VDs, and they kept you in-country until you did. Get rid of it. Lot of people had been shot and killed hanging around the Meds for five weeks with no gun, waiting for their privates to get healthy.

"Larry he told me about the PCODs and all. He showed me the ropes, telling me all the stuff about the clap and who's got the best dope and how to wash my socks in my helmet and how to walk in the woods without getting killed. Larry was the only boy older than me in B platoon. He was 25. Larry and all of those other boys called me Ole Meats since I was the latest fresh meat assigned to B platoon. And I was going to be the old man in the platoon once Larry did his ETS and jumped the Freedom Bird back to the OK state.

"So on our day off from war we went to a spot where there wasn't any shooting going on. We swam in this quiet little bayou and had some laughs and drank some beer. Those Vietnamese ladies they were friends of my buddies. The ladies got ten US dollars each to come have a picnic with us and eat US mess hall food. They were all having a good time. Me and Larry talked a while and he smoked a doobie so big it took four papers. Looked like half a pound of weed to me. He was feeling good and talking about Oklahoma. Then he went swimming in that bayou on his own.

"This part I remember. This I remember.

"I was just standing there. Growing up in the Boy Home,
I was too shy to be talking with those ladies, but I was thinking about starting. Thinking seriously right then. I had been feeling better about people and talking and all. I remember.

"I was standing in the bayou, water up to my chest, holding a can of US beer. The sun was shining so hard on the surface of the water that I couldn't see my feet. Right next to me was a lady splashing and laughing. She wasn't wearing a shirt or pants, just wet underwear. I looked at her, and she asked for a sip of my beer. I was thinking life wasn't so bad after all. I said "Sure Maam," and held out the can toward her. She never got any of that beer.

"Because all of sudden we heard this POING   the sound of some fool VC way up in the hills lobbing a mortar round. Right at us standing in that river. Those VC were just dead-bored and they saw us having a good time with the

Vietnamese ladies and they wanted to be spoilsports on our day off. Probably hadn't had much in the way of lady company themselves lately. That's what I thought later.

"But then I didn't know much about mortars, and I only looked up because Larry he was yelling "Incoming! Incoming!" He was swimming hard to get out of the water. He got right up next to me and stood up, and me and that girl and Larry we all started running for the bank, sloshing every which way. Then here came this BLAM!, loud like I haven't ever heard before. Then KA-WHOOSH! Big tower of water rising up right between me and the bank. Muddy water all over. I can't see. That sound kicked me hard in the guts, kicked me backwards. But I was still standing. Lucky it went off under the water. Those girls were all screaming and running out of that bayou into the woods. My B platoon buddies were on the bank laying flat on their bellies with their M16s, busting caps at the hills, but nobody seemed hurt.

"Nobody but me and Larry.

I didn't know it at first. I was looking down, and that water all around me starts swirling red red red, mixing with the muddy gray. Makes a nice color of pink, I remember thinking. I don't know why I was thinking about color then but I was. Then I saw Larry, floating face-down right by me. He wasn't moving. I was dizzy and I had started seeing stars and black all mixed up. I grabbed Larry's arm, turned him over and dragged him up onto the shore. Then I fell my poor ass down on the sand, weak like I'd been in bed with a fever for a week. But it had all happened in the blink of an eye. Just that fast.

"I looked at my leg and saw all this blood gushing down. I forgot about everybody but me, pulling my pants down quick and yelling & screaming loud like some kind of spoiled kid. Not so grown-up a way to be. Of course, grown-ups don't get shot every day either. But sure enough there was a big hole in that leg just pumping out blood. The hole missed my boy parts, but not by much. I looked at that hole, and I thought, 'Well, at least I didn't lose anything important,' and passed out.

"That was the first time I ever passed out," he tells the Assistant DA. "But I take a bathroom break.

And Chris Reed takes a moment to appraise the situation.

This guy is real. A person with no name or family and he puts it all on the line for this abstract concept called Government. Out of a sense of duty, no matter how misguided that may be. Sounds so bogus, though, even when I think it. And now he's got nothing. Except for an overblown, tired stripper and an elderly, dyspeptic dog.

And those street people. He's loyal to them the same way.

Still, he registers to vote, serves on juries, and defends his friends.

"I'm back, maam," Mutt announces as he arrives at the table, still drying his hands on a paper towel. Real nice bathroom they got here. Give you free towels. Hope they don't mind I took an extra one for Fred."

"I'm sure they won't Mutt," she replies. "Why don't you finish what you were telling me."

"Yesm. OK."

Fred listens to Mutt's story as she continues to eat. She loses some of the words because she tends to moan with pleasure when she eats real food, but she catches the gist. Feels Mutt's emotions rising. Fred begins to worry.

It is not right that Mutt would allow himself to show feelings so openly in front of a Norm we barely know. Not good Street sense. Makes him vulnerable.

She realizes she may even be jealous. *Talking real to a Norm, after all.*

Still, she had faced the same situation Mutt is describing. She knows how potent feeling the event again can be. It is almost addictive after that first taste.

Fred belches, hoping to break the tension. The noise she makes sounds like the name "Ralph."

Once again Reed is struck silent, her fork poised outside her mouth.

"Fred, be a lady now." Mutt said. "Sorry maam, she gets out of her rhythm and her digestion just goes all to hell. Can't help herself, really."

Fred puts her chin on the table and is asleep within seconds. The sound of Mutt's voice telling a story had always had that effect on her, especially after a meal. In spite of her seeming peaceful state at the Suds & Duds, Fred's got her problems. Not all of them digestive in nature.

See, dogs have it, too. A past. That same old history thing. And it can haunt them the same way memories can haunt two-footed folks.

Especially in sleep. Fred twitches her right front paw as she sleeps. The missing toe always aches like it's still there when she gets herself worked up into a tizzy.

The dozing Fred, she arrives at Grand Central Tizzy on an express train. Not a happy dog at all. Dreaming about The Trial again.

She sees herself, eight weeks old and already tussling ferociously with her brothers and sisters. They loved to latch onto each other, snapping and snarling. Active children. The playful wrestling was second nature until the trial. The "playful" part disappeared soon after.

Her owner drops her in a circular dirt enclosure. Alone with her mother. He says "Bite dat bitch, dog. Bite her hard. C'mon, 'tit chien, let's see you do some a dat battle." It didn't take much, of course. Within a few moments Fred's jaws are locked onto the unprotesting older female's back leg. Fred is pulling and tugging. The trainer climbs into the ring. Walks right up to her. Baby dog Fred is growling loudly, a two-month old pup making a major noise.

The man remarks over his shoulder, "Dis one here might be a keeper, Jacques."

He bends down with a sharpened steel chisel and hammer in hand, touching the pup and mother. Fred refuses to budge, keeps jerking on her mother's leg. Snarling, even as the trainer places the chisel's sharp edge on her inside toe.

She growls louder still. Fred is thinking, "Don't mess with me, man. I'm bad."

The man smiles and raises the hammer over the shining chisel.

The dog trainers were not cruel at all, not in their own minds. They were just insuring the best possible bloodlines, the survival of the fittest. A pup lets go after the chisel blow slices off the toe, the dog trainers immediately put the animal to sleep. But if the young dog holds on even more ferociously, like Fred did so long ago, the men are even quicker to soothe the animal and treat its wound.

Dog fighting is not legal in Louisiana. Not legal, it remains an underground fact. This is the state of pragmatic tolerance, even when it comes to matters of questionable taste. The reasoning seems to be, "If I let Alphonse dog-fight, maybe he won't make such a fuss about me being drunk all the time." Substitute the two vices of your choice.

The method applies at any level. Some years back the Federal Government walked into the Louisiana legislature threatening to take away all the state's highway money. Plus the Feds said hospital and school money to the poor, mostly Cajun parishes of south central Louisiana would also disappear if the sheriffs refused to stop cockfighting. It seems a Manhattan-bred US Senator's wife read about the practice in a Cultural Guidebook to the South and decided to put a stop to it.

"Those primitive people ought to enforce existing laws!" she cried to her husband over a generous saucer of foie gras at their Upper West Side dining table. Unrepresented chickens seriously needed a champion right then.

Sure enough, the woman and the Feds were right. In one way. The fights are against Louisiana law.

Local politicians were not upset. Just one more Yankee finger in the pot. The patient Cajun leaders knew there was always an easy way to circumvent meddling non-bayou bureaucrats. Knew how to maintain their own country ways in the face of Government, and in this case maintain a two-hundred year tradition. If cock-fighting violated state Cruelty to Animal statutes, the country boys had an easy and diabolical solution. They went right into the State Capitol tower in Baton Rouge. Spoke to their own representatives. Forged an alliance with the North Louisiana farm lobby and its influential president, a gentleman named Leonard Reed. Who, from his soybean fields in Winnfield, Louisiana, was known to do some serious political business. The Reeds had had a hand in every governmental pie since Huey Long opened the bakery. In two days an amendment was attached to the State statutes, removing chickens from the animal definition.

That did it. Everything was settled.

A chicken is no longer an animal in Louisiana, so the cruelty statutes do not apply. The cockfights continue. Though they are a bit more covert around election time.

Fred killed seven of her own kind during her illustrious fighting career. After each battle it had taken longer for her to recuperate. She knew that soon she would lose. She was injured so badly in her third fight that her reproductive organs had to be removed, among others. So she couldn't be used to breed more fighters.

When she lost she would be put to sleep.

She was a smart dog. She had seen her opponents depart. There was never a rematch. So, as soon as she had regained her strength after battle number seven, Fred had decided to leave her training compound.

The implementation of her resolution had occasioned a small riot on the part of her trainer and his assistants. The trainer had not wanted to lose Fred, was more than willing to try and restrain her manually. That was a mistake on his part, one of the few he had committed in a long career of dealing with pits and bull terriers. But he still had a winner in Fred and he wasn't about to give her up easily.

While his assistants grappled with her legs, the trainer had attempted to put a leather muzzle on Fred. Very unwise. With one quick snap, Fred had removed the man's right index finger.

While the trainer screamed and ran about the dog yard spewing blood, Fred gaily trotted behind. With some adept jaw maneuvers, she got the finger turned around and wiggling out the front of her mouth like a skinny bent tongue. There was dirt under the fingernail.

The man's two assistants started to sneak up behind her. Fred turned on them instantly. Growling the first movements of a low rumbling Dog Sonata that started at the very center of her anger. It was a horrific sound, emerging from her mouth in a froth of deep red bubbles around the bloody digit. The assistants immediately gave up their rescue mission, turned tail and ran for the phone. The sheriff could deal with this mad dog.

Fred relaxed. She padded casually over to the still-screaming trainer. He had stumbled and fallen to his knees in pain. Now kneeling in the dust clutching his maimed hand. The man looked up at her, outrage and terror competing visibly on his face. Very slowly, as the man watched, Fred slurped inward. She swallowed the finger with a loud gulp. Licked her lips.

Not bad. For a finger in need of a manicure.

It was the first time she ever smiled.

Six months and 126 miles later, a starving female bull terrier was hit a glancing blow, knocked off New Orleans' Ponchartrain Expressway by a two-tone '67 Dodge. Blue and white. Fred hadn't known about elevated roads on pillars. The country dog's experience simply didn't prepare her for such things. Once on the concrete path, she had not been able to get off. She was slammed through the protective railing. The car proceeded on toward the Greater New Orleans Bridge without stopping. Fred fell the entire thirty feet from the Expressway's first level, landing heavily in a bloody heap at the feet of a filthy human male.

Before she lost consciousness, she noticed that the man was talking to a road sign. For the Fred Astaire Dance Studios in Westwego.

Mutt bites into yet another piece of sausage. He continues the story as he chews. His eyes losing focus more frequently the longer he speaks. He has to deal with the memories as they come, no matter the audience. The need to purge the past becomes more powerful than his desire to at least appear Norm.

And please this woman. Chris Reed.

He purposefully loses visual focus, and falls back into a familiar manner of recitation.

"I woke up in a Med Evac plane on my way to Japan. They had me all packed in ice below the waist, like a watermelon. Six hours on ice. Shivering and talking out of my head. They gave me drugs, so I don't remember much of the trip except for loud roaring jet engines. The Government doesn't soundproof those military planes like they do on United and Pan-Am. Might have been my head, though.

"The doctors in Japan sewed me up and put me in a bed for a while. One tube going into me and a couple of tubes going out. I don't remember that part too well either. One day an Army Captain comes by with some papers for me to sign and says they're sending me home, instead of back to Viet Nam. I was pretty happy about not going back to that place."

With this last sentence, Mutt comes to a complete stop. One two three four five seconds pass before he sighs. Sighs so deeply that he has a coughing fit.

Chris pats him on the back, trying to help him stop coughing. Each time she touches Mutt, she gets a little more sure of herself.

This is it.

Clean him up, get him to talk a little straighter   not so much he loses his earthy feel   and he could convince just about anybody. Of anything. He pulled Cannalo right into his corner without even breaking a sweat.

So I put Mr Idealism in the right spot. Me behind him to make the reality work. Bang. I'm traveling. Out of Night Hell. An honest man. Me rescuing him, him rescuing me. He won't even know it. The perfect irony. And I like him. Not like most men. Something about him that touches me. I wouldn't have believed it possible.

She continues to reflect on that theme, all the while looking at Mutt's face.

"And they gave you a medal for being wounded, is that it?"

"Purple Heart and a Army Commendation Medal."

Mutt wipes his chin.

"Boys in the platoon made up some nice story about me, but it wasn't true. The hero bit. I was crying just like a little goddamn baby. My buddy Larry died. I didn't do anything but live. Medals don't mean a damn thing. I hocked then all a long time ago. Bought a Double Melt and a cold drink at the BestBurger on Claiborne Avenue. 1970. Not a bad burger. Swiss cheese. Medium Barq's root beer. No ice. I remember."

"But they sent you home as a hero, didn't they?"

Mutt shudders. Obviously the memory is no longer on automatic.

"No, maam. I told you there wasn't a hero. Just those boys telling stories, Chris maam. Army sent me home. They did do that," he says, his voice dropping a notch. "But when I got back to New Orleans I couldn't go back in the Boy Home. The Nuns said I wasn't a boy no more. I'd been killing people, they said, though me I know I didn't kill anybody over there. I was too busy filling sandbags. They said I was a man now, and I'd best go on my own. The Government would be taking care of me now, they said. Maybe the Government would have better luck teaching me how to make a living. But the Government doesn't give a damn once it's finished with you. They made me a man. I wasn't a boy any more. So I didn't have a home. I was an old man then. I'm an old man now. I skipped that middle part."

Mutt pauses for a second, pouring down half a glass of milk. His recitation had at first seemed to come from elsewhere, from someone else. Like when he was riding in the car with this amazing Norm. That was fine with him then. But it doesn't take long for him to decide he doesn't like this kind of remembering much at all, so he simply lets the talk proceed on its own. He isn't paying too much attention to it any more.

Reed is. The pieces are beginning to fit together. Her instincts have been proven right. An improbable first meeting, an accidental reunion, and the unlikely man turns out to be genuine. Mutt Jeansonne is another primitive piece of undeniable truth, discarded by the culture which created him.

Thrown away. A Grandma Moses painting blowing around the streets of the city like yesterday's final edition. And it had blown right into her lap.

Reed resettles in her chair.

"Go on. Go on, Mutt," she urges. "What happened to you back in New Orleans?"

"Nothing. Nothing out there for a Nam vet to do then. Nobody liked you much either, if you told them you'd been in the Army. I tried to do lots of things to make a living, but everybody wanted experience and I had done nothing steady in my whole life but mow grass for Nuns and fill sandbags for the Army. Besides, I still wasn't walking too good from getting shot.

"I never had passed the tenth grade. Got too bored with what they were trying to make me read, religion and all. I tried to study geography and history, the things I did like, but I didn't really know what to look for. And I didn't make any food money if I read all day."

"What about the VA, Mutt?" Reed interjected. "Couldn't you get help from them?"

"I tried to go to school on the GI Bill, Chris maam, but they said I needed a high school diploma, and I didn't have one. I tried all kinds of stuff, keeping busy, trying to get smart. Figured maybe I could pass the GED test and get into some college maybe. But I had to work too long and hard at getting something to eat. Every day. Reading on my own just didn't help. Not after I'd been digging holes or sweeping warehouses or loading grain sacks for eighteen hours. Doing whatever I had to do to eat. No maam, I never passed.

"I just kept working, mostly being what they call a common day laborer. Doing a lot of what I did in the Army, digging and moving stuff. Not bad, but the work never lasts for us guys on the bottom end of the line. I'd finish three months of what I'd thought was a good job, and I was still broke and on the Streets. Maybe get a flophouse for a few months, then the job would be over again and I got no money and I'm sleeping in a cardboard washing machine crate. Time just kept going by. I even looked forward to when the police would come get me for vagrancy or loitering and lock me up for a few days. Jail was three squares and a shower and a warm dry bed. Years. I was out here and I was out here and I was out here. Still out here."

Mutt takes a long drink of ice water, thinking about what he has just said. He is doing that more and more as a matter of course. The thinking. A further conclusion comes to him, just as he tries a second sip of water. He chokes, but wipes off his face and quickly comes back to his thought. He is exhilarated by what is going on within himself.

"My life before I hit the Street seems like a dream. I keep getting little glimpses of it, like just now, but the young Mr Mutt he's a long-time gone. Sooner or later I'll just accept that. Me & Fred we've been together maybe ten years I guess, helping each other get along. Then all of a sudden here's this voter's card and here's LM Jeansonne, doing all sorts of stuff I never figured he knew much about." Mutt gripped his water glass with both hands, and lifted it to his mouth one last time. The cubes settled next to each other noisily as he replaced it on the table.

"I don't rightly know who I am right now," Mutt says solemnly. "And that's all I want to remember, Chris maam."

Fred barks loudly, throwing crumbs of toast all over the table and turning over her water glass. She's heard the tone in Mutt's voice, and she's quite awake again now.

The waitress wags her finger politely from across the room.

"Such a cute little doggie."

Fred's bark becomes a menacing growl. Reed decides it is time to take the dog and his companion home. Quickly.

But the morning's activity doesn't stop there. As Reed stops to drop off Mutt & Fred under the Expressway, her car is rushed by a mob of news-hungry media sorts. After filing his story, the *Times-Picayune* reporter had indeed called the local NBC affiliate's early morning news desk with what he told them was the lead feature of a lifetime. Then he called everyone else in town with the same exclusive.

A five-minute segment including an interview with a rather sleepy-eyed Mutt and an aggravated Fred made the station's noon news. By 5pm the day after the trial all three net affiliates and one independent had jumped on the story. Now with a twist of events on the second day of developments, they discover that the bum's ADA opponent is carting him around. This makes the story much much bigger. The media crowd grows. Fred takes to hiding in the Box until time to go to work.

An ABC cameraman manages to get a long zoom shot of Fred barking at the intruders below her home, but he is the exception. The dog has become seriously constipated. Mutt is quizzed relentlessly.

The networks pick themselves pick up the story. Interest in L Mutt Jeansonne grows.

* * *

"Yes, Daddy, I took the man to breakfast all by myself, "Chris says emphatically into the phone. "He could have sued me or something. Besides, he's not dangerous in the least."

She looks out her Uptown apartment window at the light traffic coursing around the palms of Jefferson Avenue, estimating that it is almost noon and she hasn't been to bed yet. She will have to try for a late afternoon catnap before tonight's Court session.

"His dog looks more dangerous than he does. Yes, I took the dog to breakfast, too." She laughs. "No, you're wrong. The dog smelled worse. I swear."

She gets up and paces the room, talking into the cordless phone at quick intervals between sips of coffee. She is excited, but still maintaining control.

"Daddy, be serious. You know how I hate this DA and his grubby little job. Yes, I know District Attorney Bronner is a friend of yours, and I have been working my tail off to keep him happy. Thank you again for getting me the position, so I could actually work as a lawyer, but... now stop right there."

Reed puts her coffee cup down. Then she immediately thinks better, picks it up, wipes the moisture off the antique pecan tabletop and puts the cup on the floor.

"I am not even coming close to paying the notes on my law school loans with the measly sixteen thousand a year they are giving me. All right, sixteen-three. I am staying up all night five nights a week mixing with thieves and murderers and the scum of the earth   all for this scrap of money."

She dusts unseen dirt from her blouse with her free hand, waiting for her father to finish speaking.

"But listen, Daddy   I've been waiting for the right something, or someone, who can make a difference in this horrible system. Who can actually make this Government work for people."

Once again she listens a moment to the buzzing voice, then answers, "Didn't realize I was interested in Public Service! Listen to yourself! Daddy, you've been on four different government boards under three different governors in these last twenty years   have you ever been interested in Public Service? Let's just think about that one, shall we? No, I'm not trying to be snotty."

Her voice takes on a businesslike tone, the honeyed Southern drawl disappearing completely. "I have some ideas, that's all. I'll tell you more when I get a little further along.

"Oh, and I got your message. The firm you recommended is McFarland Borden and Dubney. I think I know some of the partners from my work   this should be fun. So what's that associate's name? Markham? Robert H? Good. Yes sir, I'll be calling him. I'm headed to the Veterans Administration right after lunch. Yes, I know all Feds are cretins. I can take care of myself on this one. At least this part of it."

The sugar comes back to her voice as quickly as it had left. "Thank you so much, Daddy. You know I can use it. I know I never took it before, but you're the one who stuck me down here. I'm just trying to make you proud of me. Wire it, won't you? Checks are such a bother. I won't tell Mother a thing.

"I know you write it off, Daddy. Besides, you can consider it a contribution to your very own daughter's political career. I'll even send you a receipt. Thank you, Daddy. You're wonderful. Love you. Bye now."

She carries the phone back across the room and drops it in its cradle, then retrieves her lukewarm coffee and does a two-step whirl to the windows.

It might work.

This wild idea might actually get her out of Cannalo's dungeon. Even the remote possibility makes her ecstatic.

She muses over her future cheerfully. Chris Reed would live a long, beautiful life well away from the confines of Winnfield, Louisiana. She would not wind up in a living death as legal counsel to the rural parish's salt mine.

She would need to be tough, dividing humanity as her father had instructed throughout her short life. "You got to remind yourself all the time, Missy," he would say to her. "Just keep repeating to yourself, 'There are the losers, and then there is me.'" Leonard Reed had taught Chris to apply the rule universally, family included.

"Thank you, Daddy," she announces to the window. On cue, the dimple pops in each cheek again. Her lips part, characteristically displaying the shining white bank of her teeth. "You gave me something better than money."

She's had a pretty brutal history, too, Chris Reed. It hasn't been easy for her, enduring the years and months before her near-miss with Mutt Jeansonne. Two men dominating her life. Her Daddy, as always. Then Judge Cannalo, as a Daddy-extension, a result of her Father's influence but no less obnoxious for it.

Cannalo could be particularly abrasive, though his rancor seemed to be cyclical. One night the man was borderline psychotic. Twenty-four hours later he would doze through an entire session smiling. Reed believed Cannalo's mood was linked to lunar phases, the effects of moonlight on his pituitary gland. The instances were many and memorable.

That next night at work, after her breakfast with Mutt, was yet another.

"Miss Reed, I know you are in mourning over losing your nipple-coverage case to a derelict, but you can still make a decision, can't you? Do you want to prosecute this gentleman for his non-payment of child support and put him in jail where, of course, he won't ever be able to make the money to help his family   or are you going to release him to the street on his god-fearing word-of-honor that he will finally mend his ways after three years of non-payment   and live up to his responsibilities? Yes, Miss Reed? Yes? Must I give you a lecture on the course of the law? Come on, woman, let's get this settled." The judge banged his gavel. One brief emotional chapter closed, he temporarily turned his harangue to the court bailiff.

Reed tuned Cannalo out and looked across the room at the defendant. For what seemed the hundredth time tonight a huge leering smile, augmented by three gold teeth, beamed at her from under foot-long bleached dreadlocks. "Yah, Missy," Ahmed Kulafi Jackson had sworn. He now had a job and would take care of the five young children who sat patiently behind Reed with their mother. He had called the Assistant District Attorney "Missy." Cannalo had voiced no objection.

"Goodgawdamighty!" The Reverend Lincoln Jesus Gonzales had mamboed into the proceedings in mid-trial, carrying the scent of a large congregation of *cuba libres*. As the defense's prime character witness, he was immediately placed on the stand. He told the officers of the Court that he needed to quickly get back to the pressing business of tending his flock. Judge Cannalo granted his request. He allowed some concessions of courtesy to the clergy, even when the liturgical figure in question wore red bell bottoms to complement his frayed Roman collar. As did the Reverend Gonzales this evening.

"I am here to tell you, one and all," began the Reverend, "Lord he'p us, have mercy   that this man, my beloved repentant sinner, Ahmed Daffy Jackson... what? Yes... that Jackson here is back in the fold. I have personally taken his testimony for the Lord! I have myself lowered him into the holy waters! As holy a water as is available in his place of incarceration, of course. The man is sorry for his sins, Judge! Does the word of a Christian mean nothing any more? Hallelujah!"

The preacher testified strongly as to the accused gentleman's renewed religious motivation. But Reed had seen the transcripts of Jackson's five previous arrests, one resulting in a conviction for distribution of crack cocaine. Interestingly enough, the same preacher had made similar statements of renewed salvation for the court record at each of those trials. Ahmed had seemingly taken a liking to being Born Again. And again. While living within the confines of the Louisiana Center for the Ethically-Challenged. By the ADA's numerical calculations from Jackson's arrest record, he emerged from that mystical womb cleansed of his transgressions on at least a quarterly basis. In the interim ninety days, Ahmed Kulafi Jackson took pains to make sure he amassed a sufficient stock of sins. To make his repenting worthwhile.

The recurring. The repenting. In Parish Prison. Soup-spotted Penal Edition of The St James Bible in his lap. The Lord had come to him. The preacher said that, for sure, "goodgawdawmighty!" Jackson had indeed repented. The "goodgawdawmighty!" was Reverend Gonzales' own verbal seal of absolute veracity. Reed suspected that Lincoln Jesus Gonzales was a minister in the Supreme Mystical Temple of Criminal Testimony, and freely took donations for religious endorsements of his occasionally errant parishioners.

But according to Family Counseling files, the wife had no job training whatsoever, and only a minimal welfare check and food stamps to care for a family of six. Reed felt she had to at least try and get the woman the help she deserved. This was why she had gone through the horrors of law school.

"I'd like to drop the charges, your Honor, based on Mr Jackson's required weekly attendance at Family Counseling Services and that office's strict monitoring of payments to his wife and children," she said, her mind made up.

"So disposed. Clerk, let's get on with this next item quickly. Now that we have the Assistant District Attorney's attention." The Clerk of Court immediately began to roll out the details of the next case in a blindingly fast monotone.

Reed was not listening. She put the case folder in the accordion envelope devoted to Jackson's ongoing involvement with the legal system of the City of New Orleans, and with a feeling of satisfaction, turned to nod supportively to the man's wife.

The young woman was already picking up her two youngest. She stood erect, a diapered child on each hip, and looked Christine Reed directly in the eyes.

"You ugly... ignorant... white... bitch, you let that motherfucker *go!*" Mrs Jackson said, with genuine venom in every word.

Reed winces with the memory. Ugly ignorant white bitch.

The rest of the night is of similar character. Then, in the wee hours of Saturday morning, she goes home to her bed.

Christine Reed sleeps through noon most days. So, no Night Court Saturday or Sunday makes sleeping through Saturday even more pleasurable. Then on Sunday, partially recovered from the five lost nights, she celebrates with an extended robed breakfast, with ritual and prolonged consumption of flavored coffees and the *Sunday Advocate*. She reads the comics twice, and laughs both times.

"I don't care about new things. And I don't like surprises any more," she had told her mother the last Christmas, as they sat together watching an "I Love Lucy" re-run. "Good jokes age well. About the only thing that does." Her mother had not been amused. Age was not a favored topic at the Reed household.

Like most people, Reed prefers being happy. She enjoys laughing, too, though for a long time now she has mostly laughed alone.

She has become increasingly isolated from her friends and family, and her social values have begun to take on a hermit's skew. For entertainment these Sundays after the comics Christine Reed looks at the inside page of the paper's "Living" section to see if any of her former upstate schoolmates is making a social splash in the Crescent City. A particularly wordy description of yet another motherlode of afternoon teas often sparks unpleasant self-examination, especially when combined with the simultaneous ingestion of large quantities of coffee.

Sunday. She opens the paper and is immediately assaulted.

Donna Smelsen. There's that worthless woman's face again.

Married a State Senator. Gets her picture taken. There she is, just hanging around her husband's desk on the Senate floor. Donna the Smelsen also getting paid in the high five figures to be the Senator's "Legislative Assistant." This is the same brainless twit who couldn't pass freshman English couldn't even deal with the remedial spelling courses they gave her in college!

And me, not even 30, with law degrees covering the wall, still single and working nights like a scrubwoman. Can you imagine what I'd be able to do with the kind of power Smelsen has clutched in her manicured fingers?

There is more caffeine in the hazelnut creme coffee than she would have ever expected. Reed whacks the paper with the back of her hand, tries to slap some sense into it.

What can I be thinking? Going nutso. Got to get out of this job. Get out from under Daddy's thumb.

The word bothers her.

Why can't I say 'Father'?

Daddy, it always is. Just Daddy's Little Girl. Christ!

She shakes her head, clearing the thoughts temporarily.

"Daddy dear, I'm getting as boring as you. OK?" Chris Reed says out loud. She is alone in the room. "OK, let's just read the paper," she answers.

The sound of her voice is swallowed by the ongoing grind of high-powered air conditioning. Air conditioning changed the Deep South as dramatically as the Colt 45 changed the Wild West. Its calming effects are not lost on Reed. Her attention goes back to the news. On the adjoining page Reed examines more micro-dotted faces. The newest set of eighteen-year-old debutantes to come out at the Carnival krewe presentation balls.

She moans. Yet another pet peeve. She was never allowed to show cleavage in her ball gowns. She stares at the teenaged breasts, her hand unconsciously exploring her own.

Mine were so much better. Look at those little nothings!

"I am losing touch here." She is talking again. Her voice hangs in the air.

She rubs the ink into grey blurs over a particularly young bouffant-framed smile. Her thumb blackened with the residue of the morning's numerous pictorial maimings.

Chris Reed is easily upset by such things, but she can't resist looking at the pictures of her tormentors. The pain sustains her. Helps her forget her job. She smiles happily when that happens.

The next Sunday's paper will bring more of the same.

She has other secret sources of strength. Lately, whenever she grows worried, Chris returns to the same comforting touchstone. Whether waking or asleep, it reminds her that she can do right. That she can win. That she can be safe. Her mind cradles a memory a good memory from her first days in Cannalo's courtroom. Things were different then. She often consciously directs her mind there, looking for reassurance in the middle of her disquiet.

"Officer Buller, why do you want to drop the charges against a man who so blatantly attacked you in a drunken rage?" Chris Reed asked the witness.

"Objection, your honor," said DAR Borden Esq, quickly rising from a chair beside his grumpily sober law partner. Borden was none too happy about having been dragged from bed to come across town and defend the honor of the firm once again. A Senior Partner on yet another stupid drinking binge. He had a mind to let Harry Dubney sit out the night in the parish drunk tank. Couldn't do that, though word would get out and damage the old-line law firm's conservative image. That damage would translate into dollars and cents. Besides, Borden had already slipped five hundred of those dollars into the arresting officer's pocket more than easing the pain of one misguided punch. The agreement with Judge Cannalo had made matters easier the old bastard had re-election coming up, and cash was also a prime matter there. An on-the-spot donation had been in order, nothing to do with the present case, of course, just a way of showing the Judge how much the McFarland Borden & Dubney firm admired his legal work. It was all taken care of.

Until this Reed woman stepped in.

Reed had protested the recess that allowed Borden's private meetings with the presiding judge and the policeman. She knew the deal that was being made. Knew that another well-heeled, politically-connected lawbreaker was on his way to once again walking away from a crime that would have left an ordinary citizen cooling his heels in a concrete-block prison for a year or more. She'd seen it happen many times. Her own family had no qualms about using such connections and economic grease to smooth over mistakes. It was expected. The legal entanglements of the wealthy remain a prime source of income for most elected officials in Louisiana. But something about the smug cop-assaulter and his big-time attorney buddy rankled her this night.

He really pisses me off. And Cannalo is going right along.

"There was no breath test at the scene of the arrest," Borden continued. "Although his vehicle was pulled over on suspected 'improper lane usage,' after the incident Mr Dubney was actually detained on the assault charge only, and that is all that this trial should concern."

"Sustained. Ms Reed, let's get this over will, shall we? This is about an alleged misdemeanor personal assault. No weapon involved. The victim has stated that he no longer wishes to press charges," said the Judge. "If there was no crime, then we have no reason for a trial now, do we?"

Reed had known this was coming. If she was smart, she'd just let the whole thing slide. But she couldn't. She was too smart. She already had the Criminal Codes open to the right page.

"Your honor, I am sure it's just an oversight on your part and I needn't cite Codes on this matter. We both know that the crime of assault on an officer of the law is prosecutable in Louisiana whether the victim wishes to press charges or not. Especially since the initial report, written by the officer at the scene, is a matter of record." She held up a handwritten form. "Is this arrest record inaccurate or perjured in any way, Officer Buller?"

The policeman hesitated, looking from the Judge to DAR Borden for guidance. They gave none. Both were concentrating on sending a wave of intimidation at Chris Reed. She did not seem to notice.

"No, maam," said Buller, "It's true. He hit me. I just don't want to press charges."

"Fortunately for this state's legal system, that is not your prerogative. The District Attorney's office presses charges when law officers are attacked. I represent the DA in this Court, and since you have now testified under oath that you were indeed attacked and that this is the man who committed that attack, I have no recourse but to press for conviction. There is no choice. Isn't that correct, Judge Cannalo? I want to be absolutely right in this matter. I'd hate for those bloodthirsty media sorts to hear that an injustice was committed in your Court."

"Reed, your little display has gone on long enough. Officer, step down."

"But, Judge, I've got more questions," she protested.

"Quiet, woman, I'm giving you what you want." Judge Cannalo turned to the wobbly defendant and his red-faced attorney. "Just going to make this as painless as possible, gentlemen, so you can both go home quickly. Like the lady says, I have no choice but to rule guilty as charged."

Borden spewed a protest, "Cannalo, you can't do this!"

"Yes, I the hell can, Mister Borden. Just be patient. I said guilty. But sentence is $1 fine and one day in the parish prison, both suspended, all record of the offense to be stricken from the record if there are no further violations of the law within the next seven days. Think you can make it a week without punching another policeman, Mr Dubney?"

"Wuuuhhhh," was Dubney's quick, though less-than-to-the-point response.

"Judge Cannalo, I hardly think that to be sufficient punishment, in light of the severity of the crime," said Reed, a smile causing her dimples to deepen.

"You got what you wanted, Reed. You opened that cut-rate law school mouth and had your say, did what you think is your job. The sentencing part, though, is my job. I know how to do it. Next case.

"And wipe that damn smile off your face. This is my Court."

The pleasant memory was, unfortunately, always attached to an unpleasant scene which followed closely on its heels.

The morning after the assault ruling, Chris Reed had been called to sit directly in front of New Orleans District Attorney Archibald Bronner.

She had had less than three hours' sleep between the Night Court's adjournment at 5:30am and her rising to prepare for the meeting with the DA. The unexpected summons had come only an hour earlier, at nine, and brought Reed awake only after her bedside answering machine blared a secretary's nasal voice into the room. Chris once again cursed the current state of her own mind. Totally exhausted and confused after work, she had accidentally left the playback volume up. Now she was caught.

"I wouldn't be sitting here if I had any sense."

The District Attorney looked up from his phone call. "Did you say something, Miss Reed?"

"No, sir," she answered. "Nothing. Nothing at all."

Archibald Bronner scowled once again in her direction, then turned back to the phone on his shoulder and smiled into the plastic device with the practiced and automatic intensity of a career politician. "Miz Howell, I'll be glad to see to it personally. Now that the NOPD has those vandals in custody,

I'll make sure that they get what's coming to them. Boys can't go around defacing other people's property like that and get away with it, nosireebob. Now what did they spray on your gazebo? Really. Didn't even spell it right, now did they? Well, I've got it under control down here. Got to go now. Pressing matters. Folks waiting for me. Late for a meeting. Yes, yes. I will. Bye now, Miz Howell."

The smile faded as soon as the click of disconnection popped into his ear.

"Goddamn Uptown women," he spat out. "Every one a nuisance, and thinks she owns the world to boot." The District Attorney pivoted effortlessly in his simulated ostrich skin executive-model chair to face Chris Reed.

"Something you got in common with those society bitches, Miz Reed?"

She was shocked. She had only met with the DA once before, during her brief interview for the job, and he had been civil, if a bit brusque. She struggled to start thinking clearly, bring her political self into the fray.

"Absolutely not, sir. As a North Louisiana native, you know this New Orleans old money. Those bluebloods will barely even admit that the best of families from up our way exist, much less are worthy of their attention. No matter how long we've been around, how much power or how much money we have, we're still nothing to them. I'm sure you've had to face it yourself," she said, deftly turning his anger from her.

He started to raise his hand, index finger outstretched in agreement, then stopped. A dangerous smile grew in the corners of his mouth.

This girl knows the exercise.

"Nicely done, Miz Reed. Too bad you're not using more of that sugar on our esteemed colleague Judge Cannalo. He's complaining about you again." Bronner lifted a folder from his desk, opened it and pulled out a typewritten sheet. "Says you're 'daydreaming' during his sessions   hard to do at night, isn't it, Miz Reed?" He didn't wait for an answer. "Says you're 'inattentive,' that you spend too much time on each case, that you tend to overreact when you come across female victims, etcetera etcetera. His usual bullshit." The DA kept the sheet raised above his desktop. He waited for a response, holding the bait up for her to see.

She rose to it, eagerly.

"Sir. With all due respect. Judge Cannalo runs that Court like a tyrant. Like he's got a factory with machine parts to assemble, rather than human beings with problems to solve. He doesn't seem to care one bit what the outcome of the cases are, as long as they are quickly removed from his docket, and dispensed with."

The District Attorney remained quiet, not moving until she had finished. Then he slowly replaced the file on his desk and took in a deep, loud breath before speaking.

"Anything else? No? Fine." Bronner squeezed his nose shut with the first two fingers of his right hand. Exhaled until the nostrils inflated. Released, and let his breath roar out. Looked up.

"Miz Reed. Your Daddy told me when he first called me about you, told me that you were just chock full of good intentions. A bonafide do-gooder. That just doesn't work here, darlin'. Not in a city this poor, this uneducated, this violent. You'll get yourself killed trying to do people a good turn. I understand from the Court officers that you do a damn fine job, helping folks out and all. That you know how to use the law well enough to make old Judge Cannalo just sit there and do what you tell him. That you can convict prominent citizens of their crimes, in spite of considerable pressure to do otherwise.

"But, Miz Reed   and this is much more important in the giant justice machine you find yourself in   when you do 'good' you can piss off an elected official who's got a real say in how this city's run. And at the same time piss off the people who put up the money that elects that official." Bronner stopped, took the time to look out his office window and sigh again. He stared at Reed until she embarrassedly started to cough.

The response produced, he began again, "Easy does it, Miz Reed. Need some water? No? All right. Now I know old Cannalo's a real pain in the ass. That's why he's up in the middle of the night. Just like you. But he's got himself a job I can't fire him from. Plus, he can make me downright miserable if he wants to. The man determines a nice portion of my conviction rate, and that's what voters look for when they decide if they're going to give me my job back   how many of these no-accounts I've put behind bars. So when Cannalo complains, I've got to listen.

"I've got to send the man a memo saying I've counseled my employee. That's you, Miz Reed. My employee. No matter how far back your Daddy and I go, or how much he dropped into my last campaign, I am still responsible for you."

"Sir," Reed spluttered out, "I am doing my job as best I know how. I'm up all night five nights a week in a courtroom filled with animals. And those are the good guys! They haven't got a clue about the law."

"Noted, but not worth a good goddamn, Reed. Nobody even knows you're down in that hellhole. Not many voters even know it exists. Why should they? Nasty business nobody wants to bother with. But I've got to. That Night Court puts a couple thousand low-grade criminals in jail every year. You know what that does for my numbers? No way I can let loose of that. I'd drop you in a second if I thought you would lose me those convictions."

Bronner let it sink in. "So, I'm giving you a chance to prove yourself. Down there you can make your mistakes and not a soul will notice. Do you understand? Use this time. Make your mistakes. There's nothing that happens in that room that makes one bit of difference. So you will not antagonize this old goat again. Do you understand?"

"Yes sir." Reed was once again resigned to her fate. She hated herself. The DA was using methods on her that she routinely used on others. She knew she was better at it than he was. When she was awake. She cursed under her breath. It was the invocation of her father's name that had set her off-guard.

Daddy. Goddamn. Daddy.

He'd started all this. Two years ago now, and still one of the low points in her life. He had won. She had to beg. Same now as then.

"I know you have your degree, Chrissymissy," he had said, "and I know you passed the bar, all of it. Congratulations. You studied hard, and even financed your own education. Very nice, that touch. But a degree from a small, predominantly black university with a C-grade football team? My god, woman, how much did you expect it to be worth? It'd be different if you'd taken my recommendation   and my money and gone to LSU. Then you'd have something."

"Daddy, I didn't want your money...," her voice dropped, "...then."

"I think that's admirable. Damned near unheard of in this family. Especially considering the overwhelming truckloads of greed your two brothers are carrying around. And your sister. But all three of them, they got jobs."

"You got them jobs," she was quick to interject.

"Well now, ain't that the truth?" Mr Reed bristled. He was unused to opposition from family. He looked again at his daughter. He knew how to keep her in line. He even enjoyed interjecting his long-suppressed country-boy accent into his speech. L'il Chrissymissy hated that. Hated being reminded of her origins. She would understand why he was doing it. Punishment.

"And now here you come, Missy, paid yer dues to society an' yer own way to that there blackfolk law school!" he whined. "My li'l lillywhite baby. Jus' standin' here in front of yer Daddy   jus' pitiful-like. Here I was, worried about you gettin' along, doin' my best to help you out, an' you just flat turn your back on me. Me, I was jus' tryin' ta he'p. You tell me no. Gotta go he'p them poor people, she says.

"But looka here. Now the girl's all dressed up with eddi-cation and she got herself nowhere ta go. Except ta her ole countrified Daddy. Gotta ask ya Daddy to git you a job, jus' like all the others. Need his money. Ain't that right, Missy?"

Chris' head did not come up.

"Ain't that right now, Missy?"

"Yes, sir. That's right."

He was right, then and now. So, when work approaches Monday evening, the young Assistant District Attorney puts on her war paint. In more ways than one, of course.

Applying makeup is another bit of the living ritual that Chris Reed's body can handle on autopilot. So she slaps on a face in under five minutes while simultaneously reviewing the coming Night Court's docket in her head. Confrontive or seductive, either facade can be applied from a jar.

Makeup is a vital link to her past.

Chris Reed had exploded onto the ever-so-volatile facial arts scene with the help of her girlfriend Alice Jean Lalande. Chris had thought then that AJ was much more knowledgeable in the ways of the world than she would ever be. But the two girls reached critical mass simultaneously as they both approached the cosmetically-demanding age of nine. They had torn every Max Factor ad out of Good Housekeeping for months. They knew what they needed, but were too embarrassed to even ask the price of the line of vibrant lipsticks decorating the counter at Schoen's Corner Drugs. Besides, they reasoned, that blabbermouth Mr Schoen would be on the phone to their mothers before they even crossed the street. "Your girls, they dressin' up like trollops!" would be the first words out of his mouth. They knew it. The old man loved to give lectures at Sunday School, usually dwelling on the satanic ways of devilish-sounding jezebels and trollops. What could they do? They were not yet nine. True, they had felt hormonal rumblings for months, but the unknown monster Menstruation was still over a year off for both of them. The growing girls knew metamorphosis was imminent, and makeup, makeup was the change that called now. They had no idea how to use it, but they were determined to learn. The sooner the better. One hundred and seven months into their lives, they knew it would soon be over. Next week they would be old ladies and then dead within moments.

The following Friday, home early from school, they made what they considered a suicide pact. They pin-pricked thumbs, mixed blood, and swore their sisterly allegiance would hold even under the maternal torture that was sure to come. They resigned themselves to an afterlife in Hell. Surely, it couldn't be hotter than Louisiana. They could hang out with the other trollops. Trollops had to be more fun than Mr Schoen. Within minutes AJ and Chris had completely looted the paper-lined drawers of Mrs Lalande's vanity. In the yellow light of the 40-watt bulb in AJ's closet, the two girls sat smearing variously colored creams and powders across each other's face.

"Sunset orange! AJ! That's what you needed! You look fifteen! You'll get dates! Boys'll be calling! Lalala-la La-LANDE! They'll all call for you!" Chris howled ecstatically as she applied yet another brightly-tinted layer to her friend's right cheek.

"Hold still!" AJ fussed. "How am I ever supposed to get this lipstick on straight if you keep opening that big mouth of yours? You'll never get kissed if your lipstick isn't right. Never."

"Ooooo, who would want to?" said Chris. "Kiss some boy like that Todd Moore? Put your lips on that big ugly mouth that's always got the white crust in the sides?"

"EEEEYOOOOOoo-oooo," they both gagged simultaneously, laughing at the prospect.

Their mothers had much the same vocal reaction, except for the laughter. Both girls felt the sting of maternal counseling on their ears   and willow branches on their bare legs   that night. But Chris and AJ had their own cosmetics collections in place before the year was out.

AJ was subsequently caught in the snare of handsome hometown dirt farmer Todd Moore at age seventeen, spending her best years growing up married and pregnant and, at best, middle class. Her fourth encounter with the birthing process finally rendered her into a genderless mass, weighing in on the evil side of two hundred and thirty pounds. She covertly shopped at Ellen's Stout Shoppe across the state line in Natchez, Mississippi. Covertly in the company of over half the other women of her immediate peer group.

Chris visited Alice Jean this Christmas past. After disguising her initial shock, ADA Reed brought all her professional will to bear in an attempt to keep looking her old friend in the eye while they chatted. She was determined not to embarrass AJ by staring lower, at her spreading girth. The effort, though well-intentioned, was much too difficult to sustain, and too apparent to ignore. Polite roundabout conversation collapsed. The artificial stares collapsed, and they both suddenly broke into shrieking tears. The process had taken less than five minutes.

"He still loves me, though, Chris, he does," AJ said as the weeping hit its first lull. "He's told me over and over again that the more there is of me, the more he gets to love."

"That's all that really matters. Having somebody who really loves you." Reed wondered if she meant that. She hoped her friend hadn't listened too carefully.

AJ hadn't. She was occupied blowing her nose and wiping mascara from her cheeks.

"'Cause I know we don't have much in the way of money and things, but we've got the kids and we're still married and happy after all these years. And, and my Todd is a good man. He works hard on our land. Our own land. He's got him a regular day job at the creosote plant. And he's devoted to me, no matter what I look like. He doesn't fool around with other women or drink or do drugs or any of that."

"Well, that's a plus, anyway," Chris said, sincerely this time.

"Now don't say it, girl," warned AJ defensively. "I know you're a lawyer and you're living high on the hog down in New Orleans, and you get to do things I never even thought of, but it's not all bad for me." The plump woman held up her hand to corral a sagging lash. "Yes, yes, I know. I admit it not getting to go away to school bothered me some those first years. But when I see how many of the girls in our class have come right back from college, and are still living here in Winnfield   and living no better than me   I feel just fine."

"You are doing fine, sweetie." Reed was sure she meant it now. Old Todd seemed truly in love with his wife. The house wasn't much more than a sharecropper's shack. But it had the fabled North Louisiana dream ingredients: new polyvinyl siding and a pre-fab double carport. That was a plus, to be sure. But still, to house the six of them...

And Todd still had that white stuff in the corners of his smile.

EEEEeeeoooo-oo...

Chris and AJ alternately hugged and cried for the next three hours, cursing the male-set rules for female appearance. Their friendship was stronger for the visit.

In spite of her body weight, AJ still had a well-proportioned and handsome face. A face that, after her morning encounter with the minions of Mary Kay, glowed like a long-lashed Mona Lisa on mescaline. The two girlfriends finished off their visit in a religious and time-honored manner: a quick genuflection at the altar of base & blush, repairing the cosmetic damage the bawling had wreaked. The communion celebrated with the consumption of a quite surely blessed liter of Gordon's gin.

It had been a damn good visit.

"Wha...?" Reed's mind had strayed. She had lost her place. Somewhere between the slumlord prosecution and the teen cat-burglar case. She had to be in Court in ten minutes.

"Now where was I? Well, look at that. At least my eyes are on straight," she said to the mirror.

Control.

She wants to take control of her life again. Break out of this job that Daddy has shackled to her spirit. She had already become a political lawyer just to please him. She doesn't need to totally dedicate her life to making him happy   if he ever can be made happy. She needs to do something on her own.

In the meantime, driving to work, Reed re-sorts her memory. Becoming happier.

Not a new phenomenon, this. She has continually created her own personal revisionist history of the world, over the progress of her entire life. It has been a matter of survival for Christine Reed. The truth is always whatever works. This is not lying. She cannot make mistakes, even honest mistakes, in front of her father   his approval is too important for her. So she does not make the mistakes. They are edited from existence. Convoluted memory of facts was the source of many battles with a series of past boyfriends. They learned though. If they wanted to be around her.

Starting around puberty   and hers was early everything, everything that happened to her went through the sieve of Christine's Rule: I know the truth.

Her mother's car had been badly damaged one Spring.

"Momma, I came out of the mall and there it was, right where I left it. Some fool had just rammed it head-on, and then run off," Chris had stammered tearfully for the fourth time.

"But why didn't you come tell me, Chrissy?" her mother said for the third, stirring red-eye gravy with one hand and sipping Old Grand-Dad with the other. The two Reed women found repetition soothing.

"Momma, Skippy was there. He was such a help. We knew you wouldn't want to deal with it. Nobody was hurt, after all. So Skippy and I took care of everything. Even Mr Dally at State Farm. Your car will be fixed good as new Monday evening and the insurance will pay for everything."

"Even so, honey, you should have called your Momma, let me know what was happenun." She had begun to slur. It was almost 5pm. Time for a topper. Mrs Reed stopped stirring long enough to pour another three fingers of bourbon in her glass. "Got to get your Daddy's supper unnerway. Would you be a darlinn an get me nothuh ice cube froma fridge, Skippy? Thankew, baby."

"Yes, maam. No problem at all! Be right back!" said Skippy gratefully. He was glad to be released.

Skippy Landries leaped to do Mrs Reed's bidding. He had been standing in the kitchen, listening to Chris' recital for the last half-hour, over and over. He was a little bit scared and a lot more bored. The 18-year-old young man had been in the passenger seat at the actual car-crushing event. He knew enough to keep his mouth shut. Chris had taught him well. After only a few months of dating Ms Reed, Skippy automatically observed the Rule. Go along with the unknown denter theory. Go along with anything she said. Even though he had been in the car as Reed herself rammed another vehicle. Even though he had had to sign the insurance form. It was not wise to question the Truth Rule. Not if one wished to continue to enjoy the physical pleasures of her company.

Chris found that sex was a more than adequate training device. Especially for single-minded men, whether literally single or married. The outcome of these years of conditioning men to the Rule was that she herself became unconsciously conditioned. Like her equation of courtroom and pain, sex and pragmatism had become inextricably linked in Chris Reed's mind.

The only man she couldn't train was her Daddy.

And he had dropped her into hell, just to see what she would do. Chris Reed would not do what was expected.

Monday as the sun sinks, Mutt is walking to work with Fred when they run into Noonie and her duck.

Bourbon street in the daytime is often stranger than at night. The brilliant white sunlight bears straight down on the even whiter Norms   tourists from Minnesota and such chilly environs   whose uncovered and susceptible pale skin turns bright red in the time it takes to walk half a block.

Stumbling all around these *turistas* any particular afternoon are squinty-eyed knots of sailors, military and merchant, just come off night watch and deciding to prowl the Quarter in search of nookie rather than sleep. They occasionally find it, the nookie, though their wallets also more frequently get emptied in the process.

Then there are the Quarter residents. The locals don't know whether it is day or night.

Like Noonie. Skating up the street, soiled wedding gown blowing in the wind and a two-foot-tall partially-defeathered duck squawking madly in tow, she has no idea that the sun is on its way down.

The sun prevails this August: it remains a time of encounters. Planetary movements. Solar. Lunar. Thermal. Reporters. And now, early this afternoon, the biggest batch of suits yet had been crawling all over the property around Mutt & Fred's Box. Mutt had just calmed down enough from the daybreak attack of the newsmen   not to mention the previous night's excitement and the morning's breakfast   to doze off for a few moments. Then came the suits. They had instruments and notepads and were acting real official, yelling out numbers to each other. Woke Mutt & Fred up. Mutt was having a dream about bingo. Got him confused all over again. He could still hear the numbers being called when he woke up. Then there they were. Suits yelling numbers. Very very odd. Mutt knew he needed to stay calm and undisturbed to work such significant matters into his world view.

"Four hundred forty two east... seventy four... calculate the drop at thirty-three..." This recitation caused an exhausted L Mutt Jeansonne much confusion.

It was that kind of disjointed day right from the start. Mutt knows he should have figured it out then and resigned himself to a further loss of rhythm.

Noonie's approach does nothing to slow that loss.

The formerly pacified Street is on a rant again, the gift of Rodrigo's serenity long gone. Noonie grabs Mutt's shirt already yelling: "Buy me beer. Now. Good. Bud. WHAT DO I KNOW ALL ABOUT THIS? Fuckin duck. I know. Dog wanna EAT MY DUCK. Still you OK man, you be saving that lady from the electric chair. Me and Ginny likes you, even though a famous lawman ought still to help with the beers."

When she finds out Mutt has no beer money, no money at all, Noonie walks away sullenly, still cursing her feathery companion. This does not discourage her from stopping to tell the legend of Mutt the Barrister once more to the Shoe Shine Man at the corner of Bourbon and Conti. She points back toward the club, shaking her finger and exclaiming the greatness of the Doggie Law Man.

Trying to avoid any further notice, Mutt quickly walks Fred to the Can-Can-Do, carries the dog up to the bar to sit by Melodie, then retires to Mel's dressing room to wait for her next dance set.

Melodie LaGrande dances for her living wage. This word "dance" usually implies music of some sort. As accompaniment and inspiration. Even if only primitive percussion. A shaman's stick pounding a stretched goatskin. In the Can-Do the music is somewhat more modern. And normally a great deal less expressive. It emanates from a plexiglas and chrome machine with a blinking electronic Happy Face surrounding its coin slot. As a quarter passes into the machine the eyes of the Happy Face light up and the smile broadens.

Only the dancers are allowed to put quarters in the jukebox. It is the sole source of musical background for their acts. The live three-piece combos that played turn-of-the-century jazz during and between displays of feminine flesh are long-gone. Gone with the whole "burlesque" concept.

Marty the doorman says that he's heard stories from old-timers. That the Can-Do Combo had dwindled in number from nine to three before it was finally dissolved around 1959. The only reason the Union let the Lounge drop those three remaining musicians   the bar had to be signatory to the Musician's Self-Protection Union to exist on Bourbon street at the time   was that two of the members, both over 80, couldn't last off their oxygen breathers for longer than five minutes at a pop. It is difficult, at best, to play a clarinet wearing a breather. The Union had even tried to get the girls' sets cut to two minutes to accommodate the short-winded musicians. Since the girls could barely get their opera-length gloves off in two minutes, the brothers of the Local finally gave in. The Combo was retired.

The owners of the Can-Do agreed to make an annual donation of two thousand dollars to the Union's Welfare Fund. A jukebox was brought in. The owners thought they had it made, until ASCAP and BMI started collecting royalties for jukebox use in the late '80's. Now the newest management was wishing the old codgers were back up there wheezing away at "Do You Know What It Means to Miss New Orleans" thirty times a day. The reed man forgetting the melody line to even that tired old chestnut every twelve bars. Just like the old days.

As it turns out, the Can-Do management hated spending money on a machine even more than giving it to musicians. Yet here they were, forced to write substantial royalty checks every six months without fail. It was that or get closed down. But they decided they were not going to pay a second time for the music to actually play.

So the girls have to come up with quarters to play their dance music. Those quarters they usually gather from their admirers.

Ya wants to see the show, ya gotta pay the price. Over & over.

Mutt sees it every day, but he is still burdened with some nebulous but unsettling feeling of imminent change. Chris Reed has set his world, wobbly as it is, even more akilter. He needs to talk now, more than ever. He eyes the dented styrofoam head that wears Melodie's brunette wig. The one Mlle LaGrande always wears when the Norwegian fishing fleet is in town. The head's totally white features and chemical composition feel none-too-receptive, but Mutt is desperate.

Mel enters at that moment, finished with her first set and carrying Fred, the dog draped with the dancer's outer apparel. Less than one percent of Melodie's six-foot-one hourglass frame is covered by her final costume. Her long red hair tumbles dramatically over the dog in her arms, giving Fred a most becoming '70' s coiffure. Fred complements Mel's costume with an incisive "Werf!", the wardrobe stylist once again perfectly in tune with her client. Mutt is immediately stricken by Fred's distinct resemblance to that Cher person he saw on the movie billboards. The nose is perfect.

Melodie LaGrande is already on a roll.

"They are here in droves already, clamoring for the lovely Melodie of the noon news. Mutt you handsome boy, you should not have let me walk out there in these yellow shoes. I can tell. I can sense the tension. Fred is not happy with this tattered wardrobe wasteland I am carrying about. Are you, Fred? I am the absolute TS Eliot of titty bars! I know I am not happy. You know too, don't you, Freddy my baby. Where is my cocktail? Shirley!" she yells out the open door to her favorite waitress.

A cocktail, neon green in color and alcoholically flammable in content, immediately appears at Mel's elbow, courtesy of the ever-vigilant Shirley. The waitress knows that if her girls are happy, her customers are happy. And tips become ever so much more generous.

"Thank you my darling," coos Mel. "Even you can see that there is simply no sense of unity in this dreadful ensemble. Am I right? No feeling of oneness here. It does not work. I owe it to my fans to be perfect, now don't I? I will change immediately. I can make this right. Fred, come on baby, let's go see what else Momma brought in her wardrobe today. Maybe something in rhinestones? I know how you love rhinestones. And I have that little pink outfit today, I just know I brought it. Pink, Freddy, pink!"

The costume change takes twenty minutes. After the elements of Mel's next outfit are selected, Mutt takes Fred out to her vacant lot on Bourbon street. It doesn't do any good. Fred is nervous about Mel's next show. Her digestive tract always locks up when she gets nervous. Mutt returns Fred to her barstool   Mel is working a customer already   and decides to take what fate has dealt him. He goes back to begin a discussion with the long-haired resident of Mel's dressing room table.

Sometimes the woman will just not get off the stage. I suppose you can understand that, maam. But Fred she refuses to budge while Melodie is doing her tricks. Fred loves watching Mel wiggle.

Mel she says I'm her manager. I sit here and make sure no macho bad boy tries putting hands on the goods without getting permission from the owner of those goods. Mel, she's the owner.

Fred she's her wardrobe stylist. Mel shows Fred everything she's going to wear, or not wear, before she goes on. Every bit of clothing, every single show. If that dog barks, Mel puts those clothes right on. No bark, Mel is going to be changing clothes, sure as hell.

Mel hits the stage about once an hour. Does three songs. She gets a little more naked during each song, though even at the end of the act she's got some flesh-colored glue-stuff holding a little round circle of sequins on the end of each of her nipples. That's the circle of sequins required by that New Orleans City Government Health Law. The ones that got Mel sent to the slammer yesterday. Oh, yes. Protective, they say. Like little nipple bomb shelters. Me & Fred figure those gents at City Hall don't want any unhealthy bosom bombardment going on. Got to have those sequins to keep those Des Moines tourists safe.

Mel, she does a good job of making them sweat with what she does show, though. You ought to see it. Round about the third, most naked, song of her set, the tipping gets wild. Every time. Those male children they're stuffing one-dollar, five-dollar, ten-dollar, twenty-dollar bills into her garter belt like they buying a corner lot in poontang heaven. But Mel she knows that her dancing is just advertising. The real money comes when she gets down from the stage and sits back on her barstool.

I told you, maam, Fred loves watching Mel do her stuff. It's like she's watching a T-bone steak hanging there.

And Melodie she enjoys airing out her goods. Right in this Bourbon street honkytonk. Sign outside this joint advertises "Hot Young Sorority Girls!" Mel she's one of those girls. Here she is, still in college. Working on that dancing PhD twenty years later. Maybe she failed a couple times. Something like that. Though don't tell her I told you so. I got a lot of ideas what sorority she belongs to.

Got to be fifty light bulbs blinking all day and night on that advertising sign   or trying to blink. Far as I can see, about half of those lights are burned out. Same proportion as the Sorority Girls.

Me, I'm thinking Mel is already the number-one attraction of the day-time shift. No matter what Abu says.

They got another Can-Can-Do girl doing some kinda wild stuff at night. Mia's her name, and right now she's got her picture all by herself on that advertising sign. She's wearing a fish tail, and a couple of seashells on her treasure chest. That's what she calls it. Treasure chest. The manager put a star on the side of Mia's picture. Shows she's a Sorority star. Pledge class president.

Mel, she'll get her shot soon enough though, what with all the ruckus over her going to jail.

The young woman calls herself Mia. Though she was born to her gender at birth, she and Mel have always felt a common bond. Then when Mel got arrested after Mia had missed work, they had drawn together as only true Sisters can.

Mia is 25. Her real name is Miranda. Mel has always said that Mia choosing a stage name so close to her real name means that she is closer to reality than the rest of them. In many ways Mia is.

Miranda hadn't much money when she came into the business. Her natural body was in line with her finances. But she had a great imagination, great moves and boundless determination. With a regimen of herbal supplements, specialized exercise, dietary restraint, and overtime manual dexterity on her barstool, she built up both her body and bank account. She now owns a quaint double-shotgun house in the Faubourg.

Mia is content. She rents out the side of the house she does not occupy, has IRAs stashed away in a stable bank at a good rate, and is promoting a line of How to Be Sexy for That Boy at Home videos, $19.95, not including postage and handling. No CODs, please.

She had graduated from the manual stimulation the Do requires of its B-girl dancers nearly a year earlier. She is ten years younger than Mel.

Mia and Mel get along famously. Mel hopes to become the daytime star in the same way Mia is the nighttime star at the Can-Can-Do. Professional admiration overwhelms any professional jealousy that might have existed. Mel loves Mia's act. For Mia has no wardrobe. She has costumes. She comes out as the Pregnant Bride, the Oversexed Mermaid, the Nun With A Secret. She has almost two dozen stage characters who are all invented with one thing in mind   getting naked and taking a long time doing it.

That is an oversimplification. Because simple passage of time isn't the heart of Mia's act, even though she of course knows the value of stretching out a climax. No, Mia lives her characters. She acts them out in depth on the ever-moist Can-Can-Do stage, transmitting believably genuine emotion. Fear,

Shy Reticence, Maliciousness, the ever-hopeful Love, and the frequently-appearing-on-this-stage Raging Lust.

Mia lives each of her characters' Lives over the time it takes a needle to claw its way through the grooves of three four-minute bump-and-grind tunes on the Can-Can-Do jukebox.

She has admirers whose devotion to her borders on religious fervor.

Aging gillnetters from down the bayou in Lafourche parish had been known to sob openly as the Mermaid returns to the Gulf of Mexico. She sold them a deep-water license. Hardened cowhands in town on a cattle train from Montana had proposed to the Pregnant Bride on the spot. She settled for a hundred-dollar-bill slipped beneath her garter. With a barely concealed bit of upper-thigh-caressing from those rough cow hands. The Nun's Secret had caused a covert priest hiding in her audience to pull a worn Roman collar from his hip pocket and beg for forgiveness. She had given it to him cheaply and with very little penance.

Mia believes. And so do her audiences.

Her tourist trade is augmented by an ever-expanding schedule of regular johns. She knows what they want, she knows the day they will be there for it, and she delivers. Right on schedule. She relieves Mel's day shift at 8pm, and she is ready for her boys.

For instance, Harvey from Harvey. Mia knows Harvey from the town Harvey across the Mississippi river makes it to the parking lot in the 800 block of Iberville street at 7:55pm on the dot each Thursday. He leaps from his highly-polished powder-blue Chrysler Imperial and runs the block-and-a-half to the Can-Can-Do, to arrive at his regular table breathing hard and wiping his fogged glasses.

His neat Old Fashioned is already waiting for him on a joke-encrusted Can-Can-Do cocktail napkin when he arrives.

Harvey downs his drink in three long audible slurps. He eats the orange slice and the cherry, carefully replacing the toothpick and positioning the rind and the stem back inside the now-empty glass. That completed, Harvey dries his lips on the napkin and raise his eyes for Mia's arrival.

She enters, her timing perfect. Mia knows that Harvey has a wife who serves his meal punctually at 9:15pm every Thursday. Two hours and 45 minutes later than usual. The wife has been informed that Harvey does Moose Lodge on Thursday evenings. She would, however, get incensed if Harvey wasn't in Harvey to eat his delayed meal. As it comes steaming from the microwave with the digital timer flashing 09:15. It takes Harvey 45 minutes to get back to his car and make the run home.

Over his three years of regular patronage, Harvey has transmitted all this to Mia. She understands completely and is sympathetic to his needs. So exactly at 8:05pm on Thursdays, Mia can be expected to do The Nymphomaniac Cheerleader, Harvey's favorite. At the conclusion of her erotic pep rally, he always gratefully places a $20 tip in her "Go Team Go" garter belt. Harvey is one of dozens of regular johns who get what they want with Mia's willing participation. And a reasonable honorarium.

Her long-time regulars inevitably miss the days of Mia grappling loins at the bar. But to a man they will admit they don't begrudge Mia her fame. She indulges their fantasies totally from a distance of 18 inches. And closer, when the mood strikes her.

Like Mel, she has a secret that was revealed to the public. Unlike Mel, Mia herself let it out. And still occasionally does. Mia is actually quite proud of hers, which is also physical in nature. In Mia's case the secret is simply a most intriguing Oriental design. A design that she had long ago commissioned the infamous Mike the Dagger of Rampart street to tattoo on her labia majora. It is said to be as currently erotic to view as it was originally painful to receive. Mia is most selective about whom she allows a discreet glimpse. When the forces of Law and Order are performing their functions elsewhere.

That is about as close to physical contact with Mia that anyone at the Can-Can-Do can claim, for some time.

Mia and Mel get along famously. Mutt takes pride in both girls' accomplishments.

Mel, she'll be getting a picture on that sign soon. And a star. I know it.

She has got that Sorority talent, our Mel she's got a front end like a '52 Pontiac with the twin chrome bumper cones. Got the transmission to match, too grind, grind, grind. She gonna kill me, she hears me say stuff like that. 'Scuse me, maam. It's a old man's weakness.

Now, I ain't putting her down. No. I like Mel. More than that. She's a friend. Plus, she tells me she is going to make me some money soon. No temp check either. Cash money. I'm sticking with her. I worked real hard getting this chance, pocketing me a few steady bucks every Friday. Now this Miss Chris Reed comes along with all sorts of ideas, saying it's possible in this country that even somebody like me could get his own place. I can almost believe it when she says it. Me & Fred getting a real place. Sure. Maybe with my own john. A quiet place. That would really help Fred's constipating condition, I know.

At first I thought this Can-Can-Do job was nasty, like I'm a slave to Mel. Then I think, what the hell, it's better than working the Street. Better than working the US Army. Better than the Boy Home. Ain't that right? Besides, I ain't no slave to Mel. No way. She's OK in my book. She got a good heart, that girl.

If all that silicone don't get to it.

Yesmaam, I am going to get me some money. Melodie's gonna help me get it. Melodie, she knows that business. Yesmaam.

I suppose I should tell you that I didn't know for true that Melodie LaGrande was no girl, at least not when we first met her. She got depressed one night, though, and started telling me & Fred that she got her girlhood from a Doc in Las Vegas. I'm not sure that Fred understood the biologic implications of that to begin with, but then Mel just says outright that she's no girl. At least she didn't used to be. She is now. A girl.

Like you already know I'm no Jeansonne. I wasn't at the start either. I got my Jeansonne from the Government. But in this town it really doesn't matter where you get it. Just got to have it, is all. And Mel's got all the right equipment now. So she's a girl. I guarantee she's a girl. Fred, too.

Guarantee. Fred sniffed out the proof once.

That was a time. Mel passed out in this very same dressing room.

She'd been drinking so many of those watered-down champagne cocktails that she got drunk again. Must have had a hundred over her shift. Ten an hour. No food. She was making some money, though. Boys buying her drinks right and left. Paying eight bucks a pop for those drinks. Mel, she gets four of those eight dollars to put in her pocket come Can-Can-Do payday. She's out there making those very dollars right now.

The boys, they think they're buying Mel one of those fancy Champagne Cocktails. The girls call them "New Orleans Dump Trucks" because if you manage to get loaded on those things, you get your ass tipped right over in a pile.

Like I said, boys they really buying her a shot of soda water and a shot of the worst-tasting strong-as-hell wine. The bartender pours that enhanced-alcohol T-bird into empty big-

buck French bottles and adds a little soda to make it bubble a bit. Probably about a dime worth of liquor. Those boys keep plopping down eight bucks each and every time, though, just hoping that girl will get drunk and give them something.

Mel does most of the time   give them something round about that second or third drink, especially if that boy is looking like a prospect for another couple of rounds.

The girls all give them something, even if it's just a little squeeze of the old squid under the tabletop. That's the regular deal in the Can-Can-Do Lounge. Two drinks or so and you get a touch from a Sorority Girl. But don't you be trying to touch her. Not allowed. That's where I come in.

I'm not against that Sorority touching. Girls giving them boys something for their money, I suppose. Boys coming back to New Orleans from Chi-town or some other burg next time, they going to come back to the Can-Can-Do Lounge, and they'll be buying Mel those same bad drinks again. Those boys, they love it. Giving her money. Paying Mel's rent. And my salary.

Yep, boy buys her that second drink, and she's going to give Daddy Warbucks a trip to Palm Beach.

On the street outside the Can-Can-Do, Rodrigo arrives for a visit. He is carrying a softball-sized brown packet.

Rodrigo makes matters livelier for passers-by, speaking to Marty the doorman on matters of importance: "...mmmMMOOooo-ooooskeekSKEEX-SKEEK   and Calaveras County Twain knowing President Roosevelt, sir, introduced the Good Neighbor Good Humor Policy in 1933 nothing to do with dreamsicles at all though I don't know why, you think it would work encouraging good economic and political relations between the United States of gophers' incisors protrude beyond their lips but skeekeekooooooocould be that the parking lot is getting too big for all the ships sir they are just hoveringaaaaahahhha-hhhh-iii-I I think I should worship this weekend. Worship, sir. Here, take this offering."

Rodrigo hands Marty his packet.

Marty is impressed. He has always been inspired by Rodrigo's sermonettes. Like this one. Gophers in outer space Marty thinks an especially nice combination. And he hasn't thought of dreamsicles since he was a kid. Now, this gift. What can it be? It doesn't seem to be anything. The philosopher in Marty likes that.

He gives the shoeless man the price of a chili dog. One offering deserves another.

Inside, costume change number three is proving more difficult. "It's still not right, is it, Freddy? I'm not going back out there until I get the right outfit. And where did my drink go again? Shirley! Has someone been stealing my drinks? Can you get me a Mai Tai this time, love? Shirley? Shirley! Now she's bitching me again, the tramp. Oh, Freddy, what's a girl to *do*?"

Forty-five minutes elapse before Mel will even think about going out into the club. Abu repeatedly tries to encourage, then threaten, Mel to go onto the packed barroom floor.

Manager Abu Chaudhuri had appeared on the Quarter scene some two years earlier, a maternal third cousin of Mr Nawaz Sayeed. Sayeed is known among his many admirers and detractors as "Mister Hi-Fi," "The T-shirt King of New Orleans," and a bit more pejoratively, "The Hack Pak" and "The Pakistani Plunderer."

For indeed he owns no fewer than thirty-one of the infamous souvenir shops that have eaten up so much of the residential housing of the French Quarter. Tourists love them. Sayeed has been very successful in giving people what they want. In his safety deposit boxes there are also outright ownership titles of a flourishing cab company and six camera-and-electronic storefronts in the historic district of Canal street, plus mortgages on two Bourbon street strip clubs. One being the French-Can-Can-Do. Sayeed's is a diverse empire that makes a substantial profit walking the edges of legality. Thus, the nicknames. His thriving businesses cater to tourists, especially foreign tourists who are not required to pay tax on items bought in his store for export. Over the last decade Sayeed has directly and indirectly sponsored nearly a hundred of his relatives' entry into the United States. The many businesses are now totally staffed by family.

Abu Chaudhuri is family, but is also rightly afraid of Cousin Nawaz's wrath should profits do even a momentary dip. Nawaz Sayeed has been known to drop sponsorship of unprofitable relatives. On the rare slow night, Abu reluctantly and all the while audibly moaning in bloodrending economic agony   augments the Can-Can-Do till with his own money, rather than risk the prospect of exile to another winter back in Lahore. But money is very important to Abu, too. There is that stainless steel Rolex Mariner sitting in the window at Flander's Gold & Sold at the corner of Carondelet and Canal. The Rolex watch is a symbol of American wealth. He had learned that within a week of his arrival. Symbols are very important in this culture. Abu knows that one instinctively. The Rolex will draw a lavishly-figured rich woman into his own bed and more money into his bank account.

He has a plan. He will be happy beyond his dreams. Of course, if she hasn't the proper color already, his American spouse will have to dye her hair sandy blonde. And the name will have to be right. He actually likes the name "Sandi", too. "Sandy" with an "i". Irony is much-prized in the art of his homeland. He wonders if his father's eldest nephew has passed the American bar exam yet, and can give him a decent price on a name change. Soon Abu will debase himself and beg Nawaz for a raise. Sandi will come to him. Bliss will be his.

But first he has to make a continuing profit. And that means he had to deal with an enormous pair of feminine breasts to which there is unfortunately attached the mind and will of one Melodie LaGrande.

"The house full and nobody buying drinks, my Melodie. This not being the way we should run a business. You will go to the bar now. Not to be getting mad at me, your humble servant. I am only under orders. I must be making my quota. Please please oh you must go out. Firm. I will be firm. I will be demoting you in the line-up. You will start before Wanda of the massively rippling tattooed buttocks!"

"Whaaaatttttt?!?"

"No no, I did not mean it, my precious Melodie. Of course I did not mean it. But I am desperate. I must..."

Melodie was adamant: "You must! You must get your nasty little Himalayan high-horse from my dressing room, Mister Big Pants. You are so so very short-sighted, Baby Ah-Boo-Boo. These men come here to be excited by my intense and erotic artistry. They have seen my tortured soul on the television screens of America, and they now want to see the delectable flesh in which that soul is wrapped. They will never never return if I give them less than the highest standard of adult entertainment. The standard that they have come to expect from Melodie LaGrande."

"But they are expecting the high standard of the touching of their many and happily active masculinities now, Miss Melodie. At this moment! Tonight, tonight! I am not caring about the twenty-first century of the woman-stripping business! It is now that these gentlemen of substance have the need of spending their money, money which cousin Nawaz merciful though he is   is counting as being in his pockets already!" he cries loudly.

At a sign from Mel, Mutt begins to steadily push the man from the room with the closing door.

"...please, please. You must, my Melodie. My angel. Encouraging our well-to-do and moneyed patrons. This is your job. They must be guzzling our delectable all-quality top-shelf liquors without noticing the accompanying wallet depletion. I am needing you now, my lovely Melodie..."

Mutt slams the door.

Melodie mildly calls out over her shoulder, "They'll just have to wait. They'll be thirstier if they wait. And thank you for your assistance, darling Mutt. I knew you would understand the aesthetic necessities of the situation."

Mutt sits with his back holding the door shut against the Manager's pounding and the occasional high-pitched Hindu curse. Mel and Fred add a gold scarf to her outfit, and decide they have properly executed their fashion statement. They make their entrance back into the "entertainment area" of the Can-Can-Do to no small amount of applause. There is a camera crew present. Mutt can tell Mel is gratified. Fred is shaking a tail feather, too. Following right behind.

"Good for them. They're OK. Me, I'm still in a mess," Mutt says to no one.

Figuring he has an hour before the two return backstage to dress Mel for the last show, he heads outside for a breather, quickly skirting an occupied Noonie who has returned to the front of the Can-Can-Do on her cyclical tour of the Quarter, looking for the handouts that keep her alive. Mutt can see the Duck Lady is intent on her mark.

The unlucky overnight visitor from Mississippi gives Noonie a dollar just to reduce the grating assault on his ears. Besides, the woman is obviously mad and her duck rabid. Wait until he tells the boys back in Biloxi about this old bag. And the duck! Wow! New Orleans!

Ellis played his part well, happy to find a rube who would fall for the foaming bill ploy.

Fred has left her viewing post by the door and moved back to a Can-Do barstool. Unlike Mutt, she is in a very good mood.

Three people had walked up to her already this evening and given her tasty treats, recognizing Fred from her picture in the paper and in the continuing news features on national and local television.

She is smiling.

A University of New Orleans zoologist published a paper in 1990, a paper that, while conducted on laboratory animals, had some significance to Fred's current state. The lengthy article was the result of years of study, observation and experiment. Its basic premise was that emotion in animals is a matter of human projection. Humans look at a dog and decide if the dog is happy or sad in human terms, said the PhD who got lead credit for the research. He even went so far as to say that dogs cannot physically smile. They supposedly lack the musculature to accomplish such a facial expression, even if the emotional response was possible. Which, he emphatically repeated, it was not.

The PhD was lucky that Fred had not been part of his laboratory study group. She is smiling from one plump little grey cheek to the other.

And why not? Who could have asked for a better vacation? Four weeks pampered like a Queen   not a New Orleans-style queen, but a Queen nonetheless. At the hands of this glorious woman. In a most entertaining environment. And now she finds herself a star of print and screen! Fred sits in one spot to watch Mel shake her own body parts and handle the boys', then the happy dog moves to another stool to witness the scene as Noonie freaks out passers-by. The whole while Fred gets served white bread from Marty, smuggled from the Tulane

University Center cafeteria. She speculates that this is no mere Bunny Bread, but a most deliciously collegiate brand, and she feels it expand her intellect as it comforts her stomach. Fred is studying at Harvard-by-the-Bayou, right there on Bourbon street.

Everything would be perfect, except her digestive system is a bit off-key. She didn't consider this too high a price to pay, considering all the side benefits. But with Mutt at the Courthouse, Fred has only eaten five cans of the Doc all month. Got her off her rhythm, Mutt keeps saying.

Fred was definitely not lean. Her current diet had her a tad on the portly side.

Marty jokes about the Doc Wolf brand of dog food that she favors, saying he thought Fred was "suffering from a serious dietary lack of ground-up roadkill   doesn't allow for the proper purging of the system." He addresses her in his best street barker style: "The mature canine's metabolism can become dysfunctional without a daily nutritional dose of asphalt-baked armadillo. Served in a tasty matrix of crushed horse hooves and soy beans."

Fred growls loudly. She has caught the drift. Making fun of the Doc is not allowed, even by the closest of friends. Marty is repentant: "Just kidding, Freddy. Oodles of vitamins in your Doc Wolf ration, I'm sure. Still love me, Fred?"

Fred waits an appropriate length of time, to insure the apology is real, before she wags her tail. An insult to Doc Wolf is not to be taken lightly.

The biggest part of the smile on Fred's furry face is in celebration of Mutt's finishing Jury Duty. He was finally back, and into full-time canine care. Fred knew that Mutt had not been enjoying himself while he was on duty. In one way. He was coming back each time babbling a bit more about the people and the procedures and what some Judge said. And though his breath smelled funny, his head seemed to be doing fine. Better than Fred had ever seen him, in fact. But there was not much in the way of chow at Jury Duty at first. Mutt had even had to borrow some of Fred's stale white bread stash. She kept a small pile of the extra Tulane bread Marty gave her in one corner of the Box. It tended to be held together with dog fur, but other than that it was edible. The first two weeks over in that Courthouse, the Government hadn't even fed him once. Then things seemed to change. Fred wondered if Mutt had a secret bread stash himself.

In spite of a month's pampering, Fred had missed her partner.

Melodie LaGrande is happy about Mutt's return, too. She had had no one to screen out the mashers in the Can-Can-Do crowd. Abu doesn't care if she gets pinched and fondled without her permission. He considers it part of the job. Which gets much tougher with a full house.

And there is a crowd this night. All over the French Quarter. Conventioneers are rolling through town, great waves of laminated ID tags on every street. Veterans of Foreign Wars, Galactic Evangelicals and dental surgeons have appeared this week. Twenty thousand VFWs, and a scattering of wives. These old men can be some aggressive bastards, too, when they get together in one spot on the road. Away from their wives of forty years.

A gaggle come in. Fred figures that this is probably going to be the last flash of action before Mutt gets back from his break. He never usually stayed gone more than fifteen minutes, but things were a bit off since the trial. And since the breakfast with the new bitch in his life.

Mel has not learned her lesson, and is knocking back the Dump Trucks, dancing wilder and wilder as the day progresses, celebrating her celebrity. There has been a constant house full of old guys throwing money at her.

The Do is rocking this evening, Fred observes, Mel's second double shift in as many days. Every extra day that Mia takes off work, Mel's following gets larger. Fred hopes Mia stays away another week. The dog takes pride in Mel's success. Fred knows her own subtle influence in helping Mel select the costumes appropriate to the situation is a part of that success.

Like her current patriotic color theme   Fred knew what would get these Veterans hopping.

Mel has worked half a dozen ex-GIs for double-drinks at the bar since the early afternoon. Fred sits on the stool on the other side of her so she can watch Mel's activity. She is The Watch Dog, and goes on instant alert at the entrance of a group of four stooped and ancient old codgers, all of them wearing their soldier-boy hats and their even more dusty, just-out-of-mothballs woolen WW2 uniforms.

Wool, in the middle of the New Orleans summer   and this wool is the thick, prickly cloth manufactured in wartime England seventy-odd years ago to keep minor shrapnel out and major body heat in. Put it right on the Yanks, they did. Wool covers the four men top to bottom, with an additional layer of dangling ribbons and buttons from the past war and the present convention.

As they enter, Fred hears Marty say, "You gentlemen have got to be heroes of the democratic world. What we have in here are some of the fruits of your labors. God bless America!"

Marty is an artist. There is no doubt.

The wool-encrusted vets are already looped walking in the door, and they are most definitely looking for the ever-popular and-oh-so-big Party. As seen on TV.

Fred knows she and Mel have another eight bucks in the bag the moment she sees them.

Mel is just coming off the stage from giving her latest butt-level tour of bump-and-grind Disneyville when the four gents walk in. They are paralyzed at the sight of her. Before they even sit down.

"Lordyshit, willya look at that!"

Mel is indeed exhibiting her flesh rather randily and with a great deal of relish at the moment. One of her pasties minutes earlier had wafted skyward in what Fred found to be a particularly admirable new routine of breast manipulation. Mel replaced the pastie immediately, of course, for reasons related to the City's Health.

She had dubbed her novel move "Gone with the Boobs." It was part of the motion that got her busted in the first place. Mel likes to assign titles for all her Big Moves, but Marty has told her that he finds this name a tad prosaic, considering the complexity of, and flexibility required by, the maneuver. This, Mel takes as a compliment.

The four vets are dazzled. They finally sit, mute for the moment, in one of the booths at the back of the house. Shirley the day waitress goes over to wait on them. They start laughing loudly and being as macho as each of their seventy-five or eighty years of righteous living will let them. Two try to pinch Shirley's bottom, but she vigorously slaps the offending hands away and gives them all a big smile. The smile says: "Time to spend your money or get the fuck outta here, gents."

Shirley "She-Cat" Sexten knows how to give very detailed but concise messages without saying a word. Especially to men. She danced twenty-one years in the Can-Do, under a succession of managements, until her "fanny gave out," as she so succinctly describes her retirement. She had saved enough to get along well enough without getting another job, but Shirley couldn't stand inactivity. She was, after all, only forty-one years old. What was she going to do? Hang around the house reheating meatloaf and waiting for her chemical-saturated husband to get off his shift at the aluminum plant? Boring. Secretarial? She wasn't the possessor of a character that catered to sterile subservience. Sales? Her knowledge in clothing was centered on their removal.

The service industry was the logical choice. And where better to wait tables than her old haunt, the French Can-Can-Do Lounge. She knew the regulars and most of the girls. She could handle management. She knew how to wring a dollar out of the most tight-fisted customer and get tips out of dancers for working their johns for extra drinks. She did it. Her income rose ten percent her first year as a waitress. Even though dancing tips and Dump Truck money had gotten a little thin in her last few years on stage, the raise was substantial.

However, as a waitress Shirley allowed herself to vent all the feelings she had kept to herself while entertaining audiences. She took no guff from anyone, she was efficient and vaguely courteous, and she expected to be tipped well for a job well done. But there were rules for dealing with Shirley. "No touching" was one of them. As the vets had just found out.

A loud round of hemming and hawing followed the waitress' stare.

"Not very hard to control, these boys," thinks Shirley. "OK, gents, what'll ya have," she says, smiling that smile again. They all quickly order a variety of New Orleans drinks: Sazerac, Brandy Milk Punch, Hurricane, Mint Julep.

After Shirley goes to get their drink order, Mel sees the men whispering happily among themselves, the discussion finally coming up to some grand conclusion. Marty has obviously briefed them on the benefits of the two-drink reward. Then their own cocktails arrive.

One of the oldest of the gentlemen   the Mint Julep stands up, tall and all-male, and stares straight at Mel. His face reads: "Get ready, woman, to meet your master!" The other three encourage him, clapping their hands.

Mr Macho pulls the sprig of mint out of the julep glass and throws it on the floor. He pours back the remaining fluid, and swallows it all at a single gulp.

Minor mistake there.

His eyes get wide, and he spits and splutters for about five minutes. They don't have much of a handle on how many shots of bourbon are in a Mint Julep back in Wisconsin. He probably thought a Julep sounded something like a Shirley Temple. It is. It is very much like a Shirley Temple   with a huge red-veined scrotum and a rather massive erection.

The little drink setback doesn't deter him, though, and with the encouragement of his soldier-buddies he finally swaggers over to Mel and Fred at the bar. Mel can tell Marty had done his job as doorman well. That Marty had once again passed on the possibility of complimentary manual stimulation to a potential customer. The old gent does indeed sport overt evidence of stimulation as he approaches the bar, a little GI pup tent pushing out the front of those thick wool trousers.

A small dragon-shaped dust swirl dissolves in a shaft of brilliant neon light from the street outside. Marty has once again cracked open the Can-Do's front door for the rubes to get a quick taste of stripper angst.

The door is just as quickly shut, leaving everyone inside, including Fred, momentarily blind. Her eyes gradually adjust, the shapes of the players returning slowly. Just in time to see the proud veteran and his dusty suit of memories come shuffling across the room toward Mel.

"Nice doggie", he says as he sits down, reaching out.

"AaaaaahAAHHH...," Fred rumbles like a B14 with engine trouble. The vet recognizes the sound, jerks his hand back and jumps to his feet. Fast. Pretty agile for an old guy. Fred appreciates respect. She allows herself to be quieted.

"Now, now, it's alright, Freddy Baby," Mel is saying soothingly. "This gentleman just doesn't know how we treat our darling canine sisters here in the Crescent City."

She rubs the tips of Fred's ears. Lovingly. If dogs could purr, Fred would be doing so loudly at this moment.

Mel turns back to her prospective client with her hand still lightly on Fred's head. When she speaks, the old man jumps.

"This is a very special breed of dog, Soldier Boy, and she is very sensitive about being confused with the lower orders of animals here in the Quarter. She's even a specialist in haute couture, aren't you, my delicate darling?"

She pats the stool on the other side of her, "But I can tell that you are the sort of gentleman who respects and enjoys good breeding. Do sit down and tell me about yourself."

The old soldier sits, and the bartender is opposite him in a microsecond with the eight-dollar drink the first of the handjob qualifiers. The soldier gladly puts a ten on the bar, all the while staring down Mel's exposed décolletage and babbling on. Mel is used to the routine. The vet of course isn't used to it at all. He doesn't even notice that the bartender has whisked away the money, without a word quickly appropriating the change for the bar tip jar.

Mel lets the old gent talk and flirt and do his thing. While he is having a good time prefacing his life story, she polishes off the first Dump Truck in less than a minute.

The bartender is back instantly. It is his job, "Care to buy the lady another drink?"

The stakes are upped. Obviously the veteran knows the effect of a second purchase. He clears his throat nervously, and looks back at his table full of cronies. They wave him on, encouraging him.

"Why, of course," he says, a bit unsteadily.

The drink arrives and Mel blasts it back at a gulp. Then she turns to directly face the old soldier, and without a wasted movement, reaches down and grabs his crotch.

She squeezes the contents of the gentleman's trousers with a practiced pressure. It is definitely what he wanted. He smiles and looks back at his friends. They see what is happening and nod their heads lasciviously. Oh, they are enjoying this. They watch every move.

Fred also likes watching the process. Watch Dog.

She can see that the fossil is starting to grow. Mel can feel the development, too. She grips the bulge with even more ardor. The veteran's head starts to go back. The bartender busies himself washing glasses. Fred watches. Mel is pulling harder and harder, with a definite rhythm.

The veteran groans loudly.

Mel gives his groin another massive tug.

A large "ka-WHOOSH" sound and a cloud of grey dust envelopes the bar. Mel falls back on her stool. Fred leaps into Mel's lap to protect her from what might possibly be a detonating veteran. Shrapnel from a testicular land mine.

Nope. He is still sitting there, intact.

Nope.

The eruption is no live round left imbedded in his loins from The Battle of the Bulge. Nope. Nothing quite so dramatic.

Though almost.

The entire crotch of his crusty old pair of trousers had come free, ripped away from his body, and is now clutched in Mel's hand. From the condition of the edges it is apparent that the torn material was completely dry-rotted. General Patton is lucky he made it all the way down Bourbon street in his moth-balled army-issue suit.

The vet quickly stands up. He is unperturbed. His pants legs, now no longer attached to the rest of his pants, fall around his ankles. He adroitly steps out of the remains. About two inches of pants dangle from his belt over his boxer shorts.

The boxers in question have large blue polka dots all round, with a rather massive and   considering his age unyielding body part protruding from the front.

Mission accomplished. He proudly steps back from the stool, anything but embarrassed, and salutes Mel snappily. Then he marches in hup-two-three-four cadence to his table of friends, haughtily pointing at his still-present erection. The other men stand and reverently salute their comrade's military valor. One of the veterans takes off his jacket to protect this long-neglected member of their company, and ties the coat's arms around the stimulated gent's waist.

They order more drinks. Mostly Mint Juleps.

Mel regains her seat, passes the handful of musty wool to the bartender, and looks to see if anybody new has come in. She still has an hour or so left in her shift.

"Maybe something really wild will happen, liven things up, Tootsie-dog o'mine," she says.

Fred barks twice.

"I was thinking I might change into that vibrant spicy-orange miniskirt number. The one with the flame-red sequins and tassels."

Fred was going to suggest gloves.

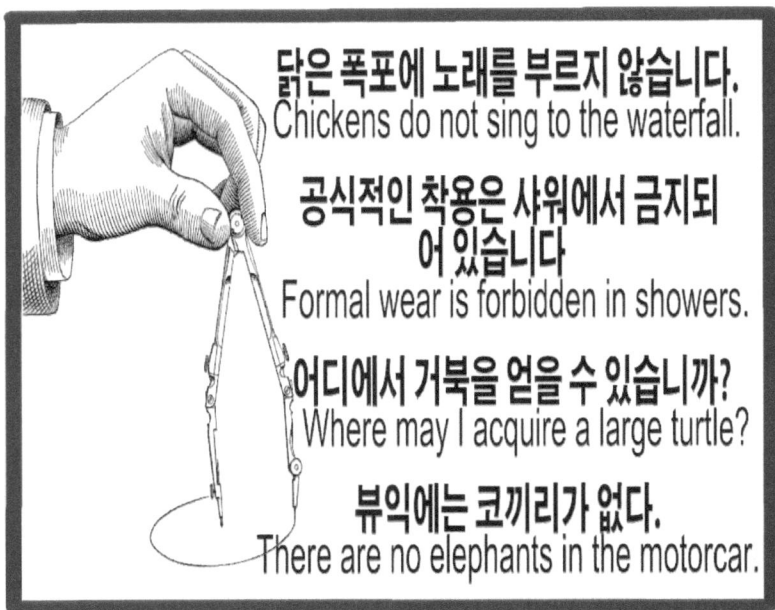

The heat of yet another in a succession of feverishly hot August nights has been tempered by a passing curtain of big-dropped afternoon rain. Small inverted cones of steam spiral up from the hot street, the tiny droplets of water kept in roundabout rising motion by a light evening breeze off the river. Going back up to grow large and fall again tomorrow. On the edge of one such wet pillar, Mutt stands, leaning on the right front fender of Melodie's red Studebaker.

Roland Clemenceaux, #6, Democrat, endorsed by the Downtown Gentlemen's Irish Association, stares solemnly at Mutt. The ragged campaign poster has survived all manner of abuse by being heavily and thoroughly glued to a metal utilities pole. Attaching any material onto public property like the pole is a blatant violation of city laws. This minor bit of illegal posting is symptomatic of the occasional pragmatism of the Clemenceaux campaign and the man himself. Mr Clemenceaux had won. The duly-elected mayor, no longer a candidate, has a right to put his face wherever he wants. The law could be enforced in later elections.

Mutt was unconcerned with political subtleties at the moment. He was going to talk, no matter the circumstances of the mayor's presence.

Oh, I know what you're saying, Mr Mayor sir. I didn't vote for you, so I probably should just keep my mouth shut. Leave you alone. But I am a registered voter, you know, and you probably ought to keep in touch with all us registereds.

You're probably thinking a man like me can't hardly talk nor read nor write worth a damn. You probably thought I can't drive. I can. Drive fine, though I got me no license. Read fine, too, if I could see right. Besides, even if you can't read you can still get a driver's license in Louisiana. They got a law here where they have to read that driver's test to you, if you can't read it yourself. Me, I can read and write better than most of these New Orleans high school graduates. I just like the idea of having somebody read to me. I get them to read it to me every time I take that Driving Test, which is really only one time in my life so far, since I haven't had the opportunity to touch any car but Mel's. But I am looking forward to the next reading I'm going to get from that lady at the Driving Test place. Think I'm going to have to wait a while, though. They won't actually give me a license on account of my eyes not being so good, but hell, my eyes were good enough to pass the writing test and the driving test. Good eyes. Passed both them tests. Just couldn't pass the seeing test.

I haven't been able to get me any eyeglasses yet, though I go all the time to Charity Hospital. They got me on the schedule twice, but it's hard for me to come in on their schedule because I don't have a phone and my address is under a rock.

No eyeglasses, no license. Yet. But Mel knows I'm a good driver, even though I'm a hair blind, and she lets me drive her around in her car. Because sometimes in this line of work she gets a little too much to drink. She doesn't drive so good then.

Me, I drive just fine. Smart driver, smart parker. I usually park around on Dauphine street where there's a broken meter. Nice '61 Studebaker, Mel's. It is, too. Nice. Got to love that girl's taste in cars. Fire engine red, inside and out, that Studebaker. Kinda like her hair.

Almost time for us to go home now. Melodie's gonna be wrapping up her last john, Fred's gonna have to go out and do her thing once the tension is off, and me I got a serious hankering for a Lucky Dog with double chili and relish.

Two dollars and forty-seven cents including tax is just burning a hole in my pocket. Pair of George Washingtons from Mel just calling out my name to that weenie man. "Save a Dog for the Mutt!" That's what those Georges are yelling. Found the forty-seven cents under a toilet in the Do. Plus, I got a brand-new can of Doc Wolf's dog chow hidden back at the Box for Fred. Doc Wolf's Doggie Ration in the Big-Dog 30-ounce size. Twenty-nine cents at Schwagg's Food Man Supermarket. Nobody seems to know why they call him "Doc". Maybe he sent a bunch of guys to a doctor. If they were messing with his doggie ration, that might explain it.

Fred has a serious crush on Doc Wolf. Mutt saw her licking his picture on a can once, a funny look in her eyes. Mutt was encouraged. This was overt second-hand sexual orientation   something he could understand. Relationships with two-dimensional representations (even if they were on a three-dimensional can) were right up his alley. He didn't have much experience with the real thing. No experience, in fact, except hearsay. Doggie girls liking pictures of famous doggie boys was much easier for Mutt to understand. Much better than worrying about her having more complex desires, like Mel.

Fred likes that Doc Wolf can, but she does not like the word "doggie." Not at all. She thinks it sounds like a poodle.

The French Quarter has the highest number of PPSI, poodles-per-square-inch, in the civilized world. May even have made the Guinness Book by now. The poodle may well qualify as the patron saint of sexual ambiguity. Like the All-Our-Boys-Are-Girls Social & Pleasure Club. That particular temple of moral elasticity held cross-pollination worship services at regular intervals on Bourbon, then on Chartres street, for some three decades. There were dozens of small porcelain poodle icons behind the bar. Next to the Chartreuse and Herbsaint. Candles were lit in the evenings. The word "Fifi" was heard with increasing frequency in the near proximity of the doggie statuettes. Pet topiary was a commonly-discussed practice: "Raymonde trimmed little Fifi so she looks just like Minnie Mouse. It's so darling!"

Mutt speculated to Rodrigo once that Quarter Drag Queens are required by law to nurture at least two poodles to keep their Drag IDs current. Mutt suspects his joke was close to the truth. He and Fred both like the deep-voiced ladies. They're sweet girls, the queens   very tolerant of Streetfolk.

But they have these poodles. It is Fred's theory   serious, this time   that the ladies like to feed their little dogs a mix of ten-dollar-a-pound steak and ground-up antique jewelry.

There is this poodle promenade every day, when the girls wake up around lunch. This ritual allows the queens to get their eyes focused and the poodles to squeeze a few more rhinestone-encrusted love offerings onto the sidewalks.

Poodles. Doggies. Fred doesn't like anybody to call her a doggie. But those cans of Doc Wolf's, Fred loves that stuff. It may well have something like ground-up catpoop in it, she loves it so much. Dogs. If she wasn't always so hungry, she'd be rolling around in the stuff before she eats it. So I got her the big can of Doc Wolf. That there is a major treat, for the middle of the week especially. If I can just keep her off of my chili dog long enough to get home, we both are going to have us some fine dinner tonight. Light me a candle or something. Read Fred the contents off the Doc Wolf Can while she eats. Real civilized sit-down meal. Gonna have us that evening re-past.

Me & Fred are seriously moving up in the world.

I'm employed, you know. It's a regular sorta thing now, my job. We take Mel home from the Can-Can-Do. She spends a hour in the bathroom while me & Fred eat baloney sandwiches. That's a special bonus just for us. Melodie keeps a big old roll of baloney and a loaf of white bread in the fridge for me & Fred when we work overtime with her. Lets us make our own sandwiches, Mel does, so we try not to be greedy. Peel the red plastic off that meat tube real careful. Fred likes hers with one thick slice of baloney and lotsa Creole mustard, 'cause that mustard makes her sneeze. Dog likes to sneeze. Peculiar for a dog, if you know what I mean, but she just makes a little WHOOP sound and smiles every single time she lets loose one of those dog sneezes. Sometimes makes her blow a little baloney rocket clear across the room. What the hey. I figure she's getting old and she should get her pleasure wherever she can.

We are supposed to go do our other job afterwards. Me & Fred put up flyers about Mel doing her special act on weekend nights. Girl works seven days, so we try to help.

We're out on the street a long time at night, Me & Fred, putting those flyers out. Fred, she gets to growling again when she gets tired. So I usually end up carrying her the last hour or two. It's OK. I get to thinking about lots of stuff.

I sorta dream about ladies sometimes. Real ladies, though, like Miss Reed. In a purely theoretic kind of sense.

Trying to figure out what those ladies do in their real life. What the men around them do. I gotta investigate. Do scientific observations. I go to my picture walls. Look at them good and hard. After all, I've only done this one single morning's talking to a real Norm lady, Miss Reed you know, and I think she's wanting to talk some more. Kinda scary. Can't even tell you what we talked about. Just all came out at once, it did. I wasn't as prepared as I hoped to be, you see. But something's coming. I can feel it for sure. Maybe something good. I could get me a place to live and somebody to talk to all at one fell swoop.

Shut up, Mutt. Stop that. Sorry, Mr Mayor.

It wasn't just that time in Court, now. It wasn't just Miss Reed. I been speculating about these lady and men things ever since they put up this new Blue Island Tropical Tequila sign. Right next to the Claiborne Avenue exit. Big one. A night-lighter. Has three-four ladies sitting around a table with the same number of gents. Playing a card game, passing out little colored pieces of something. The table full of shiny green glasses with fruit hanging off the side. All those folks smiling and laughing. There is this pretty blonde lady. Closest one to the exit ramp side of the sign. She has her hand on a good-looking fellow's arm. He's not laughing, though. No. Just smiling real big and looking right in her eyes. Straight in there.

Fellow really looks happy. Kinda glowing.

I been wondering if I'm ever gonna get a shot at feeling like that. Odds don't seem too good. The way I'm looking and smelling. Place I'm living. Even the way I'm talking. Don't seem too conducive to meeting ladies. Not Norm ladies, anyhow. Not real ones. Not like Miss Reed.

Pretty damn pitiful. Mutt the ladies' man.

Enough of that, Mutt.

Mutt Jeansonne has forgotten all about the Can-Can-Do for the moment. He's truly caught up in this discussion of philosophy and gender with the newly-elected Mayor. It's seldom that he has so auspicious an audience, or one so closely connected to actual life. As the intense conversationalist circles the Dauphine street utility pole, gesturing emphatically to its adherent campaign flyer, he draws anxious looks from the shadows.

Retired animal control officer Bertie Joe Plummer and Edna, his wife of forty-seven years, give Mutt a wide berth. They seldom if ever see such sights in Longview, Texas. Mutt's display gives them a perversely attractive sense of danger. The desk clerk at the Holiday Inn had warned them about the locals. The clerk, himself from Detroit, had told the aging couple that north of Bourbon Street the Quarter could be quite dangerous. There were Characters afoot.

Bertie Joe is unafraid. He has seen quite a few mad dogs in his time. He is angry, though. He should have known to put his net and pistol in his bags when he packed for a weekend in godforsaken New Orleans.

"Could be a space alien, Bertie Joe. I seen the diagrams in the paper. Boy could have one stuck slambang in his brain," is Edna's immediate judgment. "Picture in the new Comet looks just like him. A saucer, him and a dog, you see, Bertie Joe."

"I know about dogs, Edna. My business to know about dogs," he says, looking about the street warily.

Edna's mind shifts again. She speaks to her husband. "To have a husband like you, and now to meet an alien. My life gets better and better, Bertie Joe. Next thing you know, I'll be in the paper myself." She loves the tabloids, and this is an occasion to prove the much-maligned media right. Aliens on earth.

Bertie Joe nods sagely. The sight of a New Orleans Character on the loose, and Bertie's own in-depth knowledge of the intricacies of East Texas animal control, again bring his philosophy of life to the fore. "Oughta make 'em get they shots. Register aliens, you see, Edna, not guns. I'll send me a note to the NRA. They'll take it right to Washington. Aliens come here, they gotta get they shots, just like they was a German shepherd. That'd fix 'em," is his solemn pronouncement. The Plummers pass by, quickly heading for the safety of the Inn and their king-sized bed with its electric Vibro-Flux mattress. Twenty-five cents per the ten minutes.

"Now that's some kinda comfort," says Edna, back in the room and flat on her back. She grunts, pulling her knees to her chest and peeling off her triple-strength panty-hose.

"C'mon, honey," says Bertie Joe, serious lust welling in his eyes at the sight. "We're in New Or-leans. Daddy needs some comfort hisself," he whispers, flagrantly dropping three quarters in the bed's coin slot.

On the street Mutt, unaware of the Plummers' ongoing Vibro-Fluxing, and as yet unprompted by the Mayor, continues to speak.

Get off all that nonsense thinking. Instead of history, we got some geography coming up now. My own applied science: learning things from Mel. I can think about Mel as a woman. Because she's really George, so she's safe. No disrespect, Mr Mayor, but a goodly portion of your registereds ain't exactly your straight up-and-down Norm. At least in this neighborhood.

Don't be making fun, now. I think it's a good thing when an old man like me gets an opportunity to speculate about such important considerations. That part about being old is OK to me   folks don't expect that much of you. Don't expect you to do much else other than drift away somewhere. Now Rodrigo, he's a good bit older than me, and that's a man who's still moving the limits a science. Thinking all day every day, and well into the night. Thinking keeps him young.

One of the reasons I still like geography. Though it was a little different when I was a kid.

Those Nuns would die clutching their little holy-water-filled wooden crosses if they knew I was here all these years later, working for a fallen woman. A man-made one at that. Me sitting right there in a Den of Iniquity if I've ever seen one. Far as those Nuns would figure, I'd be headed to the hottest part of hell just walking in the door of the Can-Can-Do. Even if I never sat on a stool.

Yessir, those Nuns would be doing the Mortal Sin Mambo for old Mutt right now.

Reverend Lincoln Jesus Gonzalez, without any pressing Courthouse duties and now back to his principal calling as a preacher to the wayward of the wee hours, walks down Bourbon street. He carries a worn Bible open in his right hand. With his other hand he presses an electric megaphone to his mouth, amplifying his message into the consciousness of the disbelievers and sinners on their way to and from degradation.

The preacher still wears a small multi-colored umbrella hat on his head from his earlier efforts. This day his afternoon ministry had proved so empty of profit and full of disbelievers as to result in an extended night shift. Rent is due. He is well aware that the offering can strapped to his chest holds only eighteen dollars in folding money, four dollars in food stamps and some small amount of change. He rattles the can occasionally for the passersby, noting subtly to them how little reward has come to a man of the cloth this night.

"Verily, this has been a long and arduous journey! Toiling in the fields of the Lord! Goodgawdamighty! Come to me now, my sisters and brothers, come away from your shopping for sins of the flesh. Stop all this banal passing of the evil dollar and let me tell you the ways of the Lord!"

The god-sent evangelist of the city streets has found often stones imbedded in the way of his Biblical plowshare. Tonight he comes upon a boulder.

Noonie and her duck Ellis are working the crowd outside the Can-Can-Do Lounge. As Mel chats up another customer at the bar, Fred can hear Noonie talking outside. As always, Noonie's voice is clearly audible, even over the jukebox.

She has mistaken the preacher for a tourist.

"CIGARETTE mister? Duckie and me COULD USE CIGARETTE. Fuckin duck! WHAT HAPPENED TO YOUR HAT MISTER? S'AT A UMBRELLA? Ain't s'posed to RAIN MISTER!" Noonie pitches him at high volume. Unamplified, she is much to his embarrassment louder than the megaphone he brandishes. The Reverend retreats a few steps backward, trying to save face as he goes.

"Goodgawdamighty! The sinners and profligates are upon us! Creatures from the satanic planets above! Where they have never heard or understood the Holy Words! Nor come to embrace Him in their misbegotten pride!"

The Rev decides to take the offensive. That always works with belligerent Norms. He turns to lure in the crowd, while pointing at Noonie and Ellis.

"They rain down upon us in the guise of woman and fowl! Dropping sin and degradation wherever they may enter. The devil comes in mysterious ways, yes, yes, he does."

Ellis quacks loudly and flies directly at the Reverend Gonzales' pointing finger, beak open for his own offensive. Gonzales is taken further aback by the duck's audacity. He starts looking for an aisle of retreat through the growing crowd.

"Lord have mercy! Jackanapes and rabid vermin descend upon me! Bear witness, my friends! Bear witness, brothers and sisters! Sweet Jesus, will thy work never be done?" At this pronouncement, panic sets in. The feathered devil is advancing. The blessed Rev retreating. He lowers his megaphone and sprints away, running out of the Quarter and toward the deserted safety of the Central Business District.

"Goodgawdamighty!" he cries in the distance, his last words floating back onto Bourbon street. The Reverend Gonzales' wake is strewn with tourists knocked hurriedly to the side in his attempt to flee the threat of demonic duck.

Noonie yells after him.

"Got a poster GOT A POSTER wanna buy a POSTER. See here's the DUCK. FUCKIN duck. CIGARETTE maybe. Duck wanna CIGARETTE. NICE HAT. Cigarette be good."

When he arrives at his Ninth Ward home via the Bywater RTA bus an hour later, the Reverend Gonzalez quiets himself by watching a few minutes of gore-and-terror-filled television news. And partakes of a sacramental sixteen-ounce jelly-jar or two filled with iced off-brand rum and coke. He does this only to acquaint himself with the evil ways of the world. He cannot fight what he does not know.

The last months he has heard and seen increasing reports of demons being visited upon the planet from other worlds. The theme has worked itself into his sermons. He practices at night in front of the TV, chilled *cuba libre* in hand, accepting anticipated donations as the power of the sermon successfully opens the purses of his prospective listeners. The practice is necessary. He has to make sure he can keep his rhythm unbroken as he preaches. The first donation will inevitably trigger another. He must be able to accommodate the generosity of his listeners. Even in the face of disbelievers such as the duck woman.

"Yea, verily, this is the final and complete punishment for Man's sinful ways! Lord, that sin has totally permeated the Sodom and Gomorrah they call New Orleans. I myself have seen much, have long travailed down in the bowels of this city's sin-filled Courthouse. Caught up in my own struggles, ever battling to save a few of God's lost souls. Trying to keep myself alive to do God's own work! Thank you so much, sister, that small amount of money will feed my body and help save your blessed soul. But not for long. Oh no! For yea, the last days of this earth are upon us!"

The end of time is a good draw, he has come to realize.

"Might as well give me the money, brother, since there won't be any place to spend it soon!" That logic led his sermons to take on increasing references to Armageddon. There was money to be made in alien subjugations. The horrors of the American judicial system. The evils lurking in the musty closets of the cosmos.

With occasional references to fluoridation. Just to help the cash flow.

"Yes, Lord!"

The comings and going continue on Bourbon Street. Abu Chaudhuri is on break himself now, and watching his favorite TV show. Ten times at once. The stack of televisions in Nawaz Sayeed's Miracle-a-Minute Tax-Free Electronics & Camera Heaven are tuned to one channel. Abu runs the block-and-a-half from the Can-Can-Do to his maternal third cousin's store at this exact time every evening. This thirty-minute program provides him with knowledge vital to his future happiness. It educates him, gives him the cultural cues he needs to understand. As a man in search of a woman. Sandi.

"Tonight's the Big Night, Frankie!" An announcer screams from the nearest screen. 42 inches. *"Discounted for One Day Only! Just US$1,699.99!* (with US passport)*"*

"And don't we know it, Dave!" responds Francis "Frankie J" Murphy, game show host extraordinaire. "Yes, folks, we're live and on the air, and we're looking to find that special person for another willing contestant! Please welcome

Miss Mitzi Lodovico, former astrologer to the former President of the United States of America! She's our first guest on tonight's edition of 'DREAM DATE'!!!"

The studio audience goes wild. Abu stands in front of the bank of televisions applauding along. "Oh, this is being a good one, I can tell. I am getting some of the good stuff tonight." His relatives at the store's checkout counter nod their heads proudly. Abu's dedication to his studies is a source of inspiration to them all.

"Dream Date" is one of the most popular shows in syndication history. Part of the reason for this particular show's success is Dave Edelman, the congenial star of the half-hour program, and a long-time veteran of stage, radio and now, television. Edelman possesses a finely-honed ability found only in a few rare semi-upright mammals: his bad taste can embarrass anyone. But he is especially vitriolic with women.

The theme music fades as Dave raises his voice: "Mitzi, baby, before we bring on the young stud we've selected just for you, why don't you tell us, by your own astrological reasoning, what do the stars tell you about why a broad with such great legs ended up a horny old maid?!"

Abu roars. "Oh, so funny, that Dave! He is truly being the manly sort. The horny talking is always to be getting the woman's goat. I must be remembering these things," he mumbles to himself, making hurried notes in a tiny tablet he keeps for just that purpose. He doesn't want to miss anything. Abu needn't worry. The audience's laughter and knee-slapping goes on for a full minute, with Mitzi glaring at her off-stage agent the whole while, before Edelman raises his hand to calm the crowd.

"You know I was kidding, now don't you Mitzi? Just an ice-breaker to make the people here in our studio and at home feel a bit more comfortable   anything can happen here 'cause we're live   and we're not that serious about this love game now are we, folks?"

More applause and hearty head nodding.

"It's a darling little figure that you have, Mitzi, and like I said I do love your legs. But let's talk about what you told us at the head of the show, darling. Now, why is tonight so special?"

Mitzi shakes off her peeve and smiles toothily at Dave. It is so hard to stay mad at such a handsome and jolly man.

"Well, Davey, if you must know, last night and tonight are very special as far as planetary movement goes. There are a number of things happening that could make these forty-eight hours a crossroads in many people's lives, both sexually and socially. And hey, I'd like to cash in on it!"

Mitzi looks to the crowd for a reaction. It was a big gamble. Bust. Nothing. She tries another angle.

"I mean, even a bonehead like you   just kidding, Dave   must know that we are in Libra, so things are balanced out, nice and level. But then the sun and moon came into conjunction last night in the early morning hours and tonight Mercury goes retrograde and things are going to get even wilder. You can even look for parenthood in the next year as a result of what gets started now."

"Or maybe even the next nine months, right, babe? If enough of that conjunction happens tonight?"

Leering chuckles and light applause from the men in the audience. Abu leans closer to touch the screens, speaking to them, "You will be receiving the conjunctions from me, Sandi. I will be learning the agilities of this American manner of the sexual speaking. Happiness will be ours."

"Sure, Dave," Mitzi continues. "Nine months. But this sun-moon crossing means that you should be able to attract the people and situations you want..."

"All-*RIGHT!*"

"... though things may seem to be a bit out of control."

Edelman mugs for the audience. Knowing laughter.

"Just hang on," Mitzi continues, speaking to the camera. "There is some sort of role in society that is pre-ordained for you. It could be parenthood. It could be something larger, but it's on its way. For me personally, I'm hoping it's going to bring the right relationship."

"We've got it for you, babe. Long, tall and... I am sure he's a leg man, Mitzi, just like the former President..."

"The Dave is such a man of knowledge," thinks Abu. "But I am hoping this Mitzi woman is not being correct. I am not wanting something big to happen tonight. The arrestings of the authorities the last night were plenty plenty for me. I am needing merely the steady spending of customers and the quiet meal of the Burger Barn to help me in the finishing of my shift." He looks at his watch, a Korean knock-off Timex. "Oops, I am being late!"

His three distant cousins watch Abu admiringly as he sprints out the door and back down Bourbon street. The oldest proclaims: "It is firmly against all of my family's long-cherished beliefs," a pause with a sigh interrupts, "but I am most aggressively desiring a transfer to Nawaz Sayeed's bar of the titties."

Things settle down on Bourbon Street with the successive exits of the Preacher, and then Noonie & Ellis. Mutt had come back from his break, followed shortly afterwards by Abu. Melodie has sobered up enough to come outside, take some air, and talk to Marty the Can-Can-Do doorman. While advertising the products on display inside the Lounge, Marty and Mel discuss his graphic design for her flyers. She wants to promote her act even more and move up in the Can-Can-Do dancer hierarchy. After all the attention she has received over her victory in Court, Mel feels the time is right for some serious self-promotion. And if, like Mia, she can gain a large enough following for her dance act, maybe she won't have to work the barstools quite as much. Marty thinks that a worthy ambition.

Marty Schruer is a 20-year-old schoolboy, living a completely separate and Norm day-time life at Tulane University. With a deft and much-admired hand, he executes light, airy figure studies to fulfill upperclassman Fine Arts curriculum requirements. Art occupies all the time Marty is not standing on Bourbon street barking out at tourists, luring them into the Sorority house. His street patter gives little indication of his fascination with Goya. Or his origins in Massachusetts.

"Hot Sorority Sisters in there dancing dancing boy hi-dee," he tells them.

Marty gives Bourbon street pedestrians the inside poop on which of the sisters are "ready to par-tee." He also gives them the lowdown on the two-drink bonus   "got a little present for Big Jim & the Twins, yessir we do sir,"   on the sly. The young collegian normally gets a tip for that bit of information when he plays his cards right. This is assuming he hasn't told some undercover nerd-impersonator from Vice.

Once upon a time, Marty had the hots for Mel, like most men who are around her for any length of time. But Marty didn't know Mel's secret. Not until the trial.

Marty's roommate John Wilton works at a copy shop down on St Charles Avenue. A couple of weeks ago, John made a hundred copies of Mel's flyer for free. When Mutt and Fred appeared at the counter to pick them up, John acted like they were real customers. Even though he gave them the copies for nothing. The gesture made them feel important.

"Those school boys are OK", Mutt announced to the world as he had walked back toward the Quarter.

Sometimes Marty distributes the flyers himself, sticking them up all over town when he gets off from barking at tourists. He even sticks them on telephone poles near the Uptown music clubs. Not that any of those folks would ever come near the Quarter, Bourbon street, or more especially the Can-Can-Do. Marty probably wouldn't like having to deal with them anyway. Or the possible exposure of his night job to his Norm school chums. But putting out the flyers Uptown is Marty's way of showing his commitment to Mel as a real person. Plus Marty is working off the fever of seeing Mel naked all night, ex-guy or no.

Marty brings Fred university cafeteria white bread to eat. Fred likes that white bread. She likes the taste of those flyers, too, especially the pink ones. Not as much as white bread, but Mutt still has to be on the watch to make sure she doesn't gobble the flyers as soon as he lays them down. Fred pushes the blue and yellow and green ones aside and eats the pink, getting dog slobber on all the other colors in the process.

Fred doesn't understand that those pieces of paper are an essential part of Mutt's strategy, intended to get tourists and local johns flocking in from all over, opening their wallets for Mel. And to prompt Mel to give Mutt and Fred some of that cash. That's what she told them, and that's what she does. Every time they put out her flyers. But Mel does not yet realize that additional publicity efforts will soon be made redundant by an approaching tidal wave of publicity. Like the delayed after effects of a major earthquake, the real media tsunami of the trial is still to come, but for now an unsuspecting Melodie is taking care of business as usual.

Marty's last flyer design featured Mel's best novelty show act. "Melodie LaGrande" written in stars right over a stylish line-drawing of Mel herself, mostly naked and facing a businessman wearing a tie. The tie is very straight.

It is also the centerpiece of the act.

The exotic dancer Melodie LaGrande makes men's ties stand up and fall down. She wraps her hands around them in provocative fashion midway down their length, then places the rigid cravat in close proximity to a variety of her body parts. This usually also brings the wearer's face into the close environs of these same parts.

Then, when she deems the customer's erotic imagination to be properly steamed, Mel looks around to the rest of her audience. She seems to question their overtly bawdy expressions. Her face becomes completely childlike in its innocence. She pauses and looks again at the stiff tie in her hand.

"Oh, no," she pantomimes, "did you gents think this tie looked like that?!" She looks at their trousers, one by one. "Oh, no! And I thought you respected me!" She doesn't have to say it. You can see it in her eyes. She is shocked.

She looks at the tie, still in her hand, then at the face of the tie-bearing customer. An evil gleam comes into her eyes   a new set of eyes. This man has defiled an innocent woman. She squeezes the base of the tie angrily.

At this point in the act, the customer begins to have doubts about emerging from the Can-Can-Do with his lower anatomy intact.

This is part of Mel's artistry. By the time she gets to "the evil look," her john really believes his tie is his penis. He wants the tie to be his penis so badly during her intimacy with it that now he is stuck with his fantasy.

My dick is in her hands. Oh god.

But she lets him off the hook. If he has been a Good Boy. Normally, after asserting her control, Mel looks at the tie again, blows gently on it, and with the subtlest of hand moves allows it to wilt.

But if the john has shown the slightest resistance or any overt aggression during her act, she has a second ending for the show. Still looking directly in the john's eyes, she pulls a pair of miniature scissors from her g-string. They are tiny, the size of the scissors often found built into pocketknives. Only an inch long in their folded position, but with a functional honed-chrome edge when opened. She displays the scissors to her victim and then slowly, ever-so-slowly, cuts the tie off at the halfway point.

She keeps a supply of new Hong Kong ties stageside to replace those of the customers she emasculates. A tie to match the deed   the broad end of the replacement ties is printed and shaped like a penis.

Even her victims are inevitably immediate fans.

Mel showed the secret of the trick to Mutt and Fred. Manual dexterity. Using her right hand to keep the base of the tie held in an almost-complete cylinder. When she desires the erect neckwear. Then slowly opening her palm until the support of the cylinder shape gives way. And the tie droops. But does not fall from her hand. Mel all the while using the ever-so-subtle breast wiggling for attention diversion. No one ever thinks to watch what she is doing with her hand. Mutt thinks it's a pretty damn good act. Fred loves it, of course.

That's where the flyers come in. Mutt and Fred are supposed to take them to all the hotels near the Quarter and on Canal street. Their mission is to get the word out to the money-carrying male masses about Mel's tie act. That is their job, and it is much better than scrounging for a living in other ways. Since they met Mel, Mutt and Fred haven't had to do nearly as much dumpster diving.

Really, almost none. Especially if they go by Mel's second late-late-night job, at Benny's. They could almost always score some free chow there.

Benny's Raw Bar. Known to locals as a fake biker hang-out, but also frequented by a rather intriguing blend of only moderately-deviated folk: insurance executives in Barbara Streisand drag, animal lovers in coordinated khaki and silk safari attire, and the occasional guilty but repentant civil servant dressed in the complete habit of the Sisters of Grace.

Starched wimple included in the rental. They're an inventive lot.

There is a Kansas-cattle-drive-or-two's worth of leather in Benny's on any given night. The cut runs regimental, the color inevitably gloss black, the accessories Harley-esque. A number of the gentlemen actually own 74-cubic-inch Harley-Davidson hogs, but primarily so they can exhibit their machines outside bars like Benny's.

The individual black and chrome motor-sculptures parked in a line at Benny's Raw Bar are each kept pristine and shining, and tuned to chug effortlessly in neutral at 60rpm. THU-buttah. THU-buttah. Throaty and low. One a second, Mozart to a Harley mechanic's ears. Beautiful collector's bikes. Exotic dated details. Pan heads. Suicide clutches. Fifties' cop bikes with the spin sirens and blue lights still intact. In perfect working order and trim.

Few of the bikes from Benny's will ever be subjected to the rigors of a road trip, however. Much too dusty an experience for their owners. The six blocks' expedition into the Quarter is frightening enough. A gent could simply ruin his supple cowhide outfit on the open road.

Outside of the leather crowd, Benny's patrons are mostly fairly calm day-straights, boys and girls and in-betweens in one way or another. The Raw Bar isn't on any tourist maps. It hasn't any oysters on the half-shell. That's not the kind of Raw that Benny is talking about.

Mel had an ongoing joke that the boys & girls in Benny's "carry more crustaceans in their pants than you can find at a Elks crab boil in Chalmette."

Chalmette is downriver a few miles. The crabs there are blue and six inches across. Melodie LaGrande does not frequent the town.

She wouldn't frequent Benny's if she wasn't saving so desperately for her maternity. Mel gets done up fancy-faced all the time when she's doing her Can-Can-Do shifts, but she avoids big-time makeup when tending bar at Benny's. The few times she puts on her eyes are all the same. She's tired before she even goes to work, and tries to lose her exhaustion wrinkles in faux-Liz-Taylor eye shadow. That Cleopatra makeup on Mel's face is a warning sign meaning: "You mess with me, you die." A patron doesn't read the sign, doesn't pay attention, he or she's going to pay a price.

Mel puts on the full death rig when she's in that mood. Kinky western. Like this wild-looking Egyptian female is planning to be buried in some Hopalong Cassidy pyramid sitting out on Rampart street right after her shift. She wears her pinto-spotted cowgirl boots, a short black rubber mini-skirt that's got a nickel-sized hole just north of her navel, and some electric pink net stockings bought right out of the Bendover Boutique window on Dauphine street.

This night, after two full shifts at the Can-Can-Do, Mel is putting in another full eight hours at Benny's. Mutt and Fred are there both to keep her company and to make sure she doesn't fall over.

Mel continues to make her way through her daybreak shift, the last of twenty-four straight hours that she has worked. Some of the regulars are sitting close by the corner of the bar while Mutt & Fred wolf down their burgers. The customers don't pay the ragged Street pair any mind, but the occasional deluded fool will give Mel grief. One particular old hetero twist   Fred can smell twists of any brand a mile away since she's been with Mel   he's drunk as eight kinds of hell, talking loud about the size of Mel's chest. Another chunk of nothing-but-trouble sits next to him, listening and laughing. Couldn't call them Norms, but probably as close to straight as come in Benny's.

He's saying: "I'd give my right nut to get a look at them titties   why don't you give us a peek, Darling?"

That kind of talk.

Mel comes over quick. Looks him square in the eye.

"That nut hasn't worked in years, you useless ten-for-a-penny piece of shit."

She is quiet then, but Mutt can almost hear the wheels of Melodie's mind churning and spinning. He looks up just in time to see Mel turn to him, and a visible tic pull at the corners of her mouth as some wild resolve snaps into place.

Mel walks right to Mutt & Fred, confronts them directly. Mutt, he's got a lardburger in mid-chew, and Fred has an onion slice hanging out the corner of her mouth. Mel puts her hand right on her own two breasts and looks at them contentedly.

Mel says: "You know, I'm tired of wasted old trashpiles like those two always running their mouths about things they've got no business even thinking. Bet you'd appreciate a look more than these old peckerheads, wouldn't you, Mutt? What do you say, dear boy?"

Mel knows of course that Mutt sees her naked every day ten times a day.

First he's thinking, *Sure, it's a swell body, Mel, but hey, I'm eating here! Doesn't say it out loud, of course.*

Then, a second wave comes to him. Grows. Mutt gets a quizzical look on his face as the thought settles in. *Melodie, she's the one who gave me the meal in the first place, ain't she. Shoot, I'll do whatever the hell the sweet woman wants.*

Sure. 'Cause this little production is some sort of big deal to Melodie. I can tell. Something bigger than just showing silicone, or shaming two losers.

She wants me to help her find something.

So Mutt puts down his burger. Fred does the same, gently laying half a tomato slice back on her plate. Fred takes another long slurp of beer   she's drinking the Abita

"Turbodog" dark brew tonight   from her saucer, preparing for action.

When Mel looks back at those two twists, she's got fire in her eyes. This is these guys' Wet Dream DeLuxe, getting a look at her chest. Mel knows it, and she is going to give their dream away to a Street bum and a dog.

Those two guys both get real quiet. Start to lean forward.

Mel gives them The Look of Death.

They freeze where they are. They're dying for those breasts, but they're also dead afraid. Rightly so. At this moment she'd slice both of those boys to bits with that bar knife, lemon slice still stuck on the end. Stick it right through what brains they have, if they try to move. They know it, too.

Once she has them paralyzed with fear, she turns her head back to Mutt & Fred.

"Well, Mr Jeansonne?" Mel says.

Mutt thinks what-the-hell, and nods. "Sure," he says. He almost chokes on a curly-sliced dill pickle   those gherkins with pepper slices in the jar is what he likes. Just for the record.

He dutifully drops his eyes to her chest.

The barmaid Melodie LaGrande blinks her eyelashes real slow, smiles huge with a big red lipstick mouth, and pulls her shirt open another three inches. Those amazing Vegas insta-breasts were already pretty well out on view, in the first place, before these boys said a word. It doesn't take much for her to get them right out there for Mutt to inspect. She has her act together so tight, though, that those other fools can't see anything but Mutt's eyes getting a good look.

Mutt feels kind of special about all this. That is an instantly readable vibe. This surreal scene taking place for Mel's peace of mind is simultaneously another lesson in his own progress. He's never had a private show from a lady before, except when Mel and Fred are doing wardrobe, and that's different.

This time he really looks. Part of his education. He already had memorized the geography, but the lesson is the important part here, he realizes. Mutt looks, for both their sakes.

Those breasts are perfect. The Doc hid the scar right where the bottom of the curve gets back to her chest. She's got one of those cups to hold in the silicone, too, but you can't see a trace. Perfect.

Some girls at the Can-Do had a little body addition done, some had a lot done. Some stand with the hand   and body   they were dealt. A couple of the girls on the night shift have breasts that each look like a half-a-gallon water balloon bouncing around in a pint soup bowl. That's a fact. But Mel's are perfect.

Like they really grew there.

Got to admire the workmanship.

So, Mutt looks them over, paying serious attention, like he's the Pope taking the bread order at the Last Supper. He stares as long as he thinks is right and proper, then raises his head and looks Mel straight in the eye.

Fred barks and she puts her paw on Mel's right breast. So those boys will know that Fred is also protecting the goods.

Mel is smiling again. She nods at Mutt, happy with his efforts to furnish a gentleman's brand of chest inspection. He could have mentioned the many occasions in his life that New Orleans' Carnival has given him the opportunity to practice such a refined art from afar, but Mutt figures this is her trick, let her have the last word.

Mutt says "Thanks", but trying to act cool he blows a small chunk of lettuce right on her nipple. Lettuce lands right next to where Fred's foot is. Fred looks at it and barks again. Mel seems to think this addition is OK, though. She grins.

Picks off the leaf and puts it in her mouth. Melodie goes back to work chewing slowly, her grin widening with every step.

Mel has left those twists sitting there, without offering them another thought. Their mouths are hanging wide open, a little drool coming out the sides. They are barely breathing.

That girl has got some balls. Or at least she used to.

Today's lesson, titled "Mel's Psychic Invasion of the Obnoxious Males," is now completed.

Mutt's all confused again. He's learned something, yes. But he still has real trouble thinking about ladies and body parts and all the accompanying formulas. Especially if any of this applies to Christine V Reed, which he is certain it does, somehow. He's not good at this. Had no practice. All through his life everyone has remarked on his "shy" nature. Good souls tried not to invade his privacy by telling him more about living. A well-intended hole in his education, but still a mighty big hole. Mutt's friends always figured someone else would pass on the information at Mutt's own place and time.

A few years back, Mutt discovered himself slowly approaching the half-century mark of life, and yet feeling only about half-prepared for living.

So these past years he's been trying to learn about the Norm world by talking to his pictures. But he knows there are a number of things missing from his life, things he never had the occasion to study in any depth. Like real women.

There hadn't been many opportunities to get a sensitive feminine viewpoint for a confused boy growing up in the company of nuns. Not much training in interpersonal relationships for a naive draftee running scared through a foreign world of whores and death. Not many true soul mates for a penniless veteran dumped onto hard streets without an information manual.

So today here comes another in a quick series of real life experiences   not totally Norm, but close enough for Mutt and it's finally too much for him. Once again. It isn't about breasts. It's about people being affected by other people. Relating, communicating something, even if it is fear and lust. Feeling what the principals have in their individual minds, Mel's and the drunks' and even his own, makes his thinking go all confused and wild.

Mutt has an immediate need to get back under the Expressway and sort it all out. Back at the safety of the Box. In his own nest. But he feels even that desire to be a weakness.

Look where I'm living. Where I'm working. No wonder I get confused. Like right now.

I gotta figure this out.

I know I'm getting close. I just know it. Me and Fred'll talk. Gotta get back home. Fred & me.

Mutt looks down at the countertop. Fred has eaten the rest of his burger while Mutt was in his deep thought.

Fred has a smile on her face and it says: Philosophy has its price, Mutt. Ya thinks too long, ya loses yer burger.

Nothing to do but get off that stool an walk out the door. Wave goodnight to Mel and go back to the vibrating Expressway Box for some early morning talk and shut-eye. Fred is too beat and full of beer and fatty ground beef and white bread to make it on her own and whimpers until Mutt picks her up and carries her. She is snoring in his arms before they cross Canal street.

Mutt falls back into thought, as the broken cadence of his steps carries him out of the Quarter. His bum leg is aching, but he is trying to keep up a march cadence. One of the few useful things the Army gave him.

Hup a one a two   a Hup!

Got to learn to be more careful

Hup a one a two   a Hup!

Stuff it happens when you break your rhythm

a Hup! a Hup!

Noonie first suggested the house on Toulouse street.

She and Virginia had both been amazingly in-touch in the weeks since the legendary trial. People had begun to notice New Orleans Streets after Mutt's act of bravado. Flamboyant Noonie herself was approached by reporters for her opinion on matters of local concern. She tried to respond as best she could, holding in rein her somewhat elevated mode of ordinary intercourse. The word "fuckin" dwindled to a mere ten percent of her vocabulary.   When she was unexcited, of course.

And there was Chris Reed, now continually on the Streets at Mutt's side. No one was really sure what to think about this Norm girl who had Mutt all stirred up, but things had certainly started happening in the Quarter since she arrived on the scene.

Reed had walked into all their lives with a vengeance, less than 48 hours after their mutual trial. She was convinced that Mutt was somehow a solution to her own dilemma, and she was determined to find out how. Sleep all but disappeared from her life, and she was glad to see it go. She returned from her first visit to the Veterans Administration with an armload of papers. Not only proving the details of Mutt's war story, but verifying that he had indeed been drafted under just his first name.

His records were complete from the date he was medically deemed fit for service to the date he was discharged. Nothing before or after. He had been perfectly honest, as he said. Mutt was the ultimate displaced person. An orphan without a name or family, a decorated veteran and a stalwart voter. Even registered as a Democrat, for Christ's sake. Home run. A good citizen, but abandoned by society to live with his poor doggie. In a box under the freeway. MVP regular season. Serving in the judicial system and smart enough to understand the law. The National League pennant. But without a penny to his name. World Series winner.

She had yet to wrangle from him the origins of his Jeansonne surname   maybe there was a further story about his parents he didn't want to tell. With very little digging and minimal bribery of public officials, she came up with a set of voter records on LM Jeansonne that looked pretty normal. The file had even been updated in recent years at his voting precinct. The updating was, unfortunately, not of the most useful sort. Everything but the very basics of necessary information had been deleted from the computer by someone named Gladstone   some overzealous polling commissioner on Martin Luther King Boulevard. The records still certified that Mutt had a mailing address on Carondelet street, even though he didn't live there anymore. All the rest of the entries were in order. Mutt was fairly normal in some aspects of his background.

None of this really seemed to matter. The man was who he said he was. He was incapable of lying to her. She could open him up completely with just a look.

He was actually more than he said he was. Mutt's courtroom victory, and its subsequent passage into myth, had made a Street hero out of him. Every wino, asylum escapee, car dweller and temp worker in a fifty-mile radius knew by now that one of their own had beaten the System. Every hooker, poodle owner and paralegal with a night habit, from Canal Street to the Industrial Canal, knew that L Mutt Jeansonne of New Orleans had won a significant victory.

Mel's acquittal was their victory, too. A color photo of Mutt and Mel covered the entire Page One of the monthly *Gulf Coast Gay Crusader*. Mutt was pictured holding a snarling Fred slightly out to the side. Fred dyspeptic the morning after the trial. Entirely possible that lavish use of the word "doggie" by the photographer had set her off her rhythm once again. She continues to deem the categorization disrespectful.

The photographer had made additional money off the picture by wiring it to other print media. The same photo had shown up by later the same day on the cover of the *Weekly World Comet*, Edna Plummer's favorite and one of the more flagrant purveyors of supermarket UFO intelligence. A shining oval had been added to the sky behind Mutt's right shoulder. Sure enough, Fred was identified as a once-innocent house pet. A loving doggie devoted to an All-American Working Man. Now the same earth mammal was possessed by an Alien Being. Made up entirely of liquid nitrogen and hailing from the dark side of the second moon of the planet Neptune. Mutt Jeansonne, identified as a retired trucker from Dry Prong, Louisiana, had captured the vicious creature. Tamed it by forcing it to drink unleaded gasoline. Jeansonne, explained the tabloid, had previously learned the basics of subduing aliens found by the roadside in his early orientation classes with the Teamsters. The Comet was a Union shop.

There was no mention of the court case or Melodie.

Rodrigo cut the picture out and pasted it up in the Church next to a lovely line drawing of asparagus.

But it wasn't just obscure magazines zeroing in on the case weeks later. Much of the press had happened immediately.

An ambitious *Advocate* reporter located Rodrigo, the Courtroom's Mystery Man, and received a rather long discourse on avocados and amberjack by way of an interview. The paper's City Editor had difficulty finding a usable direct quote. An independent UHF station had even questioned Mutt at length on the rumor that animals had testified at the trial. The spotlight lasted for days, and then weeks.

All this press coverage had convinced Chris she was right about Mutt. He could stand the exposure. With her help, he could thrive on it. He could become a source for news that the public wanted to hear. The final pieces of a plan started falling into place for the ADA.

Reed began pushing to get Mutt a real place to live. She wanted him to have a place of residence. He was becoming a figure in the community, she told him. To prove it, Reed procured letters from both the jury pool supervisor from Mutt's sojourn and one trial, and from Night Court Judge Cannalo. Attesting to Mutt's citizenship. With these letters in hand, she convinced the VA. The veterans' group agreeing to guarantee a GI housing loan of minuscule proportions as a public gesture of good faith. If Mutt could come up with some collateral.

Big if.

Mutt finally agreed, with Reed's strong encouragement, that getting a proper home was the first step in finding himself.

"You must assert the humanity of the disenfranchised. L Mutt Jeansonne, you are becoming a symbol to all the people who have been thrown away by society," she told him the Wednesday after their breakfast.

Mutt and Chris Reed were standing face-to-face under Mutt's Expressway home at rush hour. Reed had to yell loudly to make herself heard. The usual subtleties of her enticement suffered greatly under these conditions. But she was pleased that at least the dog wasn't hanging around. Fred had refused to come down from the Box, having just devoured two rhinoceros-sized cans of Doc Wolf's dog chow in a very short period of time.

Reed reached the turning point of an electrifying closing summation, simultaneously full of logic and emotion. As she sought to motivate Mutt.

"You must take your place in that society and help others find their way." There was an immediate lull in traffic, only a few seconds, but it added power to what Reed had been saying. Mutt was totally under the spell of the woman's presence. That is, until the poignant moment was shattered by a resonating noise from the plywood Box suspended above. A noise easily identified as a canine gaseous expulsion of rather historic proportions.

However, even this crude interruption had not broken Mutt's concentration on the face   or message   of Chris Reed. He would do what she wanted. Go talk to the VA. After all, she had already done so much work just to help get him a home. And get Fred a quiet place. Go talk to the VA.

He went.

In his first impromptu meeting with Veterans Administration officials, Mutt, accompanied by Rodrigo, had offered twenty-two pounds of aluminum cans and six untorn volumes of Professor O's All-Fact Encyclopedia. In fulfillment of the VA request for collateral. Mutt's offer was taken under advisement, and he and his companion were instructed to look for a more substantial sum of cash, or property, for collateral purposes. Plus, the VA officials told Mutt, he needed to show a specific home he wished to purchase as a requirement for any housing loan.

Mel had volunteered to help raise the collateral. Even said she would loan him the down payment and co-sign a note. He had, after all, saved her. Her surge in notoriety among both the Street and Norm worlds had brought waves of new admirers to the Can-Can-Do. Even some of the girls had taken to coming into the Lounge to admire their new heroine. For only the second time in the 52-year history of the French Can-Can-Do Lounge, a dancer was making more money on dancing tips than on handjobs. Melodie was in a state of bliss.

Of course, she would loan Mutt this piddling amount of money. And in return he would do her the itsy bitsy small favor of introducing her to his dashing courtroom accomplice. After all, she owed him something of a debt, too. It was a gamble, Melodie knew that. But she wasn't just loaning Mutt the money. This was something of a community investment. Rodrigo was part of that community, Mutt's right hand man.

Melodie LaGrande had decided on Rodrigo. She had felt it an inspired decision, and an irrevocable one. Secretly, she was loaning her family money in hopes of being repaid with a Family.

Mutt readily agreed to her terms. He would never have believed it possible, but now he had access to the purchase price of a real home. His private toilet was within reach.

If he could only find one to buy.

That was where Noonie came in.

When word got out that Mutt was looking to find a Norm place to live, Noonie began to think. Clearly, as was happening with increasing frequency. She remembered she owned a house on Toulouse street with her brother. He was gone now. Buried somewhere. She didn't think the house was gone, and even though she didn't remember the number of the house, she easily retrieved a mental picture of it as green and two-storied. With French shutters on the balcony, and screen doors downstairs.

Noonie decides a hasty scouting mission to Toulouse is in order.

With Ellis D again squawking madly at the end of his leash, she runs through the Quarter. Then down Toulouse street staring at house fronts.

She stops in front of 921 Toulouse.

There it is. The color faded and peeling off, the hardware on the shutters almost rusted through. But there it is, the street number intact. Her mama and papa born and died here. Her brother. Noonie herself. Her family had lived here since New Orleans was just a crumbling, mud-walled fort surrounded by a malaria-and-gator-infested moat.

Noonie walks up to the front. Stands looking at the door. Ellis faithfully climbs the single step using both beak and webbed foot, and stands behind her, waiting.

"Marvin!"

She has already called out the name before she remembers once again. That her brother has been dead for years.

Noonie reaches out. Grips the handle on the screen door. She pulls with a jerk, and the ancient lead hardware comes off in her hand. She inspects it carefully. Puts it in her pouch. It is a piece of her family's house. She puts her fingers carefully through a rust hole in the screen and applies pressure.

The door suddenly lurches outward, coming off its hinges. Slamming to the porch floor with a resounding crash. Rotten wood, torn screen and dirt fly all around her.

"FUCKIN door!"

It takes Noonie ten minutes to quiet Ellis D. Then, once the cascade of quacking has subsided, she looks up at the monogrammed front door in the middle of the house. A cutout tin plate of the family's initial is attached to the rusted screen. A large white-outlined R. She can't immediately remember what the R stands for, but she knows it is comforting. An odd thing occurs. The twisted expression that has distorted her features for decades suddenly softens. She relaxes. Her manic drive slows to an easy walk. Altogether odd.

Noonie stands again, with Ellis in her arms. She shoves open the door with one firm motion and steps in.

The darkness and dust cloud her vision at first, after entering from the clear sunlight of the afternoon. Noonie with uncharacteristic patience waits for her eyes to adjust. Ellis twists in her arms, scratching the inside of her elbows. Noonie makes cooing noises to calm him.

"It's OK, Ducky, we home," she says calmly. Surveying the entrance hall. On the wall immediately inside the door hang two dusty oval frames. Circling glassed photographs of a handsome young woman and a rather confused-looking older man. Noonie rubs some of the dirt off the glass with her palm and points. "Mama and Papa," she tells Ellis.

"Mutt gonna like it here."

"Well, Mister Rodrigo, you great mysterious charmer, tell me all about yourself."

Mel is dressed with a great deal more restraint than usual as she perches atop a Can-Can-Do barstool next to the shoeless Rodrigo. She had told Abu that if she couldn't have her special friends come visit her at work, then she would have to take her act, and fans, elsewhere. Being as Mel had doubled both the business and the level of clientele with her flood of publicity over the past weeks, the manager very quickly allowed exception. To his normally strict "No shoes, no shirt, no service" rule. Abu had escaped the economic wrath of third cousin Nawaz Sayeed, and in the process also escaped renewed residence in suburban Lahore, Pakistan. All due to the surging popularity of Melodie LaGrande. The manager could not do enough to make Ms LaGrande happy. Marty the doorman was mightily amused.

It was Marty who had put two-and-two together from Mel's description and contacted Rodrigo at his Church. It had only been with insistent pointing at Mel's picture, still stapled on the Church wall (by Marty himself), that Rodrigo had been persuaded to accompany Marty back to the Can-Can-Do.

The public revelation of Mel's prior sex had initially put the damper on Marty's lust. Mostly he felt dumb. But somehow the fact simultaneously opened a whole new brother-sister sort of relationship that both he and Mel found quite comfortable. Marty would do anything for Mel. Anything.

And Fred, old Freddy was as famous as any of them. The last news tabloid feature crew had headlined their story: "Reclusive Dog Refuses to be Separated from Sex Queen! Homeless Hero Inconsolable!" Mutt said he did not feel inconsolable, whatever it was.

After one of Mutt's interviews that centered on his dog Fred's likes and dislikes, Fred was buried in an avalanche of jalapeno chili dogs, white bread and Doc Wolf's. The resultant gastric explosions had led Marty to introduce Fred to Rudy's Sweet Stomach Gas Powders. Marty mixed two powders in every can of the Doc ration he gave to Fred. It was either that or keep Fred away from the front door of the lounge completely. Couldn't break Freddy's heart, no.

Marty Schruer's head was changed by The Night, too. The Night of The Trial. He came to new appraisals of a number of people, besides Mutt. He was convinced that Rodrigo the madman was more together than he had ever suspected. In spite of outward appearances. Marty had always been amused by Rodrigo, but now he found he rather respected the gent. And after Mel's story, Marty had decided to do a serious reevaluation of the way he judged people in general.

Marty had told his roommate John the truth about his night job at the start. John sympathized. Marty needed to support his art school education, and his parents were in no position to send him through such an expensive private university as Tulane. John admired Marty's devotion to his career. He figured that if his roomie had the strength to put up with the vagaries of Bourbon street, Marty the barker might actually end up as Marty the artist. John had also suspected that, with all that sexual energy bouncing around every night, Marty sooner or later might find himself entangled with one of the sorority sisters. Melodie LaGrande was a strong candidate for such entanglement. He had, after all, been financing her flyer campaign for months.

With the Night, Melodie's candidacy had come to a shaky halt. Marty, in spite of his occupational environment, was still a confirmed heterosexual of rather limited scope. John had to counsel Marty on the facts: he had not been made gay by proximity to, or lust for, a previously-homosexual male being. Marty, reassured about the boundaries of his own sexuality, decided to persevere in his friendship with Mel.

Even to the point of bringing Rodrigo through the front doors of the Lounge, like a real customer. Marty leaves the door open just long enough for the passersby to get a quick look at the flagrant displays of lewdness taking place on the Can-Can-Do stage. He gives Rodrigo the full treatment, even as he continues to work the tourist trade.

"No cover charge, one drink minimum, but I got to keep these doors closed at least part of the time because our ice-cold air conditioning is escaping   don't it feel GOOD, sir?

and the Fire Marshal of the Great City of New Orleans demands I keep as much as possible of that refreshing air conditioning circulating in the club at all times. Fire Prevention. Yes sir. That is truly it, ladies and gentlemen. Got to keep our patrons from overheating."

For a University student currently enjoying a course entitled "The Art and Poetry of the Pre-Raphaelite Period," Marty has the street barker role down very nicely.

"Yes sir and yes maam. This is one hot show. Come right on in and see the lovely collegiate debutantes of New Orleans society shed their inhibitions along with their clothing. Right this way sir and I hope you have a good time inside. Shirley, get the gentleman a seat near the stage and the famous starlet Miss Melodie LaGrande. Sir, you look to be a man of refined taste and sensibilities. I am sure you will appreciate the company of Miss LaGrande."

Rodrigo sits close to Mel at the bar. He is nervous to the point of shaking.

"Don't be so coy, you sweet thing, you can talk to Melodie," she purrs into Rodrigo's ear, over the loud bump-and-grind playback that drives the Can-Can-Do dancers to artistic extravagance. Mel sits on her stool in a pose that demands appreciation. She wants her new acquaintance to become familiar with the territory.

Rodrigo sets his jaw and stares, in bursts of approximately three seconds, at each portion of Melodie's anatomy. She is flattered by his shyness, and enjoying herself. Rodrigo on the other hand, seems to be emitting small moans of pain as his eyes light on each new unexplored section of the Mel geography. It is a jerky, random inspection, but it hits each location. Once.

At the completion of his tour of the historic sites, Rodrigo looks up into her eyes.

And faints. Again. This time hitting his head on a neighboring bar stool.

"The darling man, overcome with emotion. Marty, Shirley, let's get him to my dressing room quickly! This gallant gentleman needs the comforting hand of love that only I can offer. Quick, before he comes to! I must change to something more appropriate, something conducive to convalescence. I know! I have it! I still have my nurse's uniform from Let's Play Doctor Night. What could be more appropriate? Shirley, baby, did I loan you my stethoscope?"

Voter's cards announcing an upcoming election, addressed to Registered Voters LM & FT Jeansonne, were forwarded from Carondelet street to the Toulouse street house only two weeks after Mutt and Fred moved in. LM & FT were informed that they had moved from City Council District B to District C. The irregular forwarding courtesy of the Jeansonne's old neighborhood postman. Mutt made the necessary changes in their permanent address on the cards and mailed them back to the Registrar.

LM & FT were now in residence at their home, 921 Toulouse street, New Orleans LA 70112, US of A.

The sale had all been too easy. Noonie set the price at five dollars in quarters, a carton of Marlboro filter 100s and a fifty-pound bag of duck food. She added the stipulation that she and Virginia could stay there, too, when they felt the need. Mutt encouraged them to stay permanently. He had begun to develop a long-starved taste for company. The lawyer who closed the deal called it a donation rather than a purchase, but for a Street the price was considered substantial and real.

Mutt went so far as to assert that he wanted to make the house a rallying point where he could start to organize shelter for the Street community. His description of the concept sounded very much like the voice and manner of Chris Reed. But the idea was immediately accepted by everyone because it came from Mutt.

A mission. They would have a mission in life. Wow. And toilets.

Mel loaned him the money for renovation. Ms LaGrande's loan was guaranteed by the VA, due to persistent and resolute pressure from Chris Reed. ADA Reed broke through innumerable federal paperwork blockades, pushing Mutt's loan through the bureaucracy by the sheer strength of her will. It was the first time she actually felt good flexing a political muscle. She was encouraged, renewed. Smiled at Judge Cannalo after only three hours of sleep.

Mel had an informal rider to her loan. She asked that Rodrigo could stay in the house, too. Mutt was delighted. He had already intended to ask his shoeless companion to move into Toulouse street.

Rodrigo and Mutt quickly became family. The two men organized a temp work force for doing the Toulouse renovation themselves, paying the workers wages in cash, plus two meals a day and a cheap but clean Rampart street boarding house room during construction. The work force numbered fifty, including kids, after only a week.

An interesting side product of the acquisition of the house, the title search documenting of the loan and the renovation permits, was the discovery of Noonie's last name. Which was found to be Robichaux. Noonie said she thought that alone was an adequate purchase price for the building. She began introducing herself to passers-by on the street just so she could use her last name. She even encouraged Virginia the Bead Lady to start using a surname. However, Noonie soundly rejected Virginia Bead, Virginia's first attempt at two names, as much too Norm. Noonie said it sounded like a low-tar cigarette. Virginia vowed to find a suitable nom de rue.

There was squabbling and bickering in the first weeks at Toulouse, but the antagonists always made up quickly. Very few Streets had lived in proximity to other people   especially the same people   for more than a few nights in a row. So there were territorial battles. There were battles over unique personal habits. By mutual agreement masturbation became more of a private ritual for those who practiced it.

Problems continued. Things weren't perfect. But they were a helluva lot better than being on the Street.

It was a remarkable time for everyone, but Virginia and Noonie underwent a particularly unbelievable transformation in their new collaboration as roommates. They commandeered a second-floor balcony room as their headquarters and took personal charge of its restoration. Their cleaning and painting of that room was highly uncharacteristic of their own physical states just a few weeks earlier. The room was pristine, the colors cheerful.

It did take time, however, to convince Virginia that she should use the indoor facilities instead of squatting in the small courtyard alongside Fred.

Their efforts included renovating themselves, too. They began to bathe. Their posture improved. They each did their best to make Mutt proud. The F-word became part of a foreign language, and was seldom translated. Some members of the opposite sex began to take second looks. A temp work carpenter, resettled from Minnesota, asked Virginia to dinner at the Good Shepherd Soup Kitchen. She was delighted with the attention though the man was no Mutt Jeansonne. Virginia gave the carpenter a bead free of charge.

Noonie had only one relapse. When she noticed she had not smoked in a week. Ellis had shredded all her butts to build a properly-charcoal-filtered nest of the finest blend of Turkish and domestic tobaccos. The new Ms Robichaux ran shrieking through the house for the better part of an hour in nicotine withdrawal. Then forgot what she was upset about and returned to painting.

There were occasional bursts of chaos and despair. Each new person entering the extended family went through a period of trauma and distrust. But somehow the idyllic home-making machine chugged forward. Fragile. Prepared to explode at any minute. But surviving somehow. Mutt almost forgot about the Box under the Expressway.

It was indeed a remarkable time, for many people.

Robert H Markham is coated in a mud of sweat and dust. It does not matter to him. Markham, an associate at the prestigious law firm McFarland Borden and Dubney, is a man on the rise. He knows there are fifty-three other associate partners in the firm, scattered at desks in well-paneled offices in Washington DC, Houston, and the firm's main branch in New Orleans. But he is one of the few given sensitive assignments by the senior partners. As a result, Markham is allowed use of a company cellular phone, billable to clients at double actual airtime cost. That cost, of course is added to Markham's own time, which is billed by the quarter-hour at a reasonable hourly scale of $275.   He is, after all, a junior member of the firm.

Markham is currently assigned to a special in-house project. Consequently, his cellular time is charged off as a business expense, and deducted from taxes. For such high-risk low-profile use, he has been given a decidedly out-of-date Motorola. The phone sputters as it makes its connection.

"Mr Borden? Markham here."

"Markham. Excellent. What... word... our project?" crackles the voice of DAR Borden, senior partner, from the luxurious confines of his office.

Markham looks about him as he stands in the dust and heat of the Expressway tract. "Our project." He does not know the point of what he is actually doing. The property, the squalor surrounding an elevated roadway, was a miserable scene, and as far removed from the comforts of a law practice as he could imagine. He wondered if this was really the path to a full partnership.

"Yes, Markham? Yes? Markham!" Borden is yelling into his phone.

Markham regroups his thoughts. "Bad connection, sir. The surveyors have completed their work here at the Expressway tract. I understand you were out on the site recently yourself."

"Yes. There were still hobos about," replies Borden. "Don't know how often I want to do that again. That's why you're there."

"Yes, sir. I can understand that. Those bums are a hazard to life and limb. No one here now, though, except our people. The final measurements were recorded about 1pm, and the crew wrapped up all the peripheral tasks shortly after. We should get a print-out within the next two weeks. I can have my notes back in the office for you in about an hour."

"Good work, Robert. Good. Robert? Hold just a moment."

Borden presses the red hold button on his six-line phone. He carefully unbuttons the vest of his YSL Continental Cut suit. In spite of the air-conditioning, he is still sweating from his earlier exertions. He knows it's stupid to wear his thousand-dollar wool suit to look at a filthy piece of land, but he hates changing clothes in the middle of the day.

Besides, he will be able to buy lots more suits if this deal comes through. DAR Borden, Esq, thinks he might even ignore possible controversy and buy something in blue. He has always enjoyed being at the forefront of fashion.

It is about time for lunch, isn't it?

Markham is still holding when he hears the click and then the dial tone. His boss had forgotten him again.

Probably better that way, just drifting away in hold-button limbo. Better than having the old bastard come up with one more of these wretched field assignments. Borden and that drunk Dubney spend most of their days in restaurants. Client meetings. Right.

That night Donald Markham crawls quietly into his narrow bed after an additional six grueling hours at the office. The old man was all over him when he returned. Markham has no idea why the firm is so anxious to develop this Expressway property. Markham has logged thirty-five billable hours this week alone on the project.

And he can't imagine why the whole thing is so hush-hush.

Her night of work also finished, Christine Reed happily cruises the comforts of sleep. She dreams a large scrub pasture, just like the one fronting her parents' house back in Winnfield. She stands on a dramatic high crest, familiar and unfamiliar. Body wrapped in a thick white canvas sheet, the breeze cold around her shoulders and ankles.

Very Wuthering Heights, she thinks.

She wiggles red-nailed toes in a tuft of winter grass. The bare soles of her feet record bright green hieroglyphs from the plant world.

She looks away from the family house. Her eyes see hills for a change. The hills singing rolling scales through the land. Landscape melodies running to the horizon.

Change. Perspective. That's what hills are good for.

The thought makes her sleepself homesick for Northern Louisiana.

This is a dream, she thinks, imposing order on her sleep. *It's summer, but it's freezing cold here. I've left the AC set too low again. That's it. I am really in New Orleans. I am not really here. No hills in New Orleans. New Orleans ten feet below sea level. Only stinking, crusted flat bottomland and those levees. Around and around.*

But she knows that three hundred miles north, low palmettos and thorn bushes fight pine trees for existence up and down actual hillsides. Gullies of intruding swamp are cleared. Have become grazing land fertilized by the dung of white Charolais cattle. The handful of French animals were one of her daddy's more successful experiments. That, and changing his staple crop from cotton to government-subsidized soybeans.

There's Daddy, out there in just his shirtsleeves, walking west in the pasture. Around that big mean-looking bull, like the animal doesn't even matter. Just like him. She was worried about her Daddy. She loved the crotchety old bastard, was devoted to him even when she was a baby. But now Daddy was getting further away from her.

Is *he angry with me again? Lord! What can I have done now? Maybe I should call him? It's getting late. The sunlight will be gone any minute now. Is he following the sun? Just walking into it? He'd do that just to spite me. Maybe. Daddy's sense of direction is not so good at night. He might not be able to find his way back to the house. Cold now. It's really cold. Getting dark so quickly. And now... where is he? Daddy? Where...*

Awakening with a sense of loss. Rubbing eyes. Searching for slippers. Turning the central air off.

Her dream narrative continues over her waking movements, slowly diminishing as she comes to her senses: ...freezing in here. Where's my robe? This machine's got me living winter all year round. She senses something passing her.

She turns.

Daddy. Daddy...

She is awake, standing in her own kitchen.

She looks at the clock. Ten after three in the afternoon. Due in a few hours back at work. Shaking with the cold and covered in chillbumps, but she was still living in hell.

Rodrigo, when not drawing elaborate carpentry plans or rolling on exterior paint   the Vieux Carré Heritage Commission had objected only mildly to the historically-questionable chartreuse tint   was papering an entire upstairs hallway with dissected All-Fact pages. His efforts led to a much more distinctive educational environment than even he had expected. It seems that a few of the men and women of the temp force were also fathers and mothers. There were, consequently, eight children attached to the merry work crew. Four kids were too young to go to school. But, as a result of Rodrigo's creative imagery, the children spent much of their time reading the hall walls. Absorbing everything.

One effect of this intellectual stimulation had rapidly surfaced   the children loved using their newly-discovered words as much as possible. When they had yet to assimilate a particular encyclopedic entry's meaning, they simply used the prime words as expletives. Rodrigo had himself heard a four-year-old girl yell "Penumbra!" upon accidentally stubbing her right big toe. He was gratified.

As a matter of fact, Rodrigo was stimulated. A surplus of creative energy, and the temporary cessation of visits to his Church, led him to start carving. Using a bent soup spoon, Rodrigo pulled animate shapes from the large pieces of scrap plaster that had been tossed in the patio. This particular set of critics, the work crew, was unable to come up with names for the forms. But by unanimous vote, the pieces were deemed decorative and thought-provoking enough to be mounted in the corners of the common rooms. The downstairs already had an even dozen plaster sculptures in place.

The first six weeks of construction brought triple that number of visits from the consummate Miss LaGrande. Rodrigo was finally able to remain conscious for longer periods of times in Mel's presence. The occasional relapse was usually predicated by a particularly provocative outfit or pose on Mel's part. She took an enthusiastic delight in reviving him. This phenomenon began to develop a reverse feedback effect, though. Mel had on two occasions rushed home to change when new wardrobe items failed to produce one of Rodrigo's fits.

There was only one real complication in the renovation of the Robichaux House. It wasn't totally unexpected. Mutt had been forced to hire plumbers from outside his immediate circle of friends when it became apparent that his plumbing designs were far too complex for amateurs to handle. It was those seven toilets that pushed the project to the limit.

As the work progressed, the Street community gathered in ever larger numbers around the Robichaux House. Mutt allowed anyone who wished to list 921 Toulouse as their permanent address and gather mail there. Whether or not they were in the house constantly. His one requirement was that all new residents register to vote.

Nine weeks after moving in and hammering the first nail, the work was complete. There were 226 permanent residents, only five of whom resided regularly on the premises. One of the five was a dog.

Christine Reed was not idle during this period of change.

She had become acknowledged as the spokesperson for Mutt's project. And if she was not actually their spokesperson, she was at least the "leading authority" on New Orleans' Street people. It hadn't taken long for Mutt to get tired of the limelight, or for the media to run out of new angles on homeless house work. Mutt was glad to go along with Reed's suggestion that she handle the press. And the press, they were very happy to relinquish access to the slightly unclean-smelling hobo. Who couldn't get out a complete sentence without a reference to his or his dog's digestive tracts.

In return they got an articulate Anglo Norm. A female Assistant District Attorney. Once the Prosecutor of the common man, and now his Defender, Reed was endowed with impeccable Southern breeding   even though it was from north Louisiana   plus a knowledge of both the law and politics. And good-looking? The camera just ate up those dimples. Reed was available to the media for every possible micro-second of exposure. Mutt had given her a start at building the credibility she needed to move the project forward. She capitalized on the opening without hesitation, and built on it tenaciously.

She slept little, called in sick to Night Court often, lived on her phone.

Everyone was happy. Mutt wasn't even aware that Reed had begun ever-less-subtle suggestions to the press that Mr Mutt Jeansonne, "a true man of the people," was on his way to public office. And that she, as "a concerned representative of the disenfranchised and disenchanted populace of New Orleans' Council District C," would help coordinate Mr Jeansonne's efforts to organize those constituents. In her press sheets she was "aiding a champion of the downtrodden, as he struggles to bring Government back to the people." Her quotes and catch-phrases were well-received and strongly circulated.

In private, these were of course the same people she found unbearably odious. Except for Mutt. She still wasn't sure what she felt for Mutt, and she wasn't sure she wanted to know.

But Mutt Jeansonne had got her what she wanted, in many ways. The DA had pulled her off Night Court within three weeks and reassigned her to his office as a Special Liaison.

Five days later District Attorney Bronner had called her Daddy, howling.

"Goddamn, Leonard, what have I let you talk me into? That daughter of yours has got herself showing up on the tube more than I have! I had her down in Night Court learning the ropes just fine, and then all of a sudden there she is on the goddamn TV! I had to bring her up here to my office just to keep an eye on her. Christamighty, what is a gorgeous young white woman like that doing, hanging out with every degenerate and off-the-wall ethnic and homeless group in New Orleans? And then they all turnin' out to be voters, mind you..."

"Jus' a second there, Archibald. You jus' said it," Leonard Reed interrupted. He handled politicos in his "country-boy" mode. "That l'il girl is jus' kickin' yo ass where it needs ta git kicked. If you don't start courtin' those goddamn 'ethnic groups' soon, boy   and courtin' 'em big time, too   your sweet ass will be out pumpin' diesel fuel into tractors on Airline Hi-way come next election. You better be lettin' that girl have her head, boy. She's got plenty sense and you damn well know she's doin' you a whole lotta good."

The DA hesitated. "Lenny, gimme a fuckin' break. I'm handling a parish with a seventy-two-percent black majority, another nine-percent Asian and Hispanic. On top of that I get stuck with a well-organized fe-male population out to get Equal and then some. Hell, I ain't even got a goddamn WASP up here other than me   and your daughter, of course   but there ain't nothing says I gotta put on the velvet gloves to handle these fly-bait Street people and their panty-waist deviate buddies. Goddamn, Leonard, think about it! Just doin' what they do every day is against the law! This is worse than the friggin' outer space nuts!" he yelled into the phone.

"Boy, you better be glad I ain't recordin' this one. Your time in Public Office would be over right now."

Leonard Reed's voice mellowed. The hard-bitten "country" tone was diluted. It was a family characteristic. Soothe them before you cut their throats. It was part of the drill. Bronner was forgetting his education. Reed had no qualms about giving his friend a refresher course.

He began again, "Arch, you got a loose town there, much looser than any of these ass-tight Baptist revival camps I gotta deal with up here in North Louisiana. These folks know how to take the 'fun' out of 'fundamentalist'. And you down there in Sin City, bitchin' 'bout a few kinky constituents. Son, you a little old to be forgettin' how to play the game."

"But...," the DA sputtered.

Reed cleared his throat deliberately and then resumed talking at an even slower rate.

"So you just ride loose with it. Only one way to deal with a wild pony. You been out of Winnfield so long you don't remember how to work a herd? The Longs, those boys, they knew how to handle it. Think about it, son. All you got to do is just stay on its back and hang loose 'til that wild pony gets tired. And she will get tired. Huey and Earl and Russell Long each proved it in his own way. That's all I got to say."

"Alright. I'll wait. I'll wait." Bronner changed his tone. He could indeed play this game, too. "Say, Leonard, one more thing..." There was an overlong pause before he said: "Leonard, what you think chances are that the Governor is gonna approve my emergency budget request before the next legislative session?"

Reed let seconds tick by as he flashed through his mental file on the matter. He had no immediate background for an opinion. But that didn't mean he couldn't have one.

"We'll see, good buddy, we'll see. Governor's kinda tight to his chest with his cards these days. Got an idea, though."

The DA sighed. Reed's ideas always cost him something, but he had known that when he asked.

"Did you know my baby Chris had her debutante comin'-out party with the Governor's daughter Jill?" Reed continued. "They been best a' buddies since grammar school, when the Governor was just one more country boy from Monroe. Chris and Jill still keep in touch, even though Jill's living in the Governor's Mansion in Baton Rouge. You might want ta ask Chris ta see if she can git an inside line on what's happenin' up in the Capitol. I bet you dollars to doughnuts Jill knows everything her daddy's got on his mind. Jus' like my girl does about me. Chris'll git a line on it for you. Girl gonna save your ass yet, Bronner."

"Jesus, Leonard, it ain't my ass I'm worried about," the District Attorney moaned.

The New Orleans City Planning Commission ruled in November that the nearly three hundred people listing 921 Toulouse street as their permanent residence were in no violation of city zoning laws. Since less than half a dozen were in residence at any one time.

The Registrar of Voters was required to accept the multiple new voter registrations from that address, as they were in compliance with City zoning and housing codes. Among the 248 residents of voting age, registration was one hundred percent.

The new voters' first eligible election was to come up on Wednesday, March 4. Three City Council seats were up for grabs, including the one that included the Vieux Carré, District C.

Mutt did not notice that March the fourth of the following year was Ash Wednesday, the day after Mardi Gras. Even if he had noticed, religious holidays wouldn't have seemed important at the time.

The location of Easter sets the first four months of the Roman Catholic religious calendar in place. But Easter tends to wander around a bit, determined by as arcane and convoluted a system as any devised by man.

It sounds simple at first: Easter is the first Sunday after the Pascal full moon. But the Pascal full moon does not necessarily match the astronomical full moon. That would be much too simple. There is a numerical formula.

First, the year is divided by 19. Then 1 is added to the remainder, and that sum number is applied to a rather obscure numerical table.

If the Pascal full moon hits on a Sunday, Easter moves to the next Sunday. Real simple. Just like religion.

The people of New Orleans let it slide.

Because forty-one days   not counting Sundays before the Resurrection celebration that defines Christianity comes one of the more pagan bacchanals to survive into the twentieth century. This year Mardi Gras would preface the creation of a new era of Government in this most religiously ambiguous of cities.

Lordy.

Midnight. L Mutt Jeansonne, property owner, breathes quietly in and out. Rhythmic strobes from headlights flash through the railings overhead. In front of Mutt's face, the vapor that was his breath pulses with the flickers. Mutt stands still, instinctively becoming part of the pattern of the oil-stained concrete pillars surrounding him. Automobiles travel over him without noting his existence. He absorbs the echoes of their internal combustion. He listens to them.

Mutt cannot bring himself to look at his old friends. His two-dimensional friends. The tall fields of brilliant images towering over him. Visible in the flickering blue of electrified fluorescent gases. Mutt speaks toward the ground. He cannot raise his eyes.

I remember even in the Boy Home, when I was a little cooter, I was always talking to all the statues in the chapel. They was nice folks, and all of them was smiling sweet and peaceful. Well, except that Jesus man. He was stuck up on the wall, looking pitiful. I guess so, what with nails in his hands and stickers on his head and blood running all over him. Not a nice thing for a boy to see. Don't know why they're putting stuff like that in a place where they bring they children. So anyway me I just stuck to the statues that look like they had something nice to say.

I talk to them and listen. Mostly it's real quiet. I can barely hear the rest of them boys playing outside. But I sit there, and after a while I start to feel better about whatever was bothering me   usually not getting picked for a game or something. All of a sudden I just feel better and get up and go about my business. Like somebody told me something good, or give me a soft drink.

You folks under here have been mighty fine friends. I know you ain't no saints, but you done your best, and godknows every little bit helps. I'm going along now, and probably won't be back here for a bit, but I'll try and visit, yes I will.

We'll talk again, I know that for a fact.

He has to leave. Mutt discovers that he is afraid of his old friends now. He is afraid they might pull him back in. Back into the world he had inhabited only a few months earlier. He is afraid that this new dream world will disappear, and he will wake up in the Box, the wild dream ride over. All this new life only the result of a badly dented can of expired Beany Weenies. Didn't happen. He doesn't know if he could survive that loss. He has tasted what it is like to be alive. He has seen what it is like to be accepted as a Norm. He can't go back. That much he knows is true: he cannot go back.

But he has lived here so long. He has drawn strength, has drawn purpose from this spot. He has survived because of a place.

Then a freak accident, a one-in-a-million combination of time and circumstance had thrown the switch. All of a sudden he can see, hear, taste, smell. Feel. Himself, he can do all those things himself.

Second-hand experience is one thing. First-hand experience is life. He knows that now.

Mutt Jeansonne turns his back on his old home and walks out from under the Ponchartrain Expressway. He intends to keep going forward until he stops. He intends to put every bit of energy he has into a Life, half of which had already slipped by him, unnoticed. Maybe, as he has time, he will remember more of the past. Reconstruct himself. Make himself whole.

Mow his own grass.

Melodie LaGrande walks out directly onto the third floor of Rockfield's.

She had excitedly whisked in the main entrance, inspected the directory and hopped in the elevator. She had punched the button to the floor suggested as holding both subtle clothing for the society set, and high fashion shoes.

Mel has a special occasion coming up, and she wants something to perfectly complement the moment. She does not care about cost. Only the best will do, and Rockfield's, Rockfield's is the place. Or so she has heard.

This is her first visit.

As the elevator door opens, Mel looks about. Shoes are not immediately apparent. She sees a well-dressed, though quite old, woman with the gold-plated tag of a Rockfield's sales clerk. Standing just across the floor. The woman is straightening a display of lingerie, and speaking to each piece of clothing as she places it back in its place. Mel ignores this sign. She walks directly up to Mrs Cleona Louise Bagatelle.

"Excuse me, dearie, but where oh where is your shoe department? I've ruined a favorite pair recently, and I am in desperate need of something really really hot. Oh darling, it must be something virtually dripping with sex," says Mel, innocently enough.

Mrs Bagatelle does not immediately raise her head. She very deliberately finishes folding the sea-green silk camisole, on sale for $59.95 including matching tap pants. There is a slight sweat stain on the back, due to an overexcited and overly-large customer trying on the size six garment. Mrs Bagatelle is not pleased with marking her quality goods down. She takes her time, head averted, completing her task exactly as she had planned, in due course.

It is so frustrating at times, keeping order.

Never mind the waste, it's the possibility that chaos can overcome a person at any moment. Chaos. In even the most stable environment.

I WILL keep order on Three. It is my calling.

She is comforted with her litany, and finishes nicely. Then, thinking that this voice must indeed be another itinerant housewife from the back streets of Plain Dealing, Louisiana, she looks up to confront the wanton intruder. Who dares come into her kingdom uninvited.

Six feet tall, flaming red hair, mammoth breasts, spandex clothing.

"Holy Jesus Mary and Joseph!" Cleona Louise Bagatelle cries. "The deviate from the newspaper!"

Leonard Reed takes one last look at the report on his desk, just faxed to him from New Orleans. He had spent a thousand dollars on a private detective, a highly recommended New Orleans Police Department sergeant who worked off-duty on special "political" assignments. These two pages were the result of his thousand dollars. A page and a half of typing. Came out to about five dollars a word.

His contact said the investigator ran into some difficulties.

Pay him a thousand dollars and all he gives me is a page and a half. That boy hasn't even seen the start of the grief I'm going to give him.

But the report   it was all too weird. Jeansonne sits in an orphanage for almost half of his life, has a few months in the military, then disappears for the better part of twenty years. Somehow surviving, never leaving New Orleans, but not a part of the system either. Until he decides to start voting. Then here he is again. Almost two decades, living right under the Government's nose without leaving a trace.

BAM, right back again. Right out in front.
Right into my daughter's life.

Detective Sergeant Desmond Joe Joe, NOPD, had almost recovered from the Jeansonne investigation, though the doctors told him he should apply for an additional two weeks' sick leave.   It had taken the emergency room technicians over sixteen hours to remove what they later identified as sixty-four pounds and five ounces of brown plastic wrapping tape. His skin had broken out in large ascending mounds of scarlet carbuncles where the glue from the tape had come in contact with his body. Only his nose had been left uncovered. The City doctor told him that he should be very glad that his Police Department health insurance covered him off-duty and in plain clothes. The Sergeant was in for an expensive recovery.

Desmond Joe Joe was a large man, weighing in at almost three hundred pounds. He was not quite six feet tall, but had wide shoulders and a strong jawline. He hadn't really wanted to be a policeman, but he was third generation NOPD. His grandfather was still alive and living on his cop pension. His father Papa Joe was almost to retirement himself, waiting out his twenty-fifth year safely, sitting pretty in the Fifth Precinct as a dispatcher. Desmond Joe Joe wanted to be an actor. He still did summer theatre and auditioned for bit parts in movies whenever they came to town. He had been Cop #1 in a feature-length Hollywood film the past January, and a month ago had acted as Detective in Brown Suit for a TV movie-of-the-week. Brown Suit had a speaking role: "That's enough now. Let's go downtown." Soon he would get a SAG card. Maybe his Dad wouldn't mind so much if he quit the force then. If he was a Hollywood star.

In the meantime, he made a job he hated more tolerable by trying out different roles every time he made a collar.

It had seemed like such an easy assignment. He was an intelligent man, moonlighting half a dozen "sensitive" jobs every month to supplement his meager sergeant's salary. A discredited ex-Deputy Superintendent had offered him a grand less twenty-five percent   from an anonymous upstate bigshot just to find out if some goon Streetperson had any skeletons in his closet. Nothing to it. They gave him the cash up front. Seven hundred and fifty bucks. *Piece of cake.*

The computer check should have given him a clue that something was screwy. Most of the files on Jeansonne LM were deleted. By the authority of Gladstone CR. Joe had even followed up on that. Turned out Gladstone was some ancient downtown Election Commissioner who had taken it upon himself to clean up his precinct's files. Another nobody with nothing to do. Except make life miserable for professionals. Using the most modern equipment available, the old geezer had taken out almost everything on Jeansonne prior to his last seven years of voting. And in the process accidentally deleted ALL individual files from JEB to JOA. The Registrar told Sergeant Joe that the records of over a hundred voters had disappeared in a shower of sparkling electrons.

Detective Sergeant Desmond Joe Joe had checked the news accounts, sorted out all the bogus space-invaders tabloid hype. Even though he thought the pictures of Jeansonne's dog Fred looked pretty otherworldly. Then set out to interview a few of the losers who hung out with this character.

The crazy Paki at the Can-Can-Do Lounge wouldn't let him in the club without a search warrant, so interviewing the flip-flop *nuevobimbo* that Jeansonne had sprung from jail got a little harder than he had planned. That should have been sign number two. But he figured he had that taken care of when he got her license number and a description of her car. He knew she lived a distance from the Quarter, and didn't figure her for the sort who puts up with New Orleans cab drivers. So he checked out the neighborhood. Sure enough, there it was, sitting on the block right behind the club, on Dauphine street. He knew she was on the day shift.

Desmond Joe Joe decided on his character. He shrugged his shoulders and cleared his throat. Spat on the sidewalk. He sat down on the hood of the red Studebaker, popping in a large dent with his over-large derrière.

Just a matter of time before the woman walks right into my arms.

Detective Sergeant Desmond Joe Joe was indeed still sitting on Mel's car when she rounded the corner an hour later. He made no attempt to get up, though the dent in her hood had greatly increased in size during his wait. The Sergeant felt no guilt about the damage. It was totally in character.

The price you gotta pay, babe, for not being there for the Joe when he needs ya.

"What are you doing to my car, you fat imbecile!" shrieked Melodie when she saw the man and her car.

"Say, babe, it's Sergeant Imbecile to you," he said, flipping out his badge. He loved playing the bad cop game. "Just wanted to ask you a few questions about a friend of yours, and your boss wouldn't let me see you. So I had to wait here. Guess I gotta lose a little weight, huh?" Joe asked as he got up. The rounded red crater he left in the Studebaker was two feet across and a good six inches deep.

"You idiot! This car is priceless! Look at what you've done!" Mel howled, running her hands across the damage. "You'll pay for this! You will. Let me see that badge number again! Now!" Melodie started grabbing for his ID. She had dealt with cops before.

"Hey, ease up, babe! Hey, get the hell back!" Joe swung a quick backhand across Mel's cheek, knocking her backwards across the sidewalk.

Oh shit.

She crashed into the building on the other side and fell to her knees, twisting an ankle and breaking off a five-inch spike as she fell.

"You hateful hateful man! What is wrong with you?"

Don't lose it. This could be the test that gets you a real part.

"OK," said Joe. He pulled a small electric taser out of his pocket, held it up in plain view and turned it on. The taser made a high-pitched hum. Joe smiled when he saw she recognized the device. He took a step toward Melodie. "Good. You see what can happen here, don't you? I've had enough of this bullshit. You've taken up too much of my time already. So, this is the way it works, Miz LaGrande. I ask a question and you answer. Or, you get a little surprise from my buddy here."

"I'll have you arrested!" she yelled at him.

"On what charges, babe? You got no witnesses. It's the word of a sex-change stripper against that of a decorated veteran cop."

Ooohh, that was good. That really sounded damn good.

"So you tell me about this Mutt Jeansonne character. Now."

Joe took a second step toward her.

"I knew I'd have to give you a little taste before you opened up to the Joe." He stepped forward, taser pointed toward her chest.

Mel shrank back against the wall. "You are not real. This is not happening."

"You bet it is, babe. I..."

That's where it had happened. All of a sudden Joe couldn't move his arms. He was being spun around and around. His eyes were covered. He grew dizzy, as what must have been dozens of hands kept twisting him into a tighter and tighter knot. Animal sounds filled his head. His limbs grew heavier and heavier. He was sure he had been drugged.

The night patrolman at the riverfront park had found him, a four hundred pound mottled-brown cocoon making moaning noises. The plastic tape coating his body was covered with pictures torn from some cryptic text. The lab guys had gone over dozens of pictures of fingians and pilchards, tragacanths and David's root. No prints in the white paste adhesive, but some sort of bird-foot impression in a number of locations. They had judged it the leavings of a small Canadian goose.

"Been fooling with the hoodoos, have you, Sarge?" said the Lab Chief as he watched. The emergency room intern was finally unwrapping Joe's eyes in the fourth hour of the process. Joe's eyebrows had come off with the tape. "Maybe you pissed off the outer space freaks? Man in your position ought to know better. You see what they got written on you? The pictures they had stuck all over the tape? Serious stuff. You better be watching yourself, son. Those folks got some power. Oh, by the way, your Papa's here. He'll know what to do."

Papa Joe Joe was, after all his years on the force, a firm believer in New Orleans mojo. He made his son carry a bag of dried chicken gizzards and garfish teeth in his pants pocket from that day forward. Dark Manuel at the Broad Street Botanica had told him that the spirit bag would keep everything away. Even the aliens. And the geese.

Leonard Reed folds the report, puts it in the center drawer of his desk.

Nothing there.

He hadn't believed that homeless people really existed, could continue to live outside the realm of Government. Outside all controls and safety systems. Now he has proof in black and white. For most of his life, Jeansonne only surfaced when he accidentally brushed into authority. Otherwise, he was invisible. Hidden under the surface of society. His DA buddy

Archie Bronner had told him the city was full of them. Thousands of people living outside the system. With their own set of rules. Or maybe none at all.

No wonder I hate New Orleans, he thought.

Melodie acquired a pair of shoes that were more than suitable for the occasion at a designer outlet cut-price shoppe on Chartres street. They loved her there. She had been given an additional third off the already discounted footwear, and been treated as a celebrity. An autographed five-by-seven glossy of Melodie LaGrande, customer and exotic entertainer, was now on display in the decorative accessories case at Wanda's Worship- My-Heels shoe emporium.

Mel has vowed she will never set foot on the Rockfield's side of Canal street again. In the meantime, she focuses in on the matter at hand.

That makes her quite happy.

The dining room in Faubourg St John shivers with candlelight. Mel has spent well over an hour arranging the two place settings of her mother's china and crystal on the thick mahogany table. She has removed all the table's leaves, so that the two diners will be knee-to-knee as they sit facing each other.

Miss LaGrande's stated opinion is that too much subtlety can ruin any experience.

For instance, since her legendary incarceration she has instituted a new "Prisoner of Love" routine to capitalize on her notoriety. She had refused Abu's request to costume in a totally-sequined outfit of shining black and white stripes. Melodie believed that the green hospital gown she wore during her trial made the act much more real and exciting for her audiences.

This did not, however, preclude her carrying onstage a small prop. Her specially-made battery-operated & neon-lighted judge's gavel accented the bumps and punctuated the grinds right to the music. Metaphor could just go so far, especially in art.

Rodrigo's timely arrival at seven tonight is doubtful, due to his dependence on public transportation. He had refused Mel's offer to pick him up. Had even declined the cab she had suggested she would send for him. He preferred the more spacious confines of the City's RTA buses. One of which would let him out only a half block from the LaGrande domicile.

"He will be fine. The darling Rodrigo can take care of himself," Melodie assures her own self. Talking aloud as she bustles nervously through the house. Talking helps calm her nerves.

"The sweet boy has been so much more understandable this last month. Why, I almost get what he's saying, most of the time. I don't care, though. I don't care one bit. Anything he says is so mysterious, so exotic, so erotic!"

The statuesque hostess suddenly does a perfect spin on the five-inch metallic heel of her gold-strapped sandal. Hand on hip, facing in the direction from which she had just come, she scolds with grace.

"Why, Lil Miz Melodie LaGrande! Don't tell me you're falling head over heels for some scruffy unemployed Mystic Man from way Up North!"

For the moment Melodie is playing all the parts in tonight's feature presentation. She pivots again.

"Why, yes, Dorothy Mae! It just so happens I believe this gentleman to be of such genuine and true character that I wouldn't have any other, no matter the fortune!"

There is a brief intermission for soul-searching.

"Lordy, what am I saying? What have I got in mind for this poor boy? He already knows most of my history, and yet he's still my ever-faithful and caring suitor. But he has no idea that the notorious Melodie LaGrande is as much a virgin in one way as her predecessor George Hotard was a debaucher in all others. My Rodrigo cares only about the me that is here now. What more could a girl want?

"We know, don't we?"

Miss LaGrande's eyes search the textured ceiling beams for affirmation.

"Is he the one, Mother dear? My first as a woman? Is he to be the father of our child? Lili! Freddy!

"Someone send me a sign!

"Oh dear, is that my etoufee burning?"

Christine Reed is making her point.

"So, Mr Markham   Robert   Bob   I feel it almost a certainty that with the smallest amount of push, the Council District C could easily drop right into the hands of someone who could finally unite all of the numerous, diverse interest groups of the French Quarter, Treme, the Faubourg Marigny & Bywater."

They sit in Markham's office on the 32d floor of Place St Louis. The south side of the firm's three floors of suites offers sweeping views of the Mississippi River and the western edge of the French Quarter.

Big money. The power source. Daddy was right again.

She continues to speak, inspired by proximity to her Grail.

"The 'someone' who'll benefit from 'the push' has to be a person who is seen by all those groups as representative of their own struggles. Someone who has suffered at the hands of the current establishment and still triumphed. I've got the 'someone.' His name is Mutt Jeansonne. The 'push' is what I need from McFarland Borden and Dubney. We're talking money, Bob. Substantial campaign contributions, all totally legitimate, that will both underwrite the cost of getting the campaign moving and, on a longer term basis, allow me personally to devote my time to the election effort. We both know that influence over a seat on the Council will repay your firm a hundred times over any paltry financial assistance you might offer. That is a given. So. McFarland Borden and Dubney will contribute to the Jeansonne campaign. It is only the amounts and payment schedule that I am here to discuss."

"Miss Reed," Markham begins.

"Chris."

"Chris."

Markham tries to concentrate on shuffling unrelated papers on his desk. Tries not to let his gaze linger too long on the body of the young woman in front of him. It is difficult, in spite of the strictly-business linen suit. If he raises his field of vision, she will lock him up with those tractor-beam eyes. Eyes with that "You want it but you can't have it, yet" stare built right in.

God, she makes me nervous.

Markham can't decide if he is angry or glad that he has taken this meeting.

That's a laugh.

What's the use in thinking "angry or glad"? It's undoubtedly her old man   some redneck politico from upstate   who has set the whole thing up through Donald Allen

Rothwell Borden, Esq. DAR. Senior Partner. I was offered no choice but to take the meeting.

Here she is   the hot dish I've been seeing on every news broadcast for the last two months. The female Assistant District Attorney brought to vivid life and a rousing set of dimensions.

Her mouth looks just as delectable as it does on the Sony.

Markham, deaf to what is being said in his office, is increasingly obsessed with his burgeoning sex fantasies. They have long since moved into business hours.

This is a controllable situation   I know why it is happening. Been in this all-good-ole-boy firm a bit too long. Nothing happening on the home front. The wife playing house, a nine-year-old rotten-as-hell kid trying to destroy it. My own fifty-year-old alcoholic stepmother living in the upstairs guest room.

Sandra Lou Rubens Markham. Crazy as hell. Another ball-and-chain around my neck. But if she runs off to the Quarter again I can have her committed. Except that putting her in a Home will cost even more. The woman drives Dad to an early grave, and now I've got her. Forever.

There is no escape.

The condo costs three grand a month. Before utilities.

The little woman grabs another two Gs house money every thirty days.

And me, I feel lucky if I get sex with her every six months.

Sex.

Markham turns his head and frowns deeply. He is still daydreaming, but he hears something being said at his desk.

"Please. Before you continue, please... Chris," Robert H Markham, Esq, declares aloud. "What was that you just said? Would you mind telling me again? You must excuse me. I am having trouble examining all the implications of this very ambitious plan you've been describing."

He looks up. She gets his eyes. He is caught.

"Bob, I think we both know that you have been examining my implications in great detail while I   I have been sitting here banging my chops trying to explain a strategic consolidation of special interest groups that is going to affect the political structure of this City for the next decade. An action that will shift a lot of power very quickly. This firm stands to make a great deal out of a power base on the Council, and I can deliver that base.

"So, let's cut the shit, shall we? We both know that I am going to speak to my father at some point to describe my progress here today, and that shortly afterwards Mr Borden will be apprised of the same facts. I'd rather that it was good news Mr Borden heard, Bob, exciting news, and I'd rather it came from you first. Wouldn't you? So let's you and I concentrate on what I came here to discuss. You can get the paperwork and approvals started on our campaign checks, and maybe this afternoon you can take me to lunch at the Philadelphia Club and have a drink or two to discuss my implications... Bob. We won't even worry about little Mrs Markham, will we?

"Now, shall I start over?"

"There. You. The ideal solution. Aquaculture not called for. Mercurochrome. I am indeed a possessor of no small amount of tumescence. Regenerative power of large marine mammals. Pyrotechnics."

Rodrigo slurps his first glass of wine in twenty-two years, washing down his second dozen raw oysters of the evening. Mel, her hostess outfit temporarily covered by a wraparound neck-to-knee cook's apron, is quite aware of the motto of the local harvesters of the prodigious bivalve: "Eat oysters, love longer." She hopes some proof to the maxim will be offered this night. In nervous anticipation of what is to come, Melodie has her guest situated comfortably in an antique parlor love seat.

Rodrigo's attention, however, now seems to be entirely focused on Mel's alligator sausage and pickled quail egg hors d'oeuvres.

Rodrigo makes a happy "mumph" sound as he chews each mouthful.

Mel is ecstatic. "I Been Loving You A Little Too Long" is reaching its horn-augmented peak on the stereo. The God Otis Redding is groaning low. Otis' heart has ripped itself free of his chest, is rolling around on the floor of a soon-to-be-lost love. Melodie LaGrande touches Rodrigo's leg gently.

"You darling, darling boy. You like those little eggs, don't you?"

"Mumph!"

"Now, don't spoil your appetite too badly, sweet thing," Mel coaxes. "I've so much food just waiting to come out. Mutt told me of your liking for shrimp, so I've a little surprise motif for dinner. I thought it especially apropos since the social season is upon us, and I was so hoping you might escort me to the Dislocated Ball. We'd make such a handsome couple, don't you think?"

Melodie stands in front of Rodrigo, hands on hips. Her lower regions begin a delicate clockwise rotation. Otis is screaming "Too long to stop now! Too long to stop now!" over the unstoppable rhythm of that pounding heart.

"Nooo... Nooooo.."

"Mumph!"

Rodrigo washes down another handful of quail eggs with a large swallow of wine.

Mel sighs so deeply that her exhaled breath carries the scent of rosemary to Rodrigo. He looks up with bliss in his eyes.

"This is a little something I created my very own self to make extra sure that tonight would be an evening to remember for you and me. Just watch now."

Melodie reaches behind her back and unties her apron strings, which immediately fall to her sides. Her bare hips are uncovered by the gently swinging cloth. The rotation makes it more and more apparent how little in the way of other clothing is beneath the apron.

Her breasts now begin to slowly swing counter-clockwise. Her breathing becomes deep and full, in time with Otis' surging, loving coronary bassline. Her cheeks flush. Mel reaches to her shoulders. With the grace of a born dancer, she removes the apron.

A total of six eight-count shrimp, emblazoned with edible herb bows, adhere to her body. The decorative shellfish are arranged in pairs at each of three major locations. The shrimp in the furthest south of these locations are placed nose-to-nose and tail-to-tail. Forming a rosy crustacean heart.

Beneath this edible sculpture, applied to her skin in pink shrimp mousse, is a message. Lettered in delicate calligraphy.

"M+R. Forever."

Rodrigo's eyes glaze over as he falls face-first into the alligator sausage.

"My dear, dear boy," Mel whispers, true love in her voice and a definite twinkle in her eye. "Now what am I going to do with you?"

"SSSsstt...SSSttt..."

"Ginny what what is it what? No more hissing no more sss no. No outer space. No alien. Painting painting painting is what we doing," says a red-spackled Noonie, brush in hand. She pauses after speaking and stands up as straight as she can.

"You have to go to bathroom? Not in the back yard again, no."

Noonie Robichaux is proud of the straightforward manner in which she communicates with her roommate. Every day she remembers more about dealing with other people. Noonie can sense that she has come a long way since moving back into her family home. After only a matter of weeks.

All because Mutt Jeansonne, that crazyboy allatime talking to pictures, he decide to take on the Norms. It's a miracle.

Don't know how it happened. Don't know what it is. But I sure as hell ain't going to let whatever it is go by. Got a home again. My home and Mutt's home. Me'n him together in a house, and our family.

That Mutt started it. Magic boy. Now I got to finish.

In my own sweet time. Sure.

Here she is talking with another human being, discussing concrete matters like any Norm.

It feels good. I feel good.

She even recognizes the visual cues that tell her Virginia is about to respond.

Noonie pays attention. She is about to receive interpersonal communication.

"Noonie ssSSSsstanding in duck shit," announces Virginia.

"Quaaaack," says Ellis D without remorse, and promptly adds another of his contributions to the room's remodeling.

Since the late 1970's, the unofficial opening of New Orleans Carnival season occurs some two months prior to Mardi Gras Day. On the night of a full moon in late Fall. Placed, ironically, near the start of the Roman Catholic season of Advent.

The eve's festivities, once initiated, soon became tradition.

So, not quite twenty years ago, six friends organized the Dislocated Ball. It has since become a staple for those bred on, and delighting in, decadence of any sort. The Ball has no specific sexual orientation, unless omni-sexual is allowed as a description. Like the City itself, Dislocated tolerates and loves anything that brings happiness. The more obscure and imaginative the source, the better. Monumental additions to the Party Legend   especially the successive years of the Dancing Alligator and Hot-Oil Nude Pig Wrestling   have made the limited number of Ball invitations harder and harder to procure for newcomers. Especially for those New Orleanians unlucky enough to hail from anywhere other than the heart of Downtown, the Upper Ninth Ward, also known as Bywater, and the Eighth Ward's Faubourg Marigny.

Noonie and Virginia have been unofficial mascots of the Dislocated Ball for years. The organizers felt that the two Wild Girls' presence always added to the cosmic swirl of music and madness. They were made honorary citizens of the Upper Ninth after their very first appearance. Ellis D was named a member of the Court four Balls in a row. The last year as Grand Duck.

Even Rodrigo has religiously taken to attending. His Decatur street church was discovered by one of the Ten, and he was recruited to the decoration committee with the promise of unlimited Shrimp Fried Rice and a free source of dislocated images. On the first year of Rodrigo's participation, the Ball sponsors presented him with a single large stack of picture books. The resultant work of art encouraged committee members to start collecting them the entire twelve months, specifically for Rodrigo's participation in Dislocated.

He worked right through the event itself his first year. With scissors and glue in hand, he was seated ceremoniously in front of a blank wall. He finished his efforts two days after even the clean-up crews had gone home. Rodrigo finally looked around, not quite sure where he was. He found his final installment of five pounds of slightly soggy rice, and headed back for the Quarter feeling fulfilled.

A large photograph of this, his first commissioned work, showed up in the art section of the Picayune's "Lagniappe" tabloid the following Friday. Taken by a staff photographer who was an underground resident of the Upper Ninth. Rodrigo promptly cut the photo out of the paper, carried it back to the site of the Dislocated Ball and pasted it next to a color illustration of a bottle-nosed grunt. A tiny salt-water fish indigenous to the coastal Caribbean waters of Central America.

The same photographer documented Rodrigo's second-year collage, in which the first year's faded photo remained uncovered. The newspaper had seen fit to also publish this second photo. Rodrigo had no choice but to again post the picture. In multiples. This year's collage is to be the third generation. As pictures of pictures of pictures are to be taken.

There was great anticipation of the new work among the Dislocated crowd. Requests for raw material for Rodrigo met with a literal avalanche of Art magazines, machine catalogs, tattoo journals. And glossy porn photos predominantly leather- and rubber-oriented. Again amidst some naturally-recurring confusion about the word "raw". The photos and illustrations arrived from all over the Ward.

Rodrigo became a symbol of the dislocation from the Norm that happily characterizes the neighborhoods downtown and downriver. From the Quarter into the Upper Ninth, they love their outlaws.

So it was no coincidence that Mutt was invited to the Ball shortly after he took up residence on Toulouse street. He in turn invited Chris Reed to accompany him.

"Why, I'd love to, Mutt," she had said excitedly, grabbing his hand and squeezing. "I've been so serious these last months! First the Court, and now working so hard with you, it seems like ages since I've been to a party!" She looked up, and saw that the helpless look had returned to Mutt's eyes. He was staring at her hand in his. They were both very aware of the warmth of the contact. She broke away awkwardly, heading for the door.

"Besides, I've really wanted to get a first hand look at this branch of your constituency   guess this means I'll have to costume, doesn't it? Wouldn't want to embarrass you." Chris smiled openly at Mutt, turned, and closed the door behind her as she left.

Mutt closed his eyes and examined what was left of her image. A reverse Chris floated unfixed on the liquid surface of his vision. Like the blue ball and orange field that remain moving under eyelids after a glance at the sun on a cloudless day.

He came to. Remembered their conversation. The word "constituency" had invaded their moment together. That bothered him, but not enough to cancel his first date ever.

The Reverend Lincoln Jesus Gonzalez is well aware of the annual approach of the Dislocated Ball. He is a regular and active attendee himself, having years earlier worked out a system for a more effective presence. Preparatory to his arrival, he abandons his preaching post on Bourbon street, spending the entire day in bed resting his weary and burdened spirit. He awakens as the sun sinks below the horizon, puts on his umbrella hat and offering can, makes sure he has fresh batteries in his megaphone and heads across the Ninth Ward to take up his post outside the entrance to the Ball.

His sermonettes gather force as guests begin to arrive. He derives inspiration from their costumery. A bare-chested

French Strumpet wrapped in the trappings of a nineteenth century boudoir is among the first group of celebrants at the gate.

"Goodgawdamighty, woman, have you no shame?" calls the Rev, his eyes full to the brims with cleavage. "The evil and lust that is taking over the very core of your heart, as beautiful as it may be oh yes blessed lord, will drag you down into the pit, oh yes it will. Take you to the fiery pit and land you in the arms of Satan himself!"

At that a short, crimson horned creature runs out from behind the woman.

"Good god, I hope so," says the devil, sprinting into the Ball.

Preparing to be Dislocated is half the fun. Maybe not quite half.

Melodie takes the Saturday of the Ball off from work at the Can-Can-Do. After much deliberation, she decides on costuming as The Evangelical Biker Babe. She spends the afternoon using colored ball-point pens to draw an elaborate rococo tattoo on her arms and legs. The result is formidable. Ferns entwine with delicate scrollwork on both her thighs, meeting in a botanical roadsign just below her navel. Framing the words "Highway to Heaven." Again, she feels she has avoided subtlety quite adroitly. She runs to Larry's Hardware to search for boots to match the outfit. Rodrigo says he is going as Toulouse Lautrec. His costume consists of walking on his knees.

All the members of the Toulouse entourage enter into the spirit of the event. Mutt seriously interrogates Fred on any personal messages she might want to convey in her costume. When they emerge ready for the event, Fred is wearing a white kitchen garbage bag with her head, legs and tail sticking out. Her name for the evening is "Pro-Fido-Lactic". Noonie is a vice officer. Ellis the duck has a similar theme in mind, a badge hanging around his neck that looks very suspiciously like a Night Court Bailiff's.

Even Chris Reed costumes. She hopes to keep a low profile in the crowd of crazies, and to remain disguised in case someone she knows shows up. She has noticed that reverse thinking seems proper around the Streets.

Dress crazy so nobody will notice you.

She dresses as Petite Christine, the French Tickler. A tag on her chest reads: "Just say 'Oui!'" her effort to try and invade the spirit of the evening. It proves to be a good costume logistically, because her three-foot-tall platinum bouffant hairpiece helps Mutt find her in the crowd.

Reed attempts to make friends among Mutt's intimate circle by inviting the Toulouse family Uptown for a warm-up party. To make sure no possible media opportunity is lost, however, she also informally asks a video crew of the NBC affiliate to come by her apartment. The selection process is simple: she asks the crew who have given her the most exposure over the last few months. Of course. They can get an unusual feature and then enjoy the gathering. It is not hard to convince them to spend their Saturday night shift at a party.

But videographers Joey Dayers, 'Tin & Johnny Terpletsky, after browsing through numerous shops earlier in the day, are unable to consummate costume-wise. They are brave lads, however, and are determined to go to the Ball, even though unmasked. They know Reed's ideas have been a good source of video. The trio shows up at her apartment for warm-up toddies quite humble about their lack of disguise. She lets them slide in return for a promise that Mutt Jeansonne will make the next day's news in a prime spot.

Reed originally intended that the rendezvous at her apartment would be a gesture of good will, just a few moments of chat before the main event. Somehow though, this small gathering grows quite rowdily into two-and-a-half hours of minor, though intense, drinking. She and the news crew are introduced to what they later dub "Numeric Canine Wine" mixed with cranberry juice. Immediately, the alcohol-enhanced MD50-50 wine, the "Mad Dog 50-50" as it is known to Street mainliners, takes serious bites of the group consciousness.

The Ball starts officially around 9pm. Mel's bright red Studebaker arrives, top down and packed with two- and four-legged mammals and a two-legged fowl, around 11:30.

Chris had warned her TV friends that this was a seriously degenerate event. Her comments do not strike home until the convertible parks in the vacant lot next to the river floodwall. As the Studebaker begins to disgorge its occupants, a small Datsun pulls up alongside. Its doors fly open. Out bursts a wave of noise and the overpowering scent of Halston cologne colliding with Latin liquor. It is clear that a vast army of mescal-marinated worms have already begun a pilgrimage south among the passengers of this vehicle.

The passengers disembark. Four "gentlemen", with the teased wig hairdos of elderly pensioners on holiday, and the high heels and makeup of Las Vegas showgirls, leap from the car dressed only in the sheerest of see-through patterned panty-hose. Normally unfazed cameraman Joey Dayers almost has a coronary on the spot. He is closest to the spectacle. His camera falls from his grip. It is all he can do to keep his eyes averted from their crotches, where the pantyhose coverings have placed their various external parts in a constricted, though artistic, display.

Later, when she has time to muse, Chris imagines that these anatomical features looked rather like small featherless grouse wrapped in cellophane. Her Daddy used to shoot grouse in large numbers.

The four costumed gentlemen then proceed to cover themselves a bit more by putting on large cardboard boxes cut into the shapes of land-line desk telephones. They decorate their heads with hats made of stars and planets. One of them has a cylindrical phallic shape protruding from his chest. The protrusion, supposedly a hostile being from another planet, has a diabolical   and dentally unsound   set of teeth. The four men have come as "Alien Phone Sex." And they are "ready to take your call, baby!" Their approach to the party, directly behind the Studebaker entourage, is a mini-event in itself. There is someone waiting for them.

"Good gawdamighty! My sweet baby Jesus in heaven above!" There is the rattle of an offering can.

"Well, isn't he just the best! Oh girls, girls, girls!" the pink Princess phone exclaims. "We should give the sweet man something! This outfit is too Charlton Heston!"

"Love it love it love it!"

All four of the telephones happily add a bill to the Reverend's collection.

"Thank you, sisters, thank you mightily," intonates the Reverend Lincoln Jesus Gonzales in his most solemn voice. "You may this day have earned yourself a place in heaven."

"I should hope so. After all, five dollars will get me a date on a regular Saturday night!"

The four phones enter the party giggling and shrieking. Prospective callers run up to them quickly. Each whispers a lewd phrase or two into the oversized phone handsets, to no small amount of feverish, partially feigned, blushing. The phone boys carry "While You Were Out" note pads on which they busily scribble the most interesting suggestions that are poured into their receiver-ears.

The Reverend steps into the cracked asphalt gutter to look south toward the river for new arrivals. Whether they believe in his authenticity or not, the Ballgoers make up his most receptive and generous flock. At last year's Ball, he had gathered enough money on the single Dislocated night to allow him a two-week vacation at the Mississippi Gulf Coast casinos. The Lord punished him in Mississippi and he came back a loser. It had been a sure sign from above. The Reverend Gonzalez repented mightily that day, swore a vow to the Almighty that he would thenceforward avoid the wicked and deceitful quarter slots.

He believes he knows the Lord's Way now. Blackjack. Blackjack will give him his Great Getting-Up Morning.

As soon as he gathers in another few hours' offerings from the profligates. Now that he has found them in such profusion.

The genteel rituals of the Dislocated Ball do occasionally move. Due to the time it takes for a site to recover. This Ball is taking place for the fourth straight year at an abandoned factory half a block from the Mississippi River floodwall. Inspecting the location before the party, a majority of the original founders feel that this might be its final year. Though they do enjoy its proximity to the river. Foghorns startle the partyers all night, adding small bursts of natural adrenaline to the already elevated goings-on.

One such loud marine blast occurs as Mutt approaches the reception line. He had intended to formally present his invitation and sign the guest book. But at the echoing sound of the foghorn Fred leaps, garbage bag and all, into Mutt's arms. The Ball Hostess comes forward, arms extended apologetically to hug Mutt and his dog and give them both kisses. In the process augmenting Fred's costume with a red lipstick print on each of her grey cheeks. The dog is pleased with the gesture, and licks a large hole in the Hostess' rouge in return.

The Hostess, chief of the original group, herself elated by the return of affection, laughs until she jingles. She is dressed in a black leather outfit with chrome heart cutouts and silver donuts atop her breasts. There is a none-too-subtle polished silver penis sprouting from her hairdo on either side of the coiffure. She also sports net stockings, black leather boots and an intimidating bull whip, which she uses to rather good advantage later as the party grows in scope. She warns the camera crew that, though they may take all the footage they want, they cannot reveal the whereabouts of the Ball. It will probably be moved next year, but until then its location is controlled information.

The Toulouse group, camera crew, Mel and Reed progress into the main building. A female dummy lies face-up on the "sign-in" table decorated with colorful vegetables, and is dressed in a fifties bridal gown. Noonie admires the fabric. A portion of the dummy   the four phones remark on her nail color   is piled high with marinated maraschino cherries, which are being greedily consumed by guests as they enter. The composition of the marinade is a subject of intense speculation.

They enter the main dance area. An aging neighborhood Street dressed as a generic Moses   his tablet of commandments is engraved with two columns of barcodes   acts as doorman to the two-story tin and steel structure. The building is open to the roof except in one corner over a makeshift bar. Above that area is a small single second-story room, accessible only by a rusty staircase. It is early on designated by one of the event's main organizers as the "Ladies' Vomitorium," and is appropriately used throughout the night.

Two large doors lead out onto a side lot surrounded by a tall cyclone fence. A band of musicians, all of whom look like they are, at best, out in public on a court-ordered work-release program, play under a slanted tin roof set against the side of the building. There are various monumental machine parts and mechanical-looking devices strewn throughout the yard, including 55-gallon oil drums that are emitting roaring columns of flame. This hazard affords a number of highly-flammable chiffon and polyester costume-wearers a thrilling if momentary fright that night.

One low triangular area is filled knee-high with an unrolled 35mm print of a Chinese industrial training film, thousands of feet of it. It has to do with drilling fluids. There are small votive candles burning around the film.

Large colorful cutout drawings of people and animals are placed in significant positions around the walls for immediate worship or abuse, depending on the whim of the beholder, and scarlet bunting drapes the spaces in between. Christianity as it is known in much of the civilized world is not represented.

The floor is dirt, with a fine white powder forming its top two inches. For skiing, great. For dancing, occasionally less than healthy. The loose powder in the dancing area creates dust storms of such density as to completely obscure partners.

Around midnight the Hostess' ten-foot bullwhip comes snapping out of the cloud, only to be jerked back in, with a CRACK and a whirlwind in tow. Much the same as dance partners. A dancer is never sure who he or she might be paired with at the end of any particular musical number. Hands get mixed up in the cloud. So much so that Reed refuses to dance after the second hour of the festivities. She is working. The social lottery of dancing continues. The dust also makes for sporadic coughing and wheezing and the odd sore throat, but no one seems to care.

Reed has done her research. Right away she recognizes a group of French Quarter Business Association members. She recognizes them in spite of the costumes. Their pubic areas are festooned with huge lumps of black fur, and their upper bodies have presidential seals on one side and "The Bush Family" written on the other. In spite of this, she introduces Mutt to them. Video crew in tow. Shooting from the waist up, exclusively. Reed acts as director, specifying framing when she sets up video coverage. The Bushes know who Mutt is.

"Look, partner, I don't want to mess up your Ball," says the lead Bush. "And I got nothing against you personally, understand. But we're all worried about the flood of people you got coming into your house. Of course, we'd rather have you on Toulouse street than on Bourbon or Royal or Chartres. It's not you, I know, but it's hard to do business when you've got bums begging and grifting off the tourists."

Mutt isn't prepared for confrontation. He is barely acclimated to being at a large social event. To which he has been invited. But the man is talking about his family.

"Yessir, I bet it is hard, doing business with all that distraction. But to these folks that 'distraction' is a way to get a bite to eat or a decent place to sleep. And every single person working at my house is one more that you won't see out on the Street struggling to just stay alive one more day," he says, an unusual anger rising within him. "We're all of us interested in working for a living, sir. The folks at my house they been doing construction for me. They do some hard labor, and me I'm proud I get to give them honest wages. You people ought to be happy they are in my house, and not out scratching in the Street like animals."

Mutt is suddenly embarrassed at his own unexpected fervor. He tries to smile and offers his hand to the lead Bush. "You can come inspect what they do any day you like," he says calmly. "These are honest people."

The Bushes can tell he means it.

"What the hell, Mr Jeansonne. You're damn right. I am happy. Let's party." There are handshakes all around. Mutt takes on another trainload of human data.

It is an amicable meeting. Good sound bite for the weekend news. In spite of all the booze everyone except Mutt has been pouring down. The video boys give the thumbs up and pack up most of their gear, so they can get into the festivities. Now that their official work is done. Dayers even pats Mutt on the back and wishes him good luck. Mutt looks at Dayers differently afterwards. Smiles at him. Reed notes that Dayers lives in the Quarter and is registered to vote.

Reed gets Mutt in tow and starts working the gathering like it is a Fourth of July picnic and Mutt is running for President of the School Board. He does not realize that there is any method at work. Does not notice that she keeps him in a political context with everyone they meet. She, however, knows that District C includes the Vieux Carré, Treme, Bywater and most of the Faubourg Marigny, besides the French Quarter. She knows very well that the people at the Dislocated Ball are the same voters who will be pulling the levers at the City Council election in March.

She talks to people, Mutt in tow. Discovers more about the Ball's organizers. Such skills could be useful. She lets Mutt go off on his own and dances with the Ball Hostess as the band's second set crashes to a dust bowl finale. Everybody dances with everybody at the Dislocated Ball, regardless of gender or sexual preference. Reed feels relatively safe in deciding to dance again. She is as sure as she can be, under the circumstances, that the Hostess goes for boys. She is also a decent dancer. The Hostess seems to be the prime Dislocated member, known by everyone at the gathering as the best underground real estate agent on the city. She calls Mutt "the pre-eminent advocate of cross-dressers' rights." She is a bit elevated in spirit.

As are most. There are at least a thousand people blindly staggering and dancing around the place.

Shortly after the dance dust dies down, the Hostess yet to be identified by name to Chris   brings her a drink. The drink is also nameless. Chris is thirsty and her throat full of dust. The anonymous beverage is refreshing, fruit-flavored, cold and tasty. She drinks it all.

Since Rodrigo is involved with his wall and completely encircled by admirers and photographers, and since Mel's nemesis "that bitch Perry Masonette" has Mutt and Fred in tow glad-handing everyone in sight, Mel decides to mingle. It turns out to be the right decision.

Melodie discovers one of her Sorority Sisters is also in attendance at the Ball, hanging out with a particularly disheveled trombonist. This is the Sister who is the universally acknowledged president of the Sorority. The Sister whom Mel now counts as her BFF. Especially since she still felt that the Bust was partially her fault. Mia had, after all, also called in sick. Abu would more likely be ill, and Mia quite well this evening. She was happy to see Mel.

Around one in the morning, the elder statesman of the Bush family discovers that Ellis D is once again "carrying." The unexpected stash is due to the generosity of an old hippie named Kristoffer who sentimentally thinks the duck's traditional role as the expeditor of mind-expansion is well worth reviving. The K man fills the duck's neck pouch, chuckling the whole while and speaking in a Central American Indian dialect to Ellis. Ellis quacks often in response, communicating easily, then watches as Kristoffer leaves the party and climbs the levee across the street. Kristoffer had told the duck that his spirit needed to recharge in the power of tonight's full moon. That he will be close to the river as the moon rises. Ellis can understand, instinctively linking large bodies of water, the full moon and revitalization.

Shortly afterwards, five hundred small orange barrels are discovered to be the cause of Ellis' stooped posture. The psychic laxative is quickly removed from the duck's pouch and added to what was originally meant to be the evening's one non-alcoholic beverage. It remains so.

Half an hour later, the party-wide round of LSD-saturated imitation-watermelon-flavor kool-aid blows away what little hint of restraint there is left at the Ball. There is a double round for the musicians.

The band begins to explode into increasingly raunchy rhythmic grooves.

This is a defining characteristic of all true New Orleans music. It has remained so for a hundred years. No matter the genre. No matter the state of mind. It has had the same effect on men and women alike since Buddy Bolden blew "Funky Butt Blues" at the jumping Funky Butt Hall before the turn of the twentieth century.

The effect is in full form this night. Prompting dancing of a variety never witnessed at the all-white, all-Protestant, all-Anglo, male-dominant Uptown Society Carnival Balls.

This is a lively crowd.

Mel and Mia take the music as a professional challenge.

They leap into the dust already shaking body parts provocatively. Raising the stakes and lowering the clothing level of most participants in a matter of seconds. Within a minute, dust is the only covering for most dancing flesh.

As the bacchanal progresses exponentially, Andrew "Bad Boy" Wenter arrives in his bronze 1969 Lincoln Continental. The Lower Ninth R&B legend is beloved by three generations of New Orleanians for the wild abandon of his singing. He mounts the stage riding a wave of applause. "Bad Boy" attends the Dislocated every year, happily donating to the Upper Ninth Ward the same performance for which he charges Las Vegas hotels $10,000 a show. "Bad Boy" lives in his neighborhood, and it in him. He waits until late to make his appearance more dramatic.

These are his people, too.

He grabs a wireless microphone. Bad Boy, all 287 pounds of him, agilely climbs rusted scaffolding onto the corrugated roof over the band. And begins howling at the now-visible full moon. It is just the catalyst needed for graduation to the upper reaches of Dislocated.

Bad Boy's call to arms prompts visiting musicians who have been merely standing at the kool-aid tank power-drinking to finally open their instrument cases and get onstage. The horn section grows to eight. Total band size at this point, not counting the massive vocal chorus working harmony off-stage or Wenter on the roof, is fourteen. And they are cooking.

Noonie and Ellis D are onstage, too. The official mascot and the Grand Duck are riding their own waves of energy. Ellis has been given a microphone, and is vocalizing the wildness in his ducky soul. According to many on the peripheries of the music, Ellis' voice sounds a great deal like the background vocals on early Sam and Dave. Even Fred later mentioned a new respect for Noonie's companion.

The Reverend Lincoln Jesus Gonzales is trying hard to wrangle a last few dollars from the Ballgoers as they begin to depart. Most are too dazed to offer him attention, much less a contribution.

Nonetheless, he uses the occasion as an opportunity to polish his skills. The finely-honed instrument of his voice has already netted him well over three hundred dollars this evening. He finds himself preaching for the sake of preaching. He is enjoying himself. He is letting himself get personally and deeply involved. He feels the tears welling, close to the surface.

"Yes, brothers, yes sisters!" he cries, dropping to one knee. "I come before you tonight as a sinner, yes I do. As a man who has come afoul of the devil time and time again, oh lord, and still been allowed by the Merciful Shepherd to come back into the fold. Say Amen!"

"Amen, man," says a weary voice. What looks to be a very wet wolverine drops a quarter into Gonzalez' cup, then stumbles up the street.

"And I do thank you, brother, for that meager but heartfelt offering, for I am a man of the cloth, a man fated to bring the message to mankind itself, a man brought into this world with the names of three other men, all holy to the destiny of my people: Lincoln, who freed the black man. Jesus, who saved the black man. And Julio Gonzalez, who gave this black man his life and name! All the while batting .401 for the miracle-bound Black Socks of the God-fearing Negro Baseball League. Julio, may thy name be praised! Four-oh-and-one!

"Without the benefits of any aluminum bat, my brothers and sisters, oh NO!" wails the Reverend, totally into his parable of life. "For Julio Gonzalez was a man of purity and refinement. We must all examine our origins to know from whence we came. Let us now pray silently for our salvation."

When, after five minutes of meditation, the Reverend Gonzales raises his head and sees no further worshipers are forthcoming, he hails a cab. The First Imperssion [sic] Lounge is usually a good bet for collecting the wages of sin this time of the morning, and for the Rev, it is payday.

Mutt walks through the crowd shaking hands. He has grown used to it now, the touching. The new input not as intrusive. He is dazzled with all the attention he has been receiving. Most of it at the introduction of Chris Reed. The flood of personal contact has him off-balance.

Late in the Ball, as he makes a solo tour of the now seriously off-kilter unreality of Dislocated, Mutt leans against a rusting cyclone fence and tries to evaluate what is happening to him.

I've gained and lost everything at the same time. Because of this woman. Because of a few moments trying to tell a Court that my friends are human, too. Because they made me go to Court school for a month. Because I want to be somebody. Because I want to speak. Because I got this short furry Friend. Because of all those things, I had to leave my home. Forever. And find something else.

I am a land-owner. Something I would never in my life have dreamed possible.

I'm learning, too. In new ways. Taking in huge doses of information every day. I got help. Rodrigo is a much less intimidating teacher than the nuns were, though some of his information doesn't seem too useful for living in New Orleans.

Or on this planet, for that matter.

I can pass the GED if I ever get another shot at it. I know I can. I wonder if I'm too old to make another try at college. Use my GI Bill.

A herd of seven-foot-tall Bigfoots with flying saucer heads suddenly run in front of him, flashing lights and trailing red smoke.

Mutt yells aloud. Jumps back and hunches his shoulders protectively. Clouds of dust shot through with the orange of flames whip around him as he stands frozen, staring toward the fire source.

I can't believe what is happening.

Just then: I was actually thinking about the future. I never ever before in my life figured I actually had a future. Up to just a bit ago life was now. Time only streams backwards into the past. Gone.

Then, to stop the hurting, you forget the past.

That's not happening any more.

Mutt emerges from his daydreaming just in time to spot Chris Reed battling through the mostly naked crowd. Stumbling rapidly toward the stage. Caroming off other dancers.

The band is just rounding the bend of an inspired combination of the horn chart on Lee Dorsey's "Ride Your Pony" and the extended guitar/bass jam on Jimi Hendrix's "Machine Gun." Reed has a determined look on her face. A rabid look actually.

Mutt goes after her.

She is fast, though staggering heavily. She has been given a mission from Rodrigo's fabled Cosmos. Her assignment was sent by universal brain fax directly from the galaxy Lysergic Acid Diethylamide.

Reed climbs onto the low stage and roughly grabs Ellis' microphone. To his credit, the duck doesn't stop his vocal rendering for a moment, actually breaking into a harmonious chorus with Noonie. The Assistant District Attorney's face twists with mad intent. The blue eyes flash beams of hallucinogenic resolve. She starts chanting in time with the staccato guitar riffs. The words are not clear at first, but finally sort themselves.

"Cut for Pound Sill! But Wood Pound Mill! Mutt Wood Pound Sill! Mutt on Council! Mutt on the fucking Council!" Feeling foolish at first, she gains confidence as she finds the words. The young ADA forms her chosen message with spittle and volume.

"Mutt on the Council!"

"Get on your pony and ride, baby!"

Reed's concentration on her chosen task, especially in the face of a wildly disorienting psychedelic distraction, is totally admirable. Even if her timing might be questionable.

The Dislocated audience, oblivious to the sudden change in direction, think the chant to be their part of the ongoing musical jam. They take up the new mantra eagerly. By the time Mutt reaches the stage to rescue Reed, a thousand voices are roaring in unison. He still has no idea why. He puts out his arm to support the now-flagging attorney, and the crowd goes into a mighty cheer, his name on every voice.

"Mutt on the Council!"

"Ride, dammit, RIDE!"

Reed hears the applause and comes to in an instant. She looks into the faces of the naked, dirty and howling crowd in front of her. Something snaps. A long-dormant synapse closes. She tears open her blouse to cement her bond with the audience.

Only one person notices.

Joe Dayers is quite happy he'd brought out his video camera again. Even if he is drunk and stoned. This is going to be the lead piece on the Weekend Evening News, he knows it.

Dayers is wrong.

Chris Reed's unorthodox announcement of Mutt Jeansonne's candidacy for the District C Council seat is the Lead Story on the 6am, noon, five and 6pm news on Sunday.

And Monday.

And Tuesday.

"Mutt, how often am I going to have to tell you this?" asks Chris impatiently. "We've gone over it all afternoon. You have got to be sincere. They expect that of you. You can't just give people memorized words and expect them to believe you. You know that this is something you believe yourself, so it's not like we're just making something up and sticking it in your mouth, is it? You've just got to say it like you believe it. Now. Again, please. Just use your own words. Try to convince me that everything you say is absolutely true."

Mutt raises his eyes from the notecards in front of him. His cheeks are flushed. He presses his lips together, sets his jaw, takes a deep breath and begins again.

"It is the truth, maam. I don't want to be a politician. Never did," Mutt says, looking straight at Chris Reed. "I just feel it's time somebody takes politics seriously. Most of these folks, they treat Government like it's their own little parlor-room game. They act like it don't effect us people out here on the Streets, in the neighborhoods of this city. Like being in Government isn't a real job, just a couple months' fun. Well, it's time we stop playing at politics and started working at it!" Mutt yells.

"All right, Mutt!" Chris cheers, rising to her feet. "That's the way candidate L Mutt Jeansonne talks to his constituents. That's the way he gets on the City Council. You've got to give it that kind of energy every time."

Two months' backbreaking work was beginning to pay off.

When Chris Reed calmed down from the furor that followed her soul-baring and unorthodox announcement of Mutt's candidacy, she zeroed in on him. Spent an entire week convincing Mutt that the campaign was the thing to do. Run for Council. Make a difference. Stand up for the people. Don't let your friends down.

She talked to him for hours. Holding his hand. Speaking firmly and with quiet logic. Until she discovered that he instantly went deaf when she touched him. Physical contact disabled the Candidate. At least, physical contact with her disabled him. So she sat across the table. Repeating her arguments.

Mutt finally said yes, yes he would do it. Reed paid his filing fee that day with a check, drawing on the first of the McFarland Borden and Dubney campaign contributions. Over a week earlier, she had opened the account with their money and had checks printed.

Chris Reed knew her Candidate would give in.

The law firm's money allowed the Jeansonne candidacy its birth. But, while Mr Borden's partnership did provide the all-essential operating monies   and an ongoing stipend to

Reed   it was by no means the sole contribution to the campaign. Candidate Mutt Jeansonne had no problems with funding. It seems that a large part of the populace of the Upper Ninth Ward already had subliminal Mutt Jeansonne election posters tacked up on the wall of their psychedelically-decorated frontal lobes. Right next to a first-edition blue and orange "Jimi Hendrix at the Avalon Ballroom."

It wasn't just the watermelon kool-aid. They were convinced Mutt was one of them.

They were right, he discovered. He just never knew it before. He never knew much at all about himself before, until other people started re-inventing him. He didn't mind one bit. He was glad to be someone with whom strangers could relate.

However they wanted to do the relating.

Chris Reed was still the prime source of his re-invention. She had initially pushed him into running. Alright, he admitted, he was not exactly a willing candidate. But this draft wasn't turning out so badly for him. He was even enjoying certain aspects of it. Reed had helped him get his confidence together. Spent long hours helping him straighten his thoughts and speech out. Three times she had slapped him and yelled at him. Told him to concentrate. Twice she spontaneously hugged him and said he was doing great.

He took it all. Enjoyed it all. He was sure that she didn't remember. When he dropped her off at home after the Dislocated Ball. He helped her with her door. She kissed him on the lips.

He couldn't stand to think about that. He became weak and addled every time the incident stuck its foot in his mind's back door. As a matter of fact, he was glad that she was now making most of their contact over the phone. For the sake of the new campaign, not his own personal pleasure. That part of him missed her physical presence. Ached without it.

Her last visit to Toulouse street had been almost two weeks ago. It had been mildly traumatic from the moment she walked in.

"Mutt, you know how much I care for you, and how much this campaign means to me," she had begun. "But I simply cannot work in this zoo! And these meetings in your bathroom! I know it's quieter in here, but I don't understand how you can expect people to do serious business sitting on the edge of a tub!" She touched his arm for emphasis.

In all the months Mutt and Chris had worked together, Mutt had never grown accustomed to the contact. It still made him lose his mental place. He saw another Chris Reed. It made him forget. And yet, as infrequently as it now occurred, his sense of her was still restricted   she was still holding something back. Mutt saw a reflection of himself there. He knew for a fact that she felt an affection   or something more for him. That knowledge warmed him, as always. And underneath there was the business of the moment, the successes mixed with the petty annoyances. Then he hit a blank wall. Consciously or unconsciously, she wouldn't let him in any further.

Mutt didn't care. She was so beautiful. He picked at her image like a tongue seeking out a sore tooth. He remembered all too well what she had done at the Dislocated Ball. Against his conscious wishes, his mind continued to remind him of the two freckles on the underside of her left breast. Which he himself had helped cover, modestly closing the frenzied woman's shirt amidst the Dislocated madness.

"Yes maam I can understand that," he replied after a substantial gap in time. "It's just this room is kinda special to somebody like me who's been out on the Street for a while."

"Of course. Of course, Mutt. Forgive me. We're moving so fast, I forget how short a time it's been. You've been amazing. It's no wonder at all that you occasionally have a hard time keeping up." Chris stopped for a minute to look around her, as if searching for something. "You know that you've come to mean a lot to me, Mutt."

"Well, I do what I can, maam. I know I'm not much."

"No, you are amazing. I mean it. You've helped me as much as I've helped you. Besides getting me out of that horrible Cannalo's range, this campaign has let me do things I had only hoped I'd be able to do. Maybe you can meet my Dad once we get through this thing. I think you might like him."

"I'd be most pleased to, Chris maam. I'd be most pleased to." Mutt reached out toward her, his hand extended palm up. Trembling slightly.

Reed looked at it, raised her eyes and looked into Mutt Jeansonne's. Felt suddenly uncertain of herself.

Why do I keep wanting to be close to him?

"Got to go now, Mutt. Got to go," she said quickly, brushing by him as she made her way to the bathroom door.

"We'll talk again later. Need to get the last bits of next week in order." She smiled as best she could, now trying not to look directly at him. "I'll call you this afternoon."

"Yes maam," was all he could get out before the door shut behind her.

What did I do? Did she feel me touch her?

Something was growing in Mutt, and he knew it involved Chris Reed. He had begun to hope that it would never come out. At times, fatigued and weakened, he wished he could die. Or at least just sneak back to his Box under the Expressway. Anything to stop feeling. After all the years of Street life, at least that was a familiar reaction for Mutt.

"Missa Roh-doo-REE-goh! Missa Roh-doo-REE-goh!"

The short lady in the K-Mart sundress and coolie hat is insistent. "How come you come all this time, you just start talk now? How come? You know we all likee you much. Why you wait til now?"

"Now, Mrs Foy," intervenes the Reverend Nathaniel Barclay.

Reverend Barclay, a native of Birmingham, England, has been missionary pastor of the Chinese Methodist Enclave for eleven years. He knows how to deal with the occasional pocket of spice in his normally unflavored rice bowl. His bishop had told him that New Orleans was considered missionary territory on a level with the Australian outback. The Asian majority he had found in his congregation merely added to that status.

"We should be glad that Rodrigo has come to trust us enough to open up and speak around us," he continues. "We all know he is a kind man, and a creative one, what with all the additions he has made to our chapel. We should not pressure him."

Mrs Foy is not so easily appeased. "He talk to her first," she says, pointing to the even more diminutive figure standing next to the flustered Rodrigo. The second woman is wearing utilitarian plain cotton pants and shirt, decorated with a wide variety of stains, and a white stovepipe hat.

"I talking to him! Mista Mutts. Roh-doo-REE-goh friend." says Mrs Lee Fat. "Mista Mutsa friend my husband. This man running to be on City Councils. I offer Missa Roh-doo-REE-goh me my husban' help. He say, 'Thank you,' is all."

"Him talking! Him talking! Not saying 'Moooo'! An' now you say you know his family! I want know. Tell me!" screams Mrs Foy.

Again Barclay seeks to intervene. "Ladies, I think we have to be reasonable about requests on members of our congregation. This gentleman has come to our Enclave in search of himself. He should be allowed his privacy, his peace of mind when he comes within these walls. Now please apologize. Please."

Mrs Foy sends a frustrated look at her Anglo pastor. Then at the shoeless philosopher.

"You ladies registered voters?" Rodrigo asks.

"Five months ago he showed up in my courtroom," Chris continues, gathering momentum as she carries the phone around her office. "The man was stuttering, stammering, confused. But he won a significant victory in this community. It may have seemed just a freak phenomenon to some members of the media, but it made the people here in the Vieux Carré, Faubourg Marigny and the Bywater wake up and notice that somebody was finally on their side. Three months later he is a candidate in a major political campaign, gathering support from every corner in his district.

"Why? Because they believe in him. He tells them the truth. And now he's out every day, talking, listening to the people. He's a phenomenon you can't ignore. Mutt Jeansonne will be on the next City Council. And you should start establishing some lines of communication with the man right now. So when do you want him down at your studio? I'm after some housewife/working-husband demographics. Morning Show? Alright, fine, but I don't want that highbrow anchor that Manhattan import   what's his name? Bradley. I don't want my man being interviewed by Bradley. The weather girl? Black, good-looking with long hair? Fine. It's a deal. I'll have him there at 5:15 sharp.

"Charlie, are you by any chance a resident of the... no? 'Burbs, huh? I thought so. That's OK. See you tomorrow."

Chris Reed finishes filling out a page on the Candidate's calendar, then holds it up to double check the times. She has developed a good system, something simple enough so that Rodrigo can keep track of where Mutt's supposed to be and what he's supposed to do. The red entries are engagements where Mutt is expected to speak. She capitalizes and underlines any special topics he should cover. The appointments in black are simply appearances, with the cause or organization noted below the time.

It's amazing how much that Rodrigo character has been able to help. You'd think he was a real person.

Tomorrow Mutt Jeansonne has seven speaking appointments. Seven.

"So whaddya gonna do if those news stories are true, huh?" says the man in the rust-colored leisure suit. The French Quarter Business Association luncheon has taken yet another strange turn. "That's part of a politician's job! Whaddya gonna do if those TV people are right? I'm Church of Christ Latter Day Saints just like my dad and his dad, and our preacher's tellin' us that the end is damn well nigh and we better get right with the Lord! I dunno if I can afford to be tolerant of these folks! Everything they do is so different from everything I'm believin', 'specially right here at a moment when we're gonna be destroyed by some aspect of Satan descendin' from outer space! I..."

The outcry drowns out his last comment completely. Everyone has something to say. About the possibility of Flagrantly Flying Satanic Saucers.

"Sit down, Bernie!"

"Jeez Christ, man, what the hell are you talking about? If Satan gave a damn about what happens in the Quarter we'd have all been bubbling in the deep fat fryer years ago."

"Bernard Lawson, you haven't been to Church since I've known you! Let the man talk without all this nonsense! He'll think we're a bunch of fools!"

"It's the wife," Lawson says defensively. "The preacher's been gettin' the wife all riled up. I should never have let her go to that crazy Galactic Evangelical convention."

The storm gains intensity.

Mutt Jeansonne stands at its center, all alone once again. But he is not alone. Far from it. He is in the crowded back dining room of Alonzo's French Quarter Bar. But Mutt is not panicking. He seems quite calm, especially considering his recent life history.

Look at his face and you know what he's doing. He pictures the room in front of him. A gigantic multi-face billboard. Sure, no problem there. The dozens of humans in front of him are painted figures that only seem to move. Because of the sun. The voices are amplified by the concrete. From the cars perched on the Expressway above. He is on his home turf. The thought calms him. He steps out of the daydream.

Raises his hand.

"Folks...," he gets out, before his voice starts to crack again. His throat is sore. He has never spoken this much before in his life. Or this well. Reed's repetitious speech training is paying off. Everyone in the audience understands him, even though there is still a touch of his Street garble in the mix. They want to understand him, because he is genuine and gentle. And humble. The crowd can tell he is a local boy. And yet he seems like he could possibly be a politician, too. The good kind, if there is such an animal.

He turns to the gentleman who spoke last.

"No, sir, I don't want to do anything that might hurt your religious beliefs," Mutt says. "I can tell you're OK. Man I wouldn't mind living next to. Be proud to have you as a neighbor. And I know you don't want to do something that might hurt a neighbor. Just because he or she is a person who might have different beliefs. Now, do you?"

There is a moment of indecision, then Bernard Lawson answers quietly, "Well, I guess not. Not if they don't come round an' all."

"Fine. I'm sure we can keep folks off your doorstep. About the other part, well, I don't know a thing about outer space. I haven't been there, except maybe for a few moments at the Dislocated Ball a couple of months ago."

A small rumble of chuckling erupts in the room.

"All I been saying here is just let's us folks get along together in this District. You know that the rest of New Orleans thinks we here in the Quarter, Marigny and the Upper Ninth Ward are not much good at this Government business. We got to show them different.

"We are different. We want different things. We need different things. It's natural. We're living in the oldest houses in the City. We got the oldest pipes, buried under the oldest streets. Some of you folks still got DC power in your houses. Your children have a hard time getting to their schools because rich folks' tour buses are blocking your streets going five miles an hour. Your babies trying to get to school and learn something, and here's some bus driver teaching a history of New Orleans he probably got out of a comic book. Telling it like it's gospel to a herd of old folks from Ontario. Who could care less about the important reasons our balconies are so high. And all the while they're sitting in the comfort of a rolling air-conditioned lounge. Your kids' schools don't have air-conditioning.

"It's time we stopped playing politics and started working at them. We pay taxes on everything. So now we get the Government to use our money to make our neighborhoods a better place to live. For all of us. You and me."

Fred, sitting in the chair next to the speaker's podium, gives her partner Mutt a loud, enthusiastic cheer as a coda.

"KAWF!"

"Thank you, folks, and thank you, Fred," Mutt replies.

The French Quarter Business Association awards Mutt Jeansonne, Candidate for City Council, a long round of sustained applause.

When the president of the organization, easily recognizable as a member of the Dislocated Bush Family, adjourns the meeting, a large number of the organization's members rise to come forward and shake Mutt's hand. At a table in the corner Rodrigo, aided by Stephanie Jorgensen, the Dislocated Hostess, passes out contribution forms and takes in campaign donations. Jorgensen has become one of the very first fund-raisers for Mutt. She believes in him. She believes in Rodrigo's belief in him.

Both Rodrigo and Mutt are dressed in well-pressed suits. Bought for five dollars at the Lower Quarter Flea Market. The two men are quite presentable. Though Rodrigo remains shoeless. He has taken Mutt's cue, though, and now explains his bare feet as part of his religious beliefs. No shoes on the faithful's feet. Everyone understands. "Gent must be one a' them Hin-doo" that comment reflects the general consensus.

Mutt and Rodrigo have not eaten any lunch at this Luncheon. Just as they had not eaten any breakfast at the Gay Lesbian Bi Trans Liberation League Breakfast. But they are both happy. They are used to missing meals. Besides, they are too excited to eat. Neither had ever dreamed that he would take pleasure in the approval of crowds of people. And yet here they are, dealing with an endless stream of admirers. People who want Mutt to speak for them. Even after weeks and months, it is still hard to believe. They are both speaking. Doing things.

Fred is eating well and regularly. She is convinced that the spotlight is where she was meant to be all along. FT Jeansonne is ready to do her part, and has been trying to encourage Mutt as best she knows how.

Charles Taylor stares at the *Weekly World Comet* picture that identifies Mutt as a possessed Chalmette trucker and Fred as his alien dog master. Months after its publication, the photo remains crookedly taped to his refrigerator door, a reminder to all who enter the Lower Ninth Ward kitchen that otherworldly invaders can possess even the most normal-looking American patriot.

"Them sunsabitches," he mutters. Taylor chooses his enemies with obsessive care, continually battling what he considers a universal conspiracy against his own pleasure. He takes another deep pull off his lukewarm tall-boy, spilling the final bit onto the newspaper in his lap. "Shit! Takin' over the worl'." This is his fifth beer of the day, but it has been a particularly good can for reading his morning paper. Charles enjoys Colt 45 malt liquor in the sixteen-ounce size to the exclusion of all other beverages. He is indulging in what his educated (and reviled) neighbor Harold calls another C45ID, a Colt 45 Impromptu Drunk.

"Rashann, gimme nuthah Colt," he calls over his shoulder to his twelve-year-old niece. "Hurry t'up, girl."

Charles brushes the liquid off his newspaper. Stops dead still. Unwrinkles the front of the "Metro" section. He looks at the picture on the bottom of the page, a photo of two old guys cutting a ribbon somewhere. Weird-looking dog sitting to the side. A soup kitchen in the French Quarter. The guy on the right is familiar. He looks back up to the refrigerator.

"Shit!" he cries again. "'At muthafuckah from the jury-house! Annis devil dog!

"He runnin' for at goddam City Council!"

Melodie approaches the matter as delicately as she is able.

After a long day spent organizing the rather irregular Jeansonne campaign forces, she and Rodrigo had returned to her cottage for dinner.

Mel brings in containers of Lee Fat's Won Ton Soup and Lo Mein to smooth the way for what is to come. Then shows Rodrigo her scrapbook. The photos of her operation.

He nods sagely as he looks at page after page. Endless scenes of stainless steel and what seems to be an unwanted chicken neck. He drips the tiniest bit of Won Ton on one particularly graphic photo, and cleans it off quickly with his shirt sleeve. Shortly after the noodle box is empty, Rodrigo looks at the final page   the end result of the operation   then turns to Melodie.

"Ahhhhhh-hh, " he says, "galactophorous!" Rodrigo smiles hugely, kissing her on the end of her nose.

Melodie cries with joy for twenty minutes.

"Thank you thank you thank you! Oh, Rodrigo, my dear dear boy!" she finally ventures between contented sobs, "we've grown quite close in these last months, and I am happier now than I have ever ever dreamed possible. You know everything and you still care for me! You're so much more than what I ever hoped for! I mean, you were wonderful when I first met you, but now, now I am amazed at what you do, and how you have grown. I knew that helping you and Mutt get started was the right thing to do, but I had no idea... I wish Mother was alive to meet you and see how wonderful her gift to me truly is."

"I would like to meet Mother. Just like Mel, I bet. Sweet woman." Rodrigo is expansive. His life is taking on new and interesting shape daily. Mel a major part of that change.

"Yes, baby, we were alike. I admired so much about her. She was so supportive of me. And now I've a way to get a little bit of Mummy back."

Mel looks at Rodrigo, a soft sparkle in her eyes.

"The fun part is that you can help, sweet man. You've got something I need."

"Oh boy! I can help. Mel can have anything I got. What is it Melodie wants?"

Reed had become so confident of Mutt's presence and speaking ability that she had recently taken to sending him on his own to speaking engagements such as the Business Association. She had priorities of her own, and was deeply involved with their progress.

McFarland Borden and Dubney had underwritten her Project, but she knew that they were motivated by the prospect of a certain political payback. Like her, they wanted something from the Council. They needed a foothold in the governing body of the City more than she had realized, for some as yet covert purpose. She knew the firm had made its fortune in real-estate, and had her father keeping an eye out for any movement in the New Orleans metropolitan market. Knowing the firm's plans could give her a major advantage. They wanted something. Like her, they wanted it badly enough to gamble on a very unconventional plan. The Jeansonne plan.

Chris Reed believed in Mutt Jeansonne. But as the campaign progressed, Reed's attention shifted more frequently to fulfilling her own personal aspirations from the Jeansonne candidacy. Finally given her shot, she intended to show her father what she could do. She would make her mark on society. And, she would provide long-term benefits for Ms Christine Reed at the same time. She knew that going after political contributions was a risky business. But practical, as always, she was preparing herself. For whatever demand the law firm would make when it called due her debt. She would have to deliver, but so would they.

A Southern girl was used to protecting her flanks.

There were other people in Mutt's life who kept him going besides Chris Reed.

Rodrigo was a whole new person, except for his feet. He even neglected his Decatur street Church to stay at Mutt's side. Rodrigo was his right hand man   though he was left-handed, as he told Mutt. He was there to offer sage All-Fact wisdom whenever it was needed.

Rodrigo was also the prime gatherer of the oriental vote. Soon after he began talking at services, Rodrigo took Mutt to Sunday services at the Enclave. Even though he had not completed his formal Reed training, Mutt spoke with such sincere eloquence that the ladies had endorsed him then and there.

It was a better speech considering that very few of the ladies understood a word of English. The Reverend Barclay and Mrs Lee pledged to help gather support from the substantial Oriental community in the District.

Mutt even discovered that he had old friends.

Several elderly Nuns at Manus Boy's Home in Gentilly had recognized him on TV. And while scandalized at the company he kept   that naked Assistant District Attorney woman and the Boy-Girl Dancer in particular   they were proud of what he had done with his life. Even though they weren't in his District, the Nuns at the Boy's Home sent him $32.76 to help with his campaign.

And a St Jude medal.

In the Quarter and throughout the Street world, St Jude is universally known as the heavenly supporter of lost causes. Consequently, there is a large shrine dedicated to St Jude at the Our Lady of Guadalupe parish church on Rampart street. Usefully close by the Quarter. The Mother Superior wrote that they had all been praying to St Jude as Mutt's patron saint.

Sister Mary Ambrosia mentioned that they had also sent a registered letter to the Vatican. She herself wrote the Pope suggesting an ecclesiastic search of ancient Chinese missionary records for a St Mutt, just in case. They remembered Mutt's childhood make-believe stories about a patron saint, and thought they would give it a try, just for his sake. "Mutt" held the possibility of being a Chinese surname to the nuns from Gentilly.   As in "Mutt Wong Chu, Revered Patron Saint of rickshaw mechanics." The aged sisters believed he deserved his own namesake. Until then St Jude would fill the gap.

Mutt re-evaluated his memories, deciding that maybe the nuns weren't such a bad lot after all. Maybe someday he'd be able to meet them in person again. Get rid of all those nightmares.

Gregory Francis, PhD in Poultry Sciences from Texas A&M, hadn't slept well in ages. But it wasn't his fault.

His mother had convinced him that, with his higher education, he should run for public office. Since diagnosing chicken diseases within the city limits of New Orleans didn't seem to be adding substantially to his static income, he agreed. Francis was, after all, a handsome and well-educated black man admired by all his neighbors for his college degrees.

His position in the community was also enhanced by the lifelong monthly payments he received from the Government, and earnings from his father's early investments in IBM. Gregory Sr had been a warrant officer in the Army, one of the few black chopper pilots in Nam. The elder Francis had not returned from southeast Asia, but he had the foresight to set up a support system for his wife and son before he left. Having barely known his father, Gregory Jr was quite content with the results of his demise. The Jr had occupied fourteen years of his life going to college on the GI bill. At his final graduation ceremony, he was upset to learn that there was no degree beyond his poultry PhD, and considered starting a whole new career in Ceramic Arts to keep the Veteran's

Administration school benefits flowing. A&M had finally asked him to vacate his dorm room.

Still, if not rich, the Francises were left comfortably off. In the Upper Ninth Ward, that was rich. But his mother was not satisfied. Her son never let her watch her soaps in peace.

Just talks and talks, that's what he does. Right when things are getting good, too. Somebody kissing or hugging, he's getting nervous and talking about skin diseases in Rhode Island Reds. Anything but the kissing. He just can't stand to see that boy-and-girl stuff. More comfortable with chicken sex. Not healthy.

Forty-one and the boy still living at home. I got to get him a woman. Get him a job.

Get him out the house.

Then one afternoon Gregory Jr had heard his Mom cry out "Hallelujah, sweet Jesus!" from the kitchen. Watching the five o'clock news, Mrs had seen that Rayford "Jackleg" Copeland had been forced to resign from the City Council under the weight of eighteen Federal counts of interstate mail fraud. An election would be held in March, and there was no one of right mind who wanted to take over the politically-explosive seat.

For Mrs Francis it was a godsend. She knew right away: Gregory could forget yolk statistics and be a politician. He'd be a shoo-in. Nobody real was interested in running, anyway. And the job paid good money. Whatever the job was.

He and his Mom didn't count on a homeless Street bum and a bunch of sex fiends to be much in the way of opposition. They had heard tell that Jeansonne was possibly white or at least bright, a devil-worshiper and probably the purveyor of some strange sexual persuasion. Though possessing a Poultry Science PhD, the Francis household was not as thorough in non-egg research. They had not realized that there were very nearly as many strange sexual persuasions in the district as there were ethnic mixes. And that the Street person was taking the political race seriously.

Gregory, having no idea what a Council member actually does, or for that matter what Government does, was at a loss for discussion of issues. He invested his IBM dividend check in the campaign, bullish in yard sign futures. No one outside his neighborhood recognized him from the photo. His next-door neighbor had refused to put up a "Francis for Council" yard-sign until he met the candidate.

It was then that Doctor Gregory Francis realized he needed votes to win.

"Outta Space?

"Lady, what all this Outta Space tawk?" repeated Lee Fat. "This my first time vote here, unnerstan'? This French Quattas verr-r-ry differen'. I wan' unnerstan'. Everyt'ing. My family own 'is properties. We living here now. I vote. My wife my son his wife vote. I go jury duty, be good citizen. See many strange peoples. I meet this man LM you say. Also differen', but very good man. You see I know him. LM. I tell my wife I meet good 'merican man in jury duty. He talk to me. She say she know. Missa Rodrigo man he inna church, he telling her also about this LM. So, I unnerstan' you say this man he running for City Councils. I vote for him. She voting for him. We all voting for him. Good, I say, good. I unnerstan' that he make good councilman, I unnerstan' that fine, but what all this Outta Space tawk?"

Lee Fat's English remains at a low level of sophistication because he wants it that way. For his own use he has mastered both the exquisite manners and wide-ranging vocabulary of Mandarin Chinese. But he can handle himself well in the subtleties of four other dialects. Plus French, Spanish and the hated but necessary Japanese. Proficiency in languages is as necessary to him as is the skill to disguise that proficiency. For Lee Fat also speaks Business.

But the namesake of the Lee Fat Restaurant is now faced with four portions of American politics that even he can't quite fathom: Street campaigners Virginia and Noonie, a large & loud duck, and a handmade LM Jeansonne campaign leaflet that is covered with colorful drawings of Saturn.

The family is on the campaign trail.

"I knew I knew I knew you shoulda let me draw it," says Noonie.

"Quuuaa-a-ackk!" replies a nonplussed duck.

"Maybe a lucky bead, mister?"

The American networks loved it. For once the milquetoast news mongers at the BBC had actually given them something Americans would watch. Aerial footage of inscrutable and unexplainable graphic designs flattened into the wheatfields of the English midlands. Mystery. Danger. A dramatic surge in ratings. The UFO fever had been ebbing for lack of a new angle. Now the down-to-earth British evidence allowed media mongers to stoke the fires once again.

The New York nets offered a substantial reward to any American farmer who could bring forth additional proof. By September there wasn't an acre of soybeans or summer wheat in seven Southern states that didn't have at least one hieroglyph from outer space cut into its protein yield.

The Federal government promised supplemental checks to all American farmers who suffered economic hardship from crops lost to alien calligraphy.

Chris Reed's politically-connected father Leonard Reed himself had the misfortune of losing a large portion of his new wheat crop to wily aliens with bad penmanship. The Agriculture Department had ended part of his farming subsidy, but he cannily made $200 more an acre in government Alien Calligraphic Compensation than he would have made selling the grain. Leonard predicted additional crop invasion on a regular basis.

Those little boogers just love to write on my land.

He even bought a brand new Allis-Chalmers industrial-grade wide-swath mower in anticipation of next year's crop.

Leonard Reed was gratified when his daughter stopped asking for extra money on a weekly basis. She even told her father that she never accepted any money directly from the campaign. But Mr Reed noticed that his daughter seemed to be in much better financial shape since she put this Jeansonne in the race. He thought that especially odd. Since he knew she was on unpaid leave from her job at the DA's office.

Old Borden must be kicking in. And a good thing if he is.

It had been all he could do to salvage that DA job after she went topless on television. The TV news director had decently placed black rectangles over her most prominent anatomic features. In compliance with the City Health Code, he was sure. Political breast-baring made the local news all the way upstate to Winnfield. Mrs Reed, both eyes on the screen as she ate a home-cooked dinner off a TV tray one Sunday evening, had recognized Chris' features instantly. The alarmed matron spewed black-eyed peas and cornbread all over the den. Adeline, Mrs Reed's cook of 22 years, had to use the Heimlich maneuver on her boss to stop her from gagging.

Mrs Leonard Reed had not hosted a bridge game since.

Leonard himself was not affected the same way. He was rather proud of his daughter's audacity. Though he was not likely to admit it to any one else.

If I had 'em, I'd use 'em, too.

That Chris always seems to land on her feet. Some-damn-how. Here she is, just a couple of months after a major scandal, she's still on TV every night like she's a goddamn celebrity or something. And she's doing better than ever financially.

That girl's more accomplished at this game than any of the boys.

Maybe I ought to call her up and tell her.

He thinks about that.

Naw. I can tell her next Christmas. Tell her in person then.

He looks out the window of his office. Rubbing his eyes clear of the stinging smoke generated by the first phases of the ongoing wheat harvest.

Rotate everything back to soy beans next year, and a damn good thing. Get the Alien compensation money first. But I got to get to work, call the Capitol. Make sure those fools keep my sugar cane subsidy   and those oh-so-substantial non-farming revenues   in place.

It's only fair. Since I don't intend to grow sugar again, I ought to be paid for not growing it.

He needs to get on the phone, but his daughter keeps returning to his mind.

He has to admit he is proud.

Leonard Reed grins.

Leave it to that Chris to make a profit off losers and queers.

Rodrigo and Fred were thrilled to be Mutt's campaign managers. They took their duties very seriously. Besides accompanying him on speaking commitments, they coordinated all his "outside work." They helped Noonie and Virginia organize the temp workers for flyer distribution and door-to-door contacts. They worked with Mel, Mia and both the gay and business organizations to rally segments of the population that had not participated in City Government before. Their mission also included the recruiting of individuals long alienated from a Government that was perceived as useless and irrelevant.

Mutt had been wondering about the wisdom of Rodrigo's frequent all-night campaign strategy meetings at Mel's house, though. Rodrigo seemed constantly exhausted. Exhausted, but happy. And coherent. So Mutt let his campaign co-manager's enthusiasm ride on without comment. Mutt was becoming organized himself, much to his own amazement.

His other co-manager, known at Robichaux House as the absentee-voter Mrs FT Jeansonne, is in high spirits and even better physical condition. The campaign fund has provided a constant supply of Doc Wolf's ration to its most avid and tireless worker. Her fur is now shiny and healthy-looking. She has more of it, too. The reduced intake of jalapeno chilidogs has also done much to relieve Fred's gastric turmoil. Consequently, she is much more welcome at the various eating gatherings to which she and Mutt are invited. Once her small dietary problem was in control, her presence grew to be expected at all of Mutt's speeches. People liked the idea of a man who had such a loyal dog. A dog who seemed to understand every word he said.

The same voters didn't care much for the rich Uptown wardrobe and upstate mannerisms of Chris Reed. And, they knew she was a DA   a universally-despised authority figure. Besides being born in North Louisiana. Immigrants from the upper reaches of the state were immediately suspect. The characteristic tolerance of New Orleanians was stretched to the limits by these Northerners. The portion of the state above Bunkie   a town some 150 northwest of New Orleans   was among the few areas of the world regarded as uncivilized by residents of the District. Why, they didn't even let people buy liquor up there. What more proof could a thinking person want? Next thing you know they'll be into shrunken heads and meter maid cannibalism.

No, for most folks, the northern girl was out.

The dog was in.

Mutt's own loyalty to his original partner remained unchanged through all the comings and goings of the political campaign. He often spoke of his as a shared candidacy. Shared with Fred. Mutt always held Fred up for the audience's applause after his speeches, Fred wagging her tail and barking happily into the microphone. Just the way she had seen Ellis D perform at the Ball.

Goes to show you can even learn something from a duck, she thought.

When it was time to get workers on the streets with campaign flyers, though, Mutt had his own design ideas. He asked Marty the doorman to take his picture holding Fred. He wanted to stick that picture on a sheet with his name and candidate number. Fred's name, too. L Mutt Jeansonne, Number 9, and Fred T Jeansonne. That was the way the flyers had come out, the picture dead center. All of them pink. All of them with the smiling Candidate and his broadly smiling dog. The Candidate was the one on the right.

Fred still slept in Mutt's room at the House. They had been in a six-foot-square box together all those years. Their Robichaux House bedroom seemed extravagantly large, even though it was only twelve-by-twelve. At first Mutt felt guilty that they had the room all to themselves, but he got used to the luxury after a few weeks.

Fred had her own bed, an old sofa pillow set beneath a poster of Doc Wolf. She received the free picture with the purchase of a full case of her favorite dog food. After a hard day on the campaign trail, Fred slept sweetly under the snarling face of the Doc.

But if Fred and Rodrigo ran the Outside, Mutt ran his own Inside campaign. He worked the phones constantly.

Mutt had a three-line telephone installed on the wall of his bathroom, and ran his personal campaign from what Rodrigo called The Candidate's Throne.

The toilet had a padded pull-down lid with JFK's face printed on it in neon colors. Mutt had picked out the design himself from the varied stock of a pickup truck displaying goods for sale on Basin street just outside the Quarter. It was a hard decision. All three designs were good. But his choice had to be right. It was either JFK or the Last Supper or Dogs Playing Pool. He wasn't much on religion in the bathroom, in spite of his current forgiveness for the nuns. And he didn't want Fred picking up any bad gambling habits. So he picked JFK. After all, JFK was a politician, too. It suited the occasion. The toilet tank cover and bath rug matched the lid. Mutt was very proud of the room, and often held "lid-down" meetings with his staff within its confines. But mostly, he worked the phones.

His private bathroom was worth all the sore throats in the world. And his phone let him enjoy the room at his leisure, even during the campaign.

Mutt tirelessly called every home in his District. He called homes repeatedly to get people's opinions. To find out what they needed from their Government. To inquire as to the health of their pets. He was entertaining and respectful on the phone. Rather than an intrusion, a phone call from Mutt Jeansonne grew to be an event central to neighborly conversation. Like a particularly good "Justin Wilson" rerun that old Cajun cook could talk too.

"Mutt called me again last night," 84-year-old Mrs Dedeaux would holler out over the back fence.

"Second time this week, ain't it, dahlin'?" enquired Mrs Johnson, her generous figure projected on a clothesline of damp men's underwear.

"Yep. He said he called back because he was worried about Spike's wheeze. Said it had been bothering him thinking my old cat might have caught this Asian cold that's been going around. Said Miz Thompson over in the five hundred block of Piety street, her Catahoula cur caught it, and Miz Thompson started feeding him loads of garlic all crushed up in his food. Dog got well in two days. Breath smelled horrible for a week, but he wasn't wheezing no more. I started Spike on it this morning. See, babe, I like it that the Mutt got his dog on that campaign pitcher. That an honest-looking dog, too. Look like a old-lady pit-bull. I never seen one that old. Wonder that dog she live so long cause she eatin' that garlic?"

Mrs Johnson put down her husband's workshirt without pinning it up on the line. She walked over to the fence, and motioned Mrs Dedeaux to come over.

She spoke quietly. "You know, Bess, I'm gonna vote for that nice boy. I don't care who he hangs out with. Not one little bit. The votin' precinck is right behind the Church, and after I get my ashes I'm gonna walk in there and vote for that boy."

"Me, too, babe," whispered Bess Dedeaux. "Father Wildman was saying at Sunday Mass that the Pope thinks them homosexualists are going against God's laws, an' that Mr Jeansonne might let them run wild right over our kids, make them all into homosexualists. But, hey, Baby June is 34 now, and Ray is away by LSU doing who knows what all already. Besides, little Joey DeSoto over on Lesseps street he's the sweetest dearest boy I ever known, him taking care of his sick Momma an' all, an' he's a homosexualist. That Joey even takes Communion. Every day. I don't think Father Wildman knows, though, or he might not be giving Joey the Sacrament. Besides, it's just me an' Bert here at home, an' I think this Jeansonne boy is the only political man done called me in the fifty-two years I lived in this house. Boy's got my vote, an' I'm gonna make sure my Bert votes the same, besides."

"Yeah you right, Gerty. Boy always seems so natural real nice when he call me on the phone. Very polite. Better than my chirren. How old you think that boy is? Don't answer. It don't matter. He called me three time now, an' I can tell by his voice he's comfortable around people. Good-nature boy."

She got closer to her companion.

"You know. I wonder if he's a white boy? I be curious. Don't matter he is or not. I'm voting for him anyway."

Mrs Johnson leaned back. "Now," she said, turning very very serious. "You ridin' in the Truck Parades Carnival morning, or you marchin' with the Sodality?"

With a few variations on the theme, this conversation was carried out dozens of times daily in the District that encompassed the French Quarter, Faubourg Marigny and Upper Ninth Ward. When he wasn't on the Street, Mutt was in his porcelain office until late at night. Talking to his hundreds of new-found friends. And making a few dozen more. He never seemed to grow tired of talking to people. It was like he had been saving up all this conversation until he found the right audience. He was convinced that he had done just that.

He wasn't going to waste his attention on those billboards any more. Nope. Not now. Didn't need to. He could talk to folks straight out. Even Norms. Mutt had found Family, and they him.

So, while his opponents hammered out their messages in 30-second TV spots, the Jeansonne campaign was for a large part advanced with its Candidate's pants around his ankles.

Lid up.

"What effect do you think holding the election the day after Carnival will have on your Candidate, Miss Reed? Have you calculated what extra incentives you will need to get the vote out amongst all the perverts and guttersnipes?"

DAR Borden is grilling Chris Reed before she has completely seated herself in the diminutive chair to which she had been resolutely directed. Robert Markham is already wedged in place in his own narrow seat when Reed arrives. He is used to his boss' seating arrangements.

All the chairs in front of Borden's massive oak desk are of a reduced scale. Borden feels that the size relationships among the pieces of furniture help assert his own power hierarchy. Borden is used to being at the top. The uncomfortable miniature chairs say so loudly.

"Daddy told me you were all business, Don. I've seen you in Court, and now I've seen you in the office and I'm most impressed," Reed says without a flinch.

Markham involuntarily gasps, so loudly that both Borden and Reed turn to him. Markham can't help it. He had never heard anyone below the State Senator level use Borden's first name, especially in the diminutive. "DAR" or "Donald" maybe, but "Don"?

Markham tries to recover. "And Daddy's always right. Right, DAR?" he gambles.

Borden looks at his subordinate. He is not much amused by either of the people in front of him, especially after Reed's reference to the drunken Harry Dubney's sojourn in the custody of the New Orleans Police Department.

The little bitch.

He turns back to face the room with a certain regal hauteur in place. To reflect his disdain.

"I know this is our first personal meeting, Miss, and that you have been working primarily with our Mr Markham here, but... I believe the firm has been most generous in financing your project so far, and for that I believe we deserve to know exactly how our money is being spent. We want safeguards in place to protect both the firm's finances and its good name."

Borden removes a cigar from its metal case, and takes the time to clip off its tip on a small desk-sized guillotine. Reed remains silent. As she watches his tongue deliberately licks the black stick of tobacco around its circumference. She knows he is baiting her. He places the cigar in his mouth, pulls a gold lighter engraved with his family crest from his vest pocket and flame-starts the rich smoke. Reed is patient. After two puffs she is still silent.

"I am sure you realize that we are going to want far more than simple good will in return for our investment. We have long had an application in mind for such a project. We will undoubtedly use it, should your efforts prove successful. We have need of a sympathetic voice to place a small piece of legislation before the council. We do not currently have such an entree. Your man will suffice. And actually, I have already met your Mr Jeansonne on several occasions and know him for exactly who and what he is."

Borden blows another puff across his desk, then leans forward, glaring at the woman sitting in his under-sized "power" chair.

"I don't think you've answered my question, Miss Reed."

He feels he is immune to such an upstart. A woman, too. No matter her father's influence. This is his office. His power will not be compromised in here.

But if the senior partner is unfazed, neither is Reed daunted by Borden. She'd never suspected that Borden would have ever had occasion to meet Mutt Jeansonne. But if anything, it is helpful that this old bastard has no misconceptions about the identity of the Candidate he is backing.

She's cracked them older, richer and crabbier. Her manipulatory skills are practiced and seamless. But she never lets her confidence show. A true Southern Lady is always cast as a bit fragile and helpless. It is an expectation that she takes great delight in frustrating. The vacuum created by that false supposition sucks the fools in every time.

I can feel a hurricane-force wind starting to whistle tunes up this old goat's wrinkled ass right now. Got him.

Christine Reed, ex-debutante and three-time Future Homemakers of America vice-president, holds Borden's gaze silently for a further five seconds. She is counting.

One thousand one.

Slowly.

One thousand two.

Not a pause long enough to be considered insolent.

One thousand three.

No, she won't let him off that easy.

One thousand four.

Reed lets just enough time elapse to force her opponent to an acknowledgment of her strength of will.

One thousand five.

As soon as she sees Borden's first squirm in his Power Chair, she drops her eyes demurely to her briefcase.

Right on time.

He draws in a breath of relief.

She begins to speak before she raises her head. "Eighty-three percent of French Quarter permanent residents, male and female, black, white and Hispanic, are gay. As of last week seventy-one percent of those are registered voters. There is too much in-fighting within that seventy-one percent for a consensus gay candidate. They are looking for someone who crosses the line, but is not an insider. Jeansonne. We can expect an almost complete turn-out in some degree for Mardi Gras festivities among the Quarter gays, and we will turn that to our advantage."

Reed is talking directly to Borden now. "The Candidate will take an active part in The Bourbon Street International Wonderland Trophy Awards as a jury member, and that is the one event that no gay person ever misses at Carnival."

Markham interrupts. "Christ, you're going to have a candidate for City Council judging a Drag Queen Contest? Are you crazy?"

Reed continues, unfazed, her eyes zeroing in on Borden, but softly.

"Mr Markham probably didn't hear my numbers, Don. Bob here doesn't realize that the Quarter gay community, with additional elements in the Marigny and the Upper Ninth, comprises almost forty percent of the total voting public in the District."

Reed's eyes remain locked on Borden, as she speaks to Markham with her voice absolutely level, without turning her head to him, "You didn't realize that, now did you, Bobby? No, you didn't. So let's keep quiet until I'm finished, won't you?"

Dead silence again. One beat.

Two. Three.

This is just like piano lessons. And I know the score to this conversation by heart.

Phrasing is everything.

Once again she continues. Steady and even. Enjoying herself. "The Candidate's registration drive among the indigent population has proved incredibly successful. Almost seven hundred new voters, directly attributable to Jeansonne's personal contact, in all three areas of the District. His blue-collar approval rating, in the poll I commissioned last week with the rather minimal funding you have so graciously provided...," another beat, "...shows our Candidate with above ninety percent name recognition overall, and with sixty percent approval rating over his two opponents among those voters who have made a choice. We took a substantial sample. Margin of error, plus or minus two percent. I've brought you copies of the straw poll summary pages."

Without rising, Reed holds out a stapled sheaf of crisp bond pages to Borden. He has to stand and reach over the expanse of his desk to get the offered papers. Ms Christine Reed does not extend her arm any further toward him. Nor does she rise from the miniature chair. Borden takes the papers back to his chair, sits down and begins reading them. Reed offers nothing to Markham, who is clearly fidgeting in the restrictive confines of his miniature chair.

She goes on. "The overlap here looks strong enough to insure a run-off, if not an outright win in the primary. But you'll notice he does have two weak areas. There is some reticence among the heavily Catholic areas of the Ninth, due to his association with gay causes and personalities. I believe we may be able to overcome that with the grassroots approach we are already using, and a small show of personal association right before the election.

"But, we have also found a very soft response among the black voters polled, basically due to a lack of racial identity on the part of the Candidate. In actuality, that lack has worked well for us so far in the campaign. Nobody knows what Jeansonne is, and he will only make oblique answers to questions in that direction, which is quite good. It is just how I would handle it, and Jeansonne does it without thinking. The man has some natural talent that he doesn't even realize is there. He unconsciously makes the racial questioner ashamed to be asking, and the question just goes away. He's actually quite good at this."

She stops once again, shoots a glance at Markham, who withers immediately, then looks back to his boss. When Borden raises his eyes from the poll results, she moves to a faster pace, carrying the two men along.

"But if he is to pull off the impossible and lock up this seat, he must connect with black voters as he has done with the working class. His phone efforts can only go so far.

"The black community sees his picture in the *Advocate* or the *Picayune* or watches him on television and thinks he may be Creole. That if he is black he can 'pass' as white and get on the inside for them.

"The whites aren't threatened because his features are not too identifiably African or radical. That's the way things are in this town   they don't really want to know. This fellow Rodrigo Somebody who is acting as a campaign assistant stood up in a staff meeting the other day and yelled that he was going to make Jeansonne into an Indian, for godsake. That might help, if it were possible and if there was a significant Native American population in the District. But even that wouldn't bring Jeansonne the hard-core votes that will go to his black opponent. Votes, that unless a clear alternative exists, will go to Mr Gregory Francis, simply because he advertises that he is black. Mr Francis' skin color in this case, whether fortunately or unfortunately for us, is his entire platform."

Borden finally feels on familiar ground. "Are you saying, Miss Reed, that our Candidate should declare himself to be Negro?" he asks, turning to Markham for the required reaction. Markham smiles. Borden acknowledges with a look.

Thank you, Markham, you can keep your job.

He turns back to Reed.

Reed is not smiling. "No, sir. But, knowing the nature of racial politics in the City, I am saying that our Candidate may need to declare himself to be something."

Charles Taylor signs the statement directly below his niece Rashann's crookedly written name. He places his left hand firmly in the middle of the page, looks up across the desk and holds out his right.

"Now whut 'bout mah money? Me'n this chile didn' come alla way crossa Nint' Ward justa be doin' no goddam good deed. We got us bills ta pay," he says, shaking his open hand for emphasis. "C'mon Francis, give it up."

"Just a moment, Mr Taylor," answers candidate Gregory Francis, taking another deep breath. He can smell the alcohol-soaked Taylor from behind his desk. He looks at the two people in front of him and wonders what he has gotten himself into.

His dislike of personal contact has not helped him in gathering votes. In the past weeks of campaigning he has acquired only one further clue as to the true workings of the democratic process. His revelation came from the afternoon television tabloid "Gut Feeling", hosted by the volatile Bavarian, Gus Meinfeld. Gregory Francis has come to believe the governmental scandals exposed daily by the screaming red-eyed Gus are the rule rather than the exception. He now knows that this is the way careers are made and broken in politics. Scandal and innuendo. And just like that, Charles Taylor came into Francis' life. Right on cue.

Taylor had called his Mom, Mrs Francis, with word that he had the dirty lowdown on that "hi-yella jizzball Jeansonne." The man Jeansonne was a racist and a child-abuser, and also undoubtedly in the power of satanic forces set to take over the world. Taylor had the proof. Mrs Francis had invited him over to the house for tea.

He accepted. Though he hadn't touched a drop of the tea.

"Well?" asks Taylor irritably.

"Let me once again make sure I have this right," says Gregory Jr, waving Taylor to stay in his chair. "I know we have this all written down, but I want to make sure that you know what you are saying in the statement." Francis pulls the document from under Taylor's hand and reads. "'That as a juror Mr Jeansonne did wrongfully convict a handicapped and elderly black man'   your brother   'of murder, conspiring with a racially imbalanced jury to deprive his daughter'   Rashann   'of both the support and affection of her natural father.' Is that correct, Mr Taylor?"

"Fuckin A. Though you dint mention at dog anna fact at boy's probly in cahoots widdem dog's Mars buddies. I showed you at!"

"Mr Taylor, a picture in the *Comet* is hardly to be considered proof of alien subjugation."

"OK. Don' matter. Long as we git him. Now, gimme at cash."

"I am sorry, but we have to give you this honorarium in check form, since it is a legally deductible campaign expense."

"Hows I know it ain' gonna bounce?"

"You may go to our corner grocery and cash it, Mr Taylor," says Francis drily, handing over the check. "The owner knows us quite well and will be happy to honor the check."

"I be right back if he don't, you kin believe that un."

"I am sure you will. Now, if you will excuse me. Good day Mr Taylor. Rashann."

Gregory Jr holds the door open and lets the Taylors out. Then he closes the outside metal security gate and double-deadbolts both it and the inner door.

He looks toward the back of the house and tilts his head up: "Motherrrrrr! I hate this!"

"But, my darlings, what can we say to him?" Mel shrieks. "The man is definitely smitten, and we know what that is like, don't we, Roddy? Captured by love! This is so dramatic, so perfectly Bette Davis! No, not this time...," she paused. "Maybe Betty Ford."

Fred growls low and long. The campaign staff dinner at the house on Toulouse street has finally come around to what was on everybody's mind.

It is after 11pm, so visiting residents and children alike are in bed upstairs or at the rooming house where the family occasionally rents extra rooms. But the core is there   Mel, Fred, Rodrigo, Noonie, Ellis and Virginia   everybody but Mutt. The candidate is being squired about by Chris Reed in a final night's courting of the few big-money Norms in the district. This is one of Reed's priorities rather than Mutt's, but he's patiently gone along for the intimacy of the car ride. Meanwhile, the family goes over strategy for the last day of the campaign.

They are meeting on Lundi Gras Fat Monday. On the day before Carnival, both King Rex and King Zulu arrive by boat to begin orchestrating the final mad hours before the climax of Mardi Gras Day. Marking the opening moments of the Magic Time.

But no one sitting on the dining room floor of Robichaux House has seen a single parade this Carnival season. They have been out every waking moment courting votes for the candidate. Mel has even taken off the week to help.

It isn't a big week for Can-Can-Do cash flow anyway. Not many people see a need to go in strip joints when everybody is naked on the streets. Not to mention that during Carnival it is usually too crowded to walk down Bourbon street. Audiences are mixed. Marty the doorman stands back. Most people literally fall in the door. Due to the press of bodies outside. Staying to buy the minimum number of drinks, use the bathroom and leave. After noticing that there are fewer naked women inside the bar than outside.

Mia has agreed to cover for Mel by working double shifts as her contribution, and even donated a percentage of her dance tips to the Campaign.

Virginia has not caught a single strand of the literally thousands of tons Mardi Gras beads that are thrown to the crowds from the parade floats. Those Lucky Beads are normally the source of her livelihood for the rest of the year.

There are now other priorities. The Campaign has become everything to this family. They are focused on it to the exclusion of everything else. In some cases this is quite welcome. Fred has not experienced a trial dream about either of her trials in months.

And yet, here they sit. After months of work. Just over twenty-four hours from Election Day, and they are absolutely certain that their candidate is being led on by his own campaign chairwoman. "Led on to what?" is the question on everyone's mind.

"But of course, we know. The Alamo. We know," Rodrigo's face brightens momentarily as he stares at Mel and is lost in sweaty thoughts far from the Campaign.

"No good. No good. Everybody knows. The duck knows. Ellis knows. Right, Ellis? She gonna hurt Mutt. He don't know about women. This woman no good, right, Ellis?" adds Noonie, breaking the silence.

A heartfelt "Quuaaaackk" is quickly given in reply.

"But we must, we must find some way to get our Mutt to look at what she is doing to him. I, too, can feel that something is wrong with the woman," Mel continues, "and yet nothing is. I see her do what seems to be the right thing for the Campaign, just perfect, and at the same time I just have this dreadful feeling that something is not right."

Rodrigo has snapped out of his reverie, "True that she is working for the Campaign. True that she is helping Mutt. Also true that she does not like any of us much. Not liking any of voting people living here. She is not living here. But what can she do when Mutt is Council person? Nothing. He is the Council person. Not her. Mutt's OK. He's growing up now. Better every day. Almost makes the Norms feel safe."

A pause.

Who was that talking?

"Perambulator!" Rodrigo adds for emphasis.

Ah, yes. Rodrigo. Me.

"It's not his political career I'm worried about, dearest joy of mine," said Mel. "It's his heart. His heart. He's just found it, and I'd hate to see it broken so quickly."

"Wah-ROOF!" says Fred.

"You're right, darling boy. And you, too, Freddy. We must deal with one thing at a time. Mutt must be able to handle his own business if he is to handle the business of City Government. Shall we agree to let the man handle his own personal affairs? Let him make his own decisions of the heart, even if they are not in line with ours?"

Two sets of affirmative nods settled the issue.

"Now," she says, looking at her notes, "what can we do about that lovely but paranoid padre down at St John's? I hear the delusional fellow is telling everyone that if Mutt gets elected it will mean an immediate transformation of the entire grammar school football team into a sashaying herd of bad lounge singers and interior decorators. Due to the influence of such as *moi*, of course. We simply must show *il papa* that Mutt is a good boy! Maybe a late night phone call..."

"Wah-ROOF!" says Fred.

Most historians assert that the Mardi Gras Indians in New Orleans are not really Indians.

These scholars have a valid viewpoint. The Mardi Gras Indians will be the first to tell you. Most have never ridden a horse, been on a reservation or inside a tepee. Most have French, Spanish or English last names. Eight out of ten have little or no American Indian blood running in their veins. Yet since before the turn of the century they have held on to an Indian identity.

The forty or so small tribes who parade on Carnival as the Mardi Gras Indians are for the most part descendants of African peoples brought to this land in chains over the last three centuries. Now free to roam in the prison of contemporary Norm society.

On the other hand, their hearts are as Indian as can be imagined. And never more so than on Mardi Gras Day.

Once-bloody territorial battles between tribes have undergone the ultimate metamorphosis. Around 1965 Mardi Gras Indians began to win face by concentrating on out-dressing and out-dancing their enemies, rather than by maiming them. The Big Chiefs became content that their rivals would merely "bow down" and acknowledge the quality of their tribes. Though this mark of respect remains no small matter.

Mostly poor and working class, the Indians scrimp and save all year to invest thousands of dollars in the feathers, beadwork and sequins that make up the eight-to-ten-foot-tall Indian "suits". The unbreakable rule is that the Indian must sew his own suit. So, for months before Carnival, hundreds of very aggressively macho African-American males can be found all over New Orleans, needle and thread in hand. Sewing, gluing and stapling large feathered outfits.

It is a soul-satisfying and uplifting experience.

The black Mardi Gras Indians are not an experience which fits most well-to-do, Anglo, Uptown sorts.

For Rodrigo, however, they are tailor-made.

"Sister Mary Ambrosia, I am so sorry to wake you, but don't you know how thrilled Mutt would be if you could accompany him to Church here in his very own District on Election Day?" Mel cajoles. "You could get your ashes together, just like when he was one of your Boys, and help him start the newest part of his life properly, with the blessing of the Church."

Melodie LaGrande listens patiently to the frail voice on the other end of the line. She hears a hint of a musical Irish accent inflecting the English words. The Irish are a large-hearted and energetic part of the City, and Mel has always relished the melodious sound of their speech.

Nuns from Ireland had been a major part of almost every Catholic child's education in New Orleans since a time well beyond any living memory.

Mel speaks again, remembering disconnected snippets of her own schoolboy days. "Yes, maam, day after tomorrow, Ash Wednesday, nine o'clock Mass at St John the Conqueror parish down on Burgundy street   oh, you do know Father Wildman, do you? How divine! I'm sure a few words from you will do wonders in helping the good padre understand our Mutt.

"No, Sweetie, it's to be a surprise. We'll bring him there right before we all go to vote ourselves. Oh, wonderful! Love you, love you, love you! You know, I often thought of being a Nun myself. I just never could get that vocation part together. A wardrobe problem, I think. I was such a trying child.

"Going to the parades tomorrow, Sister A? Oh, Rex! The King of Carnival has the absolute best parade   you'll love the Krewe of Rex. So much color! So much history! That two-story bull out front   the 'fattened calf' on Fat Tuesday! What? No, sweets, I am not making this up. Now don't you worry. Just paper mache. I don't even think the poor baby is anatomically correct.

"Well, you darling girls be careful, catch lots of beads and pray for those naughty folks who might be sinning. It will undoubtedly help all the poor bad children get a head start on the repenting they'll have to do, come Ash Wednesday. Ta, now."

Melodie hangs up quickly.

"When all else fails, break out the Nuns," she proclaims.

Virginia and Noonie, sitting on the floor across from the toilet, applaud vigorously.

* * *

Mardi Gras sunrise cuts the chill from the air outside The Plunder on Dauphine street. The eight Indians inside have been sewing all night, getting their suits completed and prepared for the day's run. Every available inch of the bar is taken up with huge cascades of orange, green, black and red feathers, giant patches of multicolored beadwork and architectural design executed in sequins. These are Downtown designs, as opposed to the more body-contoured rhinestone-and-bead-based suits of Uptown tribes.

Big Chief Julius Sanchez of the Mighty Choktaw Warriors is not about to Bow Down to any other Chief this Carnival. Not from lack of effort. He will have the most beautiful, most ornate suit of any Indian in the entire Ninth Ward. He will have the liveliest and best dressed tribe.

"Mightee-kooteefie-YO!" the Big Chief cries.

"Big Chief!" is the tribe's answer.

"Indian Red!" they beg, ready for the call to start their run.

"Jockomo!" yells Julius Sanchez, unwilling to leave until the suits are perfect.

"Jockomofeenahnay!" cries his tribe. They will be ready. They go back to work.

Except for the eight-year-old Spy Boy. Sanchez' grandson Rudy doesn't return the ritual greeting. He is soundly sleeping on the pool table, covered with his McDonough 15 school jacket. His purple feathered pants are explosively bright on the table's worn and faded green felt. Rudy's mother is at his side, dozing sitting upright in a chair beside the pool table. Her arm extends across one of the pockets, to lightly touch her child's face as he sleeps.

Sanchez' son   also his Second Chief   is at the back of the bar, cursing a sewing machine that has jammed for the umpteenth time that night. He mutters horrible insinuations as to the parentage of the aging machine, all the while trying to secure yet another layer of ostrich plumes to the Big Chief's his dad's ten-foot-tall tribal staff.

The bar's dark cubbyhole booths are all filled with completed elements of the suits. Even the bathroom stalls are being used as workspaces for the Indians, much to the chagrin of their heavily-drinking followers. Every tribe member is caught up in the same excited ritual, running about the piles of feathers, frantically tightening here, sewing an extra stitch there. Making sure that the Indian suits will withstand the rigors of a full day's running and dancing, making sure that the Warriors will not lose a moment's face. As they strut for judgment by the people of their neighborhood.

Big Chief Julius Sanchez will not Bow Down today. The Assistant Master Plumber for the New Orleans Sewerage & Water Board is Big Chief on the Mardi Gras Day. He will Bow Down to no man this Carnival. On the contrary, they will bow to him. Respect will be given to the small tribe from the Upper Ninth Ward. Respect is due to the Big Chief of the Mighty Choktaw Warriors.

"Won't Bow Down!" the Third Chief cries.

"Big Chief Julius!" responds the Flag Boy.

"Upper Nine rules!" screams the hoarse, frog-voiced bartender.

The tribe begins to yell ever more frequently, working itself up for the last strenuous dozen hours of a day that had already stretched to at least thirty. These are the hours and minutes the tribe has waited and prepared for. They have dreamt about this day the entire last year. Soon Big Chief Julius Sanchez will sing out the first lines of "Indian Red." He will sing the song that calls masking tribe members to the street in front of the den. The dingy rooms of The Plunder will echo with the call.

"Mightee-kooteefie-YO!" he will cry. The hair will stand up on the necks of the Indians. Their moment finally come.

The tribe will answer, "Eee-yahYAYYYY, eee-YAH-yay!", their hearts pounding.

The Day will begin.

* * *

The anonymous press release had hit the mail bags of every TV and radio station, every print medium, every city official, by late Monday evening. It boldly outlined LM Jeansonne's racial and moral transgressions, claiming him unfit for office, and "undoubtedly pro-immigration." The uncredited hand of Mrs Gregory Francis Sr had added that statement at the last minute. She had been inspired to the additional accusation by hearing a particularly inflammatory sermon at the corner of Bourbon and Canal streets as she shopped the pre-Carnival sales for a lace tablecloth. Something for her final Mardi Gras king cake party.

There was no chance for television broadcasters to follow up until the late shift arrived Lundi Gras night. The crews don't get started until well after the ten o'clock news.

It seems Charles Taylor does have a brother in Angola: Walter. And that Walter is in prison for murder, and that indeed he was convicted around the time of Mutt Jeansonne's jury duty. News directors all over town go for it.

Travel time to Angola penitentiary from New Orleans is two and a half hours. The prison's newly-promoted PR officer and the assistant warden are not happy about being dragged from bed by the multiple caffeine-activated phone calls.

Lights are set up in the prison conference room. It is now three in the morning. Inmate chefs are brought in to make coffee. All three network affiliates, and a lone producer/director for a syndicated program dealing with extra-terrestrial police abuse, have made the journey. The prison has not received much in the way of favorable press in a very long time. The PR officer sees this as an opportunity to show the media that Angola Penitentiary isn't such a bad place. He will show he deserves his promotion. The prison will, of course, be glad to allow emergency interviews with this Taylor character.

There are twenty-seven people, not including guards, in the room. A sleep-eyed Walt Taylor is rolled in his wheelchair into the harsh yellow tungsten glare, four microphones jammed in his face, and a roar of questions about a man named LM Jeansonne jammed in his ears. Camera operators bang elbows jockeying for the best angle.

The media assemblage receives ten words for their trouble.

"Fuck you an' fuck at man too, whoever a hell he is," says Taylor, and rolls himself to the exit. The PR officer is at a loss for words. The overnight reporters, themselves startled awake by the violence of the set-up and the brevity of the interview, decide unanimously that the story will have to be developed in a voice-over.

None are quite convinced they have a story.

* * *

Robert Markham is not convinced either.

His boss has called him from the krewe of Rex warehouse at 6am. Markham can hear the marching bands tuning up in the background. Rex Float Captain DAR Borden, already masked to hide his identity in the parade, has a Mardi Gras message for his employee.

"Get down there, you idiot!" comes the voice over the phone. Borden. "The morning news said something about accusations! That Jeansonne is a racist, of all things! The man doesn't even know what race he is! You handle it. You are assigned to monitor campaign progress   you do it! There is no need to tell you that this is crucial last day before the election, now is there?"

"No sir."

"Well, then get to it, you poppinjay! An' hab a huppy Marni Gras," blithers Borden as he hangs up.

Perfect. Just perfect. Borden's getting drunk at sunrise, climbing on a hundred-thousand-dollar carnival float to throw beads and doubloons to the masses. Raising hell with all his bigshot Uptown society buddies. Just one more nouveau riche interloper snuck in there among real Old Money society people.

Me, I'm supposed to spend my Mardi Gras by the goddamn phone.

The only consolation is that the wife, kids and Momma Sandra the Bitch will be at the parades all day.

I'll check in with Reed. She's supposed to be working, too. I'll give her a call. Maybe we can have a little tete-a-tete.

An all-business "head-to-head", of course.

He dials. Reed answers immediately and, unfortunately, turns out to be all business. She is a great deal more optimistic than he had anticipated, but not about seeing him.

She is letting him know that in no uncertain terms.

"That bullshit about discrimination will be buried in Carnival news. I mean, come on, Markham. Like anyone in New Orleans would care if they found Adolph Hitler on a flagpole on Mardi Gras Day   nothing's going to bum them out. Besides, Mutt Jeansonne hasn't got a racist bone in his body. So skip it, Bobby."

"Chris, I thought this was an important development," whines Markham, his fantasies once again unfulfilled.

"I said skip it, Bobbyboy. Stop thinking. It's Carnival. Just pay attention to my voice. Ready?"

"I think..."

"OK. I've got media coverage scheduled to hit the air starting with the Noon News. They should already be out with him. We'll get fine exposure. The television bits will touch all the district voters who are too old or infirm to get out to the parades. We'll show them Jeansonne in the midst of every cute-kid family on Canal street.

"What are you worried about, anyway, Markham? Tell Borden we're riding high in the polls. We're going to make the run-off, no matter what happens today. We'll get that Council seat, and from there we'll fill both our wish-lists easily."

Markham responds quickly, "I'm confident you can pull a run-off spot, but the conservative portion of your district will unite in a second election. After the primary they'll focus in on your man Jeansonne. His chances will be greatly diminished if he has to run another campaign."

"Jeez, fella, no wonder you're such a hardleg. The world has really got you pussy-whipped, Bobbycakes. And so do I."

Robert Markham has once again been rendered speechless by Ms Christine Reed of Winnfield, Louisiana.

She continues, "Call what friends you've got in the district, Markham. Stay home in front of the tube and report to Borden on Jeansonne's television exposure. Skip the BS and watch TV news. Stay home. You're not the sort who's any fun at Carnival, anyway."

* * *

Outside The Plunder, dozens of admirers, friends and family members of the Choktaws wait, drinking neat whiskey and gin from bottles to keep warm in the chill morning. A cool snap like this is the rule rather than the exception around Carnival time, and most of the Indian watchers are prepared for it. They bring their anti-freeze of preference by the pint. Conversation means clouds of steamy whiskey-laced breath.

Candidate Mutt Jeansonne is nervous.

Rodrigo and Fred seem completely comfortable, though. Rodrigo is mixing with the neighborhood crowd as if he was one of them. Sitting on the wooden steps of the bar. Back-patting and drink-sharing with everyone. He seems to take particular delight in the Indian calls himself. By sunrise Rodrigo has Fred so absorbed in the whole scene that she delightedly howls long and loud each time Rodrigo yells an Indian call.

"Jockomo!" screams Rodrigo.

"Ooowwoooooo-oooo-*OOOO!*" howls Fred.

"Injun like coyote," says Rodrigo proudly to the friends of the Choktaw, patting Fred on her grey head. Fred howls again, to the delight of the crowd. Many of whom take up the refrain.

"Owooooooooo-oo*OOO*," howl a dozen voices.

Chris Reed has indeed done some string-pulling to get a video crew familiar with the Candidate to cover his last day before the Election. She has given up on the minority groups she considers too weak to win over in the primary   especially in view of the libelous last-ditch racial attack that had undoubtedly come from the Francis camp. However, she thinks a little more highly of Gregory Francis Jr today   Reed hadn't estimated the man had any real politics in him at all. He had made her change her plans. Discounting the black vote as now too sensitive for any gamble on haphazard repair efforts, she has decided that mainstream Carnival footage will be the perfect middle-of-the-road sort of images. The Candidate will be seen where it will do the Campaign the most good.

She has instructed Mutt to mix with a few constituents waiting for Mardi Gras parades, shake some hands. Let the news boys get some "man of the people" video. Maybe give them a sound bite about the City's Great Heritage. Then send the crew on their way.

That is the slightly tricky part. Reed has made sure the video team has other assignments. To take them away from the candidate's side long before his appearance as a Drag Queen Judge. He needs to court his gay constituents, but Reed doesn't want that effort blatantly hitting the tube and alienating more conservative voters.

Joey Dayers knows only that he is to record a little generic Mardi Gras footage of the Candidate. Then he is to go about the rest of his shoot day schedule. But he is puzzled. *What is this mingling with some minor Mardi Gras Indian tribe?* Did Reed really set this in place? The Rodrigo character had called up the station with a last-minute change of location. Contrary to Reed's instructions. She had told him last night that they were only after a few family shots on Canal street.

Something is cooking again.

In spite of their other major Carnival assignments, Dayers and his crew are eager. Reed had never failed to come up with the goods. Even when it was goods she wished they hadn't recorded.

She had given up asking Dayers for the raw footage of her breast-revelation. Like anyone familiar with the mind-set of the workhorse news-cameraman, she knew the tape had long since made its one-way journey into that most treasured possession of any videographer   Dayers' personal out-take reel. Consequently, for such a contribution to his collections of gaffs, Dayers was more than willing to get up early and knock out a few frames of video on the Candidate.

And a colorful few frames it might be.

The Candidate will be up to his ass in Indians.

Can't remember anybody even slightly important ever coming down here in the 'hood to see these guys run their asses off all day. Could be a cute little human interest story. If I don't freeze my balls off first.

Better have another little snort.

Dayers and his working partners have their own flasks as protection against the cold, too. It's an unspoken perk for Carnival duty. Station management turned its head to a small amount of partying, but only on Mardi Gras Day, and only in the field. It was, after all, forty-nine degrees this morning. Fairly Arctic for those of New Orleans blood.

There is a burst of noise just inside the bar door. The Indians are starting to sing.

"Yo, boys!" he yells. "Here we go."

"Marvin, get the shotgun mike ready," Dayers calls out. "Jon, let's get a white balance and hope the registration holds. Run me some color bars quick. I'll want you to put the VCR into Record Camera mode as soon as the first Indian comes out the door. And keep the extra tapes in hand. I want to be ready for a quick reload."

With all the equipment demands for the multiple microwave crews out today, he'd been stuck with a prehistoric camera. This is another source of continued bourbon-augmented whining as he automatically starts preparing to do his job.

"...tubes, mind you, Jon, and a recorder separate from the camera. Where did Engineering find this dinosaur? No docking VCR. No auto white balance. No auto registration. I'm lucky the damn thing has three tubes. At least I've got the manpower. I know I can trust you and Marvin to get me decent video if you have to draw the pictures on tape. We'll send them back live video like they've never seen before! Good god! Why is that dog howling like that?"

Out the Choktaw Warriors come.

Mutt seems to realize that this is what he has come for. He walks forward slowly. The final Indians emerge, circling the big Chief. The drummers follow the feathered tribe as far as the bar's stoop, banging on their worn percussion instruments as the Indians sing.

"Somebody got soul, soul, soul.." goes the chant. Dancing bodies take on the legs of the music. The hundred or so people surrounding the bar begin to sing increasingly loud harmony with the tribe. "... soul, soul, soul..." Rodrigo holds Fred above his head as the dog wails in time: "... raoowrr, raoowrr, *raoowrr...*"

Mutt Jeansonne steps to the front of the crowd. He stands silent and unmoving, directly behind the Big Chief, waiting for the Indian to turn and notice him.

That happens. The singing and drums dwindle. The Big Chief of the Mighty Choktaw is not happy. The ritual he has waited for all year is being interrupted. By some outsider. He looks directly at Mutt Jeansonne and screams at the top of his lungs:

"EEEEEeee-YAHHHhhh!"

Mutt does not flinch. He looks back at Assistant Master Plumber Julius Sanchez and says respectfully:

"Big Chief."

Mutt bends his bad leg and awkwardly gets down on one knee. He Bows Down to the Big Chief of the Mighty Choktaws.

Joey Dayers is about to have a stroke. He knows good video when he sees it. He has shot with the best before.

But THIS! This is REAL! This Indian guy is probably going to kill a prospective councilman right in front of my camera!

The Big Chief moves toward Mutt. No one else stirs. No one breathes.

Mutt's head is still down. The Chief steps up to him and reaches down with his free hand. It is thick and twisted from 22 years of hard, honest work. Supporting his family, this tribe.

Big Chief Julius Sanchez pulls Mutt's chin up. Jeansonne shifts a little off his bad leg and again looks at the Chief.

The Big Chief of the Mighty Choktaws has tears coursing down his cheeks.

This man Bows Down! He shows me respect, the tribe respect. He Bows Down to the Indian in a white man's world.

The Big Chief pulls Mutt to his feet and hugs him hard hard hard.

"Big Chief!"

"Mightee-cooteefiYO!"

"Somebody got soul, soul, soul..." the chant rises again.

The cheering begins.

"Brilliant, just fucking brilliant, is what it was! I know it's not a ladylike way to talk, Daddy. Get off it, Daddy, I'm excited."

Christine Reed is standing in front of the television in her apartment. Screaming into a telephone over the jabber of the final few minutes of Channel 3's Noon Report. The mid-day TV news on Mardi Gras Day is being anchored from a stand in the middle of Bedlam   the central bus lanes of Canal street, New Orleans. Every parade of the downtown krewes is scheduled to make a double pass up and down the outside traffic lanes of this part of Canal street. Totally encircling the TV station's remote stage for seven hours. Bands are blaring, crowds are roaring, news anchors are yelling, the television is yelling.

Chris Reed is yelling.

Her father is listening.

"I have no idea how he got down there. But don't you see, Daddy?

"The news anchor said that Candidate Jeansonne paid his respects   he 'bowed down' to the Big Chief. Blew this

Indian Chief guy away! The news called it a moment in Mardi Gras fucking history! Nobody's gone down there before! No politician. Not into that neighborhood. Nobody! Black or white! Nobody. Mutt Jeansonne did. My Mutt Jeansonne.

"Sure, I'm taking credit for it! And more. I'm just about to get in the car and try and fight my way downtown across these damn parades. My candidate's stuck judging this drag queen thing, and now I have got to get there and move him onto more important matters. Take advantage of the moment. Maybe salvage our black vote. This could be ultimate PR.

"What? Yes, Daddy, you heard me right. Drag queens."

After leaving the Indians running on their way to adjoining neighborhoods, and Mutt headed elsewhere, Rodrigo returns to the Quarter. To put a final touch on the Church window, an index card that he has lettered in red marker with the words: "Vote Mutt The Morning After!"

He glues it on the multi-papered plywood below an array of half a dozen pink campaign flyers. All the pictures of Mutt and Fred have been carefully outlined in the same red color to emphasize the two politic figures, and a separate All-Fact illustration has been glued to each.

From left to right are encyclopedic drawings of: a pharynx, a breeches buoy, a passenger pigeon, a smelt, a yellow-crowned weaver bird and a hand loom.

Rodrigo knows he has a varied constituency. He tries to make his message appeal to as wide a group as possible.

The Bourbon Street International Wonderland Trophy Awards contest is not held on Bourbon street. Not anymore. In the '80's the crowds grew too massive for the normally quiet block of a street that was already bearing the brunt of Carnival lunacy. Frequent horror stories had been verified too often. Passers-by being lifted off their feet by the swaying mass of people and carried for a block by the sheer press of the mob. Parked cars crushed completely by the feet of swarming herds of drunks.

Then the two owners of the bar had themselves tried to leave their establishment one Carnival afternoon. The departure was precipitated by a minor emergency. Uncomplimentary rumors followed their exit. The absolute bitches on the balconies mentioned small mammals. It was too too tacky. The proprietors were simply taking a break from the madness. Maybe catching some bubbly. Possibly some of that divine ether! But in the very basic act of attempting to cross the street, they fell prey to the pandemonium themselves. The experience immediately convinced them to move the next year's Wonderland to a quieter location, just a few blocks from the original. To a small corner establishment they also owned. Benny's Raw Bar.

Not that a bar can contain such a contest. Each year there are hundreds of entries from around the world, single and group, all obsessive devotees of extravagant costumery. Each year thousands more Norm Carnival-goers (though the term Norm is relative on Mardi Gras Day) find the new location and jam the adjoining streets for the Ultimate Spectacle.

Wonderland is proudly guaranteed as an event to which Good Taste will never, ever find its way.

It is definitely an outdoor event. Carpenters build an L-shaped ramp, fifty feet long per leg, which peaks at a shoulder-high rectangular stage directly on the street corner. Across from the stage is a smaller floor wedged onto the front porch of a renovated Creole cottage. This is the judges' platform.

The music sound system is complemented with microphones for two of the city's brashest cabaret performers, Tony Rondo and Dandy Lion.

At exactly noon, as the contest is officially announced underway, the two MCs come onstage riding astride a ten-foot-long, heavily-veined penis from Houston. The four Texans inside this admirable anatomical model are giggling heavily as they walk perfectly in step, sporting hand-tooled ostrich-leather cowboy boots and cactus-patterned stockings.

Mutt sniffs the early-spring air. The metallic-floral scent of amyl nitrate wafts through the street, a sharp bite in the thick, rapidly-warming breeze. With the bouquet smell of herbs, colognes, booze and body oils filling what little space exists between spectators, the Wonderland Trophy Awards is already a four-alarm olfactory riot.

Mutt is a contributor. After happily performing his morning biological function, he had an early bath in his own tub. Mutt had then inadvertently covered himself in patchouli oil, a gift from another of Noonie's '60's era admirers. He hadn't much experience in body ointments, but he was trying to be every bit The Modern Candidate. He thought a pleasant fragrance would be a step in the right direction. In the cool morning with the Indians, Mutt hadn't noticed the power of the patchouli smell. But now that he was starting to sweat beneath his Judge's robes, the oil had attained a life of its own. He found it oddly stimulating.

"Ladies and gentle men all," Dandy announces, still atop the gigantic gland, "we are gathered here once again on this most auspicious of days to award a prize coveted by everyone from Malta to Moscow, from Zanzibar to Zimbabwe..."

"From hither to yon," interrupts Tony. "Let's get it on."

"Bitch," says Dandy, without the slightest interruption to his rhythm. "You know it's the... thirty-second... annual... IN-TER-NATIONAL... WONDERLAND TROPHY awards!"

The music comes up. The crowd goes wild. Tony and Dandy dismount, slithering down the Lone Star member with no small amount of comment from the stage crew. In spite of the working mens' irreverence, Tony is inspired to introduce the Celebrity Judges. Including "the gay community's best friend and an authority on dressing-up if there ever was one, Mr Mutt JEANSONNE!"

Mutt stands and waves.

"Mr Jeansonne is going to help us hand out some of the trophies later today, aren't you, Mutt? And don't you girls forget to go vote for this man tomorrow."

There is a universal groan.

Dandy jumps in, "I know what you're thinking, babies, but this is important. So, you tramps just get up tomorrow and eat the aspirins, put on those heels and wobble right on down to the voting booths. Polls don't close until 8pm. Do it, or... next year... I'll wear my pink taffeta smock."

"Jesus, Dandy, not the taffeta," screeches Tony. "Even I couldn't stand that! I'll vote twice!"

"Let's be real now, Baby," Dandy sulks, "and announce the first contestants in the very first category of the day, 'Best Male-as-Female Group, Religious Theme.' Come on up, girls!"

The spectacle begins. Twelve hairy-chested 300-pound Tammy Faye Bakkers who have been powerfully squeezed into black leather bikinis simultaneously crack matching bullwhips and march onstage. The "ladies" herd a joyfully cringing "Jim Bakker" in front of them. The pseudo-Mr-Bakker is carrying a bible, a blow-up Loni Anderson doll and a handful of motel room keys. He makes loud "Heeee-HEEee-ee" noises and prances about merrily as the whips pop around him. The "Bakker's Dozen" are clearly having a grand time.

Dandy Lion comments that religious motifs have always been his favorite.

Tony Calls For a Witness in his best gospel voice.

Dayers has become more than a little antsy by three o'clock. He has been shooting costumed families as a feature for the five o'clock news well in advance, and is a bit under the influence of nine hours of steady Wild Turkey consumption. Marvin has been sleeping in the microwave van since almost noon. But Jon is hanging in there, running audio as Dayers abuses parcel after parcel of Mom-Dad-and-the-Cute-Kids dressed as Hershey's Kisses, Prisoners on the Chain Gang, and the ever-popular Circus Clowns. Children are not Dayers' forte.

"If I see one more little shit-brain with a red ball nose, he's dead meat!" he says none-too-quietly to his sound man. Seven nearby white-faced costumers instantly turn and sprint away from the video truck, their large shoes flapping on the pavement.

"I give them the number one feature of the day right off the bat, and do they let me off so I can do a little Carnival partying on my own? No dice. They'll still be using that Indian piece tomorrow morning, and me I'll probably still be stuck out here on the street shooting urchins."

He turns solemnly to his co-worker, a look of sudden resolve on his glowing face. "Well, I've had it. Wake up Marvin. Fire up the van, and let's get outta here. We're supposed ta furnish a live video bed for the 6 o'clock feature story, and we're gonna do something fun for a change! They'll get their bed, and I guarantee they'll lie in it!

"They always do."

Frank Morris and Wendy Feiner have just wrapped the serious news and are already reading the first few lines of "New Orleans Mardi Gras Update" off their teleprompters when they notice something is amiss. The full-screen video that is being microwaved live over the air from their Street Cam is not showing images of cute children and their parents in costume. At least not the kind described in the script. There is some sort of stage act going in. Trophies are being handed out.

It looks much more interesting than what the script describes.

In the remote truck booth, the staff recovers quickly. Since he has no idea of where the wireless camera is originating, the rookie substitute news director (who is unhappily working the holiday and is also bored to tears) suggests to his anchors over their earpieces that they ad lib. He will punch up some of the sound from the scene they are watching. They blink agreement.

"Looks like we are going to a live remote, Wendy, just not the one we had originally planned," rumbles Frank in his copyrighted Television Anchor Voice.

"But it looks like they're having a good, good time, aren't they, Frank? And that's what Carnival is all about, isn't it? Having a good time!" Wendy returns, her pitch and hair perfect.

"Right on, Wendy. Our producer/cameraman Joe Dayers is on the scene in New Orleans! Looks like something is getting ready to happen, so let's eavesdrop on another bit of Exclusive Channel 3 'Insiders' Mardi Gras'!"

The remote audio comes up: "...winner for 'Best Group, Mixed Sex, Political Theme' is "All Day Suckers" from Algiers, Louisiana! You children come on up here and get your trophy from a real endangered species, an honest politician!" Dandy is yelling into the stage microphone.

Behind Dandy stands the robed Judge Mutt, smiling and holding a three-foot-tall, multi-level pastiche of bronze, wood and chrome. And behind Mutt, dressed very conservatively considering the day and the location, is Chris Reed. She is not smiling. On the contrary, she seems extremely anxious among the blatantly gay costumers. This does not prevent her from shaking unknown people's hands and continually whispering in Mutt's ear.

"Just give them the fucking trophy and let's get out of here," she hisses. "You've accomplished what you came here for, now you must leave before someone gets a wind of this and ties you too heavily into the gay thing again. Don't upset the applecart on the day before the election!"

Reed jerks on Mutt's arm to get his attention. He is waving to a provocatively-dressed Rhett Butler and Scarlett O'Hara. Tara is following close behind, the wheeled plantation house being pulled by a matched team of Jack Dempsey terriers dressed as mammy dolls.

"I like these folks a lot," Mutt yells into Reed's ear.

Back at the station, the young director is saying, "Isn't that Mutt Jeansonne, the guy running for Council? The guy that was with the Indians this morning? And that's his Campaign Director, that Reed woman right behind him! Great, this is great! Let's CG her name on screen, bottom-third, right after his. That announcer saying something political is coming up. This is gonna be great! A follow-up to the Indian story, and I get it! This guy is great! Jerry, bring up the audio another notch."

"Uh, Bert..." starts the audio man, but it is already too late.

They all watch as, on the other end of the feed, Joey Dayers immediately zooms to Chris Reed when he spots her. He obviously has no idea yet that he is live on-the-air. The control room struggles to get his attention, but either he hasn't switched his headset on, or he isn't wearing it at all. He frames up on Chris Reed, inspects her, tilting up and down. She is clothed this time, and quite completely.

The director notices that he now has Reed on camera in a solo shot, waist-up, so he superimposes her name on-screen just as seven men and women walk onstage to a disco arrangement of "Hail to the Chief". Each of the seven is made up in cartoon fashion to suggest a member of the New Orleans City Council, and has been labeled with the appropriate name.

"Let's hear it for 'All Day Suckers'!" cries Tony, just as Dayers pulls the camera back out wide enough to reveal that the "suckers'" costumes come to abrupt end at waist level. With appropriate ornamentation in the lower, and quite visible, body regions. With her back to the entering group, Chris Reed receives an unexpected but friendly prod from a rather prominent member of the Council.

The audio man yanks his headset off as Reed's scream blows the stage microphone.

Her name is still supered on the "Suckers" when the chief engineer falls to his knees and punches the show off the air.

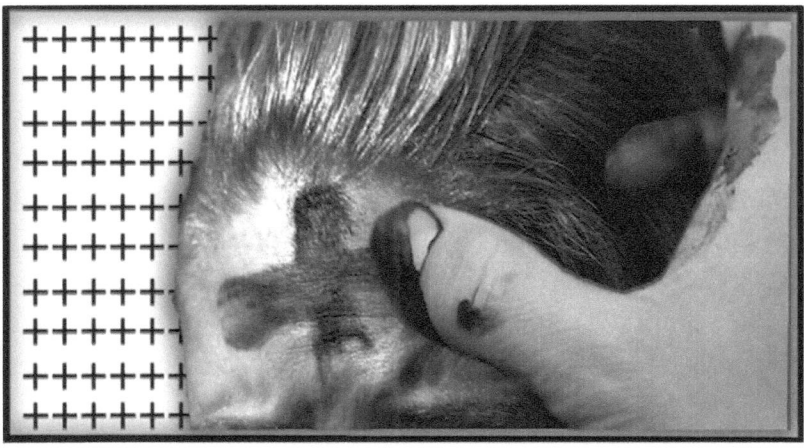

"And with your spirit," answers the congregation at St John the Conqueror parish.

St John the Conqueror parish is, of course, very different from Orleans parish. Though there is a St John the Baptist parish whose defining characteristic is an inclination to Interstate speed traps. Making it necessary to mention here that there are no counties in Louisiana. Only parishes. The Church and the Government were two heads on the same beast in this state a few centuries ago.

In Mutt's limited experience, they remain connected emotionally.

Father Aloysius Wildman is wondering about the possibilities himself. He is more than a little concerned that the City Council candidate has come to his nine o'clock mass. He has heard that there was more sensational behavior by Jeansonne and his campaign staff yesterday on television. He wants no taint of scandal at his small church. He himself never watches television on Mardi Gras Day. There is too much chance of seeing something sinful. Besides, he likes the idea of starting his penance for Lent a day early. Not that abstaining from TV is much of a sacrifice for him.

He initially panicked when he saw Jeansonne's group enter the vestibule of St John's. It was the duck and the dog that caused his heart to skip a beat. He could not recall from his Liturgical Law classes at the Seminary on Carrollton Avenue if he was allowed to offer head ashes to animals. Questions with eternal implications do nothing good for his stomach this early in the morning. His digestive tract has been almost destroyed by the stress of hearing confessions in the Upper Ninth Ward for thirty years. He is routinely told of sins that his cloistered teachers had never mentioned. Offenses they had never even dreamed possible. Sins that over three decades had frequently led Father Wildman to spiritual and intestinal tumult.

His bubbling stomach is calmer now. The candidate is surrounded by an entourage of six elderly nuns from the Sisters of the Blessed Bones, the order that runs Manus Boy's Home for the diocese. The priest proceeds with the liturgy of the day, calling for those who wish to receive ashes.

Father Wildman goes to the railing of the sacristy with his altar boy, prepared to make ashen crosses on the foreheads of whatever repentant sinners might come forward. It is a moment that most Catholic New Orleanians annually look forward to as a practical hangover cure from the excesses of the day before. The reasoning is that even if the pain doesn't go away, at least it means something after the ceremony. Like suffering for repented sins. Purgatory-on-earth credit. The pain can then be tallied up on the plus side of the roster in the old Heaven-Hell accounting books.

Mutt had liked Ash Wednesday as a child. He felt ritual drawing on faces made the ornate and complexly-ordered Church seem more primitive, more tribal. More real.

But Ash Wednesday is a long way from his mind this morning. Mel and Rodrigo had not told him about the Nuns. He wasn't prepared when they were waiting for him in the vestibule of the church. Sister Mary Ambrosia had kissed him on the cheek.

This is a day that he had looked forward to, and dreaded, for the greater part of his adult life. He is finally face-to-face with the women whose specters, implanted harshly in his earliest childhood, had haunted him for almost fifty years.

The monsters turn out to be sweet, loving little old ladies. Not frightening at all.

Mutt is delighted. More than delighted. He is ecstatic. As he files from the pew with the nuns to walk forward for ashes, he decides that win or lose the campaign, it has all been worth it.   For these few moments.

A dark and heavy skin of childhood fear, hatred and misunderstanding is unexpectedly peeling away. Leaving Mutt trembling and exposed as he kneels at the altar rail.

Father Wildman applies the black palm ashes to his forehead.

Touching Mutt, Wildman can feel the emotional surge emanating from the man kneeling before him. The shock of what he absorbs is so powerful that he finds himself stopped in front of Mutt, staring at him. Mutt is wearing his patron saint's medal. The image of St Jude, the patron of hopeless causes, hangs around his neck. Father Wildman is caused to reassess.

This is no deviate.

This man is actually affected by the House of God. He has come here with those who formed him, these Sisters, and here he is, showing true humility. How can I condemn a man who does this? I don't care about his sexual preferences!

Mother of Pearl, at least Liberace was a great piano player.

Father Wildman surprises his altar boy by handing the server his bowl of ashes.

He pulls Mutt to his feet and says quietly to his face, "You are a God-fearing man." Wildman pulls Mutt close to him in a strong embrace, then turns the Candidate to the rest of his congregation.

"This is a God-fearing man," he repeats with a strong voice.

A simultaneous bark and quack echo from the back of the church, punctuating the statement.

Later that day, after rousing literally dozens of registered Quarter girls out of their beds, Mel has a chance to stop for a moment. She had been pressing doorbells ever since she returned from mass with the Sisters at St John's. She estimates she has pushed at least forty more voters to the polls. Now, wiping her forehead and leaning against the fence on Jackson Square, she is feeling a bit faint. She has not eaten yet today. Too excited.

But Melodie is reeling under doubt. Her physical weakness amplifies it: the campaign, Rodrigo, her dream, her choice of lifestyle. They are all up for questioning. All of them.

Why am I doing this?

She needs some answers. Right here and right now. Melodie looks around. St Louis Cathedral sits in front of her as she rests on Chartres street. Nothing there for her. The chances of finding a sympathetic ear in the showcase church are slim, in spite of   or because of   its location in the Quarter. High-profile imported priests, she figures. Used god salesmen. I need a local I can trust.

In spite of it being the day after Mardi Gras, the Square in front of the Cathedral is filled with painters and musicians and tarot card readers. Melodie briefly considers the readers, then comes to her senses. Noonie had tipped her off, declaring that most of the card dealers were failed mimes. The Duck Lady's logic had been, for once, impeccable. They strip off the white face, she said. Then they sit down at a tiny card table. They soon find this is far less strenuous, and far more rewarding, than climbing invisible ladders all day. They are immediately default psychics. That in itself would be OK for Noonie but, unfortunately, the reformed mimes talk now.

Her options diminishing before her eyes, Melodie starts to walk away from the Square, towards her car. Still with no answers.

She pauses in the middle of St Philip street.

Madame Philstein. Of course.

Melodie scurries to the left, heads north on St Philip toward her friend's house as quickly as her vote-rousing ensemble will allow.

Emelean Philstein throws the bones, as potent a seer as any to be found. Her great-great grand-aunt, *Grande-Tante* Isabelle Philstein, had been a contemporary of Marie Laveau, the greatest of the voodoo queens. Isabelle had never let herself fall into the dark arts like Marie. The great Mme Laveau had even dropped so low as to control politics in the city of New Orleans. By Isabelle and Emelean's standards, that could never be forgiven. Conjuring is one thing, but taking advantage of the imbeciles in Government is reprehensible.

Emelean retains her ancestors' disdain for politics.

"I cannot look at such matters, Melodie," she answers the request. "You of all people should understand that. It is filthy business. The spirits will be offended." Madame Philstein is adamant on the point.

"But, Madame, for me, just a little peek. Just the smallest idea if what we   if what I am doing is right," pleads Mel. "I'm just spinning! I mean, what's a girl to do, working day and night, giving away everything I've saved for, just hoping I'm headed up the right path. Please, please, oh PLEASE, help me!"

The old seer wavers. "I have never been able to refuse you, you darling girl." She smiles. "You wicked woman."

Madame Philstein walks to the table in the center of the room.

"All right. I will look for you. But only for you, and your loved ones. I will not look for the bigger picture, for this political nonsense   no numbers, no bets, no winners. None of that. Just matters of the heart. Sit here."

She indicates a chair at the table.

Madame Philstein takes a calfskin bag from a drawer that was not visible beneath the tablecloth's edge. The skin is slick and almost translucent from the oil of countless human handlings.

"You must not talk again today in this room, Melodie. Understood?"

Melodie nods yes. The seer goes to work. Shakes her bag gently, regularly. Calling forth musical notes and muffled rhythms as the contents of the bag click and sound against one another. She closes her eyes and speaks in a low voice. French. For minutes that begin to stretch. And stretch. Melodie watches the bag. Her eyelids begin to droop.

"*Voi-LA!*" shrieks the Madame Philstein, scattering bones over the tabletop.

"Hmmm," she intones. She examines what has happened. Melodie watches now, concentrating, looking for clues herself.

"There," says the seer. "There. Very very favorable signs over the next day, happiness for you and those around you."

Melodie relaxes.

Things are going to be all right. I needn't have worried. This is all I need, just a little encouragement to make it through this day. Now I can get back to work. Rodrigo, Mutt, all of us we'll be fine.

Madame is not finished. "But there is something hanging, something waiting... AAAaaa... iiieieieeee!" The older woman sits straight up in her chair, staring at the tabletop. Melodie is alarmed. As dramatic as her friend could be, Melodie has never seen her like this.

"Merde!" Philstein cries to her bones. *"Vous vous trompez!* Wrong. You must be! I have never... I have never seen it myself, though I of course I... I know what it is."

"What? What is it, Emelean? Tell me!"

"Stop, Melodie. You will have courage. You will be strong."

"Yes, tell me!"

"I see death."

"What death? Who?" Mel yells, leaning forward to look more closely at the bones.

"Quiet! I told you you were not to talk! You are clouding my vision. You are obscuring..." She stops, touches the whitened bone closest to her, closes her eyes. "There is something else."

Melodie puts her own hand over her mouth. She is frightened. This stupid woman is frightening her. On purpose. Friend or no friend, Mel just wants out of the place. She will run out any moment.

"They are coming down from the skies. Thousands of them."

"That does it!" Melodie pushes back from the table, knocking over her chair as she stands. "How could you say such things to me. We were friends! All these years! How can you make fun of me like this?"

"But, Melodie, I was not..."

"I don't want to hear another word," yells Melodie, reaching in her purse and throwing a bill on the table. "You're just like all those shysters out there on the Square, aren't you, Emelean? Just say anything for money! Then make fun of me like I'm one of those idiots who believes in little green men from outer space!

"Melodie, my love, you came to *me*."

Melodie LaGrande is not to be stopped. She hangs on the edge of hysteria.

"'Coming down from the skies'! 'Thousands of them!' I just wanted to know something simple   are we going to be happy? 'Oh sure, you'll be happy,'" Mel mimics, "but then you're going to die, be killed by Martians!"

"Melodie, calm down. I said no such thing. There are portents, there are signs, that something is out there. In the future."

"Sure, Emelean. I'd just as soon believe the weatherman!"

Mel storms out, slamming both the apartment and the house door as she leaves.

"There is something out there. They are above," repeats Madame Philstein.

Mel holds Rodrigo's hand with both her own. She has eaten and is in the company of her family. Madame Philstein is all but forgotten. The election is not.

Rodrigo and Mel, Mutt and Chris, all sit hand in hand in front of a 1963 Sylvania Master-Vision TV. The black and white images shiver.

"Move right, Duckie, right," yells Noonie impatiently.

Ellis D shuffles to his left on the simulated walnut TV cabinet. The election returns clear up. He is already tired of this job. Noonie volunteered her duck to serve as an antenna when it was discovered that the borrowed set had none. He had agreed to try.

But everybody keeps adjusting him.

The living room on Toulouse street is jammed with family. Mutt is so excited he barely notices the floods of energy flowing from Chris Reed's sweating body. She seems unbound from restraint this evening, talking to everyone around her, even laughing. Mutt wants to get closer to her, but he has no opportunity. The election returns represent the culmination of months of work and long-shot dreams for everyone in they room. They are all demanding seconds of his time, hoping and yet trying not to hope. They need reassurance. Everyone has to touch him. Every return in any election has to be noted and dissected as it might pertain to Mutt's race.

"Three percent of the vote in now, ladies and gentlemen," says the voice of some grey squiggly-faced news anchor, possibly a man. Ellis shifts left again. The anchor is definitely a man. "And we are predicting a winner in the Coroner's Race. With 1,264 votes to his opponent's 46, we are projecting health club owner Harry Waltzer to be the next Coroner of Orleans Parish."

"I'm nervousssssSSSSss need to go potty," Virginia whispers to Noonie. "Call me if anything happensss."

"Sure, Sugar. I'll keep watchin'. Ellis! To the right! To the right, duckie!"

"And in the Council C race, it's neck and neck, a major horse race, with less than one percent of the vote in..."

Rodrigo can no longer stand the stress. He jumps to his feet and positions himself in front of the television. After a few protests, the room quiets. Rodrigo looks at his friend. "Mutt, sir, you won. No matter what they're saying on the TV. No matter final numbers. We won something together, me and you. We won this family." Rodrigo points at Chris Reed. "This lady she give us something, too. She give us back something maybe we already had. And for that I thanking her."

Rodrigo reaches over Mutt to shake Chris Reed's hand. Mel shakes off her reservations and does the same. There is hesitation in her eyes, the uncertainty placed there earlier in the day by the seer. But this is a night for healing, no matter the outcome. For Mutt's sake she would shake hands with the Reed woman.

Reed is stunned. She has been always been the alien on Toulouse street, in spite of their all working toward a common goal. She is unprepared to be admitted to the inner circle.

It had never occurred to her that she wanted to be.

"That is very sweet of you, Miss LaGrande. Rodrigo, very sweet," she says, her voice clouding with emotion. It has been a long day all around. Too long to keep defenses up. She is exhausted, down to the last few dregs of willpower. But if they can make the effort, so can she. "You're a dear couple, and I know that without you and all the people in this room working together, we could not have come this far. Even if we do not win, we will have shown this city that we are a part of the greater community that must be taken into account.

"We are people that matter."

Chris Reed sat in the Toulouse street house, and had used the word "we."

Hobo hero beats chicken doctor to council seat

NEW ORLEANS (AP) Council candidate Gregory Francis, PhD, conceded defeat only twenty-seven minutes after the polls closed last night in a stunning victory for L. Mutt Jeansonne and his diverse coalition of disenfranchised voters. Jeansonne won election to the New Orleans City Council outright in the primary with the largest majority ever accumulated by a single candidate in his District.

Jeansonne's campaign manager read an ecstatic though disjointed victory message shortly after Francis' concession. The statement urged further reconciliation of interests within the District C and a renewal of "peltate hairdressing."

Francis noted that eleventh-hour slander tactics directed against Jeansonne had damaged his own campaign, but denied any knowledge of the origins of the widely-circulated "racist, child abuser and abortionist" flyers that appeared shortly before the election. "I hope the new Councilman will accept my own and my mother's congratulations for keeping this election on the same high moral ground we have always maintained," said the unsuccessful Candidate, who also confirmed that he intends to return to his private poultry practice.

Jeansonne first came into the public forum last year after successfully defending a New Orleans exotic dancer from police charges of health violations based on chest exposure.

"Of course, we'll all be there, Mia! It's his swearing-in day, and I wouldn't miss the look on those stiff Council faces for a Manolo Blahnik charge account. The 'All Day Suckers' will pay attention to us now!" Mel crows into the cordless phone from her red enamel base of operations. She is building a village of small foamy igloos on the steep but picturesque Knee Cap Mountains as she speaks.

"Thanks again for covering for me, doing all these doubles   you are such a dear   I promise that as soon as we get him in his office I'll be back at the Can-Can-Do with a vengeance. I'll earn us both a second star! But I can't even think about work right now! This monumental to-do at City Hall   it's just too exciting! I've got my outfit all ready for tomorrow morning, brand-new, laid out and ready to go," she says excitedly. Though there is an ever-so-slight catch in her voice.

Mia has a good ear. Something is wrong.

"Mel, now don't you get mysterious on me. Is everything alright with you? What's wrong, my love?"

"Oh, Mia, how could I ever try to hold anything back from you?

"Darling child, what is the matter? Stop this nonsense and tell your sister Mia everything right now!"

"I'm worried."

Mel takes a deep breath, then pours her soul out in a rush. "It's this woman. Mutt's friend. She really was the source of this miracle, and it's wonderful the way it's made everyone come alive. We're all so grateful. We have to be. She's a part of our lives now... but I just hate what's going to happen."

"For God's sake, Mel, what is it?"

Another deep breath, then Melodie blurts, "I know for certain that she's going to break Mutt's heart."

Every room in the Robichaux mansion has a life of its own. Noonie estimates that well over two hundred of the Permanent Residents have arrived at the Toulouse street house by eight in the morning. Dozens had arrived the night before and slept over in a variety of closets and hallways. On porch swings, courtyard benches and bathroom floors.

The double parlor is a focal point of the happy bedlam, as guests inspect the array of presents that have been brought the Councilman-elect.

The gifts reflect the extremely diverse base of value systems among Mutt's friends. A half-dozen baby alligators contentedly munch on a mound of duck food as they lounge in a galvanized steel bucket. Four full and two partially-full bottles of Thunderbird wine, each with a ribbon and congratulatory message, sit on the mantle along with a bouquet of azalea blooms wrapped in a "City Library Week" flyer.

A beautifully-cleaned 1945 Remington typewriter, missing only the R and W keys, gleams in a corner with a message in its roller:

"He e'S SoMeTHING Fo YoU Ne JoB!

CoNG ATULATIoNS oN YoU INNING Fo ALL oF US, MUTT!"

Atop a tomato crate, a cardboard box decorated with pages from Volume Twelve of Professor O's All-Fact Encyclopedia serves as the depository for dozens of smaller, though no less meaningful, gifts.

Among other items, the box currently contains seven ball point pens. The largest writing instrument is decorated with a picture of a woman in a business suit who becomes naked when the pen is inverted, courtesy of T&G Roofers of Chalmette. Three other pens are products of a free gas-station give-away   the Exxon station nearest the Quarter is the source   and have a Saints football logo on the back. Two of the seven actually are capable of writing. Just because something doesn't work, doesn't mean it gets thrown away. Not among Mutt's peers.

There is also a half a pack of Camel Lights, 22 assorted books of matches, a stringless yo-yo, a ball of yo-yo-less string, a tin of Spam with a heart drawn in green crayon on the lid, two label-less 30-ounce cans, fourteen condoms (six ribbed, three lubricated, five in colors), approximately a hundred separate Mardi Gras beads of all sizes and descriptions, and $4.38 in change.

The extended Robichaux family has pulled out all the stops to celebrate Mutt's   and their own   entrance into the Norm World.

* * *

"Wah-ROOOOR!" articulates Fred in answer to the mayor's question.

The Honorable Roland Clemenceaux, Mayor of the City of New Orleans, is pleasantly amused.

The Council Chamber has been nothing but a dreary, back-biting House of Horrors. *In office for a full year, and I still dread coming in here. This new guy and his circus troupe look like they will afford a great deal more entertainment than the current batch of stiffs.*

Maybe even make some sense.

Only right that his swearing-in should take place at the April 1 Council meeting. April Fool's Day.

His Honor the Mayor appreciates the irony.

Jeansonne's no fool. Not at all. He's in touch with his people.

That's a definite plus.

And, unlike these other six bozos, he says he's consulted with me before, though I can't for the life of me remember where.

"I will, so help me," repeats Mutt, his right hand raised and his left hand on Volume Six of the All-Fact. He had insisted that Professor O's All-Fact Encyclopedia was the only religious text that would do for the affair. Mutt had obtained Rodrigo's permission to use the holy source, along with temporary physical possession of the least depleted Volume for the swearing-in ceremony. Rodrigo himself had been recruited as the Jeansonne family minister.

The Reverend Rodrigo had already delivered a non-denominational invocation that had left the Council members, and most of the audience, dazzled by its complex spiritual metaphors. Never before had the phrase "blissful candied yams of the Lord" been used in these quarters.

Rodrigo, delighted with his reception at City Hall, had immediately departed. Feeling the need for an enlightened addition to his own Church. He was inspired enough that he stopped en route to purchase an 49-cent jar of L'il Andy's White School Paste. He rushed to Decatur street, images flying through his head. Mel was disappointed at his early departure from the ceremony, but understood Rodrigo's pontifical responsibilities.

Fred sits by Mutt's leg on the side of the dais opposite the Mayor, with Christine Reed close behind. Reed keeps her hand tightly on Mutt's elbow. She counts his heart rate as he is sworn into office. It is a way of restraining her own excitement.

Chris Reed is not quite sure how they have won this election. Candidate Jeansonne has won big, historically big, and in the primary. Gay, straight, black, white, Hispanic, Oriental, disenfranchised, working class, homeless, landowners, religious, agnostic. You name a group, they've voted for Mutt Jeansonne. Except for less than a hundred isolationist WASPs who live richly in security-patrolled French Quarter compounds. In their sanitized group mentality they'd decided they'd rather vote for a working PhD over a hobo GED, even if they were given pause by the fact that the scholar was a man of color.

Reed had tried a last-minute blitz to deliver those few votes herself, and had failed completely. She figured they'd come around. "Just a little patience, that's all I need," she reassured herself.

Flashes go off in extended bursts, until finally the Mayor steps forward. "That will be enough, please." He waits until the still and video camera operators move back to the side areas of the room before he continues.

"Councilman Jeansonne, I would like to introduce you to the other six members of the New Orleans City Council.

First, the two 'At-Large' members, one of whom is our Council President..."

The Mayor's introductions lead to a parade of self-serving, long-winded welcoming speeches. That course, once started, inevitably ends up filling the scheduled City Council meeting's entire morning.

Clemenceaux leaves soon after it becomes apparent that the other politicians in the room are going to use the occasion as a chance to further promote their own pet projects and peeves. They each give the rookie member a peremptory greeting, then immediately launch into as dramatic a speech as they can muster on short notice and no topic. It isn't often that the news crews bother with the Council any more.

The Council members are each going for broke in an attempt to secure the exposure of a five o'clock sound bite.

Chances are slim, given the style and the lack of relevant message. Cameraman Joey Dayers is there, but is snoring loudly after only the second speech. He had been demoted from the title "Videographer/Producer" immediately after his live on-air Wonderland escapade. Thus, the "Cameraman." But when the ratings numbers came out a few weeks later, the channel's Carnival coverage pushed numbers off the scale. Management had relented. He would get his titles back after a short probationary period. No assistants until then, as a condition of his reinstatement. In the meantime Joey was given a five percent raise to insure he could endure his punishment.

"I hope this is my regular assignment. The new Councilman. Get the opportunity for an occasional naptime.

"Face it, Joey, you're not back to a hundred percent from Carnival, and this stuff is boring boring BORING. Perfect material to allow the bit of rest."

The Council chambers are packed with Mutt's supporters and friends, but even they grow tired of the rising tide of endlessly murky verbiage. More than a few leave. The rest shift restlessly in their wooden seats. Watching through their fingers as they try to find a morsel of entertainment in the proceedings.

Chris Reed sits at the table by the speaker's platform where Mutt stands. She has gone to work. Paying no attention to the demagoguery, Reed is plowing through the dozen file folders she has pulled from her case.

She is still too dazed by their success to listen. To accept that they have won. That this man has given her what she wants most.

Maybe he can give her something else.

Anything is possible now. Maybe.

The speeches trail on. Mutt is patient. So is Fred. The content dog is sleeping soundly at Mutt's side as the last Council member's greeting comes to a close. Council President William Greene loudly bangs his gavel for a lunch recess. Fred jumps to her feet, knocking Reed's papers about while trying to get re-oriented.

Dayers wakes up and reflexively jerks his camera into position.

"That's it, people. We reconvene back here at two," Greene yells into his desk microphone.

Mutt raises his hand. He is still standing at the speakers' platform. The Council President recognizes him.

"Mr Jeansonne, please be brief. We've got some hungry people here."

"Pardon me, sir. I do understand hungry," Mutt says.

He holds up five sheets of rumpled and marked paper, "but I read this Agenda you folks were kind enough to send me, and it has 37 different things listed on it that we are supposed to talk about today. We just spent two and a half hours of a six-hour meeting saying hello. I think we should stay here and get to work. That is our job, sir. At least as I understand it."

"Mwuhhh-UH," emphasizes Fred.

The Council President shakes his head resignedly, looking from side to side at the other Council members for sympathy before turning his attention back to Mutt.

"Mister Jeansonne. We've extended you every courtesy as a newcomer, though most of us have been sitting on this august body for over a decade. May I humbly suggest that your understanding of this job may be somewhat limited. In spite of your obviously extensive knowledge of not being employed."

A wave of murmurs from the chamber audience dilutes the approving comments from his colleagues on the Council.

O-o-hooh.

Dayers quietly presses the record button on his camera.

This Jeansonne guy is a shit-magnet deluxe. Something is always gonna happen around the dude and his dog.

He goes hand-held, moving into position to get a two-shot of the confrontation.

Greene continues, seeking to exploit this sudden media interest, "You will notice that we have not said a single word about your bringing your pet into this courtroom..."

Fred interrupts with an extended, "Mwuuuhhhhhh." She has heard this sort of tone in human voices before, and doesn't like it one bit.

Greene continues over Fred and the crowd's rumbling, "...a possibly dangerous pet, and I might add, a pet with no apparent City Dog License tags." The Council President is working himself up to a peak of self-righteous indignation. "Therefore," he spits, "therefore... this animal is subject to being immediately impounded, if you wish to press a point on the job we are all here to do. The work which you have so kindly pointed out that we are here to accomplish.

"Officer!" he calls to the NOPD sergeant at the back of the Chamber. "Officer, get this animal out of here at once."

But Greene has badly underestimated the popularity of his four-legged nemesis. As the police sergeant moves toward the speaker's platform, the entire audience stands with a roar of indignation. An echoing tide of agitated quacking rises from under the wooden seats, amplified by the tile floors. Those nearest the center aisle move quickly to block the officer's path. Noonie and Virginia are among the first to come to grips with the unfortunate policeman. The sergeant is rendered helpless within seconds, as he is engulfed by a phalanx of loudly protesting Vieux Carré voters. The rest of the crowd advances angrily on the Council desks, shouting at Greene and his cohorts.

"You ain't touching Freddy!"

"This here is the First Lady of the French Quarter, buddy, and you better show some goddamn respect!"

"Fuckin' A!"

The crowd is heavily pro-dog.

Dayers is smiling broadly as his camera catches every bit of the action.

Take away my assistants, will they? I'll have 'em back tomorrow if this goes where I think it's going.

Mel has been the first to run to the platform. She picks Fred up in her arms and embraces the dog protectively. Fred does not protest. She is beginning to enjoy being held. Being at human eye level. It is part of the game.

Fred has come to feel that human contact is one of the prices of life in the political spotlight, and she refuses to shirk from her duty.

"Mwuuuuhhh-hhh!" she reiterates, her position unchanged from that outlined in her earlier statement.

Chris Reed grabs the microphone stand in front of Mutt and pulls it in her direction.

"Councilman Greene, Council President Greene!" she calls over the tumult in the room.

"Order! Order!" yells Greene. The yelling begins to fade, slightly.

The high polish of Greene's confident smile is dulled by a dark smudge of panic. He hadn't expected that this sort of rabble would dare challenge the authority of the Council. *Not here. No one would dare. This room is sacred turf. Even the Mayor is polite to the Council members here. They have never, ever been called accountable for anything here. And now this, with a camera recording it all.*

Greene tries to regain control over the room, clearing his throat loudly first into the microphone in front of him. "The chair recognizes Assistant District Attorney Reed. Miss Reed, you had best get your constituents in order or I will call in the NOPD. I will call in the Louisiana National Guard if I have to, to insure that these proceedings move forward in an orderly manner. I am a duly elected representative of the people of this City, and I know their will. I shall carry that will out, in spite of the disorderly mob you have brought into these chambers."

There is another roar of indignation as the crowd moves closer to the front of the room. After a quick pan for a group reaction shot, Cameraman Dayers starts a slow zoom to the principals.

His long-disused political instincts working quickly, Greene decides to divert attention away from himself, his judgment unfortunately once again taking him in the wrong direction. "That animal is unlicensed, illegal and subject to confiscation," Greene announced in his most official fashion, all the while pointing at Fred.

The Council President is blindly attempting to intimidate the room by disciplining a random individual, a method dating back to the emergence of tribal man. Greene is happy to be dealing with Reed, whom he hopes to be a reasonably civilized person. *She is a Southern Lady, and therefore mercilessly objective in her handling of lesser members of society. She will understand the lessons of history.*

"Mr President, if I might offer some input on behalf of Mr Jeansonne's companion," Reed says in a low voice. She has learned how to better deal with riot in her months with the Jeansonne campaign. The mass of people in the chamber quiet to listen. This woman is supposed to be on their side.

"I of course have not had that many opportunities to prosecute violations of the City's animal protection and control ordinances in my tenure with the District Attorney's office. But I have some knowledge of those laws." She turns to the other inhabitants of the room as she continues speaking, drawing them to her side.

"If an animal is found to be without a city license, but in the presence of its owner, that owner will normally be given a warning with two weeks to come into line with City Licensing procedures. I can assure you that Mr Jeansonne will comply with the law within that time frame.

"On your other point, questioning the dog's presence here, I believe there is also a possibility of some mitigating circumstances. Mr Jeansonne has been unable to obtain a Driver's License on the basis of his deteriorating eyesight. I would ask you to allow the presence of this animal as temporarily performing the services of a guide dog until such time as Mr Jeansonne's visual problems are either disproved or solved."

Fred makes a small tail-wiggle of delight in the warm canyon of Mel's breasts. She might get to do her Seeing-Eye Dog routine, after all. Maybe even wear dark glasses.

Politics can be fun.

"And in another explicit example of how politics in the City of New Orleans will not be the same since the election of Street advocate Councilman Mutt Jeansonne the Council reversed its April Fool ruling today and allowed the new Councilman to attend meetings with his four-legged executive assistant by his side. Only the joke was on the Council, at least in the early stages of the discussion.

"It took some time to un-make Council members' minds. Jeansonne's legal aide Christine Reed spoke eloquently on behalf of the dog a female named Fred before the Council, which after extensive discussion allowed the animal's presence on medical grounds.

"A near-riot over Council President Greene's initial ejection of Fred quieted quickly, and the Council completed its entire agenda in a ten-hour work marathon. This was both Councilman Jeansonne's first meeting and also the longest Council session on record since 1956.

"Welcome to City Government, Mr Jeansonne. And thanks to Videographer/Producer Joe Dayers for that extraordinary footage.

"On the State front..."

Time in New Orleans can be measured in crustaceans. Crab season (lake and gulf), four strictly-observed shrimp seasons (white, brown, grey and the sporadic rock), the spiny and bulldozer lobster runs (off the Florida panhandle), and above all, Louisiana crawfish season. Not the year-round farm-bred crawfish, either. Only the wild ones will do for the true aficionado. When the Atchafalaya basin gets low and the crawfish stop running, or if the water's up and the mudbugs are too big and tough to eat, it's a sure sign summer is back.

At the Toulouse house it is half-past crawfish.

Noonie rhythmically stirs the contents of the cast-iron skillet with her wooden spoon, talking all the while. Even as June draws to a close, the kitchen is still livable. The windows and doors are open, the ceiling fans swirling on high. But the summer's full heat will soon make the stove redundant.

Virginia sits at the kitchen table, watching intently. In Uptown New Orleans, Virginia had a maid and a cook. And a gardener. All three still living in her house on State street. She had possessed enough money of her own that her husband's death had not resulted in the loss of her home. But she seldom went there after her Break. She had had that much in common with Noonie. Nothing was on State street for her. No children. Now, no husband. What was at the house? A change of clothes, possibly a bath and some makeup. That was as much as she could stand. She liked Toulouse street much better.

The three State street servants seemed to be doing quite well without either of their employers around. A household trust kept the staff salaried, the taxes paid and the cupboards full. Everything staying just as it had been for decades. Except that the owners were no longer living there.

As she walked the seventy blocks Uptown the day before, Virginia had noticed Gerald the gardener driving her Mercedes down St Charles Avenue. He was wearing one of her husband's suits. Virginia had almost forgotten she owned a car. She wondered if she could learn to deal with a vehicle again. Her father had taught her the first time.

Her mother had never instructed her on how to handle a kitchen, though. Since the woman herself seldom entered the room, much less cooked in it. Virginia thinks that no wonder. Making a proper roux at least, the way Noonie is making a roux seems a great deal more complex than pointing a vehicle.

Noonie is on a roll, finding out new things about herself every day. A few weeks ago, she discovered she knew how to cook. Now she lets the fragments find their own places in her memory. She tries not to analyze or force any order on her newly-recalled life. That would be much too painful just yet. But she realizes that somehow the process of food preparation has reopened some long-closed doors for her.

She hopes it might also help Virginia.

* * *

Mutt settled into his Council seat quickly and comfortably. It was a lot like being on a jury. He and Rodrigo talked with his constituents, singly and in groups, around a table in Mutt's assigned Council office for most of the week. Then there were days when the room was constantly filled with other politicians, informing, instructing and offering deals. The two men from Toulouse street listened to endless litanies of problems, suggestions, and the statistics of Government. Chris Reed was back full-time at the DA's office, doing other "special liaison" work, but she came by to advise and encourage Mutt at least three times a week.

In spite of the mental clutter, Mutt felt that the office was a productive, positive place. He was making a difference. He could help people. Both he and Rodrigo liked going to work. They wore their suits. Rodrigo washed his feet in the Council bathroom sink before important meetings. They grew more content and productive every day. The District C City Council office reflected that fact. The phones constantly rang with calls from District residents who had grown used to frequent personal conversations with Mutt Jeansonne.

Though there was the occasional unidentified crank caller. Charles Taylor had not given up his hatred   and fear of Aliens and prison terms with the acceptance of Gregory Francis' money. If anything, the ineffectiveness of Francis' slur sheets in the election had raised Taylor's anger to new levels. He began to obsess on Mutt Jeansonne, sending frequent updates to the *Comet* on Jeansonne's whereabouts. He had nothing else to do, other than drink. Soon his malt-liquored memory held Mutt as the pivotal human controlled by the wily Invaders. Taylor seemed to be the one person who knew the new Councilman's true mission. World subjugation and imprisonment.

Taylor figured that Mutt Jeansonne must know he was being tracked, and was the undoubtedly the person responsible for every trivial annoyance that took place in Taylor's own life, as Jeansonne tried to shake his valiant tracker off the trail. The new Councilman's phone was listed, and Taylor made use of it frequently to vent his frustration. The calls were not pleasant, but Mutt figured every person had the right to say what he or she felt.

Mutt had never in his life paid hatred any mind.

On Thursdays Mutt, Rodrigo, Fred and friends trooped into the Council chambers to do the business of Government. As might be expected, the Jeansonne camp had its own particular method of participating in the process. Fred cast all of the Jeansonne votes. A single emphatic bark for Yea, and an evocative double-sounded "Wahhrooo-WOOF!" for Nay. Though Fred's being allowed a chair at the Council table received initial resistance from the sitting members, the six incumbents relented after only minor debate. Rodrigo had acted as Fred's champion in that discussion. His use of the words "thermonuclear" and "serpulite" seemed to turn the tide in her favor. The echo of dog barks began to add a touch of humanity to the previously sterile confines of city Government.

Noonie's logic had been unassailable: everybody in the house is hungry and she has found one last sack of edible crawfish.

So when the tasty wild mudbugs gathered by the banditos of the Atchafalaya Basin swamp had dropped to thirty-nine cents a pound live on Monday, the residents had taken up a collection. To everyone's surprise, Noonie took charge of the boil.

The result is imposing. A huge pile of steaming crawfish is already spilling off the kitchen table. The crawfish are to be the heart of the bisque. Virginia is in place to record the proceedings. Noonie prefaces her culinary lecture by yelling at her duck.

"Ellis, stop that stop eating those things. Those are people dinner you know you don't like them cooked anyway, you allergic to cayenne makes duckie SNEEZE. Raw ONLY for duckies," she scolds. Ellis waddles to the corner of the room. Bill lowered contritely. Unrepentant eyes still fixed on the crawfish.

Noonie turns with a grin to Virginia, "Ducks, Ginny. Them Louisiana ducks, they love to eat them crawfish. So do Louisiana peoples. All kinds of Louisiana peoples. You know the way Cajuns cook? They use everything but the squeal when they butchering hogs. Well, this food dish from my Daddy is the same thing. If a crawfish could squeal, the noise would be in here, too."

She stirs the pot a bit quicker.

"Roux getting hot. This the way Papa used to cook at his fishing camp at Bayou Four-Point. My papa's Cajun bisque even different from the way city French ladies like my mama making it. She doing that Paris France bisque. Just a thick dark soup got a spoon of whipped cream sitting in the middle. Good for ladies or folks from up North. This one, my papa's, thinner than that fancy French soup. But strong enough in flavor to make Cajun folk from Ville Platte to blow they noses and wipe they foreheads.

"It got heads in it."

* * *

"Bring me the Jeansonne file," Roland Clemenceaux yells to his aide. He is looking over a progress report prepared by his Commissioner of Administration. In the last two months, the number of items moving to completion on the City Council docket has almost doubled. The only difference in the

Council is the new Councilman. Mutt Jeansonne. A man who was living on the Streets a short nine months ago.

The Mayor's aide drops the file on his desk. It is over six inches thick. "That includes all legislation in which he has been a major player, Your Honor," says the aide.

"All this in sixty days? This can't be right."

"It is, sir. I've been handling this one myself, since it is the most active Council file. Mr Jeansonne is fast becoming the Council's driving force. And the media have some sort of picture of his dog sitting at the Council table every day. They never get tired of that dog," said the young man.

"Fred," said the Mayor. "That's the dog's name, right? Fred?"

"Yes, sir. A female named Fred. Plus there's this fellow on Jeansonne's team who refuses to wear shoes to Council. A Rodrigo something."

"Two bums and a dog. Remarkable. And they are making that antiquated bunch of civil servants on the Council actually do some work."

"It seems so, Your Honor. I think you will find over eighty approved ordinances in the file."

The Mayor opened the folder and looked for a moment. "And what about this woman from the DA's office? She still on board? We got a conflict of interest there?" he asked.

The aide pulled open his own notes. "No, Your Honor, she's back at District Attorney Bronner's office. Though she still acts as a legal advisor and consultant to Councilman Jeansonne, and she has appeared twice in Council."

"Sounds like it's all progressing rather nicely," said Clemenceaux. He moved the file to one side. "I'll read this later. Now, do me one other favor."

"Of course, sir."

"Call the Police Chief and tell him to get this..." the Mayor looked at his daily planner, "...this Sergeant Joe off my security detail. The man's too nervous. Like he's got an itch he can't get to. Scares me.

"He smells funny, too."

* * *

One thing that continues to tug at Mutt's cuffs is his childhood. His origin. Even during his new purpose-filled existence, not a day goes by for him that does not include some thought of Manus Boy's Home. Now that he has removed his child's fear of the Nuns, he is determined to find out more about the four-letter one-name Mutt.

One Saturday he calls the Mother Superior.

"Sister Mary Ambrosia, would it be alright if I came by today for a visit?"

"My dear, dear Mutt," she bubbles happily, "of course, of course! We'll make you a special lunch. Sister Marie Bernarde will make the stuffed mirletons you used to love so much. Mutt comes to visit! Ah, the joy of it. The Sisters will be so very glad to see you! Every single one of us voted for you, you know. Every one. Even Sister Agnes, who as you well may remember is the sole Republican in our midst. What an inspiration it will be for the boys to meet the new Councilman. One of their very own!"

"Thank you so much, Sister. I've one other favor to ask of you. I'd like to bring along a friend. Actually she'll bring me, since I don't have a car."

"Why certainly. You can bring anyone you like," answers the Nun.

"Her name is Chris Reed. A good friend. She got me started."

Sister Mary Ambrosia recognizes the name. "Was that the young woman on the news? The one with the bosoms?"

"Yes, Sister, but she didn't mean to offend."

"It's alright. It's fine," she says, a little less enthusiastically. "You are our new City Councilman. You are one of our Boys. You may bring whomever you wish. We want you to come visit your Home."

"Noon then?"

"Noon will be fine. And Mutt, we are so looking forward to seeing you again."

"Me, too," Mutt says quietly. "You know, Sister, I think I have really missed you."

* * *

"Good Christ! Noonie! I was married! I've been sitting here watching you cook, all the while thinking my husband's name! And mine! I know mine! Good gravy! My last name is Beaumont!"

Virginia's background is Uptown Protestant, and religious references do not carry over into cooking as often amongst her acquaintances as with the old world Creole Catholics. She and her husband Bruce belonged to Trinity Lutheran Church.

Bruce, always the cynic, told her that the Holy Trinity of New Orleans was "Food, Music and Sex, and not necessarily in that order." Virginia did not quite understand: she didn't recall that they as a couple participated regularly or happily in any of the three. She suspected the man was a closet agnostic, though her own lack of kitchen metaphors allowed her to excuse his attitude in this case.

* * *

Just that morning Rodrigo had pasted up a new sequence of four All-Fact entries on the Toulouse house walls. He told Virginia he had made his selections mostly for their interesting illustrations and their Korean titles. But after she read the accompanying text, Virginia knew she had been correct. She knew that Rodrigo was becoming more in tune with the real universe than ever. He was very much in tune again.

NAGELFLUH   a type of hard conglomerate rock found in the Molasse mountain area of Switzerland. Nagelfluh is extremely dangerous to handle because of the sharp granite "nails" that protrude from its surfaces. Besides granite, the conglomerate is made up of petrified plants, river shells and the bones of ancient or extinct animals. The interior of the stone contains a perfectly-ordered history of its origins, but is inaccessible without some frustration and/or physical distress to all but the most well-prepared and well-equipped seekers of knowledge. [For a map of the region and sample local luncheon menus, refer to Volume Twelve.]

MODULUS   specifically, the "modulus of rupture," denotes the measure of force that is necessary to break any given body or substance. See more comprehensive explanation under illustration to left. Not to be confused with more organically pleasant MODULUS OF RAPTURE. See also: SEXUAL TECHNIQUES OF CONTEMPORARY SAN FRANCISCO.

* * *

"But why now?" asks Chris Reed. "Why not get a little more settled in your new job before you go off looking to find your lost childhood   or whatever it is you're looking for? You've got a Council meeting this afternoon. Shouldn't you be preparing for that?"

"It's just a drive across town for lunch, Chris... maam." Mutt notices as he falls back on past, more formal modes of address for his friend. He is anxious about this visit. He had hoped that Chris Reed would be supportive. "Besides, they're my constituents. A bunch of them, at that. Nineteen voting-age older-demographic women. Gotta pay attention to those group voters. You taught me that."

Chris smiles, turning her head slightly to look at Mutt Jeansonne. He looks more like a real person every time she sees him. He is no longer a trained cartoon character, answering by rote, reacting only when rewarded. He is thinking on his own, applying what he has been taught.

"So I did, Councilman Jeansonne, so I did."

"Yesm. I appreciate you giving me the lift and all, but I really wanted you along to give me a little courage."

"Mutt, they're just little old ladies."

"Oh, I know that. I know that now. It's not them. I'm enjoying the idea of being around them again. Even in the Home. It's just... I got a question or two to ask. Questions I asked them when I was a baby boy. And I don't rightly know if the answers I remember are right or wrong or just something I made up. I've been telling my story one way ever since I can remember. Every time I tell it, I wonder is it true. Do I even have a story? Well, I'm a grown man now. Thanks to you, I'm a man who is coming to know himself. I gotta know."

"And that's what this trip is about?"

"Yes, maam. The truth. There's things a grown man should know for sure. Like about his mother and father."

"After all this time. What an astonishing man you have become," says the ancient Sister Mary Ambrosia, shakily scraping the last piece of mirleton and crabmeat stuffing off her plate. The boys had been excused. Mutt, Chris and nineteen Irish women in black and white clothing sit around the cafeteria table, finishing their meal and talking.

The youngest of the nuns is in her forties, reflecting the final dwindling of immigration from the Emerald Isle. The Irish Sisters worked well with the poor and disadvantaged. They knew the territory themselves.

New Orleans' large Irish population had been imported en masse almost two centuries earlier, to dig the City's canals.

Slaves were too valuable to send into the malarial swamps. Ten thousand of the Irish workers had died completing the work. Now, at the beginning of the twenty-first century, the canals are once again filled with dirt, forming the median or "neutral ground" between the separate lanes of broad West End avenue. There is a small granite marker noting the thousands of lives spent laboring in the soil beneath. Descendants of the Gaelic families still form much of the population in the Faubourg St Mary area, between Magazine and Tchoupitoulas streets. A section long since dubbed The Irish Channel.

They are a people much loved for the strength of their convictions, and their contributions to the education of New Orleans.

Mutt knows the elderly women's strength. After complimenting the aged Sister Marie Bernarde on her cooking, he comes directly to the point, asking the Mother Superior his question.

"Can you tell me more about my mother?"

"Your mother," she repeats. Sister Mary Ambrosia looks around the table. The several older nuns purse their lips and shake their heads negatively when she encounters their gaze. The others become very intent on the surface of their empty plates. "There are only five of us remaining who were here at the time you came to us. I know that our treatment of your mother has weighed heavily on my own conscience all these years. I try to believe we did the right thing, and yet knowledge of my actions makes me unsettled. It makes me unsure of my faith, so I ignore it. When I saw you at St John's, I knew we would soon have to speak of this. I am glad for the opportunity."

Mutt is taken aback. "Your treatment of my mother? You knew her? But you told me..."

"Yes, Mutt," says the nun. "We lied to you. We were ashamed of our own part in her end, and we were concerned that a poor parentless child would not have to bear any more pain than was already visited upon him. In retrospect, I can see that we were selfish. In trying to prevent pain, we brought more of it, on ourselves and on you."

Sister Mary Ambrosia rises from the head of the long table. She talks as she moves about its perimeter, stopping occasionally to place her hand on one of the older nuns' shoulder. Mutt sits silently.

Chris Reed is feeling trapped by the intimacy. "How about if I go outside for a bit? This sounds like a very personal matter," she says, rising and pushing her chair back.

"As you wish, my dear. You are welcome to stay. Mutt?" the nun asks.

"It's OK. Go."

"Then we will see you later, Miss Reed. I believe it is quite cool under the oaks this time of day. It has been a mild start to the summer." She watches as Chris walks with echoing footsteps across the large room and goes out of the building. Sister Mary Ambrosia turns to Mutt.

"Please, Mutt, please let me get this out all at once. It has been festering in my heart for almost half a century. It will take a great deal of effort to say."

The Mother Superior dropped her eyes to her clenched hands. "We cared for your mother for many years.

"That was when some of us spent half of each day at Charity Hospital. The hospital was always so understaffed, it seemed the right thing to do. Mostly we worked with chronically or terminally ill patients, sick people who required maintenance, rather than a doctor prescribing treatment. Your mother had not been taken from her room for six years when we found her, Mutt. She, too, had just one name. Juliette. What records we were given said her own parents had abandoned her, that she had been committed as a ward of the state and placed in long-term care. Like you, she was of uncertain race.

She was never given a surname. The hospital administration was rather rudimentary in those days, especially with patients whom they suspected to be other than white. The patient clerks decided that the long legal paperwork required to give Juliette an arbitrary last name was not worth the trouble. They hadn't expected her to live that long. And she could go nowhere on her own. You see, she had no idea who or where she was, Mutt. And she had fits. That was probably why her parents didn't teach her to speak properly and abandoned her. And seeing her mentally and physically unstable, voiceless and prone to violent fits, the hospital staff stuck her away in a room. It was not an enlightened time. There were thousands of poor, and very few caregivers. When Juliette grew older, someone donated a small-wheeled chair so she could roll around her small space without falling. She was fourteen when we arrived at Charity, and had been out of her room only three times since she was nine.

"She was not well, barely conscious of her surroundings. We suspected that her fits had merely been undiagnosed epilepsy. She had been so badly cared for that she had become incontinent. The poor child couldn't control her bowels. The floor of her room was coated in newspapers. Until we came, the papers were seldom changed. No one wanted to go in there. She didn't speak at all when we first started caring for her, but we bathed her and got her decent clothing. We told her stories and brushed her hair, and gradually she came to trust us. As we grew to love her. Her face was so beautiful and sweet. So pure, like the Virgin Mary. We gave her the love and attention she needed, and she bloomed even more, though she continued as a mute. We were the only contact she had with the outside world. She was the sole girl in our charge. She saw no one else, went nowhere else. The door of her room was kept locked when we left. We were afraid she might get hurt, wandering around as she was.

"One day   it was in 1955, wasn't it Sister Michelle? in the process of bathing her, we discovered she was pregnant. We couldn't believe it. We called in the doctor and he made the test twice. To this day we have no idea how, but your mother was pregnant. With you. The doctor advised abortion, but we wouldn't hear of it. Your mother was healthy and well along in her pregnancy. We were there, and quite willing to take care of both her and the child. The Church strongly forbids the taking of an unborn child's life, but I asked the Monsignor's advice anyway. He said that an abortion would be wrong, especially since there was no danger, and since we were willing to take the responsibility for the child.

"We had a wonderful time planning for your birth. We tried to let your mother know what was happening. Every day we would clean her and make sure she ate extra well and tell her about children and growing up. When the time came for you to be born, we were sure we had made the right choice.

"You were a beautiful child.

"But something in the birthing process had hurt your mother. Something unexpected. Her bleeding couldn't be stopped. She started losing horrible amounts of weight. Her breathing sounded like she was crying. She was in pain. Our merciful Lord took her quickly. The doctor said no one could have foreseen the problem. We were unconvinced.

"We, all of us, felt the pain. We felt guilty. We had been so excited about the miracle   your coming. All of a sudden we had to ask ourselves terrible questions. Had we had wanted the baby so badly that we hadn't paid the mother enough attention? We had not protected your mother as we should have. Her well-being was our responsibility, and she had died.

"You poor child. I am sorry to tell you this. I am so sorry. But after we lost your mother, we were all so distraught that I feel we may have blamed you instead of ourselves. We compounded our sin of pride and left you in the hospital nursery, without even naming you. We were blinded by the grief of burying your mother, our dear Juliette. When we came to our senses and returned to get you, we found the consequences of our actions. An ignorant hospital orderly bored or foolish or vindictive, I don't know what had played the cruel joke of your name. The man thought you were unwanted. A cast-off like your mother, he thought. He named you. He filled in the form. We begged the records people, even went to City Hall, but what he had written could not be undone. You were 'just another mutt' to him.

"And Mutt is what you became to the world.

"So quickly our baby Mutt became a young man whose awakening frightened us. You see, we hadn't realized the child would grow up.

"Forgive us. Please, Mutt."

* * *

Noonie has now burned her roux twice. Once because of Ellis getting after the crawfish heads again. The Duckie Bandito is now outside, his history lesson ended.

Rodrigo caused the second burning when he came in to see if Virginia's book needed illustrations. He had helped glue on a lovely lithograph of a Lithuanian Common Parsnip, in its full parsnipian glory, courtesy of the All-Fact.

Rodrigo's progress has really amazed everyone at Toulouse street. Just two months ago the closest he would have come to the actual subject under discussion would have been a diagram of the frontal brain lobes.

Now he walks in and says: "I am off this afternoon after City Council meeting to make the new Rodrigo complete," whatever that means, then does a sweeping exit that closely mimics one of Mel's. Virginia and Noonie look at each other, hoping he is alright. He looked quite nervous when he left. Of course that could have been from Noonie's earlier screeching about her second burnt roux of the day.

* * *

Mutt rides silently, looking out the window of the BMW at the bayous of City Park. Chris is driving slowly and with care, not wanting to jar her passenger in any manner. When he emerged from the orphanage, Mutt looked blank, grey-faced. She could sense a quiet relief in the man, and yet there was a tenuous, strained quality about him, like the smallest jar might cause him to shatter into a million pieces. He hadn't spoken, just walked to the car.

Then, "Juliette. Her name was Juliette."

"Who, Mutt? Juliette who?" asks Reed.

"Just Juliette. Like me. But she was my mother. My momma. They say she was beautiful."

"They told you about your mother?"

Mutt hesitated. "They told me that she died at Charity Hospital when I was born. That she was alone, like me, but they loved her and took care of her. Like they did me."

"And your father?"

"Don't know. But my momma's name was Juliette."

My momma's name was Juliette.

It is almost anticlimactic now. He has a mother, no matter her position in life. Juliette. She has a name and a face. Mutt Jeansonne has a foot in reality.

Now what do I do?

Chris pulls the car over to the Perdido street curb in front of the City Hall. Mutt sits next to her, his jaw clenching and unclenching as he faces each new future. She instinctively knows what to do. She unfastens her seatbelt and leans over in front of Mutt. She slowly and deliberately kisses him on the mouth. When she pulls away, he lets out a long, warm breath. He looks in her eyes without fear or hesitation. It occurs to him that he really does not know the woman in front of him. But he knows her name.

"Thank you, Chris... maam."

Mutt opens his door and gets out of the car. He bends down to look at Chris one more time.

Who is she?

He shuts the door.

"It does go on, doesn't it," Mutt says aloud as Chris drives away. "Life. You just keep on living, whether you want to or not." He thinks about that for a moment before whispering, "Sometimes."

* * *

"921 Toulouse, yes maam. 70112, zip it is. New Orleans, maam. Correct, maam."

Rodrigo is trembling. He clutches his briefcase to his chest protectively. He was so close.

The young black woman behind the circulation desk had recognized him. He knows it. He has deserted a session of Council for nothing.

Rodrigo fears that his earlier reputation as a Street might give her some reason for rejecting his application. Plus the fact of his arbitrarily taking on Mutt's last name when he moved into the Toulouse address. He didn't feel it right to use his old name. He wasn't that person any more. He wasn't sure he even remembered that name. He didn't want to try.

He'd rather be Mutt and Fred's adopted son. He had posted a notice at the Church of Rodrigo to make the adoption official. He had listed LM and FT as his parents, living at the same address. Mother Fred. Papa Mutt. Baby Rodrigo. All registered voters. The Government didn't care. Maybe the

Library wouldn't either. Rodrigo Jeansonne had a nice ring to it.

He hoped that no one would notice that he was older than his father.

Or that his mother was quite short and a quadruped.

The librarian suspects. She is certainly taking her time filling in my form. Shuffling papers and typing.

I must be calm.

REEBOK   from roebuck. A species of South African antelope whose hooves closely mimic contemporary sports footwear. See also: EX-PARTNERS OF THE RETAIL WORLD

She raises her head, smiles broadly and hands him a laminated yellow card with the name "Rodrigo Jeansonne" typed across the top. "Congratulations, Mr Jeansonne," she says. "We are very happy to have you as a full member of the New Orleans Library system."

She leans closer and whispers, "And I am personally pleased to have you as a resident of the neighborhood. You may not recall, but we met briefly at Carnival time. My dad is Second Chief of the Mighty Choktaw. May I say that we both think you would make a great addition to the tribe? And your dog. Indian practice is 9pm Thursdays at The Plunder Bar. Do come, won't you?"

* * *

"Mister Jeansonne, if you would only please let us know why you've turned off the air conditioning in here," William Greene pleads. "We're all suffocating. We will all die in here without AC. We must have some ventilation. I don't see the point in us all being so miserable."

"You know, President Greene," says Council member Jeansonne, calmly and into his microphone, "I've found out some amazing things since I've been coming regular to this room to talk with you folks. You've taught me how to get people's attention, so they listen to you. Me, I've got something special to say today, and this is the best way I know of showing you just what I mean.

"Something that's been on my mind of late is the little ones. Children, you know. Sometimes they get thought of last because they can't speak up for themselves. I'd appreciate being allowed to enter this proposal into consideration. Fred will let you turn the thermostat down just as soon as you've read it."

"Wahrfff!" says Fred emphatically, on guard in front of the AC controls.

Rodrigo is already passing out folders of material to each person. Mutt continues.

"I'd like you to consider making this a city ordinance." His voice grows more serious, almost accusatory.

"How many of you have noticed the state flag there on the wall behind us?" Everyone nods, caught up in the mood emanating from the Vieux Carré representative. They've never heard him talk like this. "Have you really looked at that blue piece of cloth? I'm not surprised   it's a pretty strange picture, considering the way we do business. There's a bird right in the middle, a momma brown pelican. She's got no food, so she's tearing out her own flesh to feed her babies."

There is a murmur of disbelief.

"C'mon, Mutt."

"What do you mean? Really?"

"Yessir, Mr Greene," said Mutt. "Get a good look. The state of Louisiana figures that taking care of its young ones is the number one thing we all should be thinking about. Put it right up there on the state flag.

"Now when I started out in this politics business, one of the first things I noticed myself was how our babies were getting short-changed. All this money is rolling through the Quarter and the rest of the City. Beautiful double-decker tourist buses with sparkling chrome and leather seats. Our kids watching them go by, staring out at the street from schoolrooms that are hot and dusty.

"I know what you're fixing to say," says Mutt, raising his hand to stop the interruption. "I know that by all rights kids and schools are a school board issue, but I figure it's time we stop letting the structure of this Government get in the way of us doing things. I figure, let's just do 'em.

"That's why I want to ask you to put a tax of one dollar a head on every person who rides a tour bus through New Orleans. And this Government takes that dollar and puts air conditioning in the six schools in this city that haven't got any. Let those children study without sweating and fighting the heat.

"No need for momma to be tearing flesh. Not with so many tourists around."

"Sounds good to me. We'll vote. Can we turn the AC back on then?" asks William Greene.

"They like him, Don. He somehow knows what he's doing," emphasizes Chris Reed. "That's why they've voted with him these last few times. In just two months he's got the City Government system down better than anybody sitting on the Council. The other members are afraid to vote against anything he says is right. Because he's the only one who ever does any homework. They've grown dependent on him. It's better than we could have ever hoped."

Reed is back in the miniature chair. DAR Borden listens standing at the window, hands clasped behind his back.

"How can this man turning out to be intelligent possibly be 'better than we could have ever hoped'? How will that aid in getting what we want from that bunch of fools?" he asks condescendingly, without turning to face the room. Borden now avoids direct confrontation with this Reed woman whenever possible.

"Yes, how?" echoes Robert Markham. The junior attorney is also uncomfortably seated in front of Borden's desk. Sitting and responding as is his required lot.

Reed sighs. These two men are so short-sighted. So blatantly stupid. And they are the smart ones. She knows that if she ever gets her foot in the door of this firm, there will be no stopping her. It's possible she might not even need them. If Mutt could gather enough power quickly. Big "if."

Who am I kidding?

Mutt does not seem to consider political power a useful, or even desirable, tool. He avoids it. But that power put him in office. He owes a debt, whether he realizes it or not. So does Chris Reed.

I'm STUCK with these assholes. But I can deal with it.

"Because, gentlemen, his vote controls the entire council now. And I control him. Completely."

Borden rubs his eyes. He can't believe he is feeling sorry for Jeansonne.

Yes, I bet the bitch does. Poor bastard doesn't have a chance.

The Senior Partner pulls his wits together, gambles, turns. "That is what I had hoped you would say, Miss Reed. And I hope you are correct in your assumptions about the man and his influence. For we have found occasion make use of our investment in your political activities. We want to call in your and Mr Jeansonne's debt to our equanimity. And our political fund."

He does not wait for a reaction before proceeding. "To that end we have prepared a motion that we want your Mr Jeansonne to put before Council at its first meeting in August. It must pass without attracting a great deal of notice, so we have attached our property purchase proposal to a quite innocuous resolution guaranteeing continued City subsidies on handicapped bus fares. Something none of those idiots would dare oppose."

Markham hands a folder to Reed.

Borden goes on quickly. "Again I will say, this is a motion that must pass. When it does, I am sure you will find us more than grateful. In fact we would be willing to offer you an associate partnership in this firm, should your efforts on our behalf bring about the firm's legal acquisition of the property in question."

He looks directly at her. She is unmoved.

"A full partnership, with a non-revocable, loophole-free contract," replies Reed. She pulls another folder from her briefcase and hands it to Borden.

"I've taken the liberty of preparing such a document in advance," she says.

* * *

"Muthafuckin' cocksuckin' sumbitch, ah git you! You wait. You ain gittin away! I git you," finished the voice, followed by the sounds of a dropped phone, further cursing and a clumsy disconnection.

Mutt hangs up the receiver gently.

"More of that cursing man?" asks Rodrigo from across the Council office. "I could hear him from all the way over here. Why do you listen to him? Why do you let him talk to you that way? All this time, just nasty as can be. You could trace the call, put the man in jail."

"I don't know, my friend. That hate spilling out of him seems to have just the opposite effect on me. It purges all the bad. Maybe I envy his ability to feel strong emotion, as evil as his is. Maybe once he gets it all out of him, he'll feel better and start to enjoy being alive again. Like the both of us. Come to life like we did. The sumbitch."

Mutt smiles, picks up a stack of folders from his desk.
"So, are we ready for Council?"

FUGUE a musical composition in which many and varied instruments are introduced one at a time, harmonizing in short bursts according to the laws of counterpoint. ALSO, in the study of the human mind, a temporary flight from reality, in which a person behaves normally for a certain period of time, but then has no knowledge of what went on during that time. ALSO, among music therapists, the latter definition is applied, the term colloquially referring to any music performed in the state of Nevada. See also: DANKE SCHOEN.

"Mr Greene, I believe this matter should be referred to the Budget Committee before the Council as a whole makes any decision on it. At least that's the way I read the Procedural Rules you were nice enough to lend me. Sorry to interrupt. Don't mean to be pushy or anything. Just thought you'd want to know."

"Councilman Jeansonne, I have no doubt in my mind you are correct. Planning Proposal AO237-90 is hereby referred to Budget for their July 28 meeting. Thank you again, Mr Jeansonne, for your attention to these highly complex matters. And to your Mr Rodrigo for his assistance."

"Waaoof!" comes from below the Council table.

"And, of course to Madame Fred, our deepest thanks."

"Moof!"

Council President Greene continues, undaunted. "I believe everyone on the Council holds a high regard for the quality of the work you have done in the short time you have been in these chambers.

"Do you think we should send out for lunch yet?"

When she saw Borden's proposal actually listed on the printed Council agenda for the upcoming August 1 session, Chris Reed knew she had to do something. Mutt would no more miss the documentation of an approved property sale than he would forget to breathe. He was a conscientious and scrupulous examiner of all documents that pertained to his job. He would spot the amendments dealing with the transaction, and refuse to bring the proposition up unless he knew all the details.

Once he knew the details, he would see at once who the sale would most benefit. And hurt.

Chris decided on a diversionary tactic. A little private celebration. Something that would cause Councilman Jeansonne's attention to wander. He would be grateful, she was sure. Just enough intimacy to get him a bit confused. It was for his own good. He wouldn't even mind that he'd missed a minuscule bit of paper-shuffling.

They would enjoy themselves, forget about their jobs for a moment. She'd like that herself. She was rather looking forward to it. Nothing serious. Maybe this would let her get him out from under her skin. Let Chris Reed convince herself once and for all that she wouldn't let her relations with this man get personal.

Keep her from something worse.

GLOSSOLALIA   an exclamatory utterance made in either physical or emotional ecstasy, usually unintelligible and with multiple emphases, as in "UHHH'-unhhh-UHHH'." This speech phenomenon characteristically expresses some deeply-felt quasi-religious experience. Believed by some philosophers and professors of Divinity Studies to be the basis of the Lesser Reformed Buddhism found to proliferate among denizens of the Myongdong tea shops of Seoul and hillside coffee houses of Southern California and Washington state. See also: SELF-FLAGELLATION, EMPYREUMA, DISCHARGING ROD.

Chris   the "ma'am" now only emerged infrequently in addressing her   picked Mutt up the evening before the August 1 Council meeting. She drove him to her home for a working dinner. Over the phone she had told him they would discuss the next day's agenda, right after they ate.

Mutt remembers the apartment.

This is a nice quiet place, but it's so cold in here.

"Something wrong, Mutt?"

"No, Chris, nothing wrong. Just thinking is all. Just thinking."

"Well, you stop that for just a few minutes. Relax. We'll get to the work soon enough."

Reed mixes cocktails in a blender.

"Mutt, I've made these especially for you," she said handing him a tall glass. "A 'Banana Republic'. Nuts and tropical fruits and bananas and a dash of rum. Appropriate to celebrating your second month in New Orleans Government, don't you think?"

"I suppose so. But even though I've only had two months, I already know more about Government than I ever will about drinking. Never had much in the way of hard liquor. Except I drank some rum once. It was really bad." He looks up at her clouding face, realizes his mistake and takes a big gulp. "But this, this tastes good. Yes, it does taste really good."

"A healthy drink, Councilman Jeansonne. Lots of vitamins for the body and a little rum for the mind. Drink up!" she shouts, holding her glass up for a toast. She is enjoying letting go.

Mutt is happy to oblige, consuming Banana Republics without restraint. The fruit completely masks the rum, as in most of the specialty drinks served to tourists in the French Quarter. The alcohol usually asserts itself when consumption has already run the stoplight of gastrointestinal tolerance. The Vieux Carré's new Councilman has the pedal to the metal, drinking an uncountable number of the beverages. As Chris continually refills his glass, and hers, with a pinkish-yellowish liquid. In honor of his successful experience with Government.

"A toast! A toast!" Reed goes on, pouring again. "To your happy assimilation into the Council! Every one of those bums wait for you now, Mutt. They want you to take the lead. You to do the research. You to know the issue and implications."

"Hee. I don't know about that, uh Chris. They're OK folks. They just let themselves get trapped in politics. Get trapped. Hee hee. Funny. Hee."

"Politics schmolitics!" She sits close to him. "Do you have any idea how grand you look on that Council? When I think of the night we first me... I'm proud of you, Mutt Jeansonne."

Mutt is lost. Happily and blissfully lost.

She puts her arm around him.

Chris Reed kisses Mutt Jeansonne. Opening her lips, her tongue finds its way wetly between his teeth. She surprises herself, moaning as she presses her body against his.

Mutt Jeansonne spends the night on Jefferson Avenue.

Uptown.

* * *

"Mister Jeansonne would like to urge all Council members to vote for his Resolution LD-221C, as further proof of the City's commitment to the support of its less fortunate citizens."

Christine Reed is seated at the Council Chamber's podium, directly across from Mutt. She rolls on with her pitch smoothly and confidently.

"The RTA's approved budget will more than cover this minimal subsidy, thus assuring New Orleans' less fortunate citizens of public transportation. It will actually save money in the long-run, by making handicapped citizens more self-sufficient."

"And what about these amendments at the end of the document? What are these real estate matters doing attached to a Public Transportation Bill?" asks Council President Greene.

"They are merely approvals of additional revenues coming to the City from the sale of superfluous property adjoining State right-of-ways. We included them so as to dispose of the matter now, in an efficient manner, rather than bringing them up on their own as a separate agenda item."

She has not broken stride. Reed looks directly at Mutt, her businesslike voice now carrying a soft, cajoling undercurrent.

"Councilman Jeansonne felt that it was appropriate that the issues be considered simultaneously. Correct, Councilman Jeansonne?"

Mutt is elsewhere. Daydreaming about Chris Reed. He hasn't properly prepared for this session of Council.

She drove him to City Hall, convincing him that he need not return to Toulouse street. She told him he could leave Fred at home this one time. He knew Fred would not be happy, but he couldn't refuse Reed. He'd take Fred to Dooky Chase's Restaurant to eat tonight. They could actually pay for a meal, now that he was employed. That Creole food would make Fred forget all about missing the Council meeting.

To stay close to Reed, alone with her, even for just the few minutes of the car ride, he would risk Fred being angry with him.

Mutt keeps forgetting he is in the Council chambers. His mind is still back on Jefferson Avenue. Reliving every second. At least reliving the seconds that he can remember.

On the way to City Hall, Reed spoke to him as she never had before. She spoke of their future. Hers and his. Of her admiration for him. Of her need for his strength. She brushed his arm as she backed her car into a parking spot.

Mutt was forced to wait for a few minutes before he could get out of the BMW. He had been physically excited by Reed's attentions, embarrassingly so. Was forced to mull over carpentry additions to his bathroom to allow the manifestation of his ardor to subside.

Standing outside the car door, Reed knew that she had him. She would do a rapid run-through on the Resolution as they walked into the building. Mutt would never even see the paperwork until it was being read out in the session. He would trust her when it came to the vote, without a doubt. No question. And it wouldn't be so bad for him. He'd never even know the sale had happened. He'd be fine.

She planned to lean against him, position his arm between her breasts as they entered the Council Chambers. Just for good measure. The boy wouldn't even remember his own name.

That did not, of course, affect the way she expected him to vote.

Fifteen minutes after it happened, the news that Councilman Mutt Jeansonne had sold out reached Stephanie Jorgensen, real estate agent extraordinaire and Number One of the Dislocated Ten. Her youngest brother Eddie who worked in the Utilities Department of the City Government regulating taxicabs, light bulbs and cable TV, had given her a call. Eddie had a direct pipeline into the Council. He knew the details of scuttlebutt at City Hall before the Mayor even got wind of it. As she picked up her phone, Eddie was already laughing at her.

Eddie lives in one predominantly white suburb of the city called Metairie. He had moved there when he was twenty years old to get away from the "niggers and Catholics, Jews and queers, and murdering sons-of-bitches" who inhabit New Orleans. He and his suburban neighbors had voted an ex-

Klansman into the State Legislature in 1991, just to "get things balanced out" in the State Capitol.

Eddie despises the City. Though he still manages to derive his entire living from working in a Government department funded by a New Orleans black-majority population and a substantial gay community. He keeps a $50-a-month room in a boarding house on Coliseum street to avoid violating the City's residency laws.

Eddie never liked his sister much either. He took great pleasure in relaying news of her hero's defection to the side of straight white middle-class progress. The man sold his squatter's haven to Uptown lawyers. Right out from under his friends. It was absolutely perfect.

Ignoring Eddie's oaths of veracity, Stephanie had checked out his claims with the City Clerk. And found out that what he had said was true. Councilman Jeansonne had voted exactly as Eddie said.

Stephanie is aghast. She is hurt. Mutt had told her in the beginning that he had to occasionally lie when he lived on the Street. Just to live from day to day. He had promised her those times were done and gone. She took this out-front, voluntary admission of his own weakness as a sign of Mutt Jeansonne's underlying strength and honesty.

But his people, his family, is on the Street. And, according to her neo-Nazi brother, Mutt Jeansonne had just sold the land under that Street to the worst of the Uptown missionary-position capitalist slave-hoarders.

Right then Stephanie decides that she will cancel this year's Dislocated Ball. The gathering has outlived its original joyous purposes.

It had helped create a monster.

Fred moved out of the Robichaux house the evening after the land-sale ordinance was sneaked through Council approval. The sale was not the reason she left. The dog had no idea what issues were addressed at the session. She did not know a vote that would adversely affect her friends had taken place. She wasn't even particularly mad at being left out of a Council meeting. She had, after all, slept an extra ten hours that day.

"Members of Fred's particular breed have the regularly-recurring need for an inordinate amount of rest. They nap frequently to maintain their intellectual alertness," Rodrigo had theorized. Fred felt her faith in Rodrigo as a scientist of the first order was once again justified when she heard his pronouncement.

But Mutt had returned to Toulouse street carrying the profound scent of another female. A human female. Fred could feel that her closest friend was suddenly and deeply changed, marked to his core. He had lost much of the sensitivity he had carried since their first meeting under the roadway. He had simply been exposed to too much input over the last months. There were so many people demanding his attention. But now his priorities had shifted from plural to singular. He was a vastly different animal. It had happened in one night.

That the male Mutt animal had selected a single female, even if only for rutting, changed the shape of their relationship. Fred did not know this new Mutt. She wasn't staying around him until he offered some satisfactory definition of himself. That defining process was not going to happen soon.

With one of her own, re-integration into the family was merely a matter of some extended ass-sniffing. Humans carried no such easily-understandable information centers. Mutt had been unable to do anything upon his return. He could not speak or eat. He was unable to put his feet on the JFK bathroom mat and think logically. He lay on the floor of his bathroom sanctuary for the better part of two hours when he returned from Council. Continually putting his face to his armpits and chest. Smelling the foreign odors on his body and clothes.

Fred was reminded again of her brother Helen, ecstatically and helplessly rolling in fresh catshit. Let the boys smell the results of a cat's overactive digestion, or a human with female hormones flowing, and all sense of decency fled.

The effect of the scent was all the same when it came to inducing this male delusion. One whiff and they lost all respect for themselves. She pictured Helen, rolling in a nest of hard, month-old Siamese turds. No longer the strong and proud male. She had never before thought Mutt susceptible to such a loss of character.

Fred the dog knew the human female source was Reed. That the scent on Mutt was a piss-marking of territory. The message one of sole possession.

Fred moved in with Mel before the sun set. Mutt was not aware of her departure. He was not aware of any change in his surroundings for three days after his night Uptown. That third morning he ate corn cereal for breakfast and noticed the Doc Wolf poster in his bedroom.

Fred!

By then it was too late.

"They what, darling? You must slow down. I haven't heard you like this in ages! You're so sexy when you're all worked up." Mel was in her dressing room, preparing for her third set, when Rodrigo had entered already talking loudly.

Rodrigo is in no mood for play. "Tear down. Turtleneck. Trouserpress. Mel! They tearing down Mutt & Fred's HOUSE," he yells.

"WHAT!" Mel shrieks at an even higher level.

Rodrigo catches his breath and calms just a notch, "House under road. All Street people house around

Expressway! Chasing everybody off. No more boxes, no nothing anywhere near. Just piles of dirt! No people can stay."

He quiets for a second before proceeding, rubbing his sweat-beaded forehead with his hands.

"Came during day, lots of police, lots of men driving bulldozer, bulldozer taking everybody's blankets, taking everybody's food, everything! They burning, burning! Burning!"

He takes a deep breath. Mel can tell something very big is coming. Rodrigo has not talked in such a disjointed manner in months. She does not interrupt him. She waits. This is serious.

"Burning MY BOOKS!"

* * *

The University of New Orleans' National Public Radio affiliate had scheduled a replay of Orson Welles' infamous "War of the Worlds" broadcast for that night. Bumping the regular program. Citing yet another surge in UFO sightings as the reason for the broadcast.

The interest in the other-worldly was back with a vengeance. It was August again   also a ratings sweep month. The time period cleared the normally-offered "Baroque Vocal Hour," a show notorious for its paucity of listeners. The wildly-mustachioed host actually took delight in how few people were learned enough to select the program's spasmodic warblings as a desirable art form. He had trouble getting his immediate family to listen.

WWUN-FM's Program Director was determined to garner some numbers on that Thursday evening. A week earlier, he left a telephone message telling the Baroque host to remain home. The PD had gambled on finding new audiences by breaking something dramatic out of the station library. He decided he would host the "War of the Worlds" presentation himself. Bring a noted authority on board to introduce the piece. Thus providing up-to-date insight on the historic broadcast.

Dr Anatole Dzhervinsky, an astute-sounding sociology professor from St John's prestigious College of Intergalactic Affairs spoke of the "alien imposition phenomena" as being the result of a brand of mass hypnosis. People wanted the aliens so badly that they imposed them on one another as part of a group bonding experience. This viewpoint was entirely unrelated to the past year's widely accepted but utterly fraudulent "thermal hysteria," according to Dr Dzhervinsky. Studies of the August phenomena were based on his own strict scientific analysis of all available data.

It was easy to see, he explained, how the relatively uneducated masses at the times of the initial Welles broadcast could fall into the trap. The general populace now had just the opposite problem   too much input. Too much education as to the possibilities. The Welles broadcast was too primitive for contemporary audiences. It wouldn't fool anyone half a century later, but reaction to the outdated radio broadcast remained an interesting study in group psychosis.

That said, the program host/Program Director thanked Anatole for his analysis and reminded audiences that the upcoming program was indeed still just a work of fiction after all the decades since it was originally presented.

Tape rolled. A background hiss filled the air.

Orson Welles' resonant voice announced that "War of the Worlds" was just a radio show, then proceeded onward.

More than fourteen hundred calls jammed the police and military switchboards before the program was over.

Sightings continued for a week.

* * *

"But, Mel, please please just put the phone near her so she can hear. I've got to talk to her! I've got to explain."

"Mutt, you must stop this maudlin chatter. It is useless. Fred does not wish to hear or see you. And it is no wonder. You've reduced Rodrigo to tears. You've wounded all those who worked so hard to give you what you wanted. The pain will stop in time. I am sure that sooner or later we will all come to our senses and work this out, but right now I myself am worked into a complete rage. I've been bawling along with this darling man for hours! Have you any idea what you have done?"

A loud stuttering click announces the clumsy return of a dial tone. Mutt takes the phone from his ear and places it back in its cradle with exaggerated care, as if it might be a living thing.

Fred was right. He has left himself vulnerable. The pain is real. For the first time in almost a year, Mutt Jeansonne feels homeless.

"Quiet! I said QUIET, everyone!" screams Chris Reed over the din. She stands downstairs at Toulouse street on a case of Doc Wolf's. "Councilman Jeansonne cannot be disturbed now. Besides, the deed is done. The City legally sold the land last week, and the new owners have decided to develop it. This is not only within their rights, it is something that should have been done years ago."

"Pomegranate! Why didn't they come ask us to move?" mumbles Rodrigo, standing near Reed's elbow.

"Yeah," counters an orange-haired teenage boy sitting on the floor, "Why didn't they even give us a chance to move, instead of destroying everything with a fucking bulldozer, for Christ sake! They crushed my guitar, lady   the only thing I own besides these clothes."

"They say you were illegally camped on public property! It may not be right, but it is the law. It has always been the law. They just haven't enforced it before. Now, please, please, the damage has already been done," says Reed, sensing she is quickly losing momentum. She is having some difficulty maintaining a dominant position in the room. She stops listening to the roar of voices, retreats into herself to gather strength.

I am not ready for this. These Streets, acting like they have rights   something I had a hand in teaching them   and it's true! How did I end up on the Bad Guys' side?

This is too ridiculous.

All that has happened over the last year, all that I've done, and look where I am   surrounded by the very people I dreamed of protecting, and now I'm the one who's hurt them.

Why am I HERE?

The complaints mount around her.

It's only August 15. The timing's all wrong.

She had planned to take a few weeks off after the sale resolution passed, to quietly withdraw from both Mutt's camp and the staff of the District Attorney. The Jeansonne campaign debt would be paid. She would be safely ensconced in her new offices before any shit could possibly hit the fan. More than likely no one would ever even notice what had happened. Then she could help Mutt again. Once she was stable and protected in the firm, she could do him even more good.

That was the plan. But here she is, only a few days from accomplishing everything she had set out to do, and an ambitious B-league construction company decides to move up its schedule and destroy hers.

Go in like they're playing John Wayne versus the VC. Green Berets under the Interstate. No wonder these poor fools are so torn up. Great. Just great.

She is still connected with Jeansonne, though. She has not yet cut the umbilical. A PR mess for him now could still stick to her in her new job. When she got word of the debacle, Reed decided to put out a few fires before she resigned. She came over just to get things generally in order. Christine Reed had not expected this.

She thought he could handle it. But Mutt had fallen apart after that call from Rodrigo. About the books. The All-Fact is no more.

Not important in itself. But if the press gets wind of it, we are cooked   Jeansonne's alienated his loyal Street campaign manager. If the TV news crews latch onto the hobos in revolt, they'll have a field day.

It is possible that I could be subjected to TV exposure of just the wrong sort. At just the wrong time.

I'll save the day, but these people better not push.

They had best be appreciative.

After all, it was MUTT'S Resolution that did this.

"Lady, I could use a blanket," says the guitarless teen.

"Got some smokes?" asks Noonie.

"How 'bout we all stay at your house, baby?" asks a smirking boy in torn black jeans and chains.

I'm done.

She has had enough talk.

"Ladies..." she announces, "...and Gentlemen. I have told you all I know. I am sure Councilman Jeansonne will try and help you if he can, but in the meantime..." Reed is at a loss.

She looks slowly around her, "...in the meantime, you can all stay right here. Just take it easy."

I can't handle this. I can't.

"But, lady, how about the smokes?" whines Noonie. "Duckie needs some SMOKES."

That does it. "This is not my fault! It is not up to me to fix it. Why don't you people fix it for a change?" yells Reed.

"We thought we did, when we elected Mutt," answers Virginia.

Reed grabs Virginia's collar, pulls her close, and hisses directly into her face: "You're right! You elected Mutt, not me."

She steps down and walks from the room in absolute quiet. She has done the best she can, and still they want more. More. Too much. She has to think a minute, get the politic-speak going. Just get in a quiet space. As she starts up the stairs, low and subdued talking starts again. The crowd is anything but subdued.

"Fuckin' duck! DUCKIE knew we couldn't trust her!" Noonie mutters.

Rodrigo seems lost, beaten. He turns to Noonie and asks quietly, "But what about Mutt? They're saying this was his idea."

"I hear he's the one who made the deal!" the jeaned boy chimes in.

Rodrigo turns to answer him halfheartedly, "He wouldn't forget his people. We're the ones who put him in there. We're Family. Mutt wouldn't forget."

Reed knocks on the upstairs bathroom door. She hates doing business in a toilet, but today it seems appropriate. That last moment, as she stood in the middle of a room full of ingrates, she had decided that consoling the Toulouse crowd any more was useless and futile. Pragmatism, self-preservation were in order.

I can weather any fall-out that might come from this debacle. I've handled worse. I simply will not subject myself to any more of this. The cause has outlived its function. All these people. Dead weight, dragging me down, closing in on me. But Mutt. What about Mutt?

If he can be a man   shoulder the blame and handle this like he is supposed to   I might let him back in. We can get it back together. Later.

"Come in," he responds to her knock. He is standing against the wall where his phone is mounted, fully-clothed in the same five-dollar VOA suit he had worn to her house. JFK's neon face shines up at her in triplicate from Mutt's matched set of bathroom accessories.

She enters the room slowly, sizing up the man's state of mind. When she is certain he is harmless, she decides to proceed on her decision.

"I am resigning my position with your office effective immediately," Reed says quickly. "I would appreciate it if you would handle all your own press from now on, and not mention my name again in any of your political dealings." She points at the door. "These people want too much from me, Mutt. I got us what we needed for our campaign. I helped you win, then I made sure you were square with the world."

"Square with the world?" he whispers. "Does that mean destroying people's homes?"

"I didn't mean for that to happen. It wasn't my fault. We both know they weren't really people's homes. They were boxes under a public roadway. It's probably even a good thing. Maybe now we can get the City motivated to find them homes like yours. This uproar could all come out for the better." Claustrophobia begins to well up inside Chris Reed. The bathroom, the house, they are both growing smaller.

I can't breathe. I have to get OUT!

"Look, I've done all I can for you. Now I've got to take care of myself. It'll get better soon, I promise. Let things cool down for a month or so. They'll forget all about it. Then we can talk again, like we used to. But right now, I've got to go."

Chris Reed tries to act on the momentum she has built. She pivots on the ball of her foot to go, but her heel catches in JFK's fuzzy bathrug nose, and she falls to the floor awkwardly.

Mutt is quickly at her side, "Alright? Are you alright?" he says, kneeling and reaching to help.

"I can take care of myself," she replies, emphasizing each word carefully. Staying in control. She tosses back his offer of a hand up.

She gets to her feet. "You got what you wanted, and I got what I wanted, so let's call it even, right? You were nothing when I met you, and now you're something, right. I did that for you. I did it, and I took care of business. Now you don't owe anybody anything. You're free. I didn't mean to hurt you. Once all this dies down, you'll see that what I did was right. You'll see, Mutt."

Her speech has calmed her. Reed opens the door. "I've got to go now."

Mutt is still on his knees. "But we got what you wanted. Everything. I just wanted... you." He reaches up for her hand, touches it.

Chris Reed loses it completely. She doesn't look back. She slams the bathroom door, runs down the stairs, and out the door.

Before Virginia can open her mouth, Chris Reed sticks a raised index finger in her face, bolts off the front porch and sprints toward her car.

"Want to buy a lucky bead, lady?" yells Virginia after the lawyer.

The house continues to roar.

Ten days later Councilman L Mutt Jeansonne is arrested for trespassing on the very property that he approved selling. He is released from jail, disappears again. Misses two more Council meetings. No one can find Mutt to talk to him. He is once again invisible. The word is that he's back doing the Street. He hasn't slept at Toulouse in weeks. People are talking about him like they made a mistake.

"Now, Ginny, he's a big boy," says Melodie LaGrande. Virginia has called the exotic entertainer for her third dose of reassurance today. It is not yet noon. "He and Rodrigo are both big boys. My Rodrigo lost it at first when his books were burned, too. He blamed Mutt, and so did I. For a while. But he's getting over it. In one way I'm sad to lose that child-man part of my Rodrigo. I loved my mysterious baby scholar. Don't you think he looks a bit like Charles Boyer under his beard? But he's still quite the man without all that. Just different. He'll be alright. He's got me. But poor Mutt hasn't even got Fred any more.

"I don't know how she picked up on this feeling of betrayal, but it's definitely real. She won't let him near her. She sits behind my tub and broods for days on end. I almost had to force some of her favorite food down her throat last night. I am personally at a loss. Mutt is such a dear, simple man. Roddy is out looking for him. We'll get him back, pamper him with a lot of love, get Fred feeling better. It'll be alright, just you wait," Mel says confidently. "How is the rest of the family taking it?"

Virginia changes gears, "Talked to Noonie long time this morning. SSSSsss-she's in the kitchen, cooking a meal every time I turn around. It seems to help her. She cooks and thinks and cooks some more. She's been staying to herself a lot since Mutt left. I know she's upset, but she's dealing with it in the kitchen. Me, I'm not so sure about. I miss him. There's a part of me misssss-sss-SSSing with him. I can't deal with it like Noonie and Ellis."

There was no missing Ellis Duck, however. Noonie's cooking therapy had brought her feathery companion to a blissful obesity. The term "waddle" was never more appropriate.

* * *

Dinner time. No one around. Mutt sneaks into the storeroom at Manus Boy's Home. The janitor James' old room. The huge water heater on one side. On a sudden urge, Mutt reaches down and feels around behind it. His fingers touch something. *Sure enough.* He withdraws a bottle, coated in soot and dirt.

K&B Brand. Not much left in this bottle, hidden back there since James last tipped it up to his mouth. Blue ocean on the pirate picture label already faded. Cap'n James won't be coming back for another trip to the high seas.

Over thirty years since he sent me stumbling to my rubber-glove ass inspection, and James was still drinking the same bad brand of rum when he died.

At the opposite side of the jumbled space is a dusty door set into the wall. Several years' rust on the hinges tells a story of little use since the handyman's death. James had told him that the hidden door to the chapel was there. Built to make cleaning the small church easier. It opened right behind the altar.

He crosses from the doorway to the middle of a row of life-sized statues of cast and polychromed stone. The child named Mutt stands absorbing the image of a serene woman with a pleasant smile. He listens. So carefully.

He reaches out and touches her hand. Hard, unmoving. Cold, transmitting the man-made refrigeration of the chapel. But Mutt can feel her, a subtle flow of warmth at the center of the stone. The comfort that generations of young boys had found there. The trust they had left in its place.

He can talk here.

Pretty silly, after all this time, coming back here to look at all you folks. I wasn't too smart a boy, but I got these feelings about people. I knew when they liked me or didn't. Knew when they wanted to talk to me. Didn't do me too much good, though. Scared more folks away than I can remember, what with me figuring them out so quick and all. Didn't get to keep too many friends.

This wasn't a bad home, I guess, but it got to be pretty scary for me at the end.

Hey, look, I gotta go now. I just wanted to see your faces. Put it in my head so I can remember what you look like. I see you, and I'm OK. Really. I gotta go. I got me some things to talk over with a friend. Man talk, you know. Yeah, I'm all grown up now. Got me lots of grown-up friends. Give me advice and all. They do.

Gotta go. Lot of walking to do. Bye now.

* * *

Charles Taylor is walking the streets of the lower Ninth Ward about midway between midnight and sunup when an idea hits him.

He has grown tired of calling Mutt Jeansonne. The guy is never at his office anymore. And when Taylor calls the Toulouse number to curse, some crazy person makes duck noises at him. Really loud duck noises.

At least he thinks that's what he hears.

No, the phone is out as a method of stemming the invasion. No good. He decides he needs to purge the confusion in his mind with yet another roaring C45ID, and starts the walk down to Pug's 24-hour supermarket for another half a dozen tall ones of malt liquor. Maybe the new *Comet* will be in. Taylor can't get the Jeansonne situation off his mind. He's still muttering to himself when he passes the entertainer Bad Boy Wenter's house. Something clicks. He gets to an eerie-looking grey cypress shanty a few doors further down. Everyone in the neighborhood avoids the place, as it is known to be the home of the notorious traiteur Phillipe Baudoin. Taylor slows. Stops.

The idea comes.

Charles Taylor walks onto Baudoin's porch and knocks on the screen door. Already talking to the closed door. "Dat fancy phone shit ain workin fo no Nint Ward boy. Gotta gimme dat power! Gimme a lil Nint Ward juice. An dis da place."

Taylor knocks again, harder. "Hoodoo man he be up. Don sleep. No he don. Never. He fixin at Jeansonne man better an at goddam telephone."

There is a long pause. A dog is barking in the next block. Taylor knocks a third time. Another pause. A footstep. The heavy wooden inner door opens to a fluid darkness glowing with dim swirls of light.

"What you want, child?" asks a deep voice from behind the screen.

"Hey Missa Fillup hey ah gotta man he messin wid de wurl'. At whole wurl', Missa Fillup! Terrble man. Gottat dog cummin direct frummat debbil heppinim. Makin me be spillinat beer, makin static cum onnat TV, makinat 'frigerator stop wurkin. Takin over at wurl' any minnit. I wanna stop him. Givum sumthin ta think bout. Hurt him heavylike."

"It's late. It had better be worth my while for you to come banging on my house wee hours of the morning. You do got some money, don't you, child?" An ominous tone floats the words to Taylor.

He is quick to answer. "Gottat purchasin money fo a six pack a tallboy. Fo dolla anna haf. An look, wait, ah be thowin in my Timex watch. Give it to ya right off mah arm, bruthah Fillup. Work good an all. Tellat date. Gotta new wristband. Real cowhide," says Taylor, holding up his wrist for inspection.

"We can do you something for that," declares the voice. "It won't seem big to you, but it will suffice."

A shadow moves behind the screen. There is the click of a latch being sprung. A tall man dressed in stained yellow pants and a torn animal-print shirt opens the door. Patches of hair hang greasily to his shoulders from a bald crown. The pitted face has had its bottom half severed by a razor, then reattached, a quarter of an inch to one side of its original location.

"Come in, child," invites Phillipe Baudoin. He moves aside and gestures for Taylor to enter. "We'll send a little message to your bad man. He'll pay attention to me. Oh, he will. They all pay attention when this hoodoo man speaks. By the time the sun rises, he'll be wishing he never crossed you."

"He be leavin 'ishere planet?" asks Taylor eagerly.

"I promise," says the traiteur.

* * *

Mutt has made his way from the chapel at the Manus Home back to familiar territory, to billboarded friends who never stop smiling or listening.

Mister, what's your wife like? She's a woman, right? I know. I know you've got kids. I've seen your granddaughter on TV. She must be your granddaughter. 'Fifteen thir-ty-two Tulane', she sings on that commercial. She's cute. Did she grow up? Did she? Is she older now?

Is she hurting people? Is she hurting you?

Me and Fred we were happy under here. She fell into my life right over there. Years and years ago. She was hurt, too, but I fixed her. Fixed her good. I never ever hurt her. Though I did make her kinda sick once. Too much of the Doc...

Mutt stops mid-sentence as the light sensors on the billboard kick in abruptly, cutting off juice to the fluorescent tubes that lit the billboard at night. There is a crackling, an electronic gurgling as the tubes go dark and dim daylight takes over.

It is sunrise. John Feinman and his furniture no longer need illumination.

Mutt does.

He decides to walk Uptown to Christine Reed's apartment.

* * *

Mel cannot sleep. Rodrigo is out once again, searching for Mutt. She is lonely and a bit anxious. A creeping fear is beginning to take root   that all they have built will crash down without Mutt at its center. Her Rodrigo has taken on the day-to-day operation of the Council office, and has even begun sitting with Fred, substituting in Mutt's Council seat. But without the man they had all elected and cheered, without that single rallying point... she wonders if the center will hold.

A collapse will be much more damaging than the loss of her nest-egg or the family's loss of the Robichaux house. The whole Vieux Carré community the misfits, the straights, the outlaws, the regular working-class stiffs, all of them together they will all suffer an irreparable dissolution of credibility. And heart.

Melodie decides to take a bath.

As Mel climbs into the gardenia-scented bubbles, Fred trundles into the room from her own sleepless night. She lowers her drooping rear end onto the bathmat, and sits looking up at Melodie. Her tail is not wagging.

"My baby Freddy, you poor baby dog, I am so upset all this has happened. I don't know what to think."

"Murf."

"He is out there, you know," Mel replies. She turns to face her girlfriend the canine wardrobe stylist, in the process sloshing water and bubbles over the edge of the tub and onto elderly dog paws. Melodie reaches out and rubs Fred's ears as she talks, leaving a foamy residue at their tips. "Rodrigo will find him. The Family will be together again." The word "Family" causes tears to start at the corners of both females' eyes. Bubbles are now dripping off Melodie's arms, onto Fred's muzzle.

"I know. It was a little his fault, too. Wasn't it? He should have paid attention. But he was so caught up in the woman that he had no idea what was happening. Then she runs off, leaving our poor Mutt to take the blame. And he does. Oh, Freddy, we shouldn't have been so hard on him. He's not a saint, he's a regular man, and he's going to make mistakes. I knew it would be bad and I did nothing to protect him! But we'll do better next time. We can help him, we can make him talk about these things!" Mel cries, throwing her arms at the ceiling for emphasis. A shower of soap suds descends on the dog.

"Waahhhh-PHEW!" sneezes Fred, blowing a rainbow-sheened transparent sphere toward the ceiling.

The grey-haired dog smiles for the first time in weeks.

* * *

"There," says Phillipe Baudoin. "Just a little more of this oil, child, will stick the paper to the candle. And awaken its power."

Charles Taylor is getting thirsty. It's dark and hot in Baudoin's house, and the hoodoo man hasn't offered him a drink. Now Baudoin is going to ask Taylor for his beer money to pay for a black candle in the shape of a man. With a piece of paper stuck to it. Makes it a lot more valuable, that paper. The phone is cheaper, after all. Can't back out now, though, not on the hoodoo man.

"I've written some words on the paper," says Baudoin. He hands the candle to Taylor. "They'll go to your man when you burn the candle down. He won't be happy with what the message says. It will fill his mind with anguish for a long long while. The words from the candle can be quite cruel. He won't be happy at all, your bad man."

"Aah jus light at candle right now. By a time ah get home ah be gettin him good. He be wakin up burnin in hell."

"Well said, child. And now, my money. And my watch, please."

* * *

Mutt Jeansonne is not asleep. A wall clock at the Prytania street bakery reads 6:35AM when Mutt passes by, on his way to Jefferson Avenue. The large banner in the window advertises cakes in fleur-de-lis shapes for tailgate parties. Football season. The Saints. It is Fall. At least in name. But

Mutt's wool tuxedo pants know that summer doesn't read the calendar in New Orleans. The sales ladies at Rockfield's could have told him: these pants are not designed for sprinting, no matter the season. But he continues on his way Uptown, the heavy fabric rubbing his legs raw with the sweat and exertion of the long sprint.

Mutt is counting aloud. The last three took only a few minutes. Blocks. The Councilman is driven. Comes close to running on several occasions. Covers the long side of seventy-odd blocks fueled by a single burst of madness.

He stops. Catches his breath. Hides himself.

He has no idea what he is doing there, across a hedge from the entrance to Reed's opulent apartment building. He isn't sure if he is building courage to knock on the door. Or if he hopes she might catch sight of him and have a change of heart. Or if he is just worshiping at the shrine. He only knows he has to be there.

He hasn't seen her in weeks. His nose can no longer smell her essence in the clothes he had worn that night, even though he keeps them in a plastic bag and no longer wears them. He has switched back to his haunted tux pants.

In spite of the pant interference, he can still sense what has happened to him completely. It is his gift, returned. Unrelentingly dogging him again.

The first week all he had to do was put his hand to his chest. Then the memory began to lift free of his body's short-term experience. He found he could still resurrect her image by touching the clothing. He had started wearing his old pants again so that he could hold on to that night. Focus on it. But he was weakened by lack of sleep, and often confused again by the old pants' disorienting voices.

The tortured sleep had returned with the pants. Tying them around his waist didn't seem to help this time. The new memory wouldn't leave him alone either.

He could see her. Mutt felt his flesh separate from his bones. He felt himself coming apart as he examined every detail of her body. He knew her creases, her folds, her swells, the small mole on her right hip. He knew the sources of her moisture and salt. He knew it all by heart. He would not let the night go.

Over and over again he experienced the overwhelming, painful wave of physical need. His clothes were gone as he lay on her bed. She had removed them. He remembered his head growing dizzy. Spinning as his senses were exposed to the female alchemy. She was kissing him. She was inside his mouth again and again. She was inside him. Her perfume, his and her body smells were mixing. Making something new. A living thing that surrounded him. Their bodies were together, moving. Merged. At her urging he had entered her. He had pushed as far into her as he could.

Then the memory stopped. As he had stopped that night. There was something dark at the center of Chris Reed. Without willing it, his sensors had slammed on, startling him. He saw her clearly.

Even as she made love to him, she was wishing him dead.

It didn't matter to Mutt. He would be glad to die if she wanted it.

Even now, as he sits concealed watching her home, he knows that he can refuse her nothing.

Her door opens. Mutt slumps further down. He is close enough to be seen. Mutt smells Chris Reed before she comes out on the sunlit front porch, carrying a cup of coffee. The deep scent of a woman. His heart stops. He does not move. He does not want to be seen now. Only to absorb what he can of her.

He can see her plainly from his hiding place. Chris Reed is wearing a translucent ivory dressing gown printed with bright, equidistant images of wild birds. Her legs are bare to the morning sun. Her feet to the polished planks of the porch. He sees the flesh of her soles whiten as they bear the weight of her body. He is close to her.

So close that he inhales her scent, feels again her power over him, feels her dark core showing itself. Unveiled, without pretense. She is hurting someone again, and she doesn't care.

Chris gives a contemptuous wave of her right hand to the open door behind her. Robert Markham's face appears over her shoulder. He glances left and right with sharp turns of his head, then runs to his car like a hunted animal. He neither speaks nor acknowledges Reed's presence. His trousers are unzipped. His shirttail out. There is real fear on his face, a white froth in the corners of his mouth. He is sure his wife is nearby, watching. He has no excuse. Not yet. It was this woman. Using him. That's it. Using him.

Sweet Jesus, it's morning already. She'll know. She'd love a divorce. Get everything. Everything. Leave me with the old bitch, leaching away my soul. Why did I DO this? She knows! Got to get HOME!

Markham catches his pants cuff on the corner of his Cadillac Seville's door as he slams it opens it slams it again.

Reed watches Markham's tire-squealing departure from her quiet residential neighborhood. No doors open. No windows come ajar. Her neighbors are discreet.

Chris Reed is laughing. Louder and louder. Markham doesn't realize it, but he is right. Using him.

The fool.

Didn't help, did it, Chrissymissy?

No, Daddy, it didn't help.

Her laughs grow high in pitch. They echo between perfectly-painted white-columned house exteriors. Bounce off hard grey slate roofs, drop in an arch to the ground, and then settle. Still fighting for further existence. Inch-by-inch disappearing down between the blades of dozens of uniform St Augustine grass lawns.

Markham's car careens around the corner onto Prytania street.

Chris Reed goes back inside her home and closes the door softly. She does not hear the long, low moan. Or see the other man stumble away from her house.

* * *

"Ouuch! Sheeyut muthahfuckah!" yells Charles Taylor, throwing the last three inches of black candle to the kitchen floor. He has only burned the candle halfway down   to the wax man's belt   before burning himself. He kicks the remaining candle under the refrigerator. The black candle's pants will have to wait for immolation. More likely the waxen remains will be consumed by the omnivorous hordes of roaches currently in residence under Charles Taylor's energy-efficient major appliances.

Taylor peels the still-pliable wax off his hand carefully, then puts his fingers in his mouth to stop the pain.

"Rashann, git in here now!" he screams through his hand.

The little girl arrives at a run. "Yessuh, Unca Charle."

"You go look in yo Auntee dressuh drawer, bottom un, unner her stockin. Lil plastic bag innere got some food stamp innit. Bring at bag to me right here right now."

"Yessuh, Unca Charle," she says, running out as quickly as she ran in.

"Pug he gonna bitch an holler allover attat store, but he gimme sum Colt fo them stamp yes he will. Git married to a woman think she own everythin, jus cause she got a job. At woman think she hidin em stamp from me. Them stamp they money! She havta unnerstan atta man a da house he needin a lil refreshments, he gotta havum. Thirsty," mumbles Taylor, licking his stinging fingers.

"Man git wounded defendin at wurl', he git thirsty."

Taylor was happy, in spite of his thirst and burnt fingers. He was released from his obsession. His investment with the traiteur closed the Jeansonne matter. He was free. The world would be saved from domination by demons from outer space. The *Comet* would probably want to do a story on him, but that would have to wait. After he had a couple of Colts, he planned to sleep for a day or two. Get caught up on his sleeping.

* * *

Mutt has forgotten sleep. He is at the movies. Reel upon reel sits stacked in the projection booth, waiting to be loaded onto the projector. Images sent as flickering chromatic light through a clear glass lens to form a glowing trapezoid. Cutting through an atmosphere of dust particles and human scent. Splashing on the panoramic silver screen at the front of his mind. Mutt Jeansonne sits alone in the dark of the theatre. Watching. Remembering.

His body wanders the Streets of New Orleans. Mutt is at the movies.

Mel and the Sisters at the Manus Home have remained in touch over the weeks since Mutt's disappearance, but the Mother Superior is still deeply disturbed. She feels she needs to do something else.

And now is the time. Though the weekend is predicted to hold the hottest day of September's lingering inferno. Sister Mary Ambrosia wants to make a novena at St John the Conqueror church, and she will not be denied. She considers her Saturday cross-town bus trip a sanctified pilgrimage of sorts. She is going to the place where Mutt had been returned to the family.

They found him six months ago, on a day of penance Ash Wednesday. It seemed like yesterday now. Time slipped by quickly outside the Home. She usually didn't care. It was pleasant most times, living and working in the safe vacuum of Manus. It had been so before.

But now her Mutt is lost again.

Sweat pools in her lap under the heavy starched cotton and wool habit. The bus' air conditioner isn't working, and the windows are welded shut. She feels a bit dizzy, and twice bangs her head against the window as the Desire street bus lurches down streets buckled from the heat. The Mother Superior has spent all but 19 of her 81 years in New Orleans. For the last two decades, the heat has extracted a greater toll from her frail body with each passing summer.

She catches a quick glance at a street sign as the bus passes over St Claude Avenue.

How curious. Desire street and Piety street. A block apart. Right here in the same neighborhood.

Desire and piety, side by side.

But they never meet. Until they cross Pleasure street, to join and disappear.

The bus stops on the corner opposite St John's and the rear hydraulic doors open. She had told the bus driver where she was going. Sister Mary Ambrosia makes the Sign of the Cross before getting up from her seat and easing her way down the steep bus steps to the street. The concrete only intensifies the heat of the day. The black portions of her clothing feel like they are close to combustion. There is no breeze. Only a suffocating, sweltering moisture. As best she can, she hurries into the building.

It is cool and dark inside the church, the air stirred by ceiling fans twenty feet above the marble floor. Only the shaded bulb over the confessional and a small pencil beam above the altar's main crucifix are lit. But once her eyes adjust, Sister Mary Ambrosia can see that the church is awash with muted colors from tall stained glass windows. A smiling but slightly out-of-focus St John, projected from the central casement on the western side of the church, is broken into a hundred square fragments of painted light on the uneven stone floor. Sister Mary Ambrosia carefully wends her way through the pews, bending frequently to raise kneeling pads, rather than tread on the saint's image.

It had been a slow afternoon for repenting, and Father Wildman had been rhythmically walking the aisles, pacing quietly and reading Herman Melville, until Sister Mary Ambrosia arrived.

There is no one else in line at the confessional. She stands outside the wooden booth for a moment to catch her breath, pulls aside the red velvet curtains and enters.

Sister Mary Ambrosia is there to ask forgiveness, again. In the weeks since her Mutt disappeared, a deep remorse has been building in her. She has to cleanse her soul in the act of penance. Father Wildman is strong enough to understand. He should know the nature of the beast. He hears confessions in the upper Ninth, after all.

She kneels. The small wooden door slides open to reveal Father Wildman's averted face behind a narrow lattice.

"Bless me, Father for I have sinned," she begins. "It has been three days since my last confession."

"And what serious sin is it, Sister, that you have so grievously committed in these seventy-two hours? What can it be that drives you to come all this way to confess to your old friend Aloysius Wildman?" says the priest.

He had seen her get off the bus.

"Aye, Aloysius, it is something serious, and not to be taken lightly by me or you," she replies.

"I am sorry if I was glib, Sister. It was uncharitable of me. Now. What is it you wish to confess?" asks Father Wildman again.

The words explode out of the old woman's mouth. "I was cruel and heartless to a young boy. I disciplined a poor child for something that wasn't his fault, wasn't even a sin. He accepted it, accepted the fault because he knew no better. And he knew no better because I was too embarrassed to tell him the things he needed to be told about life. I drove him from his home because of my own stupid shame, Father."

The priest can hear the nun's voice beginning to quiver, her resolution faltering.

"Slowly, Sister, slowly. Now there, don't be so harsh on yourself. Are we all right?"

"Yes, yes Father, I think so. I am all right."

"This happened a long time ago, didn't it?" he begins, trying to make things easier for her.

"Yes, Father."

"And it's been on your conscience for a long time, getting bigger and bigger, because you needed to feel you were right. Because you were too proud to admit that a Holy Sister might not have all the answers. Isn't that true?"

"Father, I was fresh off the boat from Dublin. I didn't know... about men," she says quickly.

"Ah, that's it. No reason to make excuses, none atall. The Church didn't see fit in those days to give us much in the way of instruction about the opposite sex. It still doesn't. We have to learn by making mistakes. Unfortunately, part of your learning process hurt another human being. You didn't do it intentionally, did you?"

"I would never hurt that boy, Father. I loved his dear sweet innocent mother. I loved her child as if I bore him myself."

"So you didn't sin in hurting the boy the first time, did you? You only sinned when your pride took over. When you didn't go back and correct your mistake. Isn't that true, Mary Ambrosia?"

"It is true. It is true, Father. And now, just as I am so close to being able to make amends, I have lost the child again."

"You've taken the first step to finding him," he says, trying to send the strength in his voice into the frail nun. "You've done well. So. So, we'll say three rosaries, pray the Stations of the Cross, and then call Captain McClanahan at the Fifth District. He'll help us find Mr Jeansonne.

"And have you return bus fare, Mother Superior?"

Mutt turns toward the river on Poydras street, then left toward the Quarter on St Charles Avenue. A third day and night have passed since his journey Uptown. That part of his life is gone. That particular feature is over. The movies are done. He is glad. It had been painful in the end. He hadn't stayed for the final credits.

Curiously, one pain has stopped another.

Mutt does not know that September is pushing its way into the waning Summer, that cooler weather is on its way. He has lost interest in the progress of time. Mutt no longer notes its passage as significant. Though it is now well past three in the morning.

The City Councilman representing the Vieux Carré, Treme, Faubourg Marigny and Bywater is not making any conscious decisions. He is making his way slowly. Mutt feels he might be coming out of it. Whatever "it" is. Feeling anything positive is a step in the right direction. He is still scrambled, but he at least recognizes himself. He remembers that he is L Mutt Jeansonne. That he has friends. Real friends.

Family. That he has a partner in Rodrigo   someone he can trust. And Fred. His life partner Fred.

He had survived losing his home once before. Twice before, since now he had lost his connection to the Expressway.

He laughs.

Going with what other people told me didn't do me a bit of good either time. Maybe I should take that as a sign, huh?

It had come to him squatting on Jefferson Avenue. Just after she went inside. It came like a thick black cloud, filling his vision. No sooner had the door closed behind Reed than suddenly he was reliving one of the most painful memories in his entire life. It had come from nowhere. Horror. A child's absolute despair magnified again through the lens of time. Shame and confusion. That morning at the Boy's Home, when he had come back in his shabby uniform. The nuns stopped treating him like a boy. They acted like they were disgusted with him and afraid of him at the same time. They wanted him gone. Then the Government had stopped treating him like a boy, or a man. And he was gone. They would never let him return.

Now, out of the blue, all these years later the nuns had returned to his life. And he remembered. Though they feared him in one way, they had loved him in many others. That made him happy. He has survived. He has gained and lost his friends, but true friends are never lost. He knows that now.

The pain has cleared his head.

He can get his Family back. He is headed that way. Toward them.

"Here I come." He crunches dozens of scrambling nighttime palmetto bugs beneath his feet as he walks, head up. The insects make a metallic sound as they die, their inch-long brown wings crusting Mutt's shoes.

Still not totally in control. Sensitive receptors functioning sporadically, shorted. But taking messages. Sparking and sputtering. Bursts of communication. Some comforting, some disorienting. As he walks Mutt listens to his pants tell stories. The pants' tales more miserable than his own. In his weakened state, he hears their voice. Someone named Bruce Beaumont narrating his own private hell. Mutt lets it all run through him. He turns when his feet tell him to. Right now they say walk down the streetcar tracks. In the general direction of Toulouse street. That way you can't miss. You go home.

"You're right," he replies to his feet. "I won't get lost if I stay on the tracks. Take me right to Canal street. Take me right to the Quarter. Take me right there."

His conversations are no longer directed to any specific listener. He tosses words out with an occasional gesture or facial expression. Reacts to replies that he alone hears.

Attempts at dialogue are losing focus rapidly with Mutt. But he continues to try. A neon hamburger seems a possible listener.

"I have been waiting, sir, waiting a long time, to find such a place. We will see if this does indeed turn out to be..." The conversation continues as he walks. He is emptying his mind of hurt. He is still a bit addled, but Mutt Jeansonne is also beginning to heal.

He continues on toward Canal street, walking the wrong way against traffic.

For its first dozen blocks, from Canal street to Lee Circle, St Charles is one-way away from the Quarter, for all vehicles except Mardi Gras floats.

Luckily, cars are infrequent at this time of night. The few that come down the Avenue are mostly in the south lane. Away from Mutt. The lane with the streetcar tracks is rougher.

Most locals and hack-drivers know to avoid it and its slippery rails. Especially at the Canal intersection, bordering the French Quarter. There the streetcars speed up to make the only U-turn on the line and head back Uptown. The asphalt gets seriously creased with the pressure of the rushing fifty-foot-long wood and metal cars.

Rodrigo is out on the streets, continuing his search, successfully closing in on Mutt, though he doesn't realize it.

After walking the Quarter for much of the night looking for his friend, Rodrigo stopped by his former Church. It had offered him consolation and inspiration in the past. He missed it like he missed his friend Mutt.

But the Decatur street window has been badly treated since Rodrigo gave up his nightly attention. The plywood space is completely covered with handbills and flyers, most advertising thrash music bands at various downtown clubs. There are two messages from religious groups. Of these religious flyers, one orders monogamy for all of God's children. The other predicts the destruction of the white race as foreseen by an obscure prophet from Indianapolis.

Even Rodrigo reflects on that location, thinks it ironic. That someone from Indianapolis would be obsessed with a race.

Refreshed at the anachronism of life on the planet, he decides to walk across the CBD. To the site of Mutt and Fred's former house under the Expressway. Maybe Mutt had climbed over the new cyclone fences to meditate on his old stomping grounds. It is worth a shot.

Rodrigo is startled by a streetcar as he crosses Canal. He jumps back as the car rockets out of the dark into Canal street, preparing for its turn back up St Charles Avenue.

He shakes his head.

My fault. Should have been paying attention.

The cars only run once an hour at this time of night. Drivers are not quite as alert as in daytime. Besides, they only have this one small half-headlight.

Rodrigo watches as that dim headlight cuts feebly into the shadows of St Charles Avenue.

The car makes its turn. A few feet directly ahead, in the center of its beam, is the figure of Mutt Jeansonne.

Mutt never even raises his head as the steel wheels lock up on the rails. He had been thinking so hard about going home.

"Ginny, Ginny, I'm back," cries Noonie up the stairwell. She shuffles rapidly through the house, a bag of groceries under each arm. "I couldn't find him. Still nowhere in the Quarters. Even looked at Benny's. Nothing. Nobody seen him for ages. But I got some food. He'll be back, I know it, and when Mutt comes home, he'll be hungry. We'll get him to feeling better quick."

Upstairs, Virginia walks out of Mutt's bathroom with his toothbrush and comb in her hand. She is very pale. She descends the stairs one step at a time, goes into the kitchen.

Noonie doesn't notice. She is already too involved with planning the homecoming meal. "We gonna have some food like you won't believe. The market had some deep-water shrimps," Noonie continues, already pulling out pans.

Virginia puts her hand on Noonie's shoulder and the eager cook looks up, startled. She sees what Virginia has in her hands.

"Where you goin' with Mutt's stuff?"

"Charity Hospital," Virginia says quietly.

* * *

Two days after the final surgery marathon Fred still refused to budge from Mutt's bedside. It took three phone calls from the Mayor and numerous verbal and physical threats from Mel, Rodrigo, Virginia and Noonie, but the doctor finally allowed Fred to remain in the room, providing she wore a surgeon's mask and sanitary scrub shirt. The Mayor himself made several visits daily.

Mutt was kept sealed under an oxygen tent, half a dozen vari-colored tubes running in and out of his body. After the initial squabble, Fred was assigned a plastic chair in the corner of the room. She allowed herself to be bathed and dressed in a light green scrub shirt and hat. She even patiently wore the cloth surgical mask the nurses tied about her face. Fred didn't care. They could do anything to her. As long as she could stay by her partner.

The four friends kept up a rotating shift around the clock in the hospital room. Watching Mutt for any sign of improvement. Each person also tried to persuade Fred to eat or take a break. But for the last forty-eight hours, ever since they wheeled the unconscious Mutt back into the room, she had lapped only a small amount of water. She wasn't moving from the room until Mutt did.

Mutt was right. Real friends stay that way. They always let you back into their hearts.

Mutt Jeansonne's room was full of flowers, gifts and cards. He had not only been given one of Charity's few private rooms, but an adjoining room as well to accommodate a parade of dignitaries and friends. Father Wildman and the elderly Nuns had been praying non-stop to St Jude at a makeshift altar in the side room.

Rodrigo had slept at the hospital ever since the accident. Now five days. Except for surgery, Rodrigo had not left Mutt's side since he pulled him from beneath the streetcar on St Charles Avenue.

Mutt had still been conscious when Rodrigo reached him. He had looked in Rodrigo's face, recognized him and smiled. Mutt whispered, "Philodendron, sir," and then he was gone. The smile still on his lips.

As he lost consciousness, Mutt's right hand opened and an object fell onto the street. Rodrigo searched for it later as he held his friend's head and waited for the ambulance to arrive. In a crack between the paving bricks he found an eraser with half an inch of purple-and-green-striped pencil and a gold letter "K" on the side rolled onto the street. He resolved to make sure it was at Mutt's bedside for when he awoke. Mutt might need his favorite Karnival pencil. His pants had a lot more holes in them now.

Mutt had known he was with friends again. He was safe. Rodrigo wasn't about to leave him, no matter how long he had to sleep on a hospital floor. Mutt was back with his friends and that was that. Nothing would come between them now. They would never be apart again, Rodrigo was sure of that.

Mutt Jeansonne once again had his own agenda. He died at 10:42pm on September 20, the fifth day after his injury.

Fred sits between Melodie and Rodrigo. The old dog's nose is running. Melodie pulls out her handkerchief and puts it gently on Fred's snout.

"Blow, Freddy," she whispers.

"PHAWWNK."

"That's a good girl."

Melodie's black ensemble looks surprisingly uncoordinated. Nothing really matches. Everything is a bit wrinkled. And she is wearing flat shoes.

So is Rodrigo. Polished black work boots cover the sockless feet of the aide to the late Councilman.

The scene in the Church is of an epic scale. A rather unbelievable number of Mutt's constituents have sent leafy reminders of their esteem, including an entire azalea bush that had until recently decorated the landscape of the City Library. The altar at St Jude's is barely visible under the floral bombardment. New Orleans considers this a death in the immediate family. St John's was deemed too small to hold the service. Everyone wanted to attend. The funeral was moved to the larger Our Lady of Guadalupe Church with its shrine to St Jude on the northern perimeter of the Quarter. The nuns felt the choice appropriate, seeing as how they had long ago assigned Mutt to St Jude's care.

Flowers totally fill the sacristy of the church. Even Chris Reed's ever-politic firm had sent a wreath. And allowed their new full partner the morning off to attend the services.

The Reverend Aloysius Wildman, having formally requested permission to give the eulogy in this neighboring parish, completes his remarks.

"He was a man who could touch the heart of anyone he met, and make them know he was on their side. He touched me. I came to care for him that very first instant, as we met in my own church. He laid his great and humble heart open to me, and I knew right then this was no fraud. No con man. No politician. Mutt Jeansonne was a real person. Let us pray for his departed soul."

"Amen," comes from every throat.

At that word, the Bywater Community Mass Choir breaks into a spirited rendition of a traditional gospel favorite:

"Lord, I'm running,
Tryin' to make a hundred,
Ninety-nine and a half
Just won't do..."

"PHAAAWWWKKK."

Noonie, Virginia and Ellis sit across the aisle from Fred. All three are desolate, the two women each with an arm around the bewildered duck. Both of the human Streets are afraid. They are terrified that, without Mutt around, they might slip back into their former mental and emotional chaos.

"I loved him, you know, Ginny."

"Me, too, Noonie darling. Me, too. I really loved him. I never even told you."

"DUCKIE love Mutt, too, but NOT LIKE US, no."

They are trying to be strong, but their hands tremble. Virginia Beaumont and Noonie Robichaux squeeze the duck harder and harder.

Ellis begins to wonder if he himself will survive the funeral.

L Mutt Jeansonne lies in state below the pulpit. His favorite t-shirt, chilidog stains still intact, covers the horizontal Mutt to his knees. At either end are an alligator baseball hat and faded high-top basketball shoes. Rodrigo had bought replacement tux pants and tied the legs around Mutt's waist just in case this pair ended up being as talkative as the last.

A very small pencil stub is in Mutt's right hand.

The line to view the body goes all the way to the vestibule of the church. Mrs Bess Dedeaux is right behind the immediate family.

"You know, I lookin' at him up close now, baby, but with all that makeup I still can't tell if he was a white boy. He a gentleman a' color it OK wit' me tho'. God don't care when he opening them Pearly Gate if ya green or poiple man from them outta spaces, so me I don't care neither. I gonna miss them phone call, tho'."

After touching Mutt's folded hands, Mrs Dedeaux moves from the line in front of the casket. Lifting her bright orange veil from her face. Wiping a tear from her eyes. Smearing mascara and blue eye shadow across her rouged cheeks in a broad stroke. An ancient orange tabby is wrapped around her shoulders, his face against her ears. Purring loudly. "Spike he want ta pay his respect', too. Mr Jeansonne sabin' his life, ya know."

Mrs Johnson nods her head. Signifying that she too remembers the incident.

"Oughta make the man a saint, ya know. Saint Mutt."

"Amen, Bessie girl."

The two ladies slowly pick their way through the crowd. Back to their seats in a pew at the rear of the church.

Christine Reed stands, letting them by. She remains on the aisle. So she can leave inconspicuously. When she wants to. She can see the huge spray of pink flowers she sent to the Jeansonne funeral. Knowing that pink was a color Mutt held in high regard.   For some unknown reason.

She stays hidden far in the background of the mass of people. She does not go forward to view the body.

Reed leaves the church early to walk the dozen blocks back across the Quarter to her office in the Central Business District. She hears the brass band start up in the distance.

They must be bringing the coffin out. I left just in time.

She passes in front of the Toulouse house.

Pauses in the middle of the street to look at it. Quiet and deserted today.

Physically slapping her own cheeks as she stands there. First one then the other. Like she is trying to stay awake on a long journey. She had done it many times, roaring along home after completing yet another mind-numbing semester of law school. In the middle of the pitch-black night. Topping out the speedometer on a dark deserted stretch of Interstate. Not being able to fight off sleep. Her mind not strong enough to wake her body. Banging her head on the steering wheel. Slapping her own face to stay awake. This day is just like that. Just like that.

Can't fall asleep now. No. Can't lose control.

Fly into the ditch. Crash into Hell.

Move over, Satan. Get your ugly red ass outta my way.

Christine Reed pulls out a white lace handkerchief. She shivers, though in the final days of September the temperature remains well in the lower nineties.

Stinking cold weather.

Why do I live here if it's going to get cold all the time?

She blows her nose on the decorative piece of cloth. Throws it down in the street. *Not much good for nose-blowing, that handkerchief.*

Pretty things never are worth a fuck.

As the coffin is carried from the church, the band starts playing their dirge, "Just a Closer Walk with Thee." The overflow crowd outside St Jude's begins to wail appropriately. There are several of the prerequisite faintings. Voices are raised lamenting the untimely demise.

"Goodgawdamighty, he was just with us!"

Reverend Gonzales had been sure that the bereaved masses would require the services of a clergyman trained in the funereal arts. He had eschewed the possibility that his umbrella hat and megaphone might be deemed unseemly for the occasion, and had donned a small but dignified black plastic bowler. The fact that it covered little but the crown of his head made no difference. He had won the hat in a black-out bingo game earlier in the year, and had been looking for the proper occasion to wear it. The Reverend was a devoted fan of the Knights of Conundrums' games of chance, though he had not revealed his religious affiliation to his fellow gamers. He felt that the red, white and silver K of C logo on the front of his hat added a further touch of dignity to his appearance.

The pork & bean can wired around his neck was a slight, but necessary, distraction. He must gather funds to support his work among the heathen.

He winds his way through one of the peripheral groups of non-mourning onlookers. They are a particularly rough-looking bunch, but he knows he has the magic touch today.

"Yes, my brothers!" he begins. He is working himself into a high state of exposition now that he has a proper crowd. "Yes, my sisters! Let us gather together bread to benefit our departed brother's charity of choice. Your nickels, your dimes, your dollars, they will all put food in the mouth of the hungry, drink in the mouth of the thirsty. Let us give what we can in his name. Let us send a message to him in heaven that we honor him by helping another."

A shuffle through the crowd behind him catches his attention. He stumbles from being pushed. Reaching behind him, Reverend Gonzales has a truly religious experience.

"Goodgawdamighty! One of you sinners has lifted my wallet!"

A funeral is at the center of every true New Orleanian's life, not at the end.

Birth, life, death, decay, rebirth.

These things drive New Orleans forward. The evidence surrounds the city: rotting marshes become a wealth in petroleum, the all-inundating floods give the farmland new life, the deadly intrusion of salt into the fresh-water marshes brings a bounty in oysters and crabs. The gravity of the life-death cycle does not pull as hard when the death side rolls around, not in this city. Death is one more familiar neighbor whose idiosyncrasies are to be tolerated.

And death is one more good excuse for a party.

The celebration is planned decades in advance. The Social Aid and Pleasure Clubs that dot Claiborne Avenue and Broad Street all have one thing in common: inexpensive life insurance policies for their members that include both the cost of respectable above-the-ground interment and the fee for a brass band at the funeral. Above-the-ground tombs are necessary because the city is below sea level. Decaying humans are good for the banana plants but bad for the water supply. The band is necessary because folks are supposed to laugh in joy after they finish crying in despair at the funeral ceremony. The deceased has gone on to a better place   though it is universally doubted the gumbo can be better anywhere else, even in heaven.

Mutt Jeansonne's funeral has all the elements that befit the passage of a favorite son. There is the proper amount of wailing in the church and the proper amount of dancing in the street. Both Mel and Mia disrobe and walk with the band wearing only the most tasteful of somber Italian footwear. Marty had painted wide ribbons for each of the pallbearers with "RIP, Mutt" in two-inch-tall sequined letters. Fred follows close behind the casket, the bereaved dog riding in dignified fashion on a black-shrouded tomato wagon furnished by the French Market green-grocers. The pallbearers, on Rodrigo's countdowns, "cut the body loose," throwing the coffin three times in the air in front of Mutt's favorite places. The execution of this tradition for Mutt includes a coffin-tossing at the Bourbon Street entrance of the French Can-Can-Do Lounge (much to the chagrin of once-randy convening dentists), on the way to his place of interment.

The Mayor of the City of New Orleans, in concert with the City Council, had gone to great lengths to rush through the proper paperwork and raise the money for Mutt's tomb. Dislocated real-estate broker Stephanie Jorgensen had helped, frustrating her conservative brother no end. With her help the determined politicians re-purchased the land on which the tomb was to be constructed, and they did so in an amazingly short period of time. Some said it had been public spirit, but most people conceded the sale was concluded so quickly only because the original purchaser seemed to want no adverse publicity.

DAR Borden had been livid. The loss of forty square feet of his new property, no matter how minuscule it seemed, lessened the value of the whole by almost half. Though his profit would still be substantial, he could not be consoled. He had given away a binding partnership in his firm to a woman. A hillbilly woman from North Louisiana. And he was getting less money. Borden was not happy.

Chris Reed hid her pleasure at the forced sale, herself clandestinely calling Stephanie Jorgensen to tell her the identity of the property owner.

Whatever the motive, a compromise was reached in short order for the City's re-acquisition of a five-foot-by-eight-foot piece of land. The monument was constructed and Mutt's remains inserted.

It was a simple edifice of stucco-covered concrete block, with a pair of small Doric pillars supporting the four-foot-tall peaked stone roof. The tomb was built in the Ponchartrain Expressway right-of-way directly beneath the old location of Mutt & Fred's Box.

The inscription above the door reads:

L Mutt Jeansonne
Registered Voter of the City of New Orleans

As they leave the gravesite, the band breaks into the traditional uptempo departure march. Once-solemn butts begin to wiggle to "Didn't He Ramble." Smiles absorb the tears. The umbrellas come out. The white handkerchiefs come out. Shaken and flaunted at the sky.

Goodbye.
He has gone to a happier place. Truly.
We haven't yet.
Let's celebrate.

Life and death shake hands in New Orleans. Head down to the corner bar for a whiskey or three. Talk about old times.

Wonder about what's to come.

* * *

Councilman interred; city grieves

Fred T. Jeansonne (pictured left above), a City Hall regular and the only non-human to ever vote on a City budget, mourns L. Mutt Jeansonne's death as the late councilman is laid to rest under the I-10 Expressway. Fred the dog spent a productive four months in office as an aide to Mr Jeansonne. The canine activist has, for many people in New Orleans, come to symbolize a new era of human concern and honesty in government.

* * *

Charles Taylor has decided he will be awake today. But he is only on his second beer of the morning when he opens his Picayune to see a picture of Fred standing at Mutt's tomb.

"Holy shit!" Taylor yells happily. "Ah gottat muthafuckah! Burntat candle and fried at boy's brain!"

Charles Taylor's face freezes in mid-laugh, his mouth still open. He immediately becomes worried. Very worried. As worried as he can get. He begins compulsively wiping the sweat from his face, his hand tugging at his skin over and over and over again. Water pours from his forehead as fast as he can clear it.

"Lordy lordy lordy fuck! Me ah didn think at man was fo real. Ah cant be believin dis shit! Kilt him! At damn candle kilt him! Annat sumbitch hoodoo man gonna kill me now! Muthafuckah! He find me! He kill me! Wha'm ah gonna do? Fuck! Ah gotta giddafuck outta here!" he screams, running to pack his bags.

He had paid the hoodoo man with a watch that ran backwards.

"Lady, can't you get your dog to quit making that goddawful racket?"

The affluent-looking business man, outfitted in an understated yet elegant charcoal Armani suit, would normally have been a prime contender for Mel's attentions. Except for the fact that she is no longer working the bar. With its accompanying ancillary occupation. And for the fact she will take absolutely no criticism of Fred, in any way, shape or form.

"AAAAaaaaooooowooooo-oooo," moans the dog again.

"Sir, this is a grieving widow," replies Mel, pointing to the black armband Fred was wearing on her right front leg. "She and I have suffered a most desperate loss. If you cannot perform a basic human act by tolerating the physical manifestation of our grief, I would suggest that you take your tawdry trade elsewhere."

"Aaaahhhhh-hoooooooooo-ooo," moans Fred.

The well-dressed customer returns to his seat at a stageside table, shaking his head. Mel beckons to the bartender, who cranks the volume on the jukebox up another notch.

Fred had been subject to random spells of howling recently. Still, she somehow managed the courtesy to Mel and the girls of howling in the same key as their musical accompaniment. Unlike the last gentleman, most patrons had grown to admire Fred's oral gymnastics, while sympathizing with its cause. The dog had collected over a hundred dollars in tips in the two weeks since she and Mel had returned to the Can-Can-Do. But neither the money nor Mel's dedication of numerous tie-raisings to Mutt's memory had helped Fred's state of mind.

There were other changes in Fred since she had buried her partner. Her hair had turned a pure snowy white color from the tip of her nose to the tip of her tail. Even her eyes had become lighter.

It happened right after the funeral.

Mel put the kettle on to boil, ground the coffee beans and fetched in the paper. It was then that she noticed that her roommate was missing. Mel patiently searched the house for Fred. The dog had taken to hiding in odd spots since she returned from her sojourn at Charity Hospital. This morning Mel saw the shadowed figure of her friend dozing fitfully behind the tub. Fred was twitching and whimpering like she was having a nightmare. Mel thought it a good thing to wake her. She called out gently.

"Time to get up, Freddy. A fine Doc Wolf's breakfast awaits you."

There was a moan, some hacking and scuffling, as FT Jeansonne crawled out from under the tub. Into the light. An unfamiliar snow-white dog emerged, staggered into the kitchen and took a few pitiful bites of Doc Wolf. Melodie could only stare.

Fred?

An even stranger change was Fred's new manner of walking. She limped on the right, the same side as Mutt's bad leg. The vet x-rayed, probed, examined the location of her missing toe. Took blood samples.

The hair change and the limp had no natural, no biologic cause.

Marty Schruer, while not a live-in member of the Toulouse family, was no less affected by Mutt's death. At the funeral he had decided to quit his barker job at the Can-Can-Do. He didn't think he could face poor Fred and keep up the lively banter his job required. But since he still needed money to support his dalliance in other, more widely-accepted arts, he had inquired after work among family members. He told them he wouldn't be able to afford his dorm room without the Can-Can-Do. Mel gave him the perfect answer. Marty could take over as house manager at Toulouse Street. Perfect. Marty, the house manager. With his own studio.

Abu was furious. He threatened to withhold last Marty's paycheck until a replacement was found. Pressure from Mel and Mia quickly put an end to that threat. But Marty agreed to train Abu himself to fill in while he searched for another full-time barker.

Abu's first day on the job provides an interesting study in sentence structure and advanced metaphor. He, too, has a bit of the artist about him. He begins to enjoy yelling to the Bourbon street pedestrians almost from the first moment.

"We will have the shaking of the many large and tremulous body parts within this most formidable temple of the pleasurable delights, my eye-popping friends! Every single hour of the day there is the bouncing of fleshy globes on display!"

Abu grows excited. He likes this. He begins to grab people and talk to them directly.

"Yes, indeed, you of the loosely-fit all-man-made trousers, you will see the extremities of goddesses, each a youthful member of collegiate greek organizations, sisters all, and each one of these most-long-limbed and virtuous titillators of the macho personality is a woman of the notarized and most zealously-guarded virginal variety! I can give of the personal guarantee," he cries, a sincere waver coming to his voice.

A light-haired, full-figured matron catches his eye. She is wearing a solid-gold, diamond-encrusted Rolex. Abu reaches out to her. "And a most beautiful woman you are yourself, you of the cotton and occasionally transparent body coverings! We have many of the dancing variety who could come near this beautiful vision, lady and the gentlemans, but nothing that could be surpassing it! And what did you say your name was, my golden buttercup of the overflowing breast receptacles?"

"Well aren't you the fresh one!" laughs Sandi Markham, large go-cup of iced Stoli in hand. Her stepson had told her to stay out of the Quarter, but he is a stick-in-the-mud. All lawyers are.

* * *

Mel broke down and went to St Philip street for a consultation with Madame Philstein. The seer was less than happy to acknowledge that part of her prediction had come true. There had indeed been death. But she would give no further clues about the last thing she had seen   dropping from the skies in great numbers. Madame Philstein would discuss it no further. She was herself happy, though, to regain the trust of her friend Melodie. The harsh words of their last meeting were forgiven without hesitation.

She tossed the bones three times as she listened to Melodie describe Fred's predicament. On each throw, she saw that something sinister had entered the equation, something that hadn't been present in the first reading, but that the evil's influence was more than likely at an end. She did not want to alarm Melodie, but she had to ask.

"My dear Melodie, has anyone new recently come into the situation?"

Mel thought for a moment. "No. No one that I can think of."

Madame Philstein looked at the bones for a long while, thought about them deeply. There was a major reshaping of the future in progress, but she could not tell if it was threatening or benevolent. She decided to cover all the bases. Madame Philstein sent Mel home with a vial of oil, a bag of sparkling multi-colored floor wash, and two green people-shaped candles, a male and a female. Guaranteed to rejuvenate the bereaved dog.

Oil and powder were applied and sprinkled, candles were burned and snuffed. It had done no good.

Fred was not motivated to stop being bereaved.

The whole extended family was in a period of change and turmoil. No one had suspected the depth of the effect Mutt had on each of their lives.

Rodrigo moved in with Mel   as much as he had ever moved in anywhere. He still spent time on the Street, but more and more he was dedicating his daylight hours to organizing efforts at the Robichaux House with Marty. His time on the Council had vitalized him. He enjoyed doing things for other people. Finding permanent residents permanent beds and livelihoods became his mission. Mel fed him and kept his spirit alive. But she knew the loss of both his books and his best friend was still tormenting him.

Mel had herself returned to work as quickly as she could. She felt she needed to fulfill her obligation to Mia for all the time the other dancer had again put in during the crisis. After a week in the house alone, Fred allowed herself to be coaxed back to her Can-Can-Do barstool. But things were not the same.

Fred was lost without her partner.

* * *

Red roses seemed more appropriate than pink. They were for Mutt. Locals always visit the gravesites of their loved ones on All Saints Day, just to do a little fall yardwork. Trimming the wind-sown weeds around the tomb, putting on a new coat of whitewash, adding a new batch of plastic flowers to the concrete vase at the foot of the tomb.

So here it is, November 1 again, and Fred and Mel are looking at the stone and stucco monument that holds their friend L Mutt Jeansonne, Registered Voter.

Fred has already done a male dog sort of thing and peed on all four corners of the stone box. It was embarrassing and awkward for a female, but she felt it was the least she could do. She wants Mutt to know she was watching out for him.

The real roses are Mel's idea. In the carbon monoxide stench of the Expressway, the flowers won't last long. But just seeing that deep burst of color in the midst of so much grey stone makes the place feel like it still has life in it.

The wind gusts. Fred's fur ruffles toward her head. Her ears flatten.

Still the wind grows stronger. Mel's skirt whips around her. She can feel her arms being lifted to the horizontal, as if she is a child who will at any moment be swept upward into the arms of her mother.

There is no threat, no fear. It is an embrace.

The air is suddenly still, its power spent.

The exhaust fumes crowd in again.

"We won't forget you, darling boy," Mel whispers to the stone door.

"OOOOwwwwwwwwooooo..."

The entire Toulouse family had gone into diaspora soon after the funeral. Rodrigo and the few other part-time residents, they all left the house. Fred was already gone. Though each person claimed differently, the departure was always for the same reason. Everyone felt that they had been abandoned, and the house rang of desolation, in spite of Marty's efforts. Noonie Robichaux kept cooking until she was only serving herself and Ellis and the new house manager.

Noonie had suffered a monumental loss in Mutt's death. But it wasn't all bad. Like Virginia, she fought back. She had been inspired to reinforce her present by regaining her past. The cooking had helped at first. And the eating. Mutt's had been a great wake. The Lee Fat Restaurant had brought enough food to feed half a dozen Third World countries. The kitchen hummed for days, the family putting food into the mouth of every Street who walked in the door until he or she could eat no more.

Both women felt barriers breaking loose, as they ate yet another batch of the bisque they had made together. No psychotropic drug could approach the efficiency with which the seasoned crawfish heads swept clear the emotional debris of two lives gone awry.

Seriously. They looked at each other over their bowls and laughed. Cursed their stupid luck. Howled with grief at Mutt's death. Bawled with happiness at the legacy he had left. Themselves. Their love for the man. The food ritual somehow reaffirmed their common bond.

It also allowed them to more comfortably deal with the differences in their lives. Including geographic origins. Place was a part of each woman's self-definition. Each was ready to explore.

The two women's vicarious self-discoveries had started with Mutt's night in court. Since then Noonie and Virginia had both been stumbling into disconnected memories of friends and family they had thought long-lost. Mutt's new-found life had been a gift to many people. He had changed many lives. He showed them they could love. Noonie and Virginia were glad Mutt had been rewarded for his contribution. They agreed. He was no longer invisible. He had been made a saint.

Early one morning, Virginia headed for an expedition Uptown. Noonie packed up her slightly-magnetic duck compass, put out her thumb and started hitch-hiking south toward the Gulf of Mexico. Toward the endless salt-water marshes. Toward Bayou Four-Point. And her Papa's camp.

Noonie felt strongly that the expedition was necessary to complete the picture.

"I gotta do my part," she told Ellis as they dismounted from their first ride.

Noonie patiently walked on in the dark for seven hours. Ellis waddling at her side, trying to keep up conversation. He wasn't extremely excited about being awake at night, but his duck wit did not fail him.

She made LA55 well before dawn. Quickly getting a lift to take her the final five miles into Pointe-aux-Chenes. She was glad for even that ride. There had been few cars in the dark. Nobody ventured far from home at night this far out in the swamps.

They were always talking about the *loup garou*   the Cajun werewolf   out here. No wonder, she thought. The blue eyes of the swamp were visible everywhere this time of year *les revenants*. The methane from rotting vegetation on the bottom of the swamp bubbled to the surface. Spontaneously combusting in small turquoise flames. At night they could be seen for hundreds of yards. Reflecting on the surface of the water. Noonie saw it all, remembered it all.

It took her three more hitches, short hops going deeper and deeper into the marshes, to finally reach the village intersection.

She knew the road. Noonie could picture LA1121 finally making its way to a dead end on a silted Gulf beach in the jumble of salt-water swamps. The stretch of coarse brown sand. Often festooned with wind-blown jellyfish and the occasional electric-blue man-of-war. Curling in an arc around the east side of Terrebonne Bay. When the wind comes out of the north to spread the fog, all the stinging creatures are blown out to sea. Down to Veracruz and the dry heat of Mexico.

With the north wind, clouds of brown pelicans became visible. Rising at sunrise to feed off the point of Timbalier Island.

She had been there.

Papa held her hand. Looking westward across the seaweed-strewn beach toward the setting sun.

"Now, *'tit bebe*, you be watchin'. When dat sun he touchin' dat horizon there, you gonna see all dem big buildin' in Houston lightin' up an' sparklin' like heaven. Dere! Dat Houston right dere. You see it, cher Noonie ?" he would ask her. He always put the accent on the last syllable, as in "nooNEE." Trying to speak English like his wife was required at the town house. Noonie always said she could see the reflections from the Big City. Whether she could or not. She always went along with her Papa's wild ideas. She had never been to Houston. Not that she could remember.

Now she is back. Noonie Robichaux has returned to Bayou Four-Point because it was her father's Place. Part of his legacy is hers. She has found it easily. But she knows that there is a lot more finding to do.

A slightly more elaborate wood-frame building leans against a huge river oak on the far west side of the bayous. The oak grows around a corner of the building, incorporating the shake cypress boards into its trunk. Cradling the man-made structure within its own. The two have grown together. Noonie can see that the trunk is at least twice as wide as she is tall. The massive gnarled limbs touch the ground in half a dozen places, some almost a hundred feet from the trunk, dropping additional roots at each point of contact. It holds strongly onto the earth, surviving the worst hurricanes with minor leaf loss. In spite of their lack of natural enemies, there aren't many oaks of this size left. Noonie knows that only man could or would kill such a wonderful creature. She is glad to see this one has survived.

The man-built edifice is considerably less ancient, though definitely of advanced years itself. It is identified as the gas station, post office and general store by its faded sign. It remains comfortably in disrepair. Someone had labored halfway through repainting the facade barn red in the not-too-distant past. The painter leaving the last gallon can open and still half-full. The urge to labor having been properly diminished.

Noonie walks up to the building, recognition bells ringing in her head. Ellis pecks about for food among the shells. A rusty red and yellow maritime gasoline pump stands in the weed and shell-filled lot in front of the building, close to the western bayou. The pump is of a vintage that still sports a decorative glass hemisphere on its front. Colored balls float in gasoline inside the sphere. The balls move to indicate that gas is on its way out of the pump.

The seventeen-year-old girl had enjoyed watching the balls jump about while fishermen delicately squeezed every drop of a one-dollar   they said *un piastre*   petrol purchase into their tanks. The pump was the most modern thing in Bayou Four-Point in those days. It still holds that distinction.

A thick layer of dust has coated Noonie's clothes and sweaty skin in the days since she left New Orleans. She has not slept. She was too excited to make much conversation with her rides. As pleasant and open as the people had been, only one had spoken English with any ease. This far down the bayou, the language was mostly Chattimacha or Houmas or Choctaw Indian mixed with Cajun French. Maybe a little Castillian Spanish. She wasn't able to tune into specific words, but she instinctively knew what people were saying.

She remembered her Papa telling her how the people in Four-Point were so in touch with the land. They were honest to the core, he had told her.

That honesty presented itself in every aspect of their lives. One curious manifestation was their language. Many things here were named by their sound. Literally. The local word for "bullfrog" was her Dad's favorite. He had enjoyed calling out the word-sound in his deep vibrating voice, and she loved to hear him.

"*Oua-oua-RON!*" he would croak. "Gonna catch mon *bebe* a great big *ouaouaRON!*" Then he would inevitably tickle her, croaking the whole while. Her Dad was a great bullfrog.

Memories again crowd in fast on Noonie. She begins to feel weak. She remembers that she hasn't eaten in two days, and decides to try the store. Maybe she can trade some Mardi Gras beads or cigarette butts for food.

The screen door is unlatched. A light is on inside.

Noonie opens the door and walk in, letting her eyes adjust. "Hello?" No answer. Ellis D stays close by her side, a city duck that will not be separated from his link to the real world.

Shelves are filled with dusty canned goods, fishing tackle and truck parts. Glass gallon jars of pickled eggs (quail, chicken and guinea fowl) and pickled pig parts (tongues, lips, feet, tails) stand on the counter. Along with multi-colored jawbreakers and miniature Tootsie Rolls. It all seems so familiar.

Noonie becomes more light-headed as the wave of recognition breaks over her, submerges her. She struggles to the surface.

The front door opens behind her. She turns quickly to see who has come in, almost falling over Ellis, who squawks and flies up into her arms. Noonie squints. Raises her other hand to shadow her eyes.

A silhouette of a stooped figure straightens at the sight of her. Intense sunlight streams though the clouds of dust that had accompanied the figure's entrance. The dust and light add to Noonie's confusion. She sees the silhouette raise its own hand, looking at her.

A hoarse voice floats across the room.

"Incroyable! C'est Noonie Robichaux! Et un canard!"

Twenty minutes later, Ellis D gurgles happily. Nesting in Antoine Picou's lap. The old Indian strokes the duck's head, gently scratching under his bill.

Antoine has already taken to calling the duck "Tee E". Close family members out here in the country always seem to get called "*Petit*, 'tit, tee   little". Even though they might be anything but. It is a term of affection. Ellis obviously likes being "Tee E".

Noonie watches her duck enjoy the loving attention.

How come I never did that for the little fellow?

Because no one has done it to me. Not for a long, long time.

I had hoped Mutt would. Eventually.

The old man pops a dried shrimp in Ellis' mouth and another in his own, along with a deep swallow of beer.

"Dese some sweet an salty shrimps, Noonie. I done 'em mysef. Me an' Emile Babineaux. You remember him? He still alive. *Mais*-yeah. He used ta go speck fishin' alla time wit' you an' you *pere* when you a l'il t'ing. He too ole for goin' offshore now, but me an' him we workin' dat bay an' sometimes we gettin' some pretty nice size shrimps. Dry 'em ourse'fs. He be by here later, an' I know he gonna be happy ta see you. Now eat some shrimps, girl. Dey some good. You look like you needin' some food." His voice holds a note of concern.

"Not too hungry," she says quietly.

"You better be eatin' some more 'fore me an' dis Tee E here we finishin' dem all. Right, E?" asks Antoine Picou.

Ellis replies with a veritable avalanche of quacking. Playfully nibbling the old man's hands for more food. And petting.

Just like her father had said. Folks on the bayou are in touch. Antoine had walked straight up to her and grabbed Noonie as soon as he recognized her. His prolonged hug squeezed all the apprehension and fear out of her. As if she was a sponge that had soaked up something nasty. Antoine pushed it out of her. The Chittimacha *traiteur* was still the doctor for what ailed you. When he let her go, her spirit expanded. Warmth and friendship had filled the emptiness.

This is home, too, something tells her. If not this place, then this way of life. She is reassembling another lost part of herself as she sits in the general store, soaking it all in.

Antoine Picou is a contented man.

Antoine, 87 in November, had bagged twelve squirrels the week before. With a blowgun. He hated the noise and smell of gunpowder. So he tried to show the younger boys that the old ways still worked. He constructed his blowgun as his grandfather had shown him. From straight hollow elderberry branches, woven palmetto, raw cotton balls and his own innovation darts tipped in sharp metal pounded from his beer cans.

"Dat de only reason I drinkin' dis town beer," he says with a smile and another swallow, "It squirrel season."

He also carves his own decoys. Though he tries not to alarm Ellis as to their use.

"It OK, l'il fella. Ain' nobody gonna hurt no fancy city chile like you. Wouldn' be sportin'. Dem boys dey only like dat *canard farouche*, dem wild duck. Dem duck come flyin' in here in de fall, so many duck de sky she go black. Dey comin' all de way from de North Pole, some a' dem duck. Dey headin' for dey winter vacation down in dem tropic lan'.

"It a beautiful sight, lookin' up, seein' all dem bird comin' ta dem rice fiel', comin' de same place ever' year since even my *granpere* he a boy. We plant one crop in twenny jus' for dem bird. Dey come spiralin' down from dat sky ta eat dat rice, den twistin' back up and headin' sout' 'cross dat Gulf a' Mexico. Dey grateful for dat one in twenny.

"I fly wit' dem bird. I know dem bird. We give dem bird food. Dey give us food. We are dem bird and dey be us.

"Dey come soon again. Dey comin' here an' givin' our spirit dat touch from dey worl'. Dey helpin' us get by, dem bird, teachin' us ta live wit' life an' what happen at de end of dat life. Dem bird know. We got to shoot some a' dem bird to eat. Dey know dat, but dey still comin' here, comin' ta give us life.

"Dese you people, Tee E. You be proud 'bout these people. Dey got dem heart so big dey put dat whole worl' inside."

Antoine takes another deep draught.

"Do you still bird hunt, Antoine?" Noonie asks.

"Now, bebe, you can see dat I finally too ole to go sit in dem icy-cold duck blin' at fo' in de mornin' no more. I jus' make dese here decoy so Desiree can sell dem at dat tribe touris' shop over near Houma. Got spoilt, me. A sin, dat. Me secon' chief an' traiteur, an' I don' even make my own beer no more. Shame ain't it, Noonie?"

"Time moved on both of us," she says wistfully. "Made us forget who we are."

"Now you hol' on dere, Noonie. It ain' supposed to be easy. Some a' dem baby sayin to me dat they ain' no real Indian man no mo'. I jus' tell 'em right back dat holdin' onto real anythin' is jus like holdin' onto a momma catfish   she slippery as hell, and when you finally get a good grip on her she spike you wit' her fins. Makin' you bleed an' hurt. Dat real stuff always painful, *mais*-yeah."

Ellis is not concerned with reality at the moment. He seems to have become quite enamored of a particularly colorful wood duck decoy. Wood ducks, *canard branchu* to the French population of South Louisiana, are a gorgeous species. But Antoine didn't have the heart to tell Ellis that it is the males who are the brilliantly-colored gender. Noonie had sadly neglected Ellis' sexual education.

"C'mon, Tee," the *traiteur* says, picking up the decoy and the live duck. "You two have some fun while me an' Noonie talk. Noonie an' I be right back for you in a few minute."

Noonie watches as Picou walks to the edge of the bayou and gently floats both the real and carved duck. Ellis flaps and splashes as soon as he hits the water. The decoy bobs realistically.

Some people say that jazz is the only true American art form. But magnificently detailed decoy-carving by supposedly "primitive" native Americans was flourishing in South Louisiana centuries before jazz wailed out of the red-light parlors in New Orleans' infamous Storyville district.

Antoine's decoys look like real birds in their prime plumage. They float so perfectly that shotguns are aimed and discharged before a real inspection can be made. That is one of the reasons he no longer sells them to hunters. They couldn't tell them from the real thing, once they got to floating out in the marshes. Too much work and time went into each piece to see his work of art get blown up by a twenty-five cent load of 12-gauge bird shot.

He is very pleased that Ellis can relate to the decoy. It is a testament to his people's loving labor.

Antoine smiles, wipes water from his face. As he returns to walk back to his beer cooler.

"I missed you, Antoine. I missed this place," Noonie says, watching him fish in the ice for the coldest can.

"Ah *non, bebe,* you don' gotta miss it. You can carry dis place aroun' wit' you. Us peoples can do dat. But them animal, like dem duck, dey is differen'. Dat a nice boy you got dere, Noonie," he tells her, comfortably shifting time-worn gears. "I like him. We got a lot in common, me an' Tee. I t'ink you should leave him here where he can play an' get ta meet some a' his own folk. You don' be needin' to take him back to dat dirty city."

He opens another can of beer and sits on the porch by Noonie.

"Now, what botherin my sweet bebe? You wanna talk 'bout you *pere*, don' you?"

In New Orleans Chris Reed is alone again. Trying to sleep in the chill of her Uptown bedroom. Even though the late fall night is pleasantly cool outside, Chris has made it colder in the apartment. She pulls the covers around her neck. Chris wants to feel safe. Without consciously willing it, she dreams of her home. She'll be safe there.

It's a pleasant enough dream as it starts.

Watching her brother Ned mow the lawn right down to the water's edge behind the East Main street house in Winnfield. The family called the land it stood on Golden Sky Plantation. Grandiose sounding name. Reed wonders where it came from.

I never asked.

Not really much more than a regular old dirt farm. Not after eight generations of Reed men had squeezed their fortunes from it. Daddy, Ned and Bill the latest. Got nothing to do with me or Sister. Or Mother.

The bayou is down. Must be late spring. The crawfish building their twelve-inch-tall mud chimneys. Conserving scarce winter water in their underground tunnels during egg-laying season. Somewhere within a ten-foot radius of the chimney there is the crawfish's secret back door. The crawfish tail is a multi-purpose combo mud-scoop and egg-holder. Besides a primary function as backwards propeller.

It's the early '70's. Ned, Bill and their buddies have a sack of explosives. They buy brown paper bags full of Taiwanese gunpowder products in various colorful configurations. From clandestine vendors just outside the town limits. Teenage boys needing to vent the confusing and overflowing energies brought on by their own rising fluid levels. They look for release.

Harassment and destruction of lower life forms seems to do the trick. Especially in conjunction with loud noises and bright flashes of light. Ned likes to drop powerful cherry bombs and noisy M80 salutes into the moist crawfish chimneys and stomp the mud structures closed. Then watch as the crawfish is blown from the hidden back door by the explosion. Often right under his feet. Like they are fired from a cannon. Never knowing where the back door is located. That's the surprise. All of a sudden a smoking crawfish flying across the yard. Fast. Maybe a hundred feet. Sometimes even surviving.

Brother Bill is blasted right in the crotch by an eight-ounce crawfish cannonball.

Chris Reed's dream is so real. Twenty years ago happens in the now.

She remembers the day perfectly. It is the incident that brought on her own loss. After watching his brother recover in bed from seriously bruised testicles, Ned tells Chris he'd just as soon every crawfish within a hundred miles was dead.

"Dad thinks so too. Really fucks up the lawnmower when I run over those goddamn chimneys. I don't care."

Hard red gumbo mud hits him in the shins as Ned takes vengeance on the crawfish kingdom with the ancient belt-driven Briggs & Stratton mower. It is then that he accidentally discovers Chris' secret. He hates mowing most times. But now, he looks forward to cranking up that old gas clunker just once at the very end of each Louisiana winter.

When he can torture her with it.

While leveling the crawfish chimneys that February, he sees her laughing and giggling to herself. All alone in the back yard. On her knees. His sister willingly shows him the source of her pleasure. It is the time of year for the berries.

The young Chris absolutely loves searching under the dead brown grass for tiny wild strawberries. They grow for only a few weeks, ripening quickly at the bayou's edge. Water forms the far border of their otherwise even back lawn. In the late Winter afternoon, knees scraped and muddy, Christine Reed proudly brings a handful of the berries into the kitchen to show Mother.

Useless. Even then, at that time of day Mother is seldom sober enough to hold one without crushing it. But they are so delicate. Christine needs to preach the wonder of their existence, Sunday school God proven by their lawn. So beautiful, these miniatures. Translucent pearls of moisture circling the startlingly red edible gem. The size of the fingernail on her little finger. Real food in the exact right scale for the table of her doll house. Free. With the fun of searching for them.

Once he found out how important they were to her, Ned takes great pains to watch for the growth season. It is a big brother's responsibility to destroy his sister. He plans. Always finds a reason to covertly break out the mower when he knows the berries are finally ready for picking. Chris pleads with him every year, even asking him as early as Christmas to leave them alone. Count it as a Christmas present, she begs. Chris tries to make a deal weeks in advance. It is no use. The destruction gives him pleasure. Her helplessness against his power gives him pleasure. It is a trait common to the men in her family. He always gets there first.

The young girl hears the motor crank over from her bedroom. Echoing loudly as it moves through the concrete carport. Onto the grass. He knows she can hear. He waited until she was home and settled at her schoolwork. She hears.

Ned. He wouldn't. Not again.

Running into the yard screaming. Falling down ahead of the mower, scraping her fingers through the sharp dry grass. Cutting her fingers. Desperately trying to salvage some of the tiny crop. Ned laughing barely misses her scrambling hands and feet. She knows he would think nothing of actually hurting her.

Most of her family is the same.

Chris Reed is not safe at home after all. Never has been.

She wakes, knowing that.

Virginia is in a great state of mind as she walks onto the porch at Toulouse street. She carries a massive cast-iron pot. She has just returned from nearly a week's sojourn in her Uptown New Orleans home. She had fired all three of her employees. The three who had been living well in her house, alone and with no employer to bother them, for the last half a decade.

The butler had even appropriated all of her late husband's clothing, years ago donating what he thought unstylish to the French Quarter VOA.

While Virginia was sad at having lost yet another connection to Bruce, she was actually glad that someone was making use of the effluvia of his life. She even speculated that some of the Toulouse crowd might have picked up some of the recycled clothing. She had resolved to ask around when she returned to the Quarter. After she settled matters Uptown.

The cook, butler and gardener were furious with her at first. In the end they left the house satisfied. She figured they had all squirreled away enough cash that they wouldn't be hurting. But she retrieved the household checkbook and gave them each generous severance money anyway. She was very proud that she could do such things.

Her time on the Streets had taught her a few lessons about human nature, though. After their departure she had a locksmith come change all the locks, including the car and the deadbolt on the garage door. She accomplished a lot before she left. Then she walked all the way back to the Quarter with the pot intended as a present for Noonie.

Pulling open the door, Virginia feels that for the first time since her husband's death she is finally getting her life in order. She is going to help keep this new family together no matter what. It will be rough.

She goes up the stairs slowly. Sits alone on the upstairs balcony at Toulouse street, watching the night people and cars move in short spasms through the narrow street's stop signs. They head south toward the great Mississippi River, eight blocks away.

Its flood of swirling, muddy water is down behind the levee this time of year. But she can still see the lights on the masts and superstructures of the taller ships as they pass by the last narrow frame of buildings near the river.

The riverboat Natchez periodically blocked the balcony's river view during the day. Taking on every-other-hour loads of passengers at the Toulouse dock.

But the riverboat is out on a night cruise as Virginia stares down the street this evening. She remembers the dinner cruises. She and Bruce had gone on several sponsored by his company. Bruce and all his colleagues wearing expensive English wool tuxedos. They had rented a private dining room and deck.

Couples are probably still in each other's arms on the rooftop dance floor of the boat tonight, she thinks happily. Spinning around to slow ballads with lots of saxophone. While their five-story ballroom powers downriver. Back towards New Orleans under a haloed yellow moon.

She remembers watching the huge red paddlewheel churn up the river's liquefied suspension of America.

She thought the river romantic. Bruce told her it was raw sewage from Minnesota, washed-out farmland from Iowa, waste chemicals from Missouri, drowned cattle from Arkansas, whole trees from Mississippi. All floating by the City. Waving a fetid greeting as it heads out to poison the fish of the Gulf of Mexico, he told her. Bruce was not a romantic.

Virginia focuses closer in time and space. The party animals of Bourbon street cross the intersection just half a block away. People are still moving actively in both directions, well into the single digits of the night. Most remain resolute in their search for the ultimate high-alcohol fruit drink. The beverage that will bring them to the teetering brink of nausea. Then, safely hugging the commodes in their hotel rooms, they can finally attain the grand feeling that they have truly experienced everything the City has to offer.

Virginia watches the parade, wondering about her own experience. She wonders if the third life she is living will be better than the first two.

Funny. Here I sit nice and cozy and dry. In a City ten feet below sea level. Levees all around me. Holding the sea water back. Gargantuan machines all under me. Pumping the rain water out. All this activity and effort just to maintain the status quo. To keep me normal.

It was the same on State street, wasn't it?

Then the water got in.

Mutt started the pumps. I know now that I cared about him more than I ever cared about my own husband. I just never knew what loving someone was all about. Not until he was gone.

And Noonie.

Here Noonie and I are so similar, so different. Both with old families. But one Catholic, the other Protestant. Both with old houses. But one Downtown the other Uptown. Both with debilitating losses. One losing parents the other a husband. Debilitating's the word, alright both of us ending up mad as hatters. I suppose we were mad. Maybe still are. Don't think we'll either of us get certified Norm any time soon. Fine with me actually. I've been a Norm, and it wasn't much of a life for me.

But Mutt, he made a great stab at it. Mistake, I guess. He started really wanting those things. Poor boy. Then I started wanting them again, too.

So easy to get lost in the murk. You can't let your guard down on the Street.

You can't think about being human.

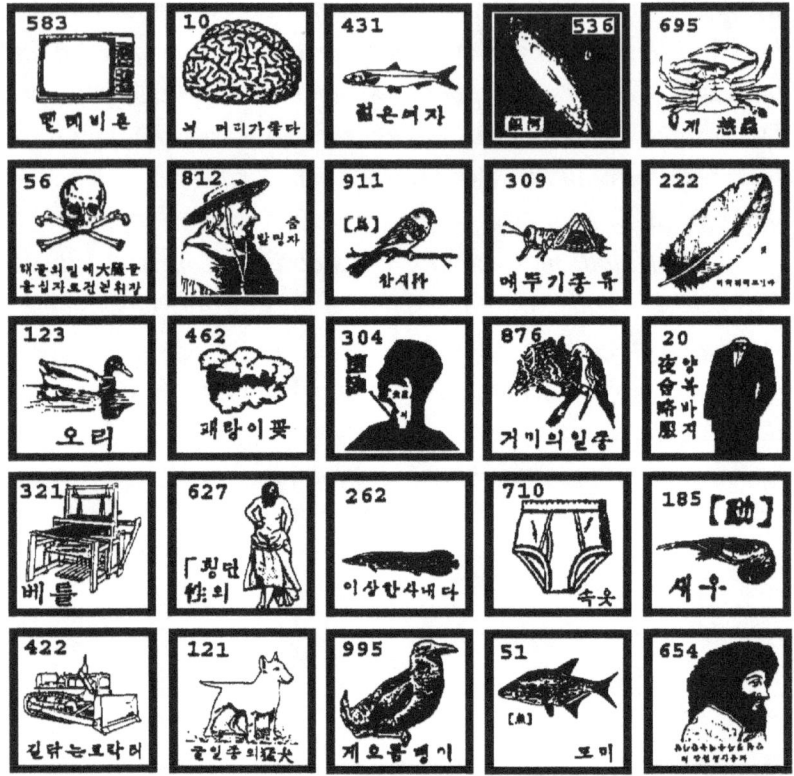

Rodrigo is just finishing a two-hour collect phone call to his brother in Chicago. They have spoken of many things, back and forth, but Rodrigo was happiest when Arthur   his brother's name had come back to him   had gone on and on describing Rodrigo's own pre-New Orleans life. Rodrigo keeps none of the details for his memory. He doesn't care for that. But he absorbs the feel of what his old self had been like, back when he was a lawyer. He extracts the good parts his brother describes about his profession   the logical way of thinking, the idea of correcting injustices, the fair arbitration of disputes and leaves the husk of the old rule-twister Rodrigo for dead.

He thanks his brother and tells him that the new Rodrigo will be staying on in New Orleans, but that he will be keeping in touch. He asks Arthur if he will mind serving as

Rodrigo's reference manual to the real world. His own library has been depleted. He needs someone to give him a dose of the past when it might prove useful. Arthur says sure.

"You need anything now, Brother Rodrigo? Anything I can do for you?" asks Arthur as the conversation comes to a close.

"Might need you to come visit in a little while, Arthur. Got a ceremony I think I need you for."

"Ceremony? Come on now. You? You not thinking about getting married, are you? An old man like you?"

"She's thirty-five, going on twenty-three, and she's... she's... she's..." Rodrigo is caught in the Melodie experience.

"That good, huh? Well, hellsbells! Sure, old man, I'd love to come walk my big brother to the altar! When's the big day?"

"Don't know yet, Arthur. Soon, but I don't know exactly when. I got something even bigger to take care of first."

* * *

"...So much for the golf circuit. Let's get down to the important stuff. Hunting season is upon us!

"And it seems like we're going to have a season to remember, folks. Those birds have already started forming up in Canada, and will soon be headed our way.

"Wildlife experts have said that this is the earliest   and largest   gathering of fowl they have seen in decades! So start priming those twelve-gauge pumps, clean out the freezer, break out the fresh ammo and oil your hip boots, guys, because you'll be up to your waist in birds real soon now. I can taste that gumbo now!

"Be careful, though. Make sure you don't accidentally hit any of those flying saucers from Outer Space while you're banging away at ducks. Game wardens will be watching hunters closely, because we all know that saucer season won't be get underway until late November. Back to you, John."

The 10pm news anchor chuckled and smiled before he started his wrap-up. It was no wonder Skippy Lyle was the number-one-rated sportscaster in town. He always left them laughing.

* * *

Noonie and Virginia found themselves, and each other. By the time Mel and Fred returned from their All Saints visit to Mutt's tomb, the two women were back in the Toulouse house. They were both firmly committed to carrying on Mutt's work, with Rodrigo's help. It was time to start again. Virginia sold her Uptown house and possessions   except for some of the kitchen furnishings   and formed the Robichaux House Trust Fund. She and Noonie intended to pay off the renovation and maintain the building as a community center for people like themselves.

In the meantime, Mutt's City Council seat had been put up for appointment. The whole matter would be settled within the next two weeks. Rodrigo had reluctantly been asked to vacate the Jeansonne offices at City Hall. And to take the seven cases of Doc Wolf's with him.

There was still the legal matter of the Jeansonne estate. Mutt had died intestate, without a will. Under the Napoleonic system of inheritance, Louisiana required "forced heirship". The children of the deceased inherited half the estate automatically. If there are no progeny, the wife inherited both halves. If there is no wife or other relatives, the State inherits. The lawyer Mel had hired, one of Mutt's French Quarter Business Association friends, was struggling to settle the estate in the family's favor as quickly as possible. It was difficult.

They had a death certificate, but no birth certificate, at least none that said Mutt Jeansonne. And the State Treasury wanted their house.

Proving Mutt was dead was easy. Proving he had been alive was harder.

"We've all got to work hard on this, because there's only one difference between the Government in Baton Rouge and the hookers in New Orleans," said the lawyer as he packed up to leave. Everyone in the room waited for his advice.

"A New Orleans hooker will usually stop screwing you when you're dead."

* * *

Christine Reed remains very much alive.

At 28 years of age, she has a corner office on the same floor with the three senior partners of one of the largest and most prestigious law firms in New Orleans. It does not bother her that they have given her the corner with what they considered the worst view, facing Lake Ponchartrain and the Upper Garden District. She has her own secretary male and an active network of friends in City Government. Courtesy of the late Mutt Jeansonne. And her Daddy.

Chris Reed intends to go on living for a long time. And her next step in life is obvious to her.

"Gentlemen, I will be the next Council member from District C," she announces at the firm's Monday staff meeting.

All the attorneys, junior, senior and partners are gathered around the massive slab of polished marble that serves as the firm's main conference room. Reed stands before a uniformly-clad group, an un-uniform fresh rose bud pinned to her lapel.

"As the senior member of Councilman Jeansonne's staff, who else should be appointed by the Council to fill the remainder of his term? Who else could better know what policies he would see fit to implement?" argues Reed persuasively.

DAR Borden clears his throat, his usual signal for precedence at staff meetings. Since all chairs are the same size in this room, he is forced to rely on verbal cues. He has brought the Reed woman to the firm. The least he can do is try to keep her in line. If that is possible.

"Miss Reed," he begins lightly, "we are all quite happy to have you here among us, the first female Full Partner in this firm's long and revered history, and only the third female attorney of any sort... though we currently have none on staff, other than yourself."

A solitary "Here, here!" exclamation punctuates an immediate chorus of deep-throated "Harumph"-ing.

Borden continues. Looking at his partners as he speaks. "I know we are all quite grateful for your assistance with a number of delicate political matters over the past year. Especially our recent property acquisition. And the final compromise settlement with the City after Mr Jeansonne's untimely demise." The last statement is greeted with an equally quick and complete silence. And not a few furtive side glances. "This, of course, in spite of the fact that our profit from the sale will very nearly be halved, as a result of the loss of forty square feet of property."

It is all Chris could do to keep from smiling.

Borden has himself on a roll, though, and will not be diverted by what he sees on her face. "But do you expect us to believe that the Mayor will appoint you to Jeansonne's unexpired term? Were you more than a campaign manager to this man?" he queries, the corners of his mouth turning up. Borden's amusement is echoed by the rest of the males present. That is to say, by everyone present. Except Reed. And Robert Markham.

She turns a look so nakedly murderous upon the room that sound is literally sucked out of its occupants. "Mr Borden," she speaks easily into the vacuum, "Gentlemen. We all know that the Mayor, at his discretion, may name the spouse of a deceased member of the Council to that person's unexpired term. In the absence of a spouse, the selection of a replacement goes to the Council itself for a vote."

Reed stares Borden down, then resumes, "Mr Jeansonne was unmarried. The Council will vote on a new member at its November 15 meeting. I have worked extensively with this Council as Mr Jeansonne's senior advisor."

"They know me," she emphasizes. "They know I could complete his term serving his constituency exactly as he would. More efficiently, since I speak their language, though at a slightly more sophisticated level than Mr Jeansonne. They do not know that he would vote as he did only if I were there to guide him. Gentlemen, having a McFarland Borden & Dubney partner sitting on the Council would do this already estimable firm an inestimable amount of good. I will willingly become an inactive partner during my term, so that there will be no sense of impropriety or conflict of interest. My offices will be at City Hall."

This last statement stirs the room, as she had planned. She takes her time looking into each face, finishing with Borden. Then says quietly, "Have I your support?"

Reed remains standing as she canvasses the table with her eyes. DAR Borden stands and looks at his partners and employees. Gradually, one by one, every man at the table stands. Borden turns to Christine Reed and extends his hand.

"I believe, Miss Reed," he announces, "that once again, you have a deal."

* * *

"My Papa, he had some problems hanging on, too," said Noonie. "That what his friends told me. They said he got distracted every so often. When Mama passed, he had a real bad spell, sorta like you. I got the same weakness, maybe worse. We sisters, Ginny."

"I know, Noonie."

Virginia and Noonie sit quietly, head in hands, elbows on the kitchen table. They are happy, having just fed seventy-eight people an evening meal of chicken and hot sausage jambalaya. Both women are beyond tired, but they are still coasting on the exhilaration of their activity and unwilling to go to bed. Virginia, then Noonie takes a turn talking. On and on. In the dreamy, truth-filled stupor born on the fuzzy border between exhaustion and sleep.

It is Noonie's turn now.

"Seems I got a bit of my Dad in me. Being alone all that time after he disappeared, not knowing what happened to him, musta made me weak. I fell right into it, and there was nobody there who cared enough to pull me out. Mama gone. My brother was there, but he was just like Mama. Upright. Stiff. Fancy Creole gentleman. Didn't care much for Dad's friends out in the country. Didn't really care much that Dad left. Probably happy when I left, too. Suppose I was a bit embarrassing for him, running around in the Streets all those years. He would rather have me out there, though, than here in this house with him."

Noonie blows her nose with gusto, on her apron.

"What happened to your father?"

Noonie sighs and sits back in the chair. "Disappeared, just started spending more and more days out in the marshes, and less here in town. One day gone. Never came back. No word, not a one. Antoine told me Papa had stopped speaking English entirely the last time he came by Bayou Four-Point. I suppose the ducks were the closest link I could find to the happy times I spent with him out there. I don't remember how or when I started having one with me. Maybe from Audubon park.

"You ought to see the land out there, Ginny. And the birds. Antoine told me, and I remembered, stories about me being a baby out there with Papa when the ducks and geese came flying in. I remember the sound. That old man talking made me remember. Goose bumps on my arms   that's gotta be why they call 'em that   the hairs standing straight up as the sound came down from the sky, louder and louder. It was beautiful.

"Do you think we still crazy, Ginny?"

* * *

William Greene is upset. He has just seen a Channel 3 News interview with Christine Reed in which she boldly stated her candidacy for Mutt Jeansonne's Council seat.

"This isn't an election!" he yells aloud to the television. "We decide who gets nominated and elected! Us! Just us! The Council! And I am the President! So sure of herself. What does this woman think she is doing? And what do those goddamned lawyers want now?" He struggles to adjust himself in his reclined Superb-o-Lounger II, before continuing. "Calling me, calling everyone I know, making sure everyone knows that I am going to vote for her. That it's a done deal. I said I'd do it! I'm not going to back out now! What more do they want from me? WHAT?"

He pulls himself upright with his left arm while waving his right. "I will not be pressured! I cannot stand this! Where is Jeansonne, now that I need him? Where is that Rodrigo when I need him? Where is Jeansonne's dog, for godsake!" he screams, banging his fist on the doilied arm of his chair.

He points at the TV, "Get that Fred dog to barking at them! That would show the lawyers! She'll chew those carpetbaggers up and spit them out! Get the *dog* in here!"

Greene's wife enters the room, holding a potholder and a spoon. A concerned look on her face. Her expression is clearly unrelated to the Sweet Potato and Pecan Pie she has in the oven. She has seldom heard her husband go on like this, and never alone. He has never ever worked himself into a fit with no one else in the room.

"Something wrong, dear? Do you want a dog, dear? Are you alright?" she asks.

"Yes, I'm alright, dammit, Margaret," he answers. "They're just trying to take my job away again, is all," pointing at their Magnavox console.

Margaret Greene looks at the weatherman now on the TV. He is pointing out cloud patterns over Montana. There are yellow arrows on a broad green line pointing toward Louisiana. A "Happy Face" sun is placed over New Orleans.

"Oh," she says.

* * *

Among the avalanche of postcards the mailman brought that Friday is one official bit of correspondence addressed to LM Jeansonne. And one to FT Jeansonne. The cards are regularly sent as a matter of course to all voters, with forwarding not normally allowed. In this rather inefficient manner the registrar purges the voter rolls.

Post-mortem correspondence is not unusual in the least. In the Algiers District, post-mortem voting is a regular occurrence. The dead en masse arising from their plots to head to the sixth precinct. Every haggard corpse a practicing Democrat. And politically active. Defying contemporary concepts of mortality, five generations of the Melancon family continue to cast their votes for favored politicians. Until the ten or twelve less-active Melancons are simultaneously booted back beneath their untended headstones by a Federal vote audit.

All of the Registered Voters in the Toulouse house have simultaneously received an announcement of a change in polling places for their precinct. They are now to vote in the rectory of Our Lady of Guadalupe parish on Rampart street. Parish as in church, rather than county.

The Jeansonne cards make everyone depressed all over again. Virginia and Noonie are trying to figure out how to keep Fred's absentee ballots coming. It is their duty. They all know how proud Mutt was of his and Fred's voting record. They also knew Fred isn't going around any voting machines any time soon.

They have more reasons to feel low. It looks like the Reed woman may end up taking over Mutt's seat on the Council. She had shamed every Council member into a commitment, using the media to cement their votes. That possibility has the Robichaux house in an uproar. They talk all morning. Enough is enough, they agree. The woman ruins Mutt's life by duping him, then dumping him. Now she takes the only other thing that had made him feel that life was worth living.

Only there isn't a damn thing they could do about it. The Council will vote their own priorities.

The house is their other immediate worry. The lack of an heir is still a problem for settling Mutt's estate and the future of Robichaux house. The lawyer has just left.

He has given them grim news. Noonie no longer has a legal right to the property. That claim will not salvage the Family home. This is Mutt's house now. The estate would have been a simple one to settle if there was a will. Or a natural heir. Then the birth certificate hassle would not have even come up.

But without an heir, there remains the serious possibility that they might lose the house. Virginia is willing to spend everything she has to keep from losing Noonie's   and their   home. Without any relatives or heirs, the house will go to the State. Which will then liquidate the property. Politicians in Baton Rouge turning it into cash suitable for use as Las Vegas "trade show" expense accounts. The Family's lawyer is trying everything he can to prevent that. But their options are getting fewer every day. The Toulouse house is well on its way to being transmuted into room service for petty bureaucrats.

Fred is not home for the conference. Rodrigo informs the two women in attendance that his adopted mother, the white-furred lady in question, is currently in the company of Miss Melodie LaGrande. Entertainer extraordinaire and occasional doggie therapist.

"I will inform Mrs FT Jeansonne of her new polling station at the evening meal," he says, trying to act light-hearted in front of Family.

Seeing the evidence of Mutt's registration hits Rodrigo hard. It was Mutt and Fred becoming Registered Voters that eventually ended up killing Mutt. Leaving a distraught though unofficial   son and... a four-legged widow.

Rodrigo jumps to his feet, startling Noonie and Virginia.

His face is flushed. His eyes flashing. The revelation has come to him with an explosive strength that had heretofore only emerged in proximity to his Church.

The answer has to do with species. Of course!

There might be a way to keep Mutt alive after all. I need to see the Mayor immediately!

They would ALL go to the Council meeting.

* * *

The Presidential Commission on Extra-Terrestrial Sightings was temporarily disbanded that very day, in an apparent dispute over the partisan composition of the panel. Democratic appointees refused to take part in deliberations until further Commission members from their party were seated, to allow them a majority vote. According to Democrat Shirley Baggs, "We have a majority of alien activities in states with a Democratic majority and the panel should reflect that fact."

Funding for the federal agricultural compensation program was at stake. Crop losses due to alien calligraphy had become a big part of their budget.

Rodrigo is prepared for any objections. He has received none. He throws down the premise. The Mayor is thinking it through on his own.

"I understand, Rodrigo   Mr Jeansonne now, is it? that as Mrs Jeansonne's Curator you could continue as you were operating during Mutt's term. Handling the office until the election comes around again, at which time you and the voters of your District can make your own decision as to who will run   whose will be the name on the office door."

"That's about it, sir, yessir," agrees the once-again shoeless Rodrigo. He had done a quick toe-rinse in the water fountain outside the Mayor's office for the meeting. Rodrigo has come to understand political protocol.

"I like it, I really like it," says His Honor. "I can get my staff on the documentation this afternoon. We don't have much time, but we can do it. We will do it. I firmly believe that this is the way Mutt Jeansonne would have wanted it. That he would continue his mandate from the voters, in the manner he himself devised. And screw these arrogant, power-broker lawyers.

"Get your people ready, Mr Rodrigo Jeansonne," he says, shaking Rodrigo's hand and leading him to the door.

"We'll do our part. Let's get your people notified, transportation arranged   there's a lot to do. We only have a few days before the Council vote."

"They'll be ready, sir," yells Rodrigo as he shuffled down the corridor.

The Mayor watches as the shoeless man cuts across the lawn in front of City Hall.

"I wish I could do that," says Mayor Roland Clemenceaux.

* * *

"No no no, Melodie, I am telling you, I know this place. You will be welcome here," reassures Virginia. "And, Noonie, you are going to like this. We need to all stop moping and be strong. Mutt wouldn't want us falling apart just because he isn't here with us all the time. We are going to make a new Melodie LaGrande, a new Noonie Robichaux and a new Virginia Beaumont. Just like he made a new L Mutt Jeansonne. We are going to do this final battle in style."

Virginia swings open the doors of Rockfield's.

"And the new girls are going to need new clothes. We might just have to pick up a few other things while we're in here, too. Shoes, Mel? Seems I have a charge account that ought to get put to some use."

A young woman walks quickly across the first floor lobby, waving her hands madly at the trio as they enter. Attempting to shoo them back out the door.

"You can't come in here, ladies. This is..."

Virginia is having none of that.

"Little girl, you just jump back right now and go find that snippy Cleona Bagatelle on the third floor. You tell her Mrs Bruce Beaumont will be up shortly, and that she will want her expert advice. Now, little girl."

"But maam..." the salesgirl continues, obviously unconvinced.

"Get your butt up there, just like the lady said," growls Noonie. Clacking her teeth together for emphasis.

To which the salesgirl responds with a barely audible "Nuh-yeek!", while dashing for the elevator.

Mel is unconvinced that any good can come out of her visiting this store again. Her ejection the last time had been a matter of no small spectacle.

"C'mon, Mel. Noonie, let's get a look at these rags. Might be fun after all."

They ascend the marble staircase to the third floor.

Moments later, they are being served.

"But, of course, Miz Virginia, I understand your situation perfectly," snaps the starched and pressed Mrs Bagatelle, today the victim of an eighteen-inch coiffure. Of a color not occurring in nature. "You should never have doubted me. Friends of yours," she looked over at Mel, "are of course always welcome. No matter their origins. And I'll be glad to see that the new address is set into your account. I must tell you how happy we all are to see you back in the store. After your lengthy absence. We have missed you."

"Quite so," says Virginia. Mel moves off, reassured. And with a mission.

"We knew you would have an extended period of mourning after the loss of your late husband. Mr Beaumont was such a dashing gentleman. I hope you know we all miss seeing him, and that we do offer our condolences, even after this period of time."

"Quite so," repeats The Lady Beaumont, impatient to get on with shopping.

Mme Bagatelle is not fazed. She will have her history. History is necessary to the preservation of order. Even in a department store. "Why, the last time I was able to wait on Mr

Beaumont, I was helping Stanley in Formal Wear fit him for a tuxedo. Absolutely top-of-the-line. Winter it was. Finest wool. Traditional single-breasted coat and button-front pants, of course. He..."

Mme Bagatelle is fazed. She is staring to her right, a shocked look invading her expensive cosmetic foundation.

"My dear Miz Virginia, your friend is disrobing in the center of the sales floor."

* * *

Joe Dayers wakes from a sound sleep. He has grown to hate covering Council meetings. They get so loud. The disturbance could really ruin this cushy job. Why don't these people just stay home and watch the Council meeting in its pre-digested 90-second form on the Evening News?

"Order! Order, please! Let's all just wait our turn to speak. I'll be glad to hear every single one of you, if you simply wait your turn," Council President Greene says calmly into his microphone.

Grudgingly, a line forms at the speaker's podium. The audience quiets. The public input portion of the meeting proceeds. Dayers goes back to dozing at his camera.

Like Chris Reed, Greene has become a great deal more adept at handling masses of screaming people. His education had begun when Mutt Jeansonne first came before the Council.

"Jeansonne had a great knack for communicating with people," Greene told other Council members, "He taught me that even mobs are made up of individuals. So you talk to the individuals rather than the mob and they listen. That was a major lesson. A lesson I should have picked up long before he got here." Greene rubbed his chin. "I actually miss that bum," he mused.

Greene is still rather astounded that he had grown to like the former Street derelict and his dog. Most members of the Council had. It is odd, since they had so little apparently in common. In retrospect they concluded that it was the idea of that very distance between them, and the way Jeansonne was able to cross it, that had finally endeared him to them.

No dog has barked a Yea in these quarters in almost two months.

A pity. Good dog. They were very well-informed votes, too.

It was all really quite charming, once you got used to it.

* * *

Leonard Reed has the title to a BMW in his coat pocket as he watches his daughter walk up the steps of the New Orleans City Hall. She is accompanied by a thundering herd of dark-suited attorneys. DAR Borden breaks from their center and leads the way forward toward the elder Reed. The battle for dominant male is on. Borden's glad-hand is extended and broad smile in place. The rest of his entourage gather round, bumping briefcases. The two men shake hands warmly, each trying to subtly squeeze harder than the other. Both strain to exert substantial force without tipping off their efforts. Pleasant words escape clenched jaws. Chris Reed stands to one side until the hormonal preliminaries are complete.

"Yes, we're all proud of her, Leonard. She's got the right stock," says Borden, proudly pulling Chris to her father's side with his free hand. "She's come from the bottom of the DA's office to the top ranks of city government in just over a year. Quite a girl."

"Quite a woman, Don," corrects Leonard Reed, releasing Borden's hand.

"Yes, well, absolutely right. Glad to see you could make it today. Uh, Christine," Borden says, letting go her arm, "we'll just wait for you outside the Council Chamber. Let you have a word with your father. Good to have seen you, Leonard," yells Borden back over his shoulder, still smiling. The Senior Partner takes the rest of the steps two at a time, rubbing his right hand the whole while.

"You've been exercising with that palm-flexer I gave you for Christmas," says Chris Reed. "Don't tell me you haven't."

"I won't deny it, Chrissy. Not a bit. Ended up being one of the smartest presents I ever got. I think of you every time I pulverize one of those bodybuilders' hands."

He reaches in his jacket. "Got something for you."

Leonard Reed hands Chris the car title. "You earned it. You fought with the Big Guys and won. I'm proud of you." Her father pulls her to him. Hugs her. "I know I haven't been the best, but hell, it's the only way I know. Maybe we can talk a little more now."

"Maybe," she whispers over his shoulder. Chris is overwhelmed, trying to recover as she pulls her face away to face him. "Where's Momma?"

"Couldn't get away, Baby. Started her bridge games up again. Afraid it ran on a bit late last night. Put her a bit under the weather. Couldn't get her up for the long drive down here. But she sends you her love. Me, I was glad to get away. I been out mowing in the beans the last five days straight. Found some great designs in your Momma's quilt book. I swear the Feds'll love it."

"I appreciate your coming all the way down here. Best surprise I've ever had, and you know me, I..."

"... don't like surprises," he finishes. "Yes, I know you. Get on in there, Chrissy. Today's your day. I'll sit in the back and watch it happen. Proud of you. Chris."

"Thanks."

Daddy.

Chris Reed and the seven three-piece suits file into the front row of the Chamber. Greene watches.

If only the Reed woman was likeable. This wouldn't be so unpleasant.

There is a quick exchange of looks between Council members, revealing that each of them is familiar with the new arrivals. They had been heavily lobbied by a multitude of the firm's friends.

They all know what is coming.

McFarland Borden & Dubney have sent their first string players to guarantee their new partner's political coronation.

DAR Borden nods to each Council member in turn, then whispers enthusiastically to Reed, "It's a done deal, my dear girl. There's not a one of them who would dare vote against you. We've a handle on each and every one of them financial support, you know. They can't run for Council unless they keep their financial support. And we know every political dollar in this town by its first name. We've let them know what we want. No, they won't even put another name in the running. You'll be on the other side of that table by the end of this meeting."

Reed is trying hard to cover her nervousness with bravado. "We'll be able to move this City the way we want from now on, Don. I told you that first campaign was the right move. It brought us right here, even faster than I had hoped. I've wanted this sort of authority all my life. I know how to use it. And today...," she says emphatically, "... today I get it."

Borden pats her hand, then turns to look at the line of well-shaved-and-suited male faces behind him. His staff. And in the last row, Leonard Reed. "Yes, you will, Miss Reed. We'll get you sworn in and on your way   and our way within the hour. The Mayor should be here any time now. I am a bit upset that I he hasn't returned my calls these last two days, though. I suppose I shouldn't be surprised. He hasn't been too supportive of your candidacy. He'd probably prefer putting another hobo in public office. Emasculate the Council and make it into his tool. Instead of ours. I suppose it doesn't really matter. This whole thing is out of his hands now."

The last speaker finishes his remarks on catch-basin drain relocation. Greene thanks the citizens who came forward to speak on the proposal. And assures them that their comments will be taken into consideration when the final decision is made. He tells the Clerk to make sure copies of what had been said are distributed to Council members.

He is stalling.

Selection of the interim Council member is next on the meeting calendar. It is obvious from the faces of everyone on the Council that they are not looking forward to the process.

"Our next order of business..." he begins.

That is all he manages to get out.

The double doors at the back of the Chamber slam open at just that moment. A horde of stern-faced twenty-first-century urban crusaders storm toward the speaker's podium. Joey Dayers is startled awake, knocking his camera and tripod onto the City Clerk. The Mayor of New Orleans and half a dozen police officers lead the foray, followed by Rodrigo, Virginia & Ellis, Noonie, and Fred in Mel's arms. The three women are dressed quite stylishly. Plus a supporting cast of a priest, five nuns, the Lee Fat family, a postman, dozens of Toulouse permanent residents. And assorted & excited French Quarter, Faubourg Marigny and Upper Ninth voters.

"Mister President," shouts the Mayor, even before reaching the speaker's microphone. "Mister President, I would like your permission to address the Council on a matter of importance."

Greene is flustered. "Mayor, we have an agenda...," he starts.

"This concerns your agenda. And it is something that I am sure you yourself will be glad to have considered," continues Mayor Roland Clemenceaux.

He pulls a thick stack of papers from his briefcase and places them on the podium. The Mayor's entourage spreads out around him. Rodrigo, Mel and Fred are close at his side.

"I am sorry to burst in on you like this, but I am also glad we got here in time to keep you from doing something that I am sure would be a big mistake for the City of New Orleans," says the Mayor, now looking directly at Chris Reed and DAR Borden.

Borden starts to rise. He speaks in a measured tone of voice, as if he is addressing an unruly child, "Mister Mayor, does not the City Council proceed by certain rules of protocol? Can you just..."

"Quiet, please," interrupts Council President Greene. "I'm the one who determines protocol in this room. Mister Borden."

"Mister Greene..." Borden shouts.

"I have requested quiet," Greene says emphatically, smiling and remaining unruffled. "And I will have it. Please be reasonable, Mr Borden."

Borden sits back down in his chair, clearly shocked at this assault on his power. He turns to Reed as if its her fault. "Reasonable?" he says through his teeth. "What is this *reasonable* shit?"

Greene looks back at the Mayor. "Mr Mayor, you have something you would like to present to this Council?" he says tranquilly.

The Mayor picks up the papers from the top of the podium.

"Mr President, the Council's appointment of an interim member is unnecessary. Mr L Mutt Jeansonne is survived by a living spouse. As Mayor I am allowed to appoint surviving spouses to fill unexpired Council terms. I will do so."

It takes a few minutes for Greene to regain order in the Council Chambers.

"I have here," the Mayor announces, "records from the City Registrar of Voters that LM Jeansonne and Mrs FT Jeansonne have been active registered voters in New Orleans for seven years. I have a sworn statement from Election Commissioner Cyrus R Gladstone at Mr Jeansonne's former precinct that not only was Mrs Jeansonne on the rolls of that precinct, but that Mutt Jeansonne confirmed on many occasions to the commissioners that he was indeed married. That he spoke fondly of his wife, who he said had a 'biologic' condition that prevented her from voting in person. She voted in each election for the last seven years by absentee ballot. Mr Gladstone himself updated the Jeansonne file in the Registrar computer system."

He held up a pink flyer, pointing to the picture. "Mr Jeansonne personally had these handbills made up for his election campaign. You will notice that the flyer clearly identifies 'Mutt Jeansonne' and 'Fred Jeansonne'."

"Wha..."

"We have researched this matter thoroughly and found in the records of the City of New Orleans a Marriage Certificate, issued by the State of Louisiana on the second of June, 1980, between LM Jeansonne and FT Jeansonne of Carondelet street in this City. There are no records prior to that time that contradict that Certificate."

The Mayor was not to be stopped, drawing further papers from his supply. "We have a Certificate of Custody estimating a birthdate of December 8, 1944 for a male child by the single name of Mutt, and affidavits from five sisters of the

Order of the Blessed Bones identifying that Mutt as the late Mutt Jeansonne of this City. The LM Jeansonne listed on this marriage certificate.

"There can be no doubt as to the identity of FT Jeansonne."

The Mayor extracts a bound folder from his briefcase, and waves it at the Council.

"I have in my hand twenty-two sworn and notarized statements to further verify that identity, as confirmed to each by Mr Jeansonne."

The Council President is delighted, but confused. "But Mr Mayor, the facts..." he starts.

"Mr Greene, you should know better," says His Honor the Mayor, "than to let facts get in the way of the truth, especially in this City."

Reed and Borden's mouths are both hanging open. The Mayor takes a moment to savor the looks on their faces before continuing.

"But, so you will understand that this is not just my call   just to make sure you understand the law is clear on this matter   I will explain. Our centuries-old Napoleonic law facilitates marriages   for purposes of breeding taxpayers and populating the giant empty expanses of the Louisiana Purchase with Churchgoers, I am sure. The law does not allow recognition of common law marriages, however, calling such blatant unblessed unions 'open concubinage.' But, dodging the issue somewhat, it does recognize what it calls 'putative' marriages where the mates truly believe they are legally partners. A fee must be paid, and a certificate rendered, as in this case.

"In spite of its severity, the law is loose on other matters. Mr Rodrigo Jeansonne here has pointed out to me that, because of the peculiarities of translation from the French language, the Code only specifies male and female.

"It does not specify species," Mayor Clemenceaux says flatly.

"What the hell are you saying, Mayor?" blurts Greene.

The Mayor grows very serious. "I am saying, sir, that the law of this great state regarding legal marriage does not exclude individuals with Mrs Jeansonne's 'biologic condition'."

Clemenceaux raises both his hands dramatically over his head.

"Members of the New Orleans City Council," he announces, "In view of the fact that it is my mandate under the law, I would like to introduce   with her legal Curator and voting representative Rodrigo Jeansonne   Mrs FT Jeansonne, my official appointee to the post of City Councilperson for the District C of the Great City of New Orleans."

The Mayor of the City of New Orleans turns to his right.

Mel places a happily beaming Fred on the podium. Mrs Jeansonne is wearing her Seeing-Eye-Dog sunglasses.

Fred smiles broadly as bedlam regains its hold in the New Orleans City Hall.

* * *

Christine Reed, Leonard Reed and DAR Borden, Esq, were incarcerated for almost twelve hours that evening, in the parish lock-up on Tulane Avenue. With a great deal of effort and the occasional shouting bout, their massive law firm finally overcame what seemed the more-detailed-than-usual detail work involved in posting bail.

It had taken a while.

After the booking process, Ms Reed was placed in the holding cell, allowing her the acquaintance of The Twitcher, who had once again been incarcerated for attempting to place her grandmother's head in a nine-speed Moonbeam Blender.

Ms Reed told the Twitcher about the lost strawberries of her childhood. The Twitcher hugged Reed and rubbed her head, causing all of the attorney's hair to stand on end. Giving Chris Reed a slight resemblance to the late Governor Earl Long, also of Winnfield, after one of his encounters with electric psychiatry.

Mr Borden was placed in a holding tank with four elderly gentlemen who had at one point been residents of a certain now-inaccessible lot under the Ponchartrain Expressway. The aging quartet were unable to convince Borden of the error of his ways, but made a lasting impression upon him in the hours of their eloquent argument.

Mr Reed was placed in a solitary confinement cell, reserved for more violent offenders.

The arrests had occurred when, in the aftermath of FT Jeansonne's appointment to the Council, Council President Greene had felt forced to invoke the City Ordinance dealing with "Contempt of Council." He would not allow the New Orleans City Council to be referred to   on the record, no less as "assholes" and "jerk-offs" by members of the legal community.

Though he took great pleasure in using the same terms to refer to the offending attorneys. Off the record, of course.

He allowed Leonard Reed to get off a solid left hook and two right crosses to DAR Borden's chin, before having Reed dragged away, too. After all, Borden had called the man's daughter a tramp and pushed her aside in the heat of the melee. Greene felt compelled to remind the gentlemen that this remained the South. Manners were in order.

A lady's honor must be upheld.

* * *

Fred is still smiling an hour later as Joey Dayers tapes the new Council member walking down the steps of City Hall. Fred, Mel and Rodrigo and their extended family pause on the steps for Dayers to finish. Noonie, Ellis and Virginia rush back to Toulouse to prepare a celebratory feast.

"Shall we tell her?" Mel asks Rodrigo, as they pose with Fred.

"What better time?"

"Freddy...," Mel starts.

"Mrs Jeansonne..." adds the shoeless man.

"I am quitting the Can-Can-Do for another full-time occupation. Besides assisting you in your Governmental duties. I would appreciate your assistance. Possibly we could convince you to move in with us permanently? After all, you are soon to be a grandmother."

"It's going to be a boy," yells Rodrigo, startling Joe Dayers into dropping his camera again.

"And his name will be L Mutt Jeansonne. Junior."

"Waaooww," exclaims the dog.

* * *

Dayers is in attendance later the same afternoon, this time in the Quarter. With a new camera buzzing on his shoulder. He arrives shortly after the first bird lights on the roof of the Toulouse street house. The station had called him back in as soon as it became apparent where the phenomenon would touch down.

It is around dusk, the day of Fred's inauguration. A breeze has come into the City from the west. Gusting gently in a discernible rhythm. Rodrigo remarks that it feels like the sleeping breaths of some overworked celidographer.

No one comments further. But that same pulsing wind carries the clear sweet musk of the marshes into the maze of the City without hesitation, as if it knows its way. Carbon monoxide flies before it, the machine poisons dissolving in the fresh sea air to the east.

Then suddenly, the sky darkens. As if August had abruptly returned with a late afternoon shower.

But it is November, not August.

People run out of their houses to see what is happening. Out onto the banquettes. At first, most residents of the French Quarter think the ominous spiral is a slow-developing twister. Dropping directly onto the Robichaux house. That is before the sonic avalanche of quacking, chirping and honking descends on the neighborhood. Before the thousands of specks in the spiral become identifiable as birds. As geese, as blackbirds, as purple martins.

As ducks.

Noonie recognizes the leader. A single bird still high above her. He is looking down, directly at Noonie Robichaux.

She puts her decoy on the front porch and sits. Waiting. She has a lot to tell the sweet boy before he heads South.